Call of Sunteri

Missy Sheldrake

First published by Missy Sheldrake November 2015
Printed by CreateSpace, An Amazon.com Company

Illustrations for this story were created using the Procreate iPad Application

www.missysheldrake.com

For my mom.

Contents

Map of the Kingdom of Cerion

Map of the Known Lands

Chapter One:

FLAME AND SEA

Tib

Filth and grunge. Rats. Rot. Bones. Cobbles. Stench. Sobbing. Striking. Silence.

"Climb the wall."

Yes, climb the wall. My feet are swift and sure in the darkness as I leap and cling to the rough stone. They find each crevice perfectly, anchoring me as I push myself up. Climbing feels good. Free. The higher I go, the better I can see the city stretched out before me. In the dye fields, they tell stories of Zhaghen with eyes full of awe. How beautiful it is. How majestic. For me, it's a place that breeds greed. Cruel. Twisted. Soiled.

"Higher."

Yes, higher. The towers are dark tonight, unprotected. Not as scary as I thought they'd be, stretching up into the sky. I creep closer to a slotted window and pause. Sniff. The air here is thick with the scent of old paper. Books. A fan of shining black hair flicks into my memory as my fingers grip the stone through soft leather gloves. My new gloves.

"Inside."

Yes, inside. My feet find the ledge and I crouch on the sill. Velvet drapes flap in the wind. Crimson, like the flowers we picked. Tucked safely into the shadows, I peer below into the darkness. It was a good climb. A long climb. Now I'm higher than any city boy could climb. Higher than I've ever climbed. Far up above the city. So easy here to ignore the suffering below. To live unaware of it. The cries of the starving, the stench of the gutters, they could never reach this far up. Only the Mages. Mages and students. Worse. Sorcerers. My hatred for them pushes me forward.

"The hearth."

Yes, the hearth. I slide from the sill and land lightly on my feet. My new boots are silent on the plush carpet. The room is still. Huge.

Dark except for dying embers crackling in the distance. Far beyond tables piled with pages and books. Shelves. Scrolls. Bottles and jars. The ceiling is high. Domed. Glass. Stars shine above. No one is here this late. The tower is asleep. Empty, except for books. Hundreds. Thousands. Ancient. Irreplaceable. Sacred. Neatly arranged on dozens of shelves. Good to hide behind. To sneak behind.

"Start it."

I take a sheaf of parchment from the shelf as I creep forward through the last row. The glow of coals lures me. The fire is dying, but soon it will grow. I light the sheaf. Watch the edges flare and curl black. I move away through the room. One by one I tuck the burning pages into place on shelves and tables. Everything is so dry and old, it catches quickly. I back toward the window, my escape. Watch the glow of flame that crawls up shelves and across tabletops. I did this. Alone. This is my revenge. Their precious knowledge, turning to char. Ashes. Dust.

"Outside."

Yes, outside. I slip through the window. My fingers find the crevices and I start my descent. Watch the smoke pour from the window. Hear the cries from inside. Fire! Fire! My feet are swift in new boots. My hands are steady. I land lightly on the cobbles and stroll away from the smoking tower. The gloves come off, tuck into my tattered bag. They're too fine for the rest of me. They'd give me away.

"On to the next."

Yes, on to the next. I step around the corner, into the gathering crowd. Necks craned up, watching smoke billowing. Some rush the doors with buckets of water, but even in this crisis they're turned away. No one notices me, the whelp in field clothes, older than a boy but not yet a man. I'm nothing to them. Unimportant. Unnoticed. I disappear as the crowd thickens around the base of the tower. On to the next.

Six pillars of black smoke rise into the night sky. Six towers burn. My work is done. The city is awake now. Watching, Screaming. Crying. Cheering. I don't need to run. Nobody suspects me. Nobody notices the poor boy in field clothes.

"Into the sea."

Yes, into the sea. I tuck my new boots safely into my bag and jump from the harbor wall into the deep. The water is warm and calm. I go under. Scrub the soot from my hands, face, and hair. Hulls of tall ships loom over me, swaying eerily. Massive dark shapes against the darker sky, anchored in the inky water. I'm a fair swimmer. I find the ship with the crest I need: purple chevron under a blue ring. I reach it and pull myself into a skiff lashed beside. Rest a moment. Listen. Way up on deck, men are talking. Watching the smoke rise. Wondering if it will delay their departure.

"Say something."

Yes, I ought to.

"Ho there, sirs!" I shout. Footsteps. Faces peering down at me. Men with trimmed beards. Hair tied neatly. Uniforms. Swords.

"Who goes?" one says. He's stern-looking. Straight as a pole.

"It's just a boy," another answers. Leans way over to peer down at me.

"You swim all that way, boy?" asks the first.

"Yes, sir. I'm a fair swimmer, sir," I say.

"What for?" the first again.

"I need passage to Cerion, sir," I reply. Try not to sound desperate.

"Passage to Cerion!" the spyglass one scoffs. More come to look over the side at me. Scoffing. Laughter.

"We're no charter, boy!" One of the newcomers chuckles. "Find yourself another ship."

"I have no money for a charter, sir. I mean to work for it," my voice is getting hoarse. My throat is dry from the salt water.

"Work for it!" More Scoffing. Laughter. Footsteps. A deep voice growls about the racket. The men go quiet. Hushed discussion of the boy in the skiff. A broad man with a pitted face and squinted eyes leers down at me. Looks me over. Calls out an order for the rope ladder.

"Climb it," he says. I do, as quickly as the flames that licked the shelves. I stand before him. Bow respectfully. "You want to work, eh?" He eyes me. "Why should I let you?"

"I'm a fast learner, sir. A hard worker. I don't complain. I'll do any task. I'm not squeamish. I'm quick. I can climb. I can swim." I say. He grabs my wrists, inspects my hands. Looks at my fingers stained red.

"From the dye fields," he grunts and lets go. "Hard working, I'm sure of it. Ever been on a ship before?"

"No, sir."

"You'll get seasick."

"I've been on a carriage before, sir. A bumpy one. Never got sick, sir."

"A carriage!" Laughter again.

"A carriage is a far cry from a ship tossed by the waves of a storm. We've got a crowd in the rows ashore, boy. Men. Strong men. All waiting to work for passage. Seafaring men. Men who know what they're doing."

"I know. That's why I swum out. I could have stowed away, but I want to work. I'll work harder than them. I'm honest. I won't argue. I don't eat much. I don't like to sleep. I'm respectful. I don't steal. I'm not afraid of anything. I'll do my work, you won't even notice me. None of them swum out. They don't want it as much, sir."

"Look at him, Cap, sir. Somethin's not right," one of the uniformed men murmurs. I cast my eyes down. Don't let them look too hard. Cap's staring. I can feel it.

"Climb the foremast," he says finally. Gruffly. "Untie the lashing on the fore moonraker. Stow it back proper again." He crosses his arms. He doesn't think I can do it. None of them do.

I've never heard of a moonraker or a foremast, but I don't question. Somehow, I know what to do. I run to the ratlines and climb all the way to the top. Even anchored in the calm, the mast rocks. I grip hard with my legs. Work the knots. Drop the edge of the highest sail. Bind it up again. Tie it. They watch from below. I'm sure they're impressed. A boy from the dye fields shouldn't know knots, rigging, and sails. They're right, I shouldn't, but it comes to me anyway. I lash it up again, exactly as it was. Make perfect knots. Slide down the ratlines. Land light and sure at the captain's feet. Salute.

"Well done," Cap says. He's impressed. Pleasantly surprised. I nod once, but don't smile. Don't want to look too proud. Powerful men don't like that. "You can stay on. Do as you're told. One wrong move and we cast you over. Agreed?" he offers his hand, and I shake it. "What're you called, boy?"

"Tib, sir."

"Welcome aboard, then, Tib," he says.

The journey is long. Days into weeks. I sleep anywhere but below. It's too cramped there. The wood encases me, reminding me of the trees, the roots, the past. The crow's nest is my favorite. I can see all around me. Watch passing ships grow and shrink. See the ocean stretch to a thin curve all the way out on the horizon. I'm talented with the lamplight. I learn how to send signals to the navy ships that follow us, too slow to keep our pace. We are their scout ship. We watch for danger.

I am invisible to those more important to me. They don't notice me. I can lurk. Pick up conversations. Learn things. One of those navy ships carries Prince Vorance, the only prince of Sunteri. He courts the eldest daughter of the king of Cerion. Her name is Sarabel. She is smitten with him. Six ships come with him including ours. Six is an auspicious number, they say. A circle number. I'm not sure what it means, but I can't ask. If I do, they'll know that I've been listening.

One month. We sail into the mouth of the river they call Jairun. I don't like it. We move slower here through the center of Elespen. The jungle creeps into the water on both sides of us. Days more of this. Days of watching jungle become village and jungle again, and then sand and only sand as far as I can see. An ocean of sand. Too much like Sunteri. Too much like the home I never wanted to see again. I feel the panic rise in me. I don't want to be in the desert.

"Sleep."

Yes, sleep. I curl up in the safety of the fore nest, and when I wake the stars stretch out endlessly above me. Noise. Lapping and chatting. Laughing and shouting. Bargaining. Unloading. The thud of the hull against the pier as they tie it up.

"Boy!" Cap shouts. I slip down the ratlines and drop to his side. The deck is deserted except for the pair of watch guards at the gangway. I stand straight and look Cap in the eye, as he has told me to do. It keeps a man honest, he says, to meet his crew's eyes.

"Sir!" I shout. He taught me to do that, too.

He tells me I'm a hard worker. I have earned five copper, which he jingles in a pouch. I like the sound of it. I have never held coin before. It has more weight than I expected. He tells me I can go ashore if I want to, and then he goes back below. I peer out at the city. Cresten. Capital of Elespen. It's different from Zhaghen. Cleaner. Brighter, even in the starlight. Noisy, but the noise is happier. They don't have towers here to watch and rule over them. Just a castle, low and sprawling. Music drifts merrily from the taverns into the street. People in beautiful colors dance in the glow of torchlight. Others toss coin at them. Even in the night, merchants in booths cook and sell. The aroma is exotic and flavorful. My mouth waters.

"Stay aboard."

Yes, stay aboard. I tie the coin to my belt and wrap the sash around it three times to keep it safe. Then I climb into the nest and go back to sleep.

I wake to the signal. The air is cooler, even with the sun bearing down. We're sailing again, flying across the water. North still, but more west now. The jungle is far behind us, just a line of deep green between the sea and sky. I train the scope behind, find the trailing ship. Read the message. Flash the mirror to acknowledge.

Two months now at sea, since we left Zhaghen. Sea and days of messages filled with nothing. All is well. All is well. Back and forth. Over and again. Still, the work is easy. Not like the fields. Freer, even confined to a ship. I keep to myself way up here, and nobody bothers with me. The main nest collects the same messages as mine. Cap tells me I'm the backup. My keen eye is valuable. I could do the main nest one day, if I stay on. He thinks I want a life of this. He doesn't know.

Cerion's cliffs are unmistakable when they appear. A white slash between the cloudless blue sky and the crisp blue-green sea. They grow impossibly high as we approach. So high it would take ten of our ship's highest masts to reach the top. As we dock, Cap pays me again. Tells me I'm welcome to stay on. I say little in the way of farewells. I know I'll never return to the sea.

The climb up the cliff seems as long as the sailing itself. Stairs and more stairs. My legs are strong, though, from climbing the ratlines. I scurry past others who trudge and cling to the ropes. The stone glints wet beneath my feet, catching the sun. Wet but not icy, which I find strange. The wind threatens to carry me off, and I keep close to the wall as it lashes at me. I have never felt cold like this before. Winter. Sunteri has no winter. The chill is painful. I am not dressed for it. I have my gloves. I have my new boots. No cloak, though. No sleeves to cover my arms.

"Climb faster."

Yes, climb faster. The work keeps me warm. Up and up I go, until I reach the top and the city stretches out before me. Low. Plain. Clean. Someone stops me. Offers me a clay mug filled with a sweet, hot drink. Kind. Smiling. Welcoming. She tells me I should visit their tavern, and moves on to those behind me without asking for payment. I sip it and it warms me to the toes.

Children run past laughing. Cloaks of fur flap behind them.

"Follow the children."

Yes, follow the children. I leave my empty cup at the stall and jog after them. The bitter cold numbs my toes and stings my fingertips, even through my boots and gloves. My teeth chatter. I rub my arms as I pass booths selling thick furs and warm knit shawls and fine winter clothes. One of them displays rolls of soft woven fabric and barrels of ground dye powders, heaping with red and blue and orange dust.

"Ten silver a scoop," a lady bundled in red smiles at me. I wonder if she knows the work that goes into one scoop. The picking, the hauling, the drying, the grinding. Thousands of blooms plucked. The workers who break their backs in the field for a loaf to feed their family and a roof over their heads.

"The children."

Yes, the children. I tear myself from the booth and chase after their laughter. When I catch up, I find them standing in a crowd lining the streets. Five of them. Two boys, three girls. I creep close to them in the crowd and stand next to a girl. She's my age. Bright red curls poke out from beneath her hat. She bumps my shoulder.

"Aren't you cold?" she asks, eyeing my bare arms. Her eyes are green. Jungle green. Pretty. I shrug.

"Raefe," she says, and tugs the cloak of the boy beside her. Older. He has his own spyglass and cranes his neck over the crowd to peer through it. He's bundled like the rest of the children. Fur wraps, thick woven hats, and bulky scarves that wind round their necks up to their noses. They have mittens, too, that make their hands look like paddles. The girls' hats and mittens are decorated with lots of colorful ribbons. I wonder what the point of that is. They can't even use their fingers. It's not very practical.

"The carriage is coming. It's slow," Raefe says on tiptoe. "Wish we could climb up on something."

"Nessa said no climbing, Raefe," says another girl. Older. Bossy. "It's too icy."

"Can you see the prince? Or the princess? Can you see her round belly?" A younger boy hops up and down beside Raefe. Tugs on his arm. "Let me look!"

"Ruben!" The prim girl scowls and pokes the boy. "Don't be disrespectful!"

"Rae." The red-haired girl tugs Raefe's other arm. "I need a cloak."

"In my bag, Saesa." Raefe leans toward her, still watching. "No, can't see inside the carriage. The curtains are closed. They might open them when they get closer."

"I want to see!" Ruben whines while Saesa rummages through Raefe's shoulder bag.

"Here," she pulls out a thick green wool cloak and hands it to me. I eye it, and her. "Don't be so suspicious," she says. "It used to be

Raefe's but it's too small now. It's still good, though. Nobody else wanted it. We all just got new ones, you see, so Nessa said find someone who could use it. It has a hood and everything."

She nudges me with it. My teeth chatter, but I still don't accept. A drink is one thing, but this cloak is expensive. A gift is a trick, my Nan would say. Don't trust it. Anyone who gives freely just wants power over you. It's true. I've seen it happen.

"Here they come," cries Raefe over the gasp of the crowd. "The curtains are open, now, too!"

"Let me up, Rae-Rae," the youngest girl whines. The ribbons on her hat bounce as she tugs him.

"Okay, but hold on tight, Emmie," Raefe says as he hefts her to his shoulders. She squeals and waves to the carriage. I feel the cloak drape my shoulders and wrap snug around my arms.

"Don't argue. You're cold, I can tell," Saesa smiles at me as she ties the laces closed. Then she ducks to peek through the mass of the crowd in front of us. I should protest, but I don't. It's warm. Nice.

"Stay with them."

Yes, stay with them. The crowd around us cheers as the carriage moves past. Through the crowd I catch glimpses of gold and purple and burnished wood. Those before us bow, and so do I as it passes. But I'm one of the first to look up.

"Hail, Prince Eron! Hail Princess Amei!" the crowd calls out. Inside the carriage, the princess waves happily. She is wrapped in clouds of lavender. Her skin is very dark. Rich and brown. Beside her, the prince looks pale but strong. He smiles and nods to those who call his name. His eyes are distant, though. Troubled. I wonder if anyone else notices. The crowd throws favors. Beside me, Saesa gasps.

"Oh, there she is! There she is, Rae!" she bounces with excitement and points to a rider far back in the escort. "Azaeli!" she calls out.

The knight is shorter than the other riders around her, but different. Her armor is blue like midnight with dazzling flecks that glitter in the sunlight. Her white cloak is trimmed with gold. The flag she waves is blue and gold check. A great two-handed sword is strapped to her saddle. Her face is covered to her cheeks with her helm. She grins and waves at Saesa, who squeals with delight.

"Azaeli."

Yes, Azaeli. I watch carefully. She's important. I understand. The others in blue and gold who ride beside her are proud. Tall. Each one is more different than the next, but something about Azaeli is special. I'm not sure what, I just know she's different from the others. I try to pick out their professions. Five warriors, one a giant of a man. An archer with painted cheeks and pointed ears. Two Mages. A lady bard with crimson hair, spiked to a point. Two healers, but one of them might not be part of the group. He's not in their colors.

A score of royal guard follow those, and behind them trail a group of peasants who chase behind the carriage, dancing and cheering.

"Will they escort him all the way to Kordelya Castle?" Ruben, the younger boy, asks.

"Just to the crossroads," Saesa answers. "Then Baron Stenneler's Guard will take them the rest of the way. Oh, imagine it! They could meet any kind of adventure out there! Bandits and Wildwoods. Or trolls! I'll bet Sir Azaeli could beat twenty trolls on her own."

"Oh, honestly, Saesa!" the bossy girl chides. "Only you would dream of being the knight. Not me," she sighs. "Imagine being the princess, whisked off to a romantic castle to be pampered and served while waiting for the royal heir to arrive. Strolling by Lake Kordelya with Prince Eron…" she gazes toward the street dreamily. "I heard it's warmer there. Better for the baby."

"What does a princess do but sit around all day? I'd rather have adventure! Azi is the first knight her age in decades! That's way better than a princess!"

"I heard," Ruben pipes up, "that the real reason is they're sending the prince away—"

"Ruben!" Raefe warns. He shakes his head as the people in front of us turn curiously. He lowers Emmie to the street and stretches his neck from side to side. "Time to go home," he says. "Take Lilen's hand, Emmie."

"Yes, don't gossip in the streets like a louse, Ruben." Lilen grabs Emmie's hand and gives the boy a disapproving look. Beside her, Saesa rolls her eyes and turns to me.

"Do you have a place to go?" she asks. I shake my head. "Come on, then," she closes her warm mittened hand around mine and pulls me along with them. I let her.

Ice. Ribbons fluttering. Red curls bouncing. Sweets. Running. Sliding. Laughter. Warmth.

"We're home!" everyone calls out as we tumble through the

door out of the cold. Inside is bright and grand. Rich. Like a palace. They all sit. Pull off their boots. Line them neatly on the side of the carpet. Fold their wrappings and stow them in the carved cupboard. I hang up my cloak but that's all. My boots are new. My gloves are new. I won't lose them.

"Stay here."

Yes, stay here. A woman with a baby on her hip appears at the top of the twisting staircase. She smiles and presses a finger to her lips.

"Garsi just went down," she says in a hushed voice. "Into the sitting room with you. Luncheon soon." Her feet are light on the polished stone stairs even holding the baby. Her dress is fine. It shimmers in the light from the high windows. "Oh, and you've brought a friend." Her smile is bright. Kind. I look down at the carpet.

"Yes, can he stay?" Saesa pleads. Lilen rolls her eyes. Raefe ushers the others to the sitting room. How strange, I think, to have a room just for sitting.

"Well, it isn't my place to say, is it? You'll have to ask Nessa. Go on, then. Take Errie with you," she says as she gives the wiggling baby to Saesa and crosses to another door. When she opens it, the mouthwatering aroma of fresh baked bread and stew seeps out into the foyer. My stomach growls. Saesa shifts the baby. Tugs my arm.

"Come on," she says. "Meet Nessa."

She doesn't tell me to take off my boots, so I don't. I walk on the thick carpet with them. I wonder what it would feel like on my toes. Soft. Like sand, maybe. The sitting room is fine. Elegant. Lots of fancy furniture and thick draperies and baubles. Expensive things. Sparkling things. Things that serve no purpose but to be looked at and not touched. The lady on the sofa fits right in. Her skirts are all ruffles that take up most of the seat and spill to the floor. Bright green, like the cloak. Enough fabric to clothe all of the girls. But they are dressed prettily enough on their own.

Emmie runs to the sofa and climbs up, trampling the gown. The lady beams. Hugs her. Kisses her face, still sticky with sweets. Sets her book on the side table as she lovingly takes the baby from Saesa. Her eyes twinkle as the rest swarm to hug and kiss and pile together around her. She doesn't shout at them or scold them for wrinkling her dress. Instead, she hugs each of them warmly.

"So, did you see the prince, then?" she asks. Her voice is soft and kind. Excited, too.

"Oh, yes, and the princess," Emmie says. She kneels on her lap, facing her. Reaches to Nessa's perfectly done hair. Twirls a lock around her finger. It's black, not red like Saesa's or blonde like Lilen's.

"And Azaeli." Saesa says with excitement.

"All of His Majesty's Elite were there. And a score of the Royal Guard, just like you thought," Raefe says as he leans against the grand hearth. I edge closer to its warmth, listening as the rest of them recount every detail of the procession. Details I didn't notice, but that seem to interest Nessa very much. The crackling fire reminds me of the towers. The flames. The smoke as it rose into the night sky. My task accomplished. My new life begun.

Stay here.

Yes, I'll stay here. Here, where they'll never suspect me. Here, where I'll be safe.

Chapter Two:

COLLECTORS

Tib

They make me sit in a tub of hot water. I scrub myself like I did in the sea. Wash away the soot and grime. I soak until it's cold and my fingers are puckered. Still red, though. The dye will be part of me forever, I think.

At luncheon I tell them my story. Not the true one, the made up one. The one I'm supposed to tell. How I was in a trade caravan, bringing dye to Zhaghen on the night it burned. I was separated from my crew by the gathering crowd. I fell into the ocean and nearly drowned. I was pulled out of the water by the navy scout ship and begged to be taken away from the fields, to start a new life. The rest of my tale is mostly the truth. Nessa is fascinated by my past. Sympathetic. She says I can stay if I want to. I do.

She asks me what ships I saw on my journey. She wonders if I saw her husband's at Cresten. She shows me a model of it as the little ones cling to the ruffles of her skirt. He's Admiral of a fleet, she says. Gone for months at a time. I shake my head. Tell her I slept in Cresten. She seems sad and picks up Garsi, who's up from her nap now. She's a fat little thing who toddles around, cooing and laughing. It's unsettling to see such a happy baby. They're uncommon in Sunteri.

Callers are announced, and when Nessa leaves to greet them Saesa fetches cloaks and takes me away to the upstairs. We pass the room where I had my bath and go up a narrow stairway to a third floor. Then up a ladder into a place that seems secret. Private. Tiny. Too enclosed. Too much like the tree. The roots. I stop. Back down. She takes my hand. I feel a little better.

"Come on, I want to show you." She tugs me.

"I don't like closed spaces," I say.

"But it isn't." Saesa pushes at the bottom of a square and it swings open with a rush of cold air. "It's the widow's walk."

She slips outside and I follow, onto a narrow balcony on the roof of the house. Manse. Lilen already corrected me twice. This is a manse. The city sprawls out beneath us, and beyond it the ocean. White specks of sails dot the gray in the distance. Six specks. Six ships.

"Those must be the prince's ships. The ones you mentioned." Saesa points into the distance. She shivers and ties her cloak on. Hands me my green one. Moves closer to me as the wind whips past, so her shoulder presses mine.

"There's the castle," she says and points northward.

It's grand. White. Nonthreatening, but strong. We stay up here all afternoon. She shows me the whole city: The Mage Academy, the arena, the guard watch towers. It's nothing like Zhaghen. Everything is bright and clean. No spires looming. No Sorcerers watching and threatening. I smile when I think of them, crumbled to ash and dust. Ruined now. Towers no more.

Saesa teaches me about the market places and the forges and taverns and dealers. She tells me about Nessa and the others. How they were all unwanted at some time, and Nessa took them in. Taught them to be collectors. Gatherers of information. Watchers. Listeners.

Tonight, she says, we'll have a visitor. A friend of Maisie's from the palace. Maisie is the woman on the stairs. The one with the baby on her hip. The baby is hers. His name is Errie. She worked in the palace once. She can't anymore. She lives here now and takes care of the others with Nessa, so she can be with Errie. Her friends come to see her from time to time. Maids from the palace on their evenings off. They'll talk about lots of things. If we sit quietly and don't ask questions, we might get to hear all of it. We'll learn about the prince, Saesa says. The one on the ship. I wonder if they'll talk about the towers.

They do, some. While the ladies gossip, Saesa teaches me how to play a game of chips on the carpet in front of the hearth. They say the fires in Zhaghen could start a war. Sunteri is blaming Cerion. Saying it must have been their spies who lit them. Demanding things. Money. Mages. Zhaghen's Master Sorcerers have disappeared. Nobody knows where they are, or if they're even still alive. I know some of them aren't. I know they were killed in some battle before the spires burned. I don't say a word. They drink spirits and talk about Prince Vorance. Rumors say he's in love with the princess. She's smitten, too, so much so that they think it might be Sorcery. It's wrong, they say, that he should come to woo her while his country is threatening war. How sad if all of it is true, and the two young lovers are simply caught in the midst of it.

The talk turns bawdy as the ladies drink more wine. Nessa sends us away. We have rooms of our own, but after everyone is settled in bed Saesa sneaks into mine. We talk until midnight about what we heard. I want to tell her things I shouldn't, but the words don't come. Tomorrow, she tells me, we'll go out into the city. She'll show me where she practices sword fighting. She'll show me secret places. She goes out and closes the door.

The room is too clean and too closed up. The bed too soft and plush. I open the window, pull a blanket to the floor, and finally fall asleep.

Nightmares. This is why I don't like sleep. My older sister sits in the field, a book balanced on her knee. She picks the red blooms idly while she reads, and tosses them to a basket beside her. A breeze fans her black hair. It glistens in the sun. I look away, across the vast field of deep red. I know what's coming. The sound of the lash. My sister's painful cries. When I look back, her golden skin is streaked with tears and blood. She fades away into the flowers, leaving nothing behind. Just me.

Later now. Years later, in our small house. It's too hot, even at night. We sleep on mats, Nan, little Zhilee, and me. The door, which is little more than a board on a hinge, slams open. He looms and we scream. The Sorcerer with skin so covered in the curls of the Mark that it's black and blue as night. He wears it as a badge. A wicked display of his power. I've seen him before. Long ago, when he came to lure my sister. Offered her knowledge. Travel. Adventure. An escape from the whip. She accepted. A gift is a trick.

I put myself between him and the others, but it's no use. He binds us with spells. Forces us to stand and dress. To walk to a carriage and get in. Nan's eyes are filled with terror. Zhilee weeps silently. I stare into her eyes to try to comfort her. It's the only thing I can do. I'm paralyzed. Can't move. Then, the roots come. They creep around us, crushing the carriage, binding us as the trees grow up into the sky. They press our faces to the hot desert floor. The sand is fine like powder. It coats my nose and mouth as I breathe it. I feel I'll die from thirst. Then the roots drip their musty, earthy water. Not too often. Not too much. Just enough so I don't die. I drink as much as they let me.

Creatures gather. White, dead-looking, tiny creatures with great eyes as black as sister's hair. They torment us. Pick at us. Tease with food. Dance. Screech. Fight each other. Pinch Zhilee. Make her cry and plead. I scream at them. Scream and rage and fight to get out.

"Tib?" Saesa's hand is on me. I kick and claw and thrash. She shakes me. "Wake up, it's just a bad dream, Tib."

My eyes fly open and look straight into hers. Green. Bright. Filled with life. I'm panting. My throat is raw from screaming. I sit up. Hug my knees. Try to calm myself.

"Did they hear?" I ask warily. My voice is hoarse. I rub my neck.

"Don't be embarrassed," Saesa says comfortingly. She gets up and closes the window. Shuts out the sun and the open space. Looks at me and remembers, and opens it again. "I have them, too. Most of us do. Even Maisie. Even Nessa."

I stare in a daze as she takes the blanket from me and puts it back on the bed. She straightens it perfectly and explains that if we make up our own rooms, the maid leaves a treat on the bed. She has clothes for me. Old clothes of Raefe's. Long-sleeved red shirt. Clean, gray trousers. She goes out to wait for me to change. I stare at the red shirt for a long time. It makes me frightened and angry, this color. I think of red powder in barrels. Blossoms. My sister. Saesa knocks and I finally put it on, and we go downstairs together.

I feel empty this morning as the dream fades. Unsure. Uneasy. At breakfast, Nessa is telling Saesa to bring me around the city. To the market. Teach me how to find things out. *Stay here.* The thought rings over and over in my mind. Nessa doesn't notice my mood. She's excited to have another collector. She wants us to learn more about the six ships. She wants information on Prince Vorance. She wants word on her husband's ship.

When breakfast is done, everyone files into the hall. The children all start putting on boots and wraps. My heart races as Saesa chatters excitedly to me. I don't hear her. I'm trying to hide my panic. *Stay here.* I can't go. I don't put on my cloak. I still have my boots on, though. I slept in them.

"Ready, Tib?" Saesa asks as she drapes my shoulders with the green cloak. She ties the ties and turns away. She crosses the threshold. I try to follow but I can't. I pause with my toes on it. *Stay here. Stay here.* I will myself to take another step, but my foot won't go. Saesa tugs my arm and I'm furious and scared. I can't leave.

"Stop!" I shout and I shove her. She stumbles down the step.

"Hey!" she cries as she catches herself on the railing. "What's the matter with you?"

Saesa frowns up at me as the wind whips past. She's wounded. Her feelings are, I mean. I can't answer, though. I don't know what's wrong, I just know I can't leave and it scares me. Raefe spins in the street and eyes me. At his hip, the hilt of his rapier flashes in the sun. I back away feeling awful. I didn't mean to be rough with her.

"I'm sorry," I say.

"It's all right," she says with a shrug. Everyone just stands there, watching me.

"Go with the girl."

Yes, go with the girl. Relief floods through me as I lift my foot and step outside.

"Sorry," I say again as she takes my hand.

"It's all right, really. Come on!" she laughs.

We run past Raefe and off toward the market. The chill wind bites at us, and before we're at the end of the row my cheeks are numb. I duck my head against it and pull my hood up around me. Saesa tugs her orange hat over her ears. Her curls shine and bounce as she walks and chatters to me. She isn't bothered anymore that I pushed her. I am. Never touch a girl, Nan always said. It's wrong. It's bad. I scowl beneath my hood. Why couldn't I step outside? It troubles me, but soon I'm too distracted by Saesa and the market to worry.

She takes me to a few different booths. Even in the cold, people are out selling and shopping. Saesa buys little things. A ribbon finds out that the Mages came to the steps last night, to clear the ice. A bundle of salt fish tells us that the prince arrived quietly along with only a few men. Saesa gives me some coppers and makes me try. I buy a smooth stone with a ship painted onto it at the next booth. The merchant tells me the prince went straight to the palace. He was all wrapped up, because of the cold. Nobody really saw what he looked like.

We go to the sea wall, where the lift arms reach out over the ocean. It takes three men cranking the wheel to hoist the platform all the way up from the foot of the cliffs. This is how freight is moved to and from the ships docked far below. She tells me to stand across the street and watch. She changes her expression to look younger. Sweeter. Wide-eyed. Innocent. She skips to the wall beside one of the men and tilts her head to the side. They talk for a while, and then she comes back to me. Tells me everything she found out.

"It took four Mages to clear the steps last night," she says quietly as we leave the market and walk toward the palace. "That's important because the Mages haven't been out for awhile. They've been keeping really quiet the past couple of months, ever since His Majesty's Elite returned from their quest. The prince insisted on using the steps and not the lift. He didn't want any special treatment or consideration. Rumor has it, he's very down-to-earth. Of course, the palace didn't want him to slip, so they sent the Mages to clear the steps. Six men climbed up with him. The rest of the crew went to the taverns. Three of his ships stayed, three left. Oh, and the one you were on is still there, too. More ships are coming from Sunteri in a month. Nessa will want to know that."

"Why are more coming?" I ask. Maybe they found out about the boy who burned the towers. Maybe they're coming to get me.

"I imagine to escort the prince back to Sunteri, with or without the princess," she says. "It'll be fun to find out how it's going between them. Lilen thinks they should be married."

"What do you think?" I peer up at the castle spires as we pass by. They're tall. As tall as the spires of Zhaghen. I bet I could climb to the top.

"I think marriage is good for princesses, but not for me. Babies and washing and cooking," she wrinkles her nose, "no, thanks. And an alliance with Sunteri would be good for Cerion, as long as they can keep their Sorcerers in check."

We walk for a while, until my toes are numb inside of my boots.

"Where are we going?" I pull my cloak tight around me as we duck into a gust of wind.

"Well, Nessa will be happy with what we found out, so now we can do whatever we want. I want to show you something," she says excitedly.

She leads me through a maze of crowded houses and shops until we reach a splintered doorway. The sign beside it rattles in the wind. It's so faded and chipped that I can barely make out the sword and anvil painted on it.

Inside it's dark, crowded, and hot. Cramped, like the roots. I hesitate in the door until Saesa pulls me through and slams it shut behind me. A broad man with a bald head leans to peer at us through stacks of weapons and wares. His eyes are hopeful until he sees us, then disappointed. Still, he smiles.

"Morning, Miss Saesa. Come to see Feat?" he asks as he ducks beneath the counter. He retrieves a bundle as Saesa leads me into the depths of the shop. It's not so bad once we're inside. It opens up a little at the counter.

"Who's your friend?" The man's eyes glint with amusement as he unravels the oilcloth and glances at me.

"This is Tib," Saesa says, her eyes fixed on the counter. "Tib, this is Mister Bren. And this," she pulls the last bit of oilcloth away to reveal a gleaming blade, "this is Feat."

I eye the blade, which is as long as my forearm and almost as broad. The hilt is banded with leather, and the cross guard has a deep chevron design. I don't know much about swords. It seems fine. Saesa is obviously very proud of it, so I make my eyes go wide with admiration.

"It's nice," I say.

"It's designed after Sir Azaeli's. She lost hers on the last quest, though," Saesa sighs, a little disappointed. "She has a new one now, but I've heard her say how much she misses the old one. This is much smaller, of course. I'm not a two-hander like she is." She traces her fingers along the hilt lovingly under Mister Bren's watchful eye. Everyone goes quiet. Finally, she reaches to her purse.

"Here you go, sir." Saesa pulls out a silver coin and slides it across the counter looking hopeful. "How much more, now?"

"One gold forty yesterday. This," he says, tapping the coin on the counter, "has you paid down to one gold and thirty-nine, Miss Saesa. You're getting there. Unless you have anything else for me?"

Saesa chews her lip thoughtfully and glances at me.

"Prince Vorance arrived last night," she ventures, watching him carefully.

"Aye, knew that," he says with a short nod. He folds the oilcloth over the blade as Saesa watches with longing.

"Surely his men will need their weapons tended. They'll need your services," she offers.

"I like where this is going." Bren scratches out a figure on a scrap of parchment pinned to the sword's wrappings. He writes the new figure beneath it. The scrap is covered in similarly crossed out amounts. Saesa has been paying for this sword for months. Years, probably.

"I can drive them to you. Bring you business," she says.

Mister Bren smirks as he tucks the sword below and then rests his elbows on the counter so he's eye-level with her.

"You do that, Miss," he says, "and I'll knock five silver off your sword for every gold spent by a man who comes in here sayin' your name. Deal?" He offers a rough hand across the counter, and Saesa shakes it firmly.

"Deal," she grins. "Come on, Tib. Let's go to the Inn."

Outside, we're greeted by a sheet of frozen rain and Raefe, who's leaning against the rickety railing under the shelter of the leaky awning.

"How's Feat?" he asks Saesa with a hint of disapproval.

"Raefe…" she sighs. "I was just…"

"Saesa."

"One gold thirty-nine silver to go," she mutters.

"Good," he says, tugging his hood down over his brow. "That should take a while. Maybe by then you'll be trained up enough for it."

"I'm ready now," Saesa says with a huff. "Hub says I'm the best in my group." She crosses her arms under her furs.

"Care to test that again?" he asks. "Or do you remember the last time we had a bout?" He steps closer so he's towering over her. Saesa purses her lips and glares at him. She doesn't say anything.

"I thought so," Raefe says. "Come on, let's go home. It's almost luncheon." He ducks into the rain and Saesa turns to me.

"I really hate him sometimes," Saesa says as she watches him saunter away. "You're so lucky you don't have a brother to boss you," she grumbles. "Come on."

Luncheon is pots of melted cheese with warm crusty bread to dunk into them, and vegetables and Saesa's salt fish, all spread out on the dining table with fancy silver and fine dishes with gold rims that glint in the candle light.

"After we eat," Saesa says to me as I stuff myself with bread and cheese, "I have my training. You could come."

"It's time Tib figures out what he wants to work towards, if he's keen to stay," Nessa says. She bounces baby Garsi on her knee while Emme clings to her arm.

"Well, he can't do swords like Saesa and Raefe and me," Ruben pipes up through a mouthful. "He's too skinny."

"I was weak when I started. Hub helped me get stronger." Saesa argues.

"Master Hubvenchlis, Saesa." Nessa corrects her.

"Master Hubvenchlis," Saesa repeats apologetically.

"What is it you like to do, Tib?" Nessa catches a bit of drool with a lace-trimmed serviette as Garsi gums a crust of bread.

"Climbing," I say. Right away I realize that I shouldn't have. It might connect me to the towers.

"Magic."

Nessa makes a suggestion that I don't hear. Everyone watches me, waiting for me to answer.

"Say magic."

Yes, say magic. No, I don't want to. I despise magic. Mages, Sorcerers, I don't want anything to do with them.

"Tib?" Saesa whispers. Nudges me. Everyone's looking.

"Magic," I say reluctantly. Most of the eyebrows around the table go up. Lilen is the first to break the silence.

"No offense," she says, "but you really don't seem bright enough."

"Lilen!" Maisie scolds. "Just because you start off saying 'no offense' doesn't make it all right to insult someone."

"Well anyway, he's too old. Mages start at six, like I did."

"How old are you, anyway?" Ruben asks me as he dunks his bread and pulls out a long, stretchy string of cheese from the pot.

"I don't know," I say, shrugging.

"You don't know?" Lilen asks with disbelief.

"You must be around my age. Twelve." Saesa says.

"Nobody ever kept track." I mumble.

"Didn't you have birthdays?" Emme asks, wide-eyed.

"Not really." I look around at them and then down at my fine plate. They have no idea. "In the fields, we work. We work every day, all day. We work and we sleep. Picking, hauling, pulling, dumping. It never stops. You're too tired for anything but bread and sleep. We don't play. We don't dance or celebrate birthdays. We work. We sleep." I pluck at my shirt. "So you can wear your red." The room falls into awkward silence. Finally, Rube speaks up.

"Well, do you have hair yet?" he asks. Nessa covers her laugh.

"Ruben!" Maisie gasps. "Where did you hear that?"

"Raefe," Ruben leans across the table. "He says you get hair on your chest when you're thirteen. I'm going to have a beard. If you don't have any, you're probably twelve. Do you?" I shake my head.

Nessa clears her throat, still quite amused.

"I'll see if I can set up an interview for you, Tib, if you're certain," she says. "Studying at the Academy is a hefty expense, but Master Rendin and I have an agreement. If you're serious and he deems you suitable, I'm sure we can work something out."

I spend a few quiet days with Saesa, gathering information, paying a silver on her sword, following her around, before Master Rendin shows up for my interview. The Mage is warm to Nessa, and she doesn't seem frightened of him at all. Not like I am. She welcomes him into the sitting room and offers him tea. It's just us: Nessa, Master Rendin, and me. I have new clothes now. Not red. Green trousers. White shirt. Blue vest. I picked them out myself. I kept my boots, though. They're good boots.

I'm not sure why Nessa made such a fuss over my appearance, when Master Rendin doesn't seem so concerned with his own at all. His hair is a great nest of white frizz that nearly covers his face. It doesn't look like it has ever been combed. His white eyebrows are so long that they creep up and tangle into the nest, and his beard goes all the way to his belt where it's caught in the clasp of it. He watches me with a twinkle in his eye as I take a seat across from him. I try not to shiver. He and Nessa make small talk until the tea comes. I'm glad. I don't want to talk to him. After a while, though, he turns his attention to me.

"Tib," he says. "Nessa tells me you're interested in an apprenticeship at the Academy."

No, I think to myself. *I don't want to do this.*

"Say yes, sir."

"Yes, sir. I am." I mumble.

"Delightful," Master Rendin smiles at me. "And won't you tell me why? What is it about magical studies that interests you?" There's an awkward stretch of silence as I try to think of a reply. Nothing about magic interests me. It only brings destruction. Pain. Mages are wicked people. Selfish. Power hungry. Nessa reaches to pat my hand, which is clenched into a fist in my lap.

"Don't be shy, dear. You can speak freely to Master Rendin," she says with an encouraging nod.

I look across at the Mage. Maybe he isn't so bad. He has none of the Mark that covered the Sorcerers who lured my sister away and later captured my family. He has a kindness about him. As I look at him, the space beside his right ear glitters. There's a silent flare. A stream of light. He doesn't seem to notice it, nor does Nessa. I shift in my seat and the answer comes to me.

"I want to learn. I want to know things. So I can help people." The beam of light pulses between his ear and the odd shimmer, and then it fades slowly away until it's gone. I glance at Nessa, who bobs her head at me again. She's looking at me with an odd expression. Nobody has looked at me that way before. It takes me some time to realize what it is. Pride. She's proud of me.

The interview goes on for a while, but not as long as I expected it to. When he's through with his questions, Nessa dismisses me. I go out to find Saesa milling nearby. When I close the door behind me, she presses her ear to it and beckons me close.

"Don't you want to know what they're saying about you?" she whispers.

"Not really," I whisper.

"Oh, Tib. Come on." She beckons me again, and I lean against the door to listen.

"I'm sure you understand our hesitation," Master Rendin is saying. "He is Sunteri, after all. After the last one we accepted…"

"Of course," Nessa says. There's the tinkling sound of silver on a cup as she stirs her tea. "I'm certain you'll make the right decision for all those involved.

"They're talking about Viala," Saesa whispers. "She was Sunteri. She went bad. The Academy has been under close scrutiny since then." The name causes my head to go light and fuzzy. I cling to the door. Close my eyes. The image assaults me. My sister sitting among the red blossoms, her black hair fanned out by the breeze, the book on her knee.

"What happened to her?" I manage hoarsely.

"Nobody knows," Saesa replies. "She disappeared. Rumor says she was stripped, but there's no proof of it. It's actually caused a lot of trouble lately."

I shake my head slowly, unable to focus on anything even as Saesa keeps talking. Viala. The name echoes through my mind and along with it the image of my sister riding away with the Sorcerers. The roots. The trees. The dust.

Chapter Three:

MEVYN
Tib

"Climb the wall."

Yes, climb the wall. It feels good to scale it to the top, up to the ledge that overlooks the ravine. I found this place on my own. It's a secret place, tucked away past the spires of the palace. Hidden by the thick trees of the forest park. The wall plunges on the other side to a river three stories down. It's dark. I can't see the waterfall from here, the one that drains into the sea behind the palace. I can hear it, though. Peaceful and soothing. This is my favorite place now. My own. I didn't even tell Saesa about it, though I've been coming here for a couple of days.

I dangle my feet over the edge. Wait. Listen. The air in front of me shimmers like it did beside the Mage. A figure emerges, pale and gaunt and only as large as my hand. His eyes are black but bright at the same time. Everything else is faded. Pale skin, yellow-white hair, faded blue pants. Reddish stubs at his back where his wings once were. Almost colorless. I press myself back against the arch. My heart races. I grip the stone, ready to climb down. Ready to run.

"Stay."

Yes, stay. His voice is in my mind and also in the air around me. Stronger than it has been. He drifts closer to me and our eyes meet. Link. I know him. I trust him. This is Meyvn. We've been through things together. Many things. Roots and sand. Towers and flames. Ships. Nessa's manse.

"*There,*" he says, both in my mind as always and also aloud. I remember him now, though he's changed a little. His skin has more color to it. He seems stronger. Not skeletal as he has been at the trees or on the ship. *How am I remembering all of this now?* I wonder. *Where have these memories been?*

"It's typical to have confusion," Meyvn says. "Don't be alarmed. You remember me now, hm?"

Memories surface and fall away in my mind. I see a time when he was nearly dead. Almost all bones. A shadow of what he had been. Dancing around my root prison. Shouting orders about Nan and Zhilee. Zhilee, little sister. He defended her. Kept the others away. What happened to her? I can't remember. He's right. I'm so confused.

"You…" I whisper. The white figures of my nightmares flash before me. "You look different. Better."

"Yes, the Mage was a great help. Thank you for that. I wondered how we would lure one in. It was easier than I expected. I was sorry to make you lie to them."

"You made me say I wanted to study there? Just so you could take his magic?" I ask, shaking my head in disbelief. I think of the Mage in the sitting room. The strange shimmer that nobody seemed to notice. The stream of light that bled from him.

"Just a little bit." Mevyn sits on the ledge beside me. Peers up at me. Watches. I can't stop thinking of Zhilee.

"It was necessary," Mevyn says. "He won't even miss it."

"What happened to her?" I ask. "My sister?"

"Which?"

"Zhilee."

"You," he says gently, "asked me to take that memory away. Are you sure you want to know?"

I push myself to remember the night that the Sorcerer came and took us. We were all under his spell. He brought us to the trees. Left us with the fallen fae, trapped in our cruel prisons. I start to shake. There was one. One white, twisted creature. One with a red slab that sent promises and commands. I could never see the writing, but I could see the gold light. I could see the reactions of the one who read its words. Anger. Sadness. Fury. Defeat. Cruelty. A fateful word. Sunset. The dread it carried with it. Then it goes black, as though nothing happened after.

Next, I'm climbing the towers. Lighting fires. Swimming to a ship.

"It's better if you don't know, Tib." Meyvn says. "Trust in me. Trust in our agreement."

"You told me to do all of those things," I murmur.

"What things?"

"Burning the towers," I whisper.

"That was your idea," he says with the same careful, gentle tone.

"Why?" I ask. I'm not sure I want the answer.

"To avenge Zhilee and your nan. To stop the Sorcerers from hurting anyone else. You came up with it."

"To avenge…" I shake my head as the realization stabs me like a knife through the heart. "They're dead."

"Dead." Mevyn whispers, shaking his head. "It's just you and I left. We're the last. The only remaining."

I think of the cruel white creatures that bound us in our root prison. How they were commanded by words on a stone. Ordered by Sorcerers who made promises and didn't keep them. Sorcerers who turned them against each other. I remember the screams. Animal. Guttural. Savage. White and bony. Fighting. Slashing. Sapping each other until there was nothing left. And Mevyn, who tucked himself beside me. Whispered ways to keep us both safe until it was over. And when it was over, he's right. No one was left. Just us two.

I bury my head in my knees and sob so hard I fear I'll fall off the edge of the wall. I remember Mevyn doing the same as we sat on the edge of the empty bowl that was once his people's Wellspring. Magic given freely by fairies, and drained by the greed of men. Reaped and ravaged by those who only wanted more power. These words. Are they my own? Are they Meyvn's? This grief, is it mine? Is it his? I can't tell. I don't know.

"The last." Meyvn sighs. "Unless…"

"Unless?" I look up. Wipe my nose on my sleeve.

"If we could get to Kythshire, they would help us. My kind flourish there. I'm stronger now. We could make the journey together."

"They would help us?"

"Yes. There are ways. Ways to restore the Wellspring. To guard it from Mages and Sorcerers. To revive my people. We could put an end to the oppression of Zhaghen. Free those gripped in its clutches. Make it a city like this one. Like Cerion, where babies laugh and no child is motherless. No one would have to suffer a fate like the one suffered by you and your departed family. We could live in harmony."

"Wouldn't it be better if Sunteri's Wellspring remained empty?" I ask. "Then nobody could use the magic or fight over it. If it stayed dried up, the Sorcerers would be powerless."

"Not so," Mevyn says gravely. "They would only move on to another spring and grow more ruthless. They tried already. They were almost able to overtake Kythshire's Wellspring, thanks to your sister. They were stopped. Thwarted, by the knight Azaeli."

"Azaeli," I remember the short knight in the procession leading the prince out of the city. Meyvn's voice in my mind, telling me to take note of her.

"They will go on, the Sorcerers of Zhaghen, until they are defeated once and for all."

"Weren't they? I thought I heard…"

"Not all. Even with the towers burnt, they survive. They spread out over the land like a sickness, leaving our oasis wasted. Ready to reap and drain and gain more. Stepstone and Elespen and Haigh. Hywilkin and Tunvidel. All of these places are threatened. War, Tib. War and death will follow in their wake, and only you and I know. Only you and I can stop them." I stare at him, wide-eyed. Terrified.

"What can we do?" I ask. I'm only a boy. I couldn't fight Sorcerers. Hide from them, maybe, but not fight them.

"We must go to Kythshire and petition for their help in restoring Sunteri's Wellspring. Together with them, we can determine a way to stop the spread of Sorcery. You and I cannot do it alone, Tib. We need allies."

"Allies," I say, nodding.

"Now, as I hate to do, but as I always do with your permission, I will clear this moment from your memory. For my protection and for yours. Do you understand why?"

I frown and stare down at the rushing water below. How many of these conversations have we had? How many times has he wiped them away? Why me, I wonder. But then, who else could he have trusted? Not a man, a grown man. No, he needed someone unremarkable. Someone who could slip in and out of situations unnoticed. He's right. We're the last. We're in this together. The last of our families.

"I understand," I say. "But wait, when will we go? Do we have to go alone?" I think of Saesa. She's always talking about adventures. She's good with her sword, surprisingly good. I've watched her training these two days. I don't see why Raefe has discouraged her. She beats any opponent they put her against.

"We shall go when the time presents itself." Meyvn says. "Who would you bring? For what purpose?"

"Saesa. She can fight. She's my friend. I don't want to leave her."

"Perhaps."

Yes, perhaps. The word echoes in my mind as I look up at the stars. My thoughts wander to the manse and to Nessa and Saesa who care about me. They're probably sleeping soundly in their beds. I wonder how long I've been sitting here. Quiet. Thinking. It feels like hours. It's so peaceful and open here that I doze off, and when I wake it's not yet dawn. Something is closed in my fist. I move my fingers and feel the coins slide together inside them. I look. Gold. Two gold. My heart races as I immediately think of Saesa. Bren. Feat. One gold thirty-two. That was the last tally.

I scramble down the wall and race through the streets, faster than a city boy could. Quieter, too. Unheard. Unseen. No one is up, anyway. It's too early. Even the sea market is deserted. My heart is pumping, maybe from the run, maybe from my excitement. Saesa will finally buy Feat. Then she can come with me when I go. Where, I don't remember. But I know what's meant to happen.

My shutters are still open. I climb up the trellis and slip into my room. Inside it's silent. I creep through the hallway and stop at Saesa's door. Listen. Breathing. She's asleep. Cautiously I tiptoe to her bed. Push the coins under her pillow. Go back to my room. Doze off again.

Saesa's squeal wakes me. I roll out of bed and rub my eyes as I go to the door. She's in the hallway, rushing toward me. Her eyes are bright. She casts a glance over her shoulder before she skips into my room and closes the door.

"Tib!" she whispers excitedly. "I don't know how, but look!" She opens her hand to show me the gold. I try to look surprised and puzzled. I hope it's convincing. She's too excited to notice, anyway. "They were under my pillow! Where do you suppose they came from? Oh, it doesn't matter, does it? Now I can get Feat!" The last part she whispers as a knock echoes from outside. Not on my door, but down the hallway.

"Saesa," Raefe calls. "You okay?"

Saesa tucks the gold into her pocket.

"Get dressed," she says to me. "I want to go before breakfast." She's too distracted to realize I already am. I grin as she jogs to my door to answer her brother.

"Over here," she says. "I'm fine." She goes out.

"I thought I heard you—"

"I was excited, that's all. I thought of something." I hear her door close, and I peek out into the hallway. Raefe has already gone downstairs. I follow and get my cloak from the cupboard. An insistent knock on the main door makes me jump.

"Who in the seven stars…at this hour of the morning?" Maisie mutters as she brushes past me in her morning coat with Garsi toddling behind her, squealing happily. Maisie opens the door. I can't see much. Chain mail leggings. The butt of a spear resting beside heavy boots. I slink back, tucking myself into the corner beside the cupboard where I'm sure not to be seen.

"City guard," a deep voice booms. Nessa rushes down the stairs. She sees me as she scoops up Garsi, and gives me a quick, reassuring smile. When she turns to the door, her smile brightens sweetly.

"Why, Freland," Nessa says with surprise, "won't you come in out of the snow?"

The boots hesitate. Stomp on the mat. Clomp inside.

"Thank you, Lady Ganvent."

"Of course," Nessa says graciously. "What can we do for you? Something warm to drink, perhaps?"

"No m'lady. This isn't a social visit. We're sent to find a boy. Around twelve, thirteen. Black hair. Sunteri features. A few around the city said they might've seen him going around with your Saesa."

"Oh?" Nessa asks. Saesa comes out from her room and peers over the railing. She meets my gaze, her eyes wide with fear. Quickly, she changes her expression to that of mild interest as she turns her attention to the scene at the door.

"He's suspected of a crime," Freland says gruffly. "Need to question him. Can't say any more than that. Have you seen him? Do you have him here?"

"Maisie, won't you get my silk purse? It's in the cupboard, there." Nessa says. Maisie opens the cupboard door. She glances at me and I give her a pleading look. They can't take me. Not now. I have something important to do. I wish I could remember what. Maisie presses her lips together. She gives a very slight nod toward the door beside me. The dining room. It leads to the kitchen. The kitchen has a back door. I look up at Saesa again. She's careful to keep her eyes on the guard. She won't give me away. Neither will Nessa, apparently.

"Sorry, m'lady. I won't take a coin for this one. My orders are from the captain himself."

"Freland!" Nessa admonishes. "I would never presume to bribe you. How could you even suggest it? Never mind about the purse, Maisie." Maisie chuckles and closes the cupboard. She turns her back to me but stays in place. Blocks the guard's view of the dining room door.

"Is the boy here or isn't he, Lady Ganvent? I would hate to have to call in a search."

"Need I remind you," Nessa's voice is low now. Firm. "That your captain ranks beneath my husband, whose house falls under sanctions that prevent such a search?

"Under the circumstances, I'm afraid it's warranted." The boots turn. The door opens again. Freland calls to others. Saesa runs down the stairs. Outside, I hear more boots. Maisie waves her hand at me behind her back.

"Run."

Yes, run. I can't wait for Saesa. I duck through the dining room to the kitchen where Bette, the cook, is working hard at breakfast. She smiles at me as I streak past and throw my cloak over my shoulders. She's used to children clambering around the kitchens, sneaking food. She doesn't think twice about it. I don't take anything, though. I just skid out into the alley and close the door quietly behind me. Outside, everything is covered in a thick blanket of white. I've never seen snow before. Great fluffs of flakes fall from the sky, swirling and floating and settling peacefully onto cushions of itself on the ground. I step down and it comes to my ankles, almost over the tops of my new boots. As enchanted as I am by the powdery soft snowflakes that cling to my cloak, I'm also aware of the problem it creates for me. Tracks. No one else has come down here. When the guards do, they'll see my footsteps in no time. I scowl.

"Just go."

Yes, just go. Just run. Quickly. I dart off into the alley. At first I don't know where to go, but then it hits me. Saesa will go to Bren's for Feat, I'm sure of it. I'll go there. I'll wait for her. Say goodbye. I glance behind me and see there are no footprints in the snow. As I run, I watch my feet. The snow pushes down and springs back up again as though untouched. A strange shimmer hovers over my boots. It reminds me of something. The air beside the Mage's head in Nessa's sitting room, maybe. The wind gusts around me and the snow is so thick that I can barely see the buildings on either side of the narrow cobbled road. I finally reach Bren's and duck inside.

Hopeful as ever, Bren leans to greet me as the bell rings. When he sees it's me, I get his usual forced smile.

"Master Tib," he says. "You're here early. And no Saesa?"

"She's coming," I reply as I shake the already melting snow

from my cloak. I try hard to seem calm, not like a boy being chased by city guards. I'm glad it's cold so my shivering doesn't seem suspicious. "She's buying Feat today."

"Is that so?" He invites me to come around by the forge to warm and dry myself and then he goes out the back door and comes back in. Putters around the shop, arranging things. We talk some, but not much. I don't know how to drive a conversation like Saesa does. When I begin to lose hope that she's coming, the bell at the front door rings.

"Ah, Miss Saesa," Bren says with a hint of relief. "We were expecting you."

"We?" She rushes to the counter. Sees me. Gasps with relief, and then catches herself as she glances at Bren. She hides her surprise quickly with a laugh. "Tib, you were right!" She turns to Bren. "He said he could beat me here. He's good at a foot race, even in the snow." Bren grunts and smiles as he ducks beneath the counter to retrieve Feat.

"Tib says it's your big day," he says as Saesa lovingly unwraps the sword. She nods her response. Her eyes are teary as she reaches into her pocket and pulls out the two gold pieces.

"Well, well. Someone's caught a windfall." Bren takes the tally sheet from its pin as I come around the counter to Saesa's side. He writes PIF across the marks. "Got enough there for a scabbard and belt, too, if you want 'em," he says to her.

"What about a knife for Tib? He needs something," she says with a worried glance at me.

"Aye, I'll throw that in," Bren says.

As the weapon smith strides around the tiny space collecting her items, Saesa moves closer to me. She's holding back from saying anything at all to me, I can tell. Afraid she'll give me away. Bren comes to her side and fits her belt. She slips the sword into its case and sniffles, grinning.

"I can't believe it's mine," she whispers.

"And for you, Tib," he says. He gives me a good knife. Nothing fancy or special. I've never had my own knife before, though. I feel a little taller as I thread it onto my belt. "Be careful with it. Both of you."

"Thank you!" Saesa cries and throws her arms around Bren, who pats her shoulder a little awkwardly.

"Don't be a stranger, you, now that you've got what you

wanted," Bren says.

He glances toward the door nervously. That's when we hear it. Marching outside. Raised voices. Saesa turns to me, alarmed. She pulls her furs tight around her arms. My heart thumps. Bren looks toward the door. His jaw clenches. He tips his head toward the back door.

"Best go out that way," he says. Neither of us thinks. Saesa grabs my hand and we dart outside. Into the snow. Right into the pair of guards standing there, waiting for us. One grabs Saesa, the other grabs me, pinning my arms.

"Thanks for the heads-up, Bren. Your reward," the guard holding me says. He tosses a pouch of coins to Bren, who's standing in the doorway, watching. He catches the pouch. He doesn't look at us. Beside him on the door frame hangs a signal flag with Cerion's crest beside a plain strip of red. The color sets off memories. Emotions. Anger. Fear. Helplessness. I snarl. Elbow the guard in the gut. Reach for my new knife. Struggle.

"Be calm."

Yes, be calm. I feel the command settle over me like the blanket of snow. Peace. The guard grabs the knife from my belt. Stows it somewhere. Clamps his hands around my arms.

"Let's go," he says.

"Bren," Saesa sobs, "how could you? I thought you were our friend!"

Bren pauses. Eyes the scene. Clenches his hand around the pouch of reward money.

"You didn't say nothing about the girl," he says. The guards exchange glances.

"He's right," mine says. "We've no orders to take her in."

"Right." Saesa's guard releases her with a shove. "You look like a nice girl. Go home. Make better choices in the future, eh? No more going around with this sort."

Saesa plants her feet in the snow. Her new sword is buried under the thick fur of her cloak, but I know she's got her hand on its hilt. The guard tightens his grip on my arms painfully. I try not to react. I try to be calm.

"Don't do anything you'll regret, you two," Bren warns. "I don't want any trouble out here." He hesitates, and then goes inside and closes the door behind him. The guards march me forward, but Saesa stands firm at the mouth of the alley.

"Go, Saesa." I say. "Go home."

The guard shakes me, "Nobody told you to talk, did they? Just walk."

"We'll get you out. We'll fix this, Tib. I promise. I know you didn't do anything." Saesa's faith in my innocence makes me feel worse than I do about the guards finding me. She doesn't know about the towers. I'm sure if she did, she'd never be my friend. Never make promises to help me. Saesa chews her lip. I see the small movement under her cloak. Her hand sliding from the hilt. She shakes her head tearfully as the guards loom closer. My feet shuffle in the snow. I look down. My boots are making tracks now. Pushing the snow, creating deep grooves. I hear her apology and nod. I don't look up though. I can't watch her leave me. Can't watch her go.

Chapter Four:
THE HIGH ROAD
Azi

"I'm just saying it's terribly boring to travel this way." Flitt chatters in my head. *"Horses take forever. Though at least the trees are pretty. Even though they're sleeping. And your mountains are covered in green even in the wintertime. Not like the Crag, which is always black and rocky. Still, we don't really have winter, except in the winter lands of course. But you haven't been there. Maybe next time when you come I can show you."*

"Mmm," I reply aloud as the fairy babbles on and on, circling around my head. I'm used to it now. I've learned to mostly tune her out.

"Try again!"

"That'd be nice." I push the thought into her mind as she's been teaching me to. I don't like the feel of it. It's too imposing.

"*Good job!*" she squeals and claps. "*Oh, here comes Stinky,*" she says as Rian trots up beside me on his steed.

"Hey, Dreamy," he says with some amusement. "You're lagging again." I look up at the prince's carriage which is several lengths ahead now, and curse under my breath.

"Charming."

The wind whips my cloak as I press my heels into Pearl's haunches to quicken her pace. Rian keeps up and behind me I hear the rest of His Majesty's Elite rush to match my pace. The Elite is my parents' guild. It's a small company, hand-picked by His Majesty King Tirnon to carry out various quests and tasks. Rian's mother, Mya, is the leader. He and I grew up side by side, often spending the weeks while our parents were away dreaming of this precise moment, when we could join them on the road to adventure. He passes me and looks back, and his grin makes my heart flutter. It's only recently that our feelings for each other have grown into something more than friendship. I worried that our affections would fade in the months following our adventures in Kythshire, but if anything our feelings have grown stronger.

The air is milder now that we've breached the crest and started downhill on the winding mountain roads. The rear window of the carriage is open to the fresh breeze, and Princess Amei looks back at us and waves. Prince Eron dozes beside her, his head resting on a thick pillow propped against the carriage wall. I wave back with my free hand and then switch the banner and flex my fingers. Rian notices.

"Want me to take it?" he asks.

"Not yet," I say. Riding point for the guild is an honor I have dreamed about for years. Even after a full day of riding with both wrists aching from the effort, I'm not ready to give up our banner just yet.

A single rider thunders past us from the front of the line and falls into step beside Mya. His name is Fenston, the Captain of the Guard.

"The forest is thinning," he says to Mya with his usual stern tone. "We'll be reaching the crossroads soon. The Inn at Westhaven is expecting us around sunset. We're keeping good time but it wouldn't hurt to quicken your pace some." He looks ahead at me and I duck apologetically.

"Ooooo, you got in trouble." Flitt giggles. *"Such a funny thing, traveling so slowly and still being concerned with the time."*

"We're not in Kythshire," I push the thought to her. *"We can't just pop from here to there."*

"Too bad," she teases. I squint my eyes and risk dropping the reins to rub my temples. I don't like this Half-Realm talking, as Flitt calls it.

"*The headaches go away after a while*," Rian's voice echoes in my head. I groan.

"Not you, too," I say. "Can't we just," I lower my voice as the Captain passes us, "talk? Out loud? Like normal people?"

"It could come in handy," Rian says. "I think it's fascinating."

"You would," I tease, "Mage. I'm taking a break from it for now. I don't like it. It distracts me."

"All the more reason to practice." Flitt again. I roll my eyes and trot up closer to the back of the carriage where Amei is watching the columns of soldiers on horseback ahead of us.

"All right, Your Highness?" I ask.

"Did I hear him say we're nearly there?" the princess asks me with a sweet smile.

"Nearly," I reply. She reaches for her husband's hand and squeezes it, and he blinks awake. I watch the two exchange a smile and then he turns and sees me. A curt nod is all he gives me in greeting, and that's just fine with me. I bow respectfully and put some distance between us. A casual conversation with Amei is one thing, but I've learned to keep a safe distance between myself and the prince.

As soon as the forest thins and the fields open up on either side of the road, we're greeted by a sprinkling of subjects who I'm sure have been waiting most of the day to see Their Highnesses ride past. They cheer as the carriage comes into view and bow when we pass by. They call out blessings and well wishes for the baby Amei carries, the new heir of Cerion yet to be born. I sit a little taller in my saddle as the crowds lining the roads grow thicker. We slow as we pass through the first village at the crossroads and the crowds cry Eron's name. He calls for his horse and leaves the carriage to ride among them, stopping to shake hands and collect favors from the adoring subjects who have gathered to see him.

"No tarnished reputation here," Rian says through the smile he's planted on his face as he sidles his horse close to mine. "Look how they adore him."

"Mama, look at the Lady Knight!" I hear a girl call out. I turn to wave to her and she squeals with delight. "She waved, did you see?" The girl's father lifts her up and she tosses a bouquet of dried flowers to me. I catch them and nod to her and she claps and squeals with delight.

"Thank you," I grin at her, flattered.

"Dead things. Ugh." Flitt murmurs into my ear. *"This is too much. I'm going. See you later!"* She darts in front of my face in a rainbow-colored blur and is gone in a blink. I look around the crowd. Just as I expect, nobody seems to have seen her. Especially in crowded places, Flitt tends to stay safely hidden in the Half-Realm. Invisible to most people. On Rian's other side, excitement is coursing through the crowd.

"Mage!" they call. "Mage! Look here! Show us a spell!"

"Rian…" I warn. Magic isn't to be used as a spectacle. It's a practical art. One that's meant to help people. To protect. Not for show. Not frivolously. Especially not now. Still, Rian gives a cautious glance over his shoulder at the rest of the Elite, who are just as swarmed by the villagers. I follow his gaze. To the cheers of those around her, Mya has taken out her mandolin and started to play a bright anthem to the Royal Family. Beside her, her husband Elliot bobs his head in time to the beat, the red fringe of his hair waving this way and that. Beyond them Bryse and Cort, both warriors, are happily accepting tankards of ale from the tavern maids who have come out to greet and watch. I laugh at Bryse, who is so large that the tankard is more like a thimble to him. My father joins the two, raising his own mug. Beside him, my mother sits tall in her plate armor. She is a paladin, and the calming aura that surrounds her stretches out over the crowd, keeping the crowd at a certain level of peace despite their excitement. Brother Donal and Dacva have dismounted. They disappear into the throngs, looking for those who might need healing.

"Just one spell, just one!" Those beside him tug at Rian's robes. I shake my head in warning, but I know it's useless. Even after all we've been through, Rian can't resist the temptation to show off. He reaches for my dried bouquet and holds it up. One by one the stems grow plump and green and the petals unfurl into fragrant, soft, colorful blossoms. As if that wasn't enough, a dozen glittering butterflies burst forth from the bouquet and flutter around us. They rest on my helm and adorn my braid as he offers the bouquet back to me.

"My lady," he grins mischievously. I take it with a roll of my eyes and a bemused smile as the crowd erupts into cheers around us.

"You're hopeless," I murmur as he leans to kiss me, causing another burst of excited applause.

"What? That was Third Circle. Barely a spell at all. Now, I could show them the Color Burst I've been working on." He wriggles his brow at me. "That's Sixteenth. But it'd probably be a bad idea, as it seems to have some sort of stunning effect."

"Probably a bad idea. Yes." I sigh at him as I turn my attention back to the road ahead.

We finally make our way through the village and travel onward, reaching Westhaven just as the sun dips below the treetops. This village is much larger than the last one we passed through, and it takes us twice as long to get through the welcoming crowds to the only inn large enough to host His Highness, his guard, and our guild together.

Normally on a quest we would camp out along the road and take watches in shifts. Rian, Dacva and I would groom and feed the horses, being the most junior members of the Elite. Here, though, our horses are led away by stable boys as soon as we dismount, and maids show us to generous rooms with plush beds and tubs of steaming water to wash in. There's very little work to do. Mum, Mya, and I room together while the men of the guild have two rooms to split between them. When we're all refreshed and changed out of our armor, we go down to the dining room where a feast has been laid out for us in honor of the prince.

Prince Eron sits at the front of the room with Princess Amei at his side. As I slide onto a bench beside Rian, I take note of the pair of guards posted at the main door and the second set standing just outside.

"Why don't we stay at Forbend Keep?" I whisper to Rian as I break off a piece of bread.

"It's too far out of the way for the princess in her condition," he says. "We would have had to ride faster, and for another half day. This place is secure enough." He brushes his fingers over his goblet before he sips from it.

"What was that?" I murmur.

"You don't miss a spell, do you?" He chuckles. "Just checking. It's all fine." He nods to the table and I understand that one spell over his cup has tested everything else laid before us. It's something my Uncle Gaethon would have done if he was here, but he put his faith in Rian to be the sole Mage of the guild on this journey. As the headmaster of the Academy, Uncle had too many other responsibilities to tend to during Prince Vorance's visit.

The ale and wine flow freely, and it isn't long before most of the party is deep in its cups, including the prince himself. Mya plays throughout the night, and there is dancing and laughter and merriment. Even Eron and Amei dance carefully, and Rian and I join them with Mum and Da. After a while, I start to notice Eron's eyes on me far more often than they should be. I make a show of laughing and fawning over Rian. When that doesn't work, I excuse myself and go outside.

In the street, Rian slips his hand into mine. We walk in silence to the outskirts of the village. When he's sure nobody is watching, he whispers a word and the air shimmers around us as we settle into the Half-Realm, the space in between our realm and the dream realm, where fairies hide. Where we can be alone.

"Sorry," I say. "I had to get out of there." I lean against him and he strokes my hair.

"I know. I saw him."

"Why does he have to be so…?" I trail off. I can't think of a nice way to say it.

"Some people just are. He's been through a lot. He's trying to fill a void."

I consider his words. Eron was recently caught in the grips of a Sorceress. Viala had managed to sweet talk and connive her way up through the Mages Circles of Cerion's Academy to Master level at the young age of nineteen. She lured the Prince with seduction and held him with intricate enchantments to help her further her plots. Rian and I discovered later that she wasn't acting alone. Her schooling was paid for by a group of ruthless Sorcerers from Zhagen, the capital city of Sunteri. They plotted to take over Kythshire, the land of fairies, in order to claim the power of its Wellspring, the source of all magic in Cerion. Prince Eron was released from her spells when Viala was stripped of her magic. In the wake of the events, he has stood many secret trials accusing him of treason.

King Tirnon is a just king, but he's also a loving father. This journey to Lake Kordelya Castle is masked as a retreat for the princess who is carrying Eron's baby, but in truth it's meant to get the prince out the city and perhaps dampen the scrutiny and accusations that continue to surround him. Certainly he was under enchantments, but even so, I don't believe the prince to be completely without faults. Rumors of his lascivious activities and the fruits of them sprinkled around the city are whispered among commoners and nobles alike. My thoughts drift back to the moments just last summer when he held me in a hidden alcove of the palace, brushed his rough chin on my cheek, and breathed hotly in my ear before I was whisked away by the younger princesses.

"I wish he could fill it without being so creepy." I frown. We circle back and settle together into an alcove just across the street from the inn. No one from our world can see us in the Half-Realm, and Rian and I have made it our refuge these past few months.

"Don't worry about him," he whispers as he slides his fingers into my hair and pulls me to him. We kiss for what seems like half the night as the merry sounds of the feast drift out from the Inn, and my thoughts of the prince are long forgotten.

"Azi, you have a Stinky Mage stuck to your face. Want me to get it off?" Flitt giggles and Rian yelps and jumps away from me.

"Hey!" Rian yelps. "I told you before, that's not funny, Flitt." He scowls and rubs his nose.

"Oh, I think it is," Flitt chirps.

"Well, you're—"

"Shh, you two," I whisper. Across the street, just beside one of the posted guards, a shadow moves. At first I think it's a trick of my eyes, an odd flicker in the torch light. But as I watch, it changes slightly. It looks almost like a woman. Or the thought of a woman that hasn't quite formulated yet. "Do you see that?" I whisper.

"Oh, it's a dreamer." Flitt hovers between us. "Someone dreaming, just wandering through." As we watch the shadow shimmer and fade, another one catches my attention just down the street. It jumps up and starts to soar, and then touches down again several paces away.

"Why have we never seen them before?" I ask.

"Well, it's difficult to see anything at all with your faces always stuck together, isn't it?" Flitt scowls.

A streak of red fur emerges onto the road in the distance, and Rian tugs at his robes to smooth them. "Here comes Da," he says, and we watch as the red blur slows until we can make out the pointed ears and yellow eyes of a fox. Elliot, Rian's father, is a wood elf and a dream messenger. He takes the form of a fox in his dreams, and goes out scouting for information and delivering messages. He pauses as he reaches us and greets us with a bob of his head before ducking past the guards and into the Inn.

"Any word from the Ring?" Rian turns to Flitt. She turns her face away from him and crosses her arms.

"I've already answered two questions," she huffs. "You owe me two now. Honestly I don't think you'll ever get it right, Mage. Typical."

"What do you want to ask me?" Rian says through clenched teeth. I turn away and cover my smile. Poor Rian is constantly being antagonized by Flitt, and my laughing only seems to egg her on.

"When are you coming back to Kythshire?" she asks. She spins in place, causing the multi-colored ribbons of her skirt to fan out prettily. Rian glances at me.

"I don't know…" he says quietly, his expression darkening.

"After we see the prince and princess safely to the castle guard." I say. "That's our plan."

"That's *your* plan," Rian sighs. "I'll wait outside."

"You don't have to. You'll be fine." I try to sound reassuring.

"Maybe." Rian shrugs. I understand his concern. Kythshire has an effect on him. As soon as anyone crosses into its borders, they're met with air thick with magic. For someone like me who doesn't study the arcane, the feeling is simply confusing. It causes mood swings and inexplicable shifts in emotion. For a Mage, though, the effect is magnified. Every time a spell is cast even outside of Kythshire, the magic that courses through a Mage is intoxicating. Within Kythshire, so close to the Wellspring, it's a constant effort for a Mage to keep himself in check. I've seen how it affects him firsthand.

"Are you really going to ask to bring *her* back?" Flitt whispers. Rian's frown deepens and I hesitate to answer. There's a long, awkward pause and he finally scratches the back of his head and steps down into the street.

"I'm going back in," he says quietly. I watch him pause at the guards, who are oblivious to him. He shakes his head and goes back down the street. When he emerges again, the guards stand at attention until he identifies himself, and then they allow him to pass.

"So, are you?" Flitt bobs before me, her multi-colored light brightening so much that I have to shade my eyes.

"I don't know." I let out a deep sigh. "It would help if they could see how she is now. To know she isn't a threat anymore. I just wish I could make Rian see that he did the right thing by the choices he made for her."

"You guys are all so complicated." Flitt clicks her tongue. "We don't bother lingering in the past. What's done is done. Water past the willow tree."

"Oh, is that right?" I cross my arms and lean back against the stone with a patronizing smile. "That must be why you're so welcoming and trusting of us humans, especially Mages, hm?" I roll my eyes.

"That's different!" she squeaks at me. Inside, Mya's playing has slowed and the laughter has died down. I can hear the murmur of more serious conversation in quiet undertones beneath the music.

"I'm going in. Are you coming?"

"No way, it stinks in there. Like ale and smoke and people-sweat. Ugh. I'll see you tomorrow."

"Goodnight, Flitt."

"Night!" She pops out of view and I'm tempted to follow her home. I've teleported to her grotto once before, but it was a dire situation. I'm not sure I could do it again. She'd probably call me rude if I did. Still, I don't want to have the same circling conversation with Rian regarding Viala that we've had these past few weeks, and I know that once I go inside, that's just where the discussion will lead.

"I don't like going back on my word," Rian whispers to me later in the hallway outside of my room. Everyone else has gone to bed, and I'm so exhausted I can barely stand.

"It's ordered by His Majesty, Rian. He just wants to see her. He won't keep her. She can go back to Iren after. You're not breaking any word by asking to take her on a journey." My eyelids are so heavy I can barely keep them open. This is exactly the conversation I was trying to avoid having again. "You never actually promised anything. You just agreed to spare her. What are you afraid of? Please help me understand."

"What if…" he starts, and then pauses. I look up at him. His brow is furrowed, his jaw clenched. "What if bringing her back to Cerion somehow triggers memories? What if she remembers her past because of us? I just feel like it's best for everyone if she's left forgotten. We should have told them she was killed. Or maybe we should have told Iren to—"

"Don't." I interrupt him with a kiss. "You made the right choice, Rian. You spared her. She isn't Viala anymore, she's someone else." Over Rian's shoulder in the dim light of the hallway something moves. A shadowy figure. As soon as I focus on it, it flickers away so quickly that I wonder if it was ever really there at all. I rub my eyes. "I have to sleep. Tomorrow is going to be awful if I don't."

I stand on my tiptoes and kiss him, and he circles his arms around me and holds me close. Neither of us wants to let go, but we do eventually, reluctantly, and retire to our beds.

Chapter Five:

LURKING IN SHADOW

Azi

"Who goes?" a guard's call jolts me awake.

"Halt, I say," he shouts. "Halt in the name of the Prince! Halt! Halt!"

"Halt!" More voices command, and with their shouts comes the whooshing sound of arrows leaving bows.

I'm disoriented at first until I see Mum bolt from her bed and grab her sword. This is our third night on the road and our third inn since Westhaven. It's much smaller than the first. Mare's Head is a small village. It's much less grand and not nearly as secure as our previous stops have been. We all went to bed on edge and still half-dressed in our armor padding knowing that it would provide at least some protection if we were to be attacked during the night. It was almost as though we knew this would happen.

The clash of swords rings out in the street outside our window, and flashes of magic burst through the cracks of the shutters. Mum and Mya rush off and I'm not far behind them, my sword raised and ready.

Rian meets us in the hallway and follows our charge, and as we descend the narrow staircase I hear him casting and feel his shield spell fall over us. The sounds of the battle are louder now, more urgent. Metal on metal. Explosions of fire and lightning. Thundering footsteps behind us tell me that Bryse has joined the defense. I glance over my shoulder to see the hulk of a man bulging out from behind his tower shield, which is taller than I am and twice as broad. Behind him Da has his hammer ready and Cort his slender, elegant blades.

We charge together into the street and the scene that greets us shocks me. All of our soldiers, every one of them, lies lifeless in the dirt road, utterly defeated. I stumble back against Rian from the shock of it.

"No," he whispers and points to the far end of the road. A

hooded figure, terrible and black, glides toward us. As it approaches, the royal soldiers rise eerily to their feet behind it and stand in formation. Each one's eyes are vacant. Dead. They remind me of the skeleton sentries that we faced at the Sorcerers' keep in the battle of Kythshire.

Mum puts her arm up to guard me and the others arrange themselves between me and Rian and the approaching Sorcerer. The marching of undead boots thumps rhythmically on the packed dirt road as they near. Bryse readies his shield. Da raises his hammer. Rian murmurs so many wards that I lose track. It's no use, though. The Sorcerer glides effortlessly through the wall that our family has created to protect us. As the robes whip around, curls of black tendrils lick at our guild members one by one. Mum falls. Da falls. Mya falls. Elliot falls. As each of them rises up again, blank-eyed, I try to charge but my feet are rooted to the spot. I can't move. My arms are heavy. Cort falls. Bryse falls. His tower shield clatters to the ground.

The hood slips from the Sorcerer's face to reveal a curtain of shimmering black hair and slanted, deep brown eyes. Viala. At her throat, a perfect diamond glitters brightly. My diamond. Flitt's tether. Anger surges through me as she glides to Rian and slips her fingers into his auburn hair. He smiles at her the way he smiles at me, like she's the only thing in the world that matters to him. Then she pulls him to her and they kiss passionately, deeply.

I wake up screaming. Instantly Mum is at my side, soothing me. She strokes my hair and I feel her calming pulse wash over the bed and settle my racing heart.

"Shh, a dream, just a dream, Sweeting," she whispers as she settles beside me. "Do you want to tell me about it?" I shake my head and close my eyes, but the image of my undead family is burned into my eyelids. I open them again, but the darkness of the room isn't much comfort, either.

"She okay?" Mya murmurs from her own bed and suddenly I feel foolish. Childish. I wonder how long I was screaming and who else heard me.

"I'm fine," I say a little more defensively than I intended to.

"Don't be embarrassed," Mya yawns and pushes herself up onto her elbow to look at me. "Dreams are important, Azi. They show us things that our hearts know, that our minds are too closed to see as truths."

I know she's trying to comfort me, but what she says only

frightens me more. I don't want any part of that dream to ever become a truth.

"Talking about it sometimes helps us work out the meaning," Mum offers gently. I shake my head and turn away from her, and she sighs and tucks the coverlet around me. "Try to sleep then. We'll reach the castle on our next ride. Be at peace." Her final words carry with them a beautiful sense of serenity. My thoughts clear as my eyes close, and the next thing I know, it's morning. I wake fully rested and eager to be on the road. Just one more day of riding and Rian and I will be able to head to Kythshire.

I've woken later than I'd like, and Mum and Mya have gone down already to breakfast. I throw a tunic over my armor padding and nearly collide with Dacva right outside of my door.

"Sorry," he mutters, his eyes fixed on the floor. Dacva and I were longtime rivals through our training in the Arms guild, where we practiced swordplay for several years in the same troop. He took pleasure in rallying his friends to bully and torment me, and I paid him back by besting him in every spar and competition that we faced each other in. Knowing how things turned out, our rivalry seems pointless now. When Dacva's guild, Retribution, betrayed the throne, Dacva took refuge with Brother Donal, my guild's cleric. He traded his sword for a cleric's mace, and he's been following Donal ever since. Now that I'm a Knight and he's an apprentice healer, I try not to play to my rank too much around him. The Elite are still wary to allow him to join, but Brother Donal insists on mentoring him. I imagine things between us will always be strained.

"Good morning," I offer and step aside to let him pass. When he nods and moves to rush on, I note the bundle of herbs he has clutched to his chest.

"What happened?" I ask him, my insides suddenly twisting with dread. I think of the dream I had last night. A dark dream. I don't quite remember the details.

"Her Highness is having pains," he whispers, nodding toward the quarters where the prince and princess spent the night. My eyes go wide.

"Is she all right?" I ask. "Is the baby?"

"I think so. I think they're both okay. Brother Donal is with her, and the midwives. And the physician." He frowns at the last. Clerics and physicians often work together, but neither one is ever very trusting of the other's methods. "We won't be riding today though.

That was agreed on early. I have to bring these." He holds up the herbs.

"Of course." I wave him on urgently and watch as he disappears through the princess's door.

"I hope the baby is okay." Rian appears beside me as if out of nowhere, making me jump.

"Rian!" I cry. "I wish you wouldn't do that."

He takes me in his arms and kisses me, and as my eyes close, my forgotten dream floods back to me. The way he looked at Viala. The way he kissed her. I break away from him and try hard to hide my disgust. It was just a dream, after all.

"Hey," he says softly, holding me at arm's length to look me over. "You all right?"

"Sure." I force a smile. "Breakfast?"

The others are already crowded around tables in the dining hall when we arrive. I squeeze into a space on the bench between Bryse and Elliot even though Mya slides over to make room for Rian and me to sit together. Bryse is laughing over some jest by Cort and barely notices me, which is fine. I don't really feel like talking to anyone. I push my breakfast of hot ground meal mixed with winter berries around my bowl as more of the dream comes back to me. The bloodied soldiers rising up into formation with the Sorceress orchestrating them. The glint of Flitt's diamond sending a spray of rainbow light across the folds of her robes.

My hand goes to my chest where I keep her diamond secure in a pouch that hangs tucked inside my shirt. The pouch is there. I pat it. It's empty. Panic grips me like a vice clamped over my heart. Losing Flitt's tether is like losing Flitt herself. She trusts me to keep it safe. It's the only way she can leave Kythshire and get to me. Me, or whoever holds the tether. I swallow the lump in my throat and nearly fall from the bench in my effort to free myself from the tight space between the two men who are oblivious to my sudden alarm.

I race to my room and search everywhere: The bed, my packs, Mum's bed, Mya's bed, Mya's packs, Mum's packs. Under furniture, inside furniture, between mattresses. It's nowhere. It's gone. I try to think of the last time I had it. Flitt came to me yesterday just before supper, so I had it here at the inn. It has to be here somewhere. I go through my bedding again. I take off my shirt and my undershirt and shake them out. Nothing. My hands are shaking so hard I have trouble dressing again. I barely hear the knock on the door and Rian calling in over the ringing in my ears. How could I have lost something so precious? More importantly, who has it now? The thought of Flitt appearing to someone else chokes me. I gasp for breath as I wrench open the door.

"What happened?" he asks. When he sees the state I'm in, his eyes widen in fear. "Azi, what's wrong?"

"The diamond," I whisper. "The tether." I hold up the empty pouch. "How did I lose it, Rian? I had it yesterday. I never took it off. I never do."

"We'll find it." He tries to calm me with an arm around my shoulder, but his touch just annoys me. "Here." His fingers close around the pouch and he whispers a spell. My hair flutters around my shoulders as a soft breeze swirls around us, carrying with it a floral scent. A tendril of light swirls up from the pouch and forms a tiny globe. The globe bobs before us for a moment, and then darts off down the hallway.

"Follow it!" Rian says. He grabs my hand and we jog after it as it weaves through the corridors of the inn and outside into the street. We lose sight of it for a moment and then I spot it far ahead, dancing its way to the north along the road.

"There!" I cry and take off at full speed. The globe speeds up, too, through the village and down the road into a thick of trees. It veers from the path and disappears again into a thicket.

"Azi!" I hear Rian call from behind me, but I don't stop. I crash through the underbrush and dodge around twisting trunks, focused only on the globe. It shoots through a thick hedge of ferns and I jump after it. I'm mid-leap when I realize my mistake. The other side of the ferns is a ravine, at least two stories deep. There's nothing I can do. The light hovers above me as I plummet, taunting me. I scream, and just as I'm about to crash to the bottom I feel myself caught and lifted. Blue energy shimmers around me as Rian's levitation spell carries me upward.

"Are you out of your mind?" He shouts as his spell settles me gently in the ferns. "What were you thinking?" I jump to my feet and turn, looking for the globe.

"It's gone," I cry.

"I dispelled the globe," Rian says. "I didn't know you'd be so careless about following it. Lucky I got here in time to catch you."

"Cast it again," I demand as I creep through the ferns to assess the climb down. Maybe the diamond is there at the bottom, buried in the thick green underbrush.

"No," Rian says firmly.

"No?" I spin to face him. "Why not?"

"Because," he says gently, offering a hand to me as though trying to tame a wild creature. His tone and manor irritate me. "I thought it would be in your room somewhere. I didn't know it would lead us all the way out here. You're unarmed and without your armor, and we're a few hundred paces off the road in an unfamiliar forest. Be smart about this, Azi. Don't overreact."

"Overreact?" I scoff. "Rian, this is important! It's gone and we have to find it. Flitt's life depends on it." I shove past him roughly and storm away toward the road.

"Azi, wait!" he calls after me. "What's with you today? You're not yourself."

"Well for starters, I don't appreciate being called stupid." I throw back over my shoulder. A bush of thorns catches my pants, scratching through to my skin. I growl at the thorns that rip into my fingers as I yank it away.

"No, it's something else. Did you have a dream last night? A nightmare?" he asks as he catches up to me. I pause. My hands start to shake again. He takes them and binds them with a strip of cloth.

"How," I whisper. "How did you know?"

"I had one, too," he says quietly and kisses my fingertips. My cheeks grow hot and I pull my hands away.

"Was *she* in it?" I don't want to say her name. He'll know who I mean if she was.

"No. Emris was," he says. I shiver. Emris was one of the six Sorcerers we defeated at the battle of the Keep at Kythshire. I can see his evil face as plain as day, blue-black and terrible with swirls of the Mark so thick that his skin seemed to undulate with it. He tried to entice Rian to join him. In the end he was defeated by a wind fairy named Shush, and Iren, the massive, statue-like Spirit of the Shadow Crag, who drained him of his magic and ground his body to pebbles and dust. Rian goes on.

"He was marching on the village with an army of Mages. I've never seen so many gathered together before. They were using unfamiliar spells. Horrible spells. He was gliding at the front of them, and you were beside him." He looks at me and swallows, and then looks away. "You were dressed in robes and covered in the Mark. I couldn't even see the color of your eyes anymore. And then you reached for him and pulled him to you and you let him…" His breathing is shallow. He shakes his head.

"It was just a dream," I say, my voice shaking. His was almost exactly the same as mine.

"So was yours," he whispers.

We stare at each other for a long time in silence. I know he's right. It was just a dream. It wasn't real. He loves me today as much as he did yesterday. Viala is gone, she doesn't exist anymore. Emris is dead, his magic embedded in a single pebble and entrusted to the fairies. To Flitt. The thought of her chokes me up again, and then I have a thought.

"Did he have the diamond? Emris? In your dream?" I search his face and know the answer even before he nods his reply, wide-eyed.

"What does it mean, Rian?"

"I don't know. But one thing is certain. You need to warn Flitt before she tries to jump to her tether. Hopefully she hasn't tried to leave the Grotto yet this morning."

He's right. I know I can get to her if I think hard enough. I just need to set an intention to see her and concentrate hard on her grotto. I've done it before. I go to Rian's side and take his hand.

"Ready?" I ask. He shakes his head. Tears prick my eyes.

"I knew it. You're not coming." I whisper.

"I can't," his voice is thick, like he's fighting his own tears.

"I need you," I say, moving closer to him.

"You don't understand," he says quietly. "I shouldn't, Azi."

"I trust you, Rian. They trust you. They said you're always welcome back. Please." I squeeze his hand. "Please. Don't make me go alone. If she isn't there—"

"She'll be there," he says firmly.

"Rian." I say pleadingly. I can't bear to leave him behind. Not for this. I can't face it alone. He reaches up and rakes shaking fingers through his short-cropped hair and lets out a long, slow sigh.

"Fine," he says finally. "Do it quick before I change my mind." He whispers a spell and I feel the air shift around us as we enter the Half-Realm.

"It'll be easier from here," he says.

I close my eyes and think of the Grotto that Flitt calls home. Nestled in a colorful corner of Kythshire, it's a beautiful, tiny space with a sparkling pool full of graceful fish and a peaceful little waterfall. Rainbow-colored willow fronds drip down to graze the water's surface, and the trees there are adorned with trinkets that chime melodically in the breeze. I think of it purposefully, and I feel the crunchy leaves beneath my feet fade away to be replaced with soft, spongy moss.

"Did you see that?" Rian asks from beside me.

"What?" I look around the sparkling scene hopefully, but my heart sinks. Flitt isn't here.

"Not here. In the Half-Realm," Rian says. "Never mind. It was probably nothing." He closes his eyes and I know that he's trying to keep himself in control. Kythshire is like a wonderful dream. The air here is saturated with magic. I can feel it surrounding us, thick and tangible, like the scent of a delicious meal luring me, inviting me to enjoy every last bite. For Rian I know it's more like he's been starved for a week and then dropped in the middle of a great feast and forced to resist it. I squeeze his hand and he forces a smile.

"All right?" I ask, and he nods. "Oh, Rian, she's not here." I pace, trampling the moss as fear and regret wash over me in waves, followed quickly by anger. I'll find whoever has the diamond. They'll pay. If any harm has come to Flitt, heads will roll. I think of my sword and wish for it and feel it at my back. For good measure, I wish for my armor as well and it appears out of nowhere, fitted perfectly as always to my body.

"Calm down," Rian murmurs as he flexes his fingers, and I'm not sure if he's talking to me or to himself. "Maybe she's dancing at the Ring?"

He points to the waterfall that acts as Flitt's entry to the pristine circle of white mushrooms where the fairies convene to discuss and dance together. We've been there a few times, but never without her.

"I have an idea." I tighten my grip on his hand and close my eyes.

I calm myself and focus on Flitt: her seven ponytails, each a color of the rainbow, her skirt of bright ribbons, her ever-changing eyes.

"Flitt," I whisper, and my feet leave the ground again.

"Well it belongs to me and I want it back. And, oof! Hey! Watch where you step, you big oaf!" Flitt's voice rings out squeaky and annoyed from the ground at our feet.

"Yeah, I'm talking to you, Stinky!" she shouts up at Rian. "What's the big idea, blinking around at full size? I thought Mages were supposed to be smart!"

Suddenly, the ground grows closer and the trees surrounding us stretch impossibly higher, and I realize that Flitt has shrunken us down to her size. I don't even care. I dive at her and throw my arms around her and sob with relief.

"Hey, that's short enough," Rian squeaks from beside me, where Flitt has shrunken him to half my height.

"That's for stepping on my foot," she sticks her tongue out at him. "Lucky you didn't step on my everything and squish me, lummox."

"It wasn't my fault." Rian makes a gesture and shoots up taller. He measures his chin to the top of my head to make sure he's got it right. "Azi was navigating."

"Typical. Always placing blame. You can let go of me now, Azi." She wriggles her shoulders and squirms out of my embrace. "Be more careful next time. Oh! And I have a petal to pick with you, Azi! What do you mean, losing my tether?"

"What?" I ask, distracted by our glittering surroundings. We're standing at the base of a great, twisting tree which has grown in an impossible way. Sections of the bark have separated and grown together again to form rows and rows of tiny doors and windows. Some of them glow with various colored lights while others are dark. Each door is decorated with trinkets and baubles, some natural, some man-made. I spot all sorts of found objects here and there: a thimble, the clip of a belt, a broken hair comb. Rough gems and cut gems sprinkle the ground around us and decorate crevices in the tree as far up as I can see. Dozens of baskets woven from golden wheat hang from a network of tiny ropes on pulleys all along the massive trunk. Odd things poke up over the edges of them: torn bits of parchment, seashells, balls of thread, feathers. What strikes me most about all of it, though, is the silence.

"Where are we, Flitt? What is this place?" Rian asks with awe, echoing my thoughts as he gazes up at the tree.

"Makers' Tree," she says, and then shouts up at the tree, "and I'm not leaving until someone tells me exactly what's going on!"

"We're not coming out with *them* here," a tiny voice calls from inside the tree.

"Yeah, make them go away first!" shouts someone else.

"Are you kidding me?" Flit yells. "If it wasn't for these two, you'd all be sapped white as pinkynut grubs! Ask Iren! Ask Crocus and Scree! Stupid Makers," she grumbles the last bit under her breath and kicks at a basket near her feet. It tips over and spills its contents: a collection of smooth chips of sea glass.

"Hey, watch it!" A blur of yellow dashes toward us and snatches up the basket and the glass, and then darts back into a nearby door.

"We're not giving it back!" someone calls from elsewhere in the tree. "You shouldn't have trusted it to someone dumb enough to lose it!"

"Hey." Rian growls in the direction of the voice. I don't defend myself. It was stupid of me. I should have kept better track of it.

"Hey!" Flit snarls and leaps up. Her wings carry her to the voice and she perches on the threshold of a bright pink door. "Take that back! I gave it to who I was supposed to give it to. It's not my fault she was stupid!"

I cross my arms and press my lips together while I listen to the fairies argue about my level of intelligence. Rian paces beside me, wiggling his fingers. I know he's trying hard to keep control. His eyes flash between wild and calm in waves.

"I didn't lose it, okay?" I finally shout. "I had it yesterday! I had it and then it was just gone. It disappeared!"

"Oh, sure, it just disappeared," a voice calls from yet another door.

"Not likely," says another.

"She was probably careless with it and dropped it," says someone else.

"Or tried to sell it. It is a diamond after all. Who chose that for a tether, anyway?"

"Dabble!" Flitt says defensively. "Dabble did, and it was brilliant of him, too." She floats back a little ways from the door. "Perfect for me. You should see how it twinkles. Just like my light. So you can all just be quiet!"

"Where is he, then? Dabble?" one of them calls. Dozens of others echo the name. They go on awhile until he finally makes his appearance, hovering beside Flitt. He's a round little thing with spectacles of shimmering mica and a beard of orange that goes all the way down to his knees in thick ringlets. His head is bald and shiny, and he wears a thick apron stuffed full of whittled twigs and strange tools carved from stone. His wide wings seem to require a little more effort than Flitt's as the two lower themselves to the ground beside us. As he comes closer, my heart races. Tucked under his arm is the diamond.

Above us, curious little faces appear in the doorways and windows. When I look up to them, some of them dart back inside timidly.

"Here you go, then." Dabble holds the tether out to Flitt and she takes it carefully from him with a pointed scowl in my direction. After a moment, she hands it over to me.

"Don't lose it again," she scolds. Protests erupt from the tree, and Dabble turns toward it.

"She's not stupid, and she didn't lose it, you cretins!" he shouts up at the hiding fairies.

"How do you know?" the yellow fairy from before peeks out of his door.

"Because I put a guard on it. A precaution for this very occurrence." Dabble adjusts his spectacles and the mica flashes with various colors.

"What kind of precaution?" someone else calls.

"What occurrence?" Rian asks.

"Theft. It's a theft prevention guard," he explains. "I magicked it so it would transport here if anyone tried to steal it. And someone did. Someone lurking in the Half-Realm. Someone with dark magic. A Sorcerer."

M. Shelbrake
2015

Chapter Six:
IREN'S WARNING

Azi

A hush falls over the tree at Dabble's declaration. Immediately, I think of Viala. I look at Rian and realize that he's probably thinking of Emris. I shake my head. Both notions are ridiculous.

"A Sorcerer? Well, you two know what to do with Sorcerers, don't you?" Flitt beams at us. "They're no match for us, are they?" She turns toward the tree. "We're not afraid of any Sorcerer!"

"Calm down, Flitt." Rian takes a step toward Dabble, who leans away slightly and adjusts his spectacles on his nose. Behind the thick mica flakes, I see the fairy's eyes flick over Rian's chest. I know what he's looking for: Mage Mark. Unfortunately, Rian is dressed for winter. His high-collared vest and thick robes could conceal any Mark from his jaw down. This past Autumnsdawn, when he was forced to hold all of Viala's magic after she was stripped, the Mark had crept up over his face. Now, I know, it's barely visible across his chest. I blush and glance at Flitt, who's watching me watch Dabble. She rolls her eyes, and it's not the first time I wonder whether she can read my thoughts.

Rian is oblivious to the two of us as he addresses Dabble.

"How can you be certain it was a Sorcerer?" he asks.

"Ah, well," Dabble glances away and takes a step back. His fingers wind into his beard nervously.

"I know! Let's play!" Flitt giggles. Rian and I groan in unison.

"Yes, you three go play somewhere else." Dabble says with relief. "Go on, now. Flitt can answer your questions. We've got lots of work to do. Always working. Very busy." Before any of us can protest, he flies up to the tree and disappears through a deep purple door.

"You heard him," someone shouts from a window further up. "Go somewhere else!"

"Nice meeting you!"

"Bye!"

"Friendly folks, aren't they?" Rian mumbles.

"Snobs," Flitt wrinkles her nose. "They think they're so smart. Brains aren't everything," she shouts up at the tree, then she nudges me. "Right, Azi?" Giggles erupt from the windows closest to us and I narrow my eyes at Flitt. "Oh come on, I was joking."

"Anyway, let's go." Rian says. "We're obviously not welcome here, and the guild will be wondering where we went." His hands are balled into fists and shoved into the pockets of his vest.

"Right." I tuck the diamond back into the pouch and push it safely under my shirt, then I turn to Flitt expectantly. "Ready."

"Ready for?" Flitt asks, wide-eyed.

"For you to take us back." Rian says.

"How do you expect me to do that?" she asks. "My tether's here." She points at me.

"You can't just…?" Rian waves his hand casually as his voice trails off.

"No, I can't just. That's kind of the point of a tether. Inside Kythshire, simple dimple. We can go anywhere you like. But to get outside, we need tethers."

"Couldn't I do it? I got us here from outside." I say.

"Go ahead and try." Flitt comes to my side and links her arm through mine. I do the same with Rian and close my eyes and think of the inn. I focus hard on Mum and Da, and try to take us to them. Nothing happens. I look up at Rian and shake my head.

"Come on." Flitt says, and without warning we're pulled away again, this time back to her Grotto. Rian grumbles and trudges out of the pool of water, dripping wet. "That never gets old." Flitt laughs.

"That's right, antagonize the volatile Mage. Never mind me trying my hardest to keep it together." With a swish of his hand he dries his robes and drops beside me onto the moss.

"Ready to play?" Flitt perches daintily on a nearby root. Her prisms of light glitter brightly over the dewdrops on the bark of the tree, and her colorful hair shimmers as she smoothes her ribbon skirt. The beauty of the scene placates me. All of my tension and anger fades away, and instead I feel a rush of love for this little fairy and her precious world.

"Yes." Rian's matter-of-fact tone snaps me back to my senses. "Why did Dabble seem so certain it was a Sorcerer who tried to steal your tether?"

"Aw," Flit tips her head back wistfully. "I was hoping you'd forget about that and ask how to get back to the inn instead."

Rian watches Flitt patiently, waiting. He knows as well as I do the rules of the game are that Flitt has to answer the question and then ask her own.

"He has ways of knowing," she replies vaguely. "Did you two have nightmares last night?"

"How did you—" I start, but Rian stops me.

"Shh! She's trying to steer us away from my question, which she didn't really give a proper answer to. Yes, we had nightmares." He taps his lip thoughtfully and winces as a spark of energy from his fingertip zaps him. "Ah!" He curses and shoves his fists into his pockets again. "All right, you're right. I can ask about the impending threat of dark magic once we're out of here. We need to leave, Flitt. What's the easiest way for us to get back to the inn?"

"Well, for you two, since you can go in the Half-Realm, probably all you have to do is step across the border of Kythshire into Cerion, and then you can think yourself back to your Mum, Azi. Or anyone, really. I think, anyway."

"All right, let's try it," Rian says.

"Wait, it's my turn to ask!" Flitt scowls, but Rian shakes his head.

"We'll keep playing once we're back," he says.

"Fine. We'll go to Iren and cross there, since it knows you." Flitt darts to us and pulls me to my feet. "Grow up."

As we grow to our normal size I reach for Rian's hand. He takes mine, his brow lined with worry. Iren is the Guardian of the North, the Spirit of the Crag who fought beside us against the Sorcerers and gifted my armor to me. We never would have been able to defeat them without Iren's help, and Iren never would have woken if I hadn't restored it. I'm actually looking forward to seeing the Guardian again, but I understand why Rian is hesitant. At the end of the battle, he chose to leave Viala in Iren's care. The Guardian assured us that she would have no memory of her previous life. The two of us trusted Iren's word and allowed Viala to live, but deep down I'm certain that Rian is just as reluctant to see her again as I am.

Before either of us can think further about it, Flitt whisks us to a place where gravel crunches under my feet and we're pommeled by gusts of wind that feel as though they'll blow us right off of the edge of the mountain. I cling to Rian and hesitate to open my eyes. I've been here before, where the Guardian of the North resides. I remember how high it is, and I don't relish the thought of experiencing that height again firsthand. It's only when I feel Rian tense beside me and Flitt burrow into my neck that I force myself to open my eyes.

At first I don't see her, but then the rocks a hundred paces in front of us shift slightly and I realize they aren't rocks at all. Her waif-like form is bundled in thick gray leathers and wools. In her gloved hand she holds a graceful long bow at the ready. The string is drawn back perfectly and the arrow aimed precisely at Rian's head. I sidestep to put myself between the arrow and Rian as she steps closer. The wind whips her hood from her face, unleashing a fan of gleaming black hair. As she makes her cautious approach, I see that on the right side of her head where her hand is poised holding the arrow, her hair is shaved close to her scalp. She looks so different from the Sorceress she once was that I can't help myself.

"Viala," I whisper. Behind me, the air around Rian crackles ominously.

"Mage!" Viala calls firmly over the wind. Her voice is the only thing that doesn't seem to have changed. "Show your hands."

Rian's hands appear over my shoulders on either side of my field of vision. Every now and then a glow of blue or a crackle of white flicks from them. Viala moves the bow slightly. Now it's aimed directly into the eye of my helmet. At my shoulder, Flitt giggles.

"*Watch this!*" The fairy's voice echoes in my mind. A flash of light glints off of the arrow's point as Flitt appears on the tip of it.

"Ki!" Flitt squeaks with her hands on her hips, and Viala's eyes widen. The former Sorceress dips to her knee without a second thought and bows her head. She lays down her bow and presses her fist to her chest.

"Your Brilliance," she says in a hushed tone, so quiet that the wind threatens to carry it away before it reaches us.

"You may rise," Flitt says with great airs, and Viala obeys. Flitt hovers above her and turns to us.

"This," Flitt gestures to Viala, "is Ki." The fairy's light grows so bright as she speaks that I have to shield my eyes to keep them from watering.

"Ki," Flitt goes on. "These are my friends. Rian Eldinae, Oathkeeper, Windsaver, Arcane Guardian, Steward of the Wellspring, and Azaeli Hammerfel, The Temperate, Pure of Heart, Reviver of Iren, The Great Protector, Cerion's Ambassador to Kythshire."

"Your Excellencies," Ki dips to her knees again and bows her head with great reverence as Flitt rambles off the titles that had been bestowed to us by the fairies at the Ring just months ago. It's the first time I've heard them used since then, and they still don't feel like they fit quite right. I'm not sure what makes me more uncomfortable, hearing them again, or seeing Ki, formerly Viala, being so submissive. I take a step closer to Rian, who rests his hands gently on my shoulders.

"Wow," he whispers in my ear. We stand there awkwardly for a long stretch, waiting for some change, but Ki continues to kneel and Flitt continues to glow blindingly bright. After a while, she winks mischievously.

"Um…" Rian stammers. "You don't need to… That is, you can, you can get up, Via—" He clears his throat. "Ki."

At his words, Ki stands and slings her bow over her shoulder. Her eyes glow soft blue for a moment and then she bobs her head to us.

"The Shadow Crag wishes to speak with you, Your Excellencies," she says. "Please allow me to guide you."

Rian and I glance at each other in disbelief as Ki turns to lead us up the mountain. She's so completely changed from the power-hungry, ruthless Sorcerer she once was that Rian and I are both in awe. This girl steps lightly over the sharp, jagged rocks along the mountainside as though she's lived here her entire life. I, on the other hand, cling to Rian so tightly that I fear I might snap his arm as we pick our way after her. Above us to the right, a sheer cliff stretches up to the sky. To our left there is a steep drop into a valley lined with golden wheat and heaps of treasure.

Just as I'm about to ask Flitt why she didn't just bring us straight to Iren, Ki turns on the path. The glow in her eyes fades as she points into the space behind us and then bows her head. Rian and I shuffle ourselves around carefully on the narrow path to look back in the direction we came from. The ground rumbles beneath our feet as the stony platform where we arrived begins to move. Even though I'm half-expecting it, I'm awed by the transformation that takes place as the craggy mountain becomes the Guardian Iren. I see now that we had arrived on its chest, and had we stayed where we were, we would have been in serious danger as the great statue-like creature sat up to greet us.

Iren is just as breathtaking now as ever. A figure of grace and strength formed from the mountain itself, its presence is commanding and powerful. Its face is smooth and beautiful, with a strong jaw and lips that curve up to hint at a smile. The most remarkable thing about Iren, though, is the single eye in the center of its forehead, which is a polished blue stone as large as I am. Gazing into it is like looking into the night sky, where the stars are flecks of gold that float aimlessly in the vast space within. As Iren sits back I feel myself drawn into the eye, my gaze locked on the slow and peaceful movement of the flecks.

"Thank you, Ki. You have done well." Iren's voice booms over the wind. "Come." It beckons her closer and Ki slips past us to climb deftly up to Iren's knee. It looks at her and smiles, and she grins. I've never seen her smile so brightly. She seems genuinely happy.

"My friends," Iren turns its attention to us, "welcome. You have met Ki. She is a great aid to the North Border." Iren says. I look across to Ki, who stands a little taller at Iren's praise.

"She's…" I start, but I don't know quite what to say.

"Remarkable." Rian finishes for me.

"Ki, rest now. I will do the watching." Iren smiles at her and she nods and slides into a stony fold of Iren's tunic where she curls up comfortably.

"How did you do it?" Rian asks Iren as Ki drifts to sleep. "She seems as though she's always belonged here."

"Memory," Iren replies. "Memory molded, formed, guided, taken and given. Memory is a most precious commodity. It empowers us. It makes us who we are."

"Do you see now?" I ask Rian, "She isn't Viala anymore. She never will be."

"Indeed. The woman you once knew is no more. The Sorceress is gone. Forever changed." Iren looks down at Ki with a fatherly affection. "Made new."

Drawn to the kindness Iren exudes, I let go of my grip on Rian's arm and step closer to it. The Guardian's great hand scoops me up gently and sets me on its other knee. The Oculus looks me over and draws me in again.

Flashes of my recent memories rise and fade in the space between us like actors on a stage. I see myself riding through the streets of Cerion bearing the Elite banner, with crowds of people cheering as the Prince's carriage passes through. We're in the woods, and Eron sleeps as Princess Amei looks back to speak with me, her hand on her round belly. We're in the village, and Rian's enchanted bouquet glitters in my hand as I blush at him. We're dancing in the tavern, and I'm avoiding Eron's eye. I'm talking to Dacva in the hallway as he carries herbs to Amei's room. Rian and I are hidden in the safety of the Half-Realm, lost in each other's embrace, locked in a deep, passionate kiss.

Rian clears his throat loudly and the images fade as I tear my gaze away.

"You are well, Azaeli, my friend." Iren says to me and I nod, a little disoriented.

"Yes, thank you," I press my fingertips to my cheeks, which are hot with the most recent memory Iren drew out. My eyes meet Rian's, who's also blushing. He grins and shakes his head and we both laugh, embarrassed. Still, somehow what Iren does doesn't feel like a violation of privacy. It's more of an act of protection, as if it's looking in on me to make certain I'm safe and content. There's an unspoken understanding that this exchange is required if we're to be in Iren's presence.

"I am glad you have come," Iren says. "And Rian Eldinae." It offers its hand to Rian, who climbs into it a little hesitantly and is neatly placed beside me on its knee. Their gazes lock together and I watch the same exchange, though the figures that dance between them are more distant and faded than they were in my own display. I see Rian in a dark room, facing several Master Mages. He looks exhausted, harried. I know of this memory, but to see played out it this way gives it a life and makes it even more real.

When we returned to Cerion after the battle with the Sorcerers, Rian told me he faced many long days of questioning. Within the Academy walls, they secretly drilled him on everything from Viala's stripping to the details of the time he spent in Kythshire. While I watch the memory, the thing that impresses me most of all is how true he remained to the fairies, and how hard he worked to keep their secrets safe. He was as tight-lipped as he could be about what he saw within the borders. I glance at Flitt who's hovering beside me and watching the memory with fascinated awe.

Iren lingers for a long time on the grueling questioning that Rian faced, and then the memory changes to our conversation in the inn regarding Viala. I shift uncomfortably as I watch myself trying to convince Rian that taking her away from here would be okay, and I watch Iren's face to gauge its reaction. It remains stoic and interested, and the memory fades between them as the observation ends. To my surprise, it doesn't address that conversation at all.

"Rian Eldinae, you remain a true ally to Kythshire." Iren nods respectfully. "For that, I offer you knowledge. A warning." Iren says with a foreboding tone. I shift closer to Rian and slip my hand into his. "Do not linger in the Half-Realm. You consider it a safe place, but it is not a haven. Be vigilant there."

"I understand," Rian says. "Thank you, Iren."

I try not to scowl. Ever since we were accidentally given access to the Half-Realm we have used it as a tool, a way to keep ourselves safe and unseen. I wonder what could possibly harm us there, and then I immediately think of the dark figure that I saw in the hallway at the inn, and the strange dreamers that leapt and soared in the city streets while Rian and I watched.

"As always, you are welcome at the Crag," Iren says, "but you have come today for passage, which I grant unto you. Be safe, my friends. Remain on the path." It presses its finger to the gravely ground and the pebbles sparkle with a soft white glow that snakes away through a nearby crevice. Iren picks us up and gently deposits us onto the path. "Be safe," the Guardian repeats.

We say our farewells and follow the trail through the crevice and down the mountainside before anyone breaks the silence. Rian is the first to speak.

"That was interesting," he says thoughtfully. I think back on the encounter.

"Which part?" I ask.

"You didn't ask to bring Via— Ki."

"Oh." I say, thinking back. "I guess I forgot. It wasn't the right time, anyway. We can come back for her. That was the plan, wasn't it? After we see Amei and Eron safely to the castle."

"Mm." Rian gives a noncommittal reply and then pauses. "Here's the border."

"I'll see you later," says Flitt, breaking her own unusual silence.

"You're not coming?" I ask.

"Nope, you go on. I'll find you later. Hold on to that tether this time!" She pokes at my chest and then disappears.

"She's so odd," I say, closing my hand over the pouch.

"You say that like it's a revelation," Rian laughs. He runs his hand though the air in front of us. "All kind of wards and protections here. I'd imagine they keep the fae in as much as they keep others out.

"What are you saying?" I ask incredulously. "They're trapped in here?"

"They don't seem to see it that way, but essentially…yes." Rian pulls his hand back and inspects it.

"Is it safe to cross?"

"It should be if we stay on Iren's path like we were told."

"Let's go together, then." I link my arm through his and we take a giant step together across the border. As soon as we cross, the white path fades away.

We're greeted with a rush of air so cold that my nose and mouth sting with my first breath. Other than the cold, there is no difference here on the other side of the border. The trees are the same, and the landscape is just as sloped and rocky. A twig cracks nearby and Rian whispers a spell of protection which shimmers around us both. I reach for my sword and draw it from its sheath silently as frosty leaves rustle nearby. We watch silently, waiting for whatever is making the sound to reveal itself, and both breathe a sigh of relief as we catch a glimpse of familiar red fur.

"Elliot," I reach my hand out to the fox and it trots up to greet me and nuzzle my hand. "Great! He can give us a ride back if we shrink down." I remember the journey Elliot brought me on recently, to show me the corruption of Zhaghen and the distress of the fairies in Sunteri. We were able to cross continents in moments with me riding on his back. I crouch to stroke the thick fur at his neck, but when he looks up at me I pull my hand away. His eyes are wrong. They're colorless and milky. Rian's hand clamps over my shoulder and I squeeze my eyes shut as I feel the ground shift beneath me. Midway there, Rian whispers the revealer. When I open my eyes again, we're in a hidden alcove just outside of the inn.

"That wasn't Da," he whispers as he pulls me into the street. We pause at the guards posted at the inn door just long enough for them to wave us through. When we duck inside we find Elliot and Mya sitting at the table, going over a list of supplies. Elliot looks up and smiles at us.

"We were wondering where you two wandered off to," he says. "Never mind, you're back in time for lunch." He pats his stomach and grins.

"Right. We've got some things for you to take care of after." Mya shuffles the lists as Elliot pats the bench beside him to invite us to sit, and Rian and I exchange a worried glance. If Elliot has been here, wide awake, then who was the fox in the Half-Realm waiting for us to cross the border out of Kythshire?

Chapter Seven:

INTERROGATION

Tib

Clanging. Shouting. Marching. Stench. Creaking hinges. Slamming door.

The candlelight is harsh after so long in the darkness. I try to remember how long. Hours, not days. Hours since they put me in here in this tiny room. Musty-smelling, like the roots. Dry, like the sand. Cleaner, though. I panicked at first when they left me here. Couldn't breathe. Couldn't think. Be calm, a voice told me. Breathe. I did. It didn't help much. I cower from the approaching flame. Can't see the man holding it. My eyes aren't used to the light yet. He drops a tin plate onto the rough table with a clatter. I jump and flinch away. Eye the dish. My stomach growls.

"Eat," he says. Pulls up a stool to sit. His uniform is neat. Blue and purple. Cerion's colors. Not city guard. Palace. Palace guard. He nudges the dish toward me. "You don't eat it, I'm taking it away. Don't know when you'll get another plate. Go on."

There's bread. Meat. Hard cheese. I pick up some of that, the cheese. I sniff it before I take a bite. It's good. Better than I've had before, even at Nessa's. The meat, too. It's fresh and hot. Lined with fat. I clean my plate too quickly. He waits awhile before he starts the questions.

"You like to climb?" he asks.

I don't answer. I mop the last of the fat with my bread. My stomach churns. The towers. The fire. I can't swallow. I feel his eyes on me. Try to look innocent, like Saesa with the dock workers. Shrug my shoulders.

"Sometimes." I say. My voice comes out thick. Guilty.

"Yeah?" He pours me a cup of something brownish from a pitcher. At first I think it's ale, but it's too sweet when I sip it.

"What is this?" I ask.

"Cider," he says. He blinks at me in disbelief. "You never had cider?" He peers into the pitcher and swirls it, then looks at me again.

"No, sir." I remember my sirs. Nessa says politeness can get you out of a pinch. "Thank you, sir."

"How old are you, boy?" he asks.

"Twelve, sir." I drain my cup and he fills it again.

"From Sunteri?"

"Yes, sir," I admit. Not like I can hide that, looking like I do.

"How long have you been in Cerion?" he asks. He leans back on two stool legs. Puts his hand casually on his sword hilt. It's a big one. Way bigger than Saesa's.

"About a week, sir." I gulp the sweet cider. My mouth is so dry. "I came in with the fleet."

"And you been staying with Lady Ganvent that whole time?" he asks.

I watch him carefully. He watches me, too. I wonder why he's asking questions he already knows the answer to.

"Yes, sir."

More watching. More silence. His eyes bore into me. I look into them like Cap taught me to. Honest men are brazen. Only men with something to hide look away.

"So, climbing," he says finally. Slaps his hand on the table. My heart races. I can smell the smoke. Feel the stone through my gloves as I grip to scale the tower. "You like the aqueducts?"

I look up. Meet his eyes again. I'm unsure what he means. "Sir?"

"The aqueducts. The arches next to the castle. Along the river. You like to climb them?"

I stare at him. Nod slowly. "Sometimes."

"It's illegal," he says sternly, then looms over me and speaks very slowly. "Against the law. You understand?" He leans back. Crosses his arms. Looks menacing. Relief floods through me. This isn't about the towers. It's about the arches. My secret wall.

"I'm sorry. I didn't know, sir." I try not to smile. Try not to grin. He's not smiling. I've seen that look before. I wonder what the punishment is for climbing the aqueduct. I'm not afraid of lashes. I can take them. I took seventeen once.

"Yeah, well…" his voice trails off. He's still suspicious. "What are you doing in Cerion? Why'd you leave Sunteri, anyway?"

"To get away from the dye fields." It isn't a lie.

"You belong to someone back there?" He drums his fingers on the table. My mouth goes even drier. I don't like this question. I shrug.

"Answer," he says.

"Used to." I stare at my empty plate.

"Well, what's that mean?"

"Am I in trouble or not, sir? I climbed the aqueduct. I already said so." Just punish me, I want to say. Punish me and get it over with.

"You're in trouble if you don't answer the question," he glares. "And watch your tone, you. What's it mean, you used to belong to someone?"

I eye my empty cup. He doesn't fill it again.

"I asked you what's that mean?" he says again. He's losing his patience.

"She died. No one else to claim me, so I left. Before someone else could." I meet his eyes. Don't look away. It's not a lie. Not all of it, anyway. He sighs. Shakes his head. Hides his pity quickly, but I still catch it.

He asks me question after question. What did I see on the scout ship? What messages were passed? Do I have any reason to believe that Prince Vorance is involved in Sorcery? Did Cap pay me? What did I hear at Lady Ganvent's? What did I see? I give him his answers. Mostly. Try to protect Nessa and her secrets. Even ask him if he's got any news about her husband's fleet. He hasn't. By the time he's through with his questions, we feel like friends. Until he gets up.

"Let's go," he says briskly. I imagine it's time for my punishment. I wonder what it'll be. He takes out his keys. Unlocks the door. Barks a command at the guards outside: "Northwest Tower."

They march me along stone-walled corridors. Clean but rough. Low ceilings. The musty smell fades as we walk, replaced by citrus oil. The guards in front push open a door. I blink at the sunlight filtering in through the high windows. The drapes are open, but there's no draft. Outside, snow billows past the windows. Lighthearted. Carefree. My boots slip on the polished wood. The ceilings are high here. Ornate. Carved with figures and faces that peer down at me. I feel small. Alone. I've felt alone ever since the cell. More alone than I've felt in weeks. It makes me more uneasy than the thought of the punishment I know is coming.

A garden. Inside. With songbirds and flowers. It smells like wet earth and green plants. Reminds me of the jungles of Elespen. Of Saesa's eyes. It's warm in here. The air is thick and humid. I peer up at the glass ceiling and see men with brooms brushing away the falling snow to let the sunlight in. I slow my pace to watch them and I'm prodded forward by the guard who questioned me. Rushed through too quickly. If this was my palace, I'd stay in the garden. It isn't my palace, though. It never will be. I'm not lucky enough to have been born here.

So many things catch my interest as I'm rushed through the twisting corridors. Silver and gold. Jewels. Pictures made of colorful thread that hang from the walls. Statues carved of white stone. Swords and shields and suits of armor. We climb a staircase carved with golden flowers and draped with purple carpet. The more I see, the less important I feel. I'm confused, too. If they're going to punish me, why show me all of this? Why bring me through into the depths of the palace? Wouldn't it be better to do my lashings somewhere else? Anywhere else? My stomach flips nervously. I try hard not to think of the fatty meat and cups of cider heavy in my belly. I don't want to ruin the carpet.

We finally stop at a door carved with dainty figures of winged ladies. They remind me of bony white creatures with black, empty eyes. Roots. Sand. I look away as the guards in front of me knock. The one who questioned me is behind me. He clamps a hand on my shoulder. The door swings open and a lady in a fine gown gives me a disapproving once-over. She looks at the man behind me, shakes her head, and steps aside to let us in, wringing her hands.

Inside is too pretty. Frills and ruffles everywhere. Lace curtains and shimmering sky-blue silk stretched across the ceiling. Walls painted with trees and flowers and butterflies. Poufs of pillows like mushrooms all around the green carpet. A girl sits on one of them, watching me. Her eyes are red. She's been crying. The guard pushes my shoulder down until I'm on my knees. A glint in her hair makes me finally realize who she is. I bow my head and my thoughts race.

"Is this the boy you saw, Your Highness?" The guard asks. His tone is different with her. Softer. Kind. She doesn't answer right away. Instead, she crosses the room to me. Her dress glitters with tiny jewels, bright against the deep green silk. She circles me and bends and takes my arm to pull me up.

"What's your name?" she asks.

"Tib, Your Highness," I whisper, confused.

"Tib, I'm Margary. You may call me Margy," she says brightly. She offers her hand to me. Tiny. Gloved. I look at it, and then at her. I'm not sure what to do.

"You may kiss it," she says. I glance up at her. Not sure I heard her right. She nods, and I do as I'm told. Press my lips to the soft fabric over her knuckles. She smells like flowery perfume. I feel ridiculous. The lady who let us in shakes her head and click her tongue. Behind me, the guard shifts. He squeezes my shoulder to remind me he's still there.

"Thank you, Finn," the princess says to the guard. "You may wait outside." The room is silent. "You too, Tirie."

"Your Highness, I must insist—" Finn starts to protest, but the princess raises her chin at him and he thinks twice. "Please, Highness. For your safety."

Margary looks up at me. She's not much older than Emmie. Maybe as old as Ruben. I'm not sure. Her eyes are brown with bits of orange. Puffy. Mournful. I wonder what a princess living in a palace like this could have to be troubled about.

"He won't hurt me," she argues.

"I must insist," Finn repeats. "I could lose my position, Highness." That works. Her eyes go wide. She chews her lip.

"Very well," she says. "Stand over there please, Finn."

She points to a far corner and the guard goes as he's ordered, to stand beneath a painted willow. Tirie gives me another appraising look and then goes out, closing the door behind her. The princess takes my hand and pulls me to the opposite corner. She drops onto a pouf and points to another. "You may sit," she says. I do. She leans in close.

"I saw you," she whispers. "Last night. You and him." She watches me hopefully.

"Me and?" I have no idea what she's talking about.

"Him," she says insistently.

"Who, Highness?" I frown. I was alone last night, all night, on the arches. Before I went home to bed. She sighs impatiently.

"It's okay, you can tell me. I know about them." She leans toward me, waiting.

"Know about who?" I shake my head slowly. Glance at the guard. Wonder whether the princess is not quite right in the head. She scowls.

"Here, look." She takes my elbow. Pulls me up. Brings me to the window and points down at the arches, to the spot where I dozed last night. "See? I was watching you. You and him. He looked sick. Is he?"

"Princess…" I shake my head. "I climbed the aqueduct and I'm sorry, but I did it alone, I swear. Nobody else was there." She huffs impatiently. Takes me by the sleeve. Pulls me back to the mushroom poufs.

"Please," she whispers. "I promise it's okay. I know about them. They've been helping me. We help each other. But now he's disappeared and I—"

Voices outside the door interrupt her.

"I found it! Your Highness! I found it!" The princess jumps to her feet as the door swings open and a page stumbles through it. He's waving a tattered looking baby doll. "I found it!"

She rushes to him. Takes the doll. Her shoulders slump. Quiver. She hands it back to him. Shakes her head. Tirie rushes in and embraces her. Comforts her.

"It's not…it's not it." The princess weeps.

"Shh, Highness. There, there."

"I thought for sure," the page turns the doll in his hands and then drops them to his sides, disappointed. "I'm sorry, Highness."

"You may go, Nate," Tirie says over her shoulder as she rubs the princess's back.

"Keep…keep looking. Please." Margy sniffles.

I watch him go in disbelief.

"What's the big deal? It's just a doll," I murmur. Tirie throws me a look. The princess curls into her and sobs.

"How could I lose it, Tirie?" Margy sobs. "How could I?"

"Shhh, now, little one. All of the pages are looking, and Master Anod said he'd try a location spell if he can find the time later."

"Nobody understands," Margy whispers.

"Of course we do, dear. Of course we do."

I shift uncomfortably, watching the scene in disbelief. All of this fuss over a toy? The door is still open. I inch toward it. Finn shakes his head at me.

"In the meantime," Tirie is saying, "they're working on a new poppet for you. You should see it! So many pretty little dresses and even tiny shoes. It was supposed to be a surprise, but we don't like seeing you so upset."

"I don't want…" Margy stops herself. Sniffles again. Wipes her eyes with the back of her glove. "I want Sara," she whispers.

"Oh my darling, your sister is riding with Prince Vorance, remember? You can see her at supper."

"Then I want Mama," she rests her head against Tirie's arm.

"Their Majesties are tending to the marriage contract with the advisers. They can't be disturbed." The princess sniffles again. Her glistening eyes rest on me.

"Then I want Tib to stay, and we want cakes and nectar."

"Your Highness, it isn't wise—" Finn starts, but Tirie throws him a look.

"Of course, sweet heart." The woman says, stroking the girl's hair. "I know it's hard, everyone leaving, everything changing. But it's how things are. People grow up and they go away. But we'll make sure you aren't lonesome, all right? Your cousins will be here soon. You won't be alone."

I shove my hands in my pockets and shift uncomfortably while the princess tries to compose herself. I don't want to stay here. I have things to do. Important things. I wish I could remember what. I think of Saesa. She was going to be part of it. I wonder what she did after the guards let her go. I wonder if she's trying to get me out. I wonder if Nessa will let me come back.

Margy calms down after a little while and Tirie leaves to call for the cakes. Finn stays. Watches. I go back to the mushrooms and sit when the princess beckons me.

"It's not just a doll," she whispers. "I haven't lost my mind." She moves closer. Leans toward me until I can almost smell the salt in her tears. Whispers so quietly that I have to watch her lips to make out what she's saying. "It's his tether. It's gone, and now he is, too." She searches my eyes and I watch her blankly. I don't know what to say. "You really don't know, do you? But I saw you. I saw you both. I thought you knew. I thought you could help."

"I'm sorry," I say. "I swear I don't know what you're talking about. If I did, I would tell you."

I'm glad when she says she wants her cakes in the garden. She calls it an atrium. When we go down, a table is laid out for us. Finn isn't far away, but it's much grander here. The princess doesn't need to whisper so low to be secret. She stops asking me about the arches and instead wants to know where I've been staying. I tell her about Nessa and the others, and soon her tears are forgotten. There's something about her. Something sweet that makes me want to keep her happy. To see her smile. So I keep talking.

The cakes are so sweet that they tickle my tongue, and the nectar is, too. I stuff myself full of both while the princess chatters away at me.

"Saesa is the eldest one, the one with the sword?" She asks. I shake my head.

"Raefe is the eldest. Her brother. Then Lilen."

"The Mage student, right?" She leans back in her chair and rubs her belly. "Oh, I ate too many…"

"Me too," I laugh. "Yes, Lilen studies at the Academy."

"But Saesa's the one you fancy." She grins at me. I shrug. "Oh, I can tell," she says. "You get the same look that Sara gets when she's talking about the prince."

"Maybe."

"I wish I could learn swordplay, like her." Margy says. "Like Azi." She sighs and looks out at the snow. "I wish she was here."

"Saesa?"

"Azi. She'd understand," she sighs. "Never mind." She gets up from the table and when Finn clears his throat, I do the same. "I want to go for a walk," she declares to him. "Outside."

"But Your Highness, it's snowing." Finn waves to someone outside in the hall, and Tirie rushes in.

"Yes, I know," Margy says. "If Sara can ride in the snow, I can go for a walk. I'm strolling Tib home. To Lady Ganvent's. It isn't far. Send a page to announce me."

"Your Highness, it's…" Finn trails off as Margy presses her lips together and her nostrils flare out. I've seen that look before. It's the one Emmie makes right before she starts to scream. The first time I saw her do it, I was amazed by how effective it was. Finn and Tirie don't let it get that far. Tirie calls for preparations for the princess, and Finn calls for the guard.

Not long after, we're strolling together under a canopy carried by four strong lads. Ten guards arrange themselves around us, with Finn at the lead. Tirie and three attendants walk beside the princess, who chats happily with me as we go. Several paces ahead, men work with shovels and brooms to clear snow from our path. I can't help but be amused by all of the fuss. It isn't far to Nessa's at all. Something else lifts my spirits as we leave the palace grounds. The feeling of loneliness that had settled over me fades.

"You're safe."

Yes, I'm safe. I grin. I'm safe, and I'm going home. I wasn't caught for burning the towers after all. I can start my journey. Do that task I was meant to do. Whatever it is. With Saesa. Our adventure.

"Wait! Your Highness!" The procession stops and Margy turns. I follow her gaze back to the palace gate. There, a man in orange robes flails his arms as he slips on the icy cobbles.

"Dumfrey!" Margy giggles as his slip turns to a glide and he stops gracefully beside her.

"Mage."

Yes, Mage. I scowl.

"Who's your friend?"

"This is Tib. Tib, this is Dumfrey. He's one of the Mages who works in the palace. Show him a spell, Dumfrey."

"I'm sorry, Princess," he says gravely. "You know I'm not allowed. Especially not now." He bows to me. His pointed hat flops over his long nose and he pushes it back again. "Well, maybe one. A good one." He wriggles his fingers and I shy away. "What's wrong Tibble-dibble? Don't like magic?" I shake my head. "Well, this one will keep you safe." He moves his arms in a wide arc.

"No!"

"No!" I scream. Try to run. The guards catch my arms. The spell shimmers around the canopy. I feel something strange, like a piece of me has been broken away. Terror strikes me straight through the heart. I start to panic. I can't breathe. Something is gone. Something important. I check my arms, my legs. No, it isn't that. It's something else. Someone. Someone I can't remember. He was here, and now he's gone.

"No," I cry, trying to fight free.

"Let him go!" the princess shouts, and they do. I fall to the ground. I feel empty. She crouches beside me. Scoops something into her cloak. I don't see what it is, but she cradles it gently. Hides it from the rest. Offers me a reassuring nod. "I knew it," she whispers. "Don't worry. I have him. He's safe."

"It was just a ward, Princess. I swear it," Dumfrey says. "A protection spell, to keep you all safe outside of the palace."

"See, Tib?" Margy plasters on a smile. "It was just a ward. It couldn't hurt you. Dumfrey's a good Mage. He was just watching out for us." She offers me a hand up. Keeps the other one hidden under her cloak.

"Go on to the Ganvent Manse, Dumfrey. Let them know we'll be along," Finn says.

"Yes, yes, of course," the Mage mumbles, then hurries off in a blur of orange.

"He didn't mean anything, Tib." Margy says as we continue on. "He was just trying to keep us safe. He didn't know."

"I don't like magic," I pant. Try to catch my breath.

"Lots of people don't," Margy says. "But it's like everything else. Some is good, some is bad. You just have to look out for the bad and stick with the good."

Chapter Eight:

MARGY'S SECRET

Tib

"Her Royal Highness, Princess Margary Plethore," someone announces as the canopy halts in front of Nessa's Manse. The guards in front of us part and stand in rows up the stairs. Nessa opens the door herself and dips into a low curtsy as the princess climbs the steps. Past her, inside, I see the others all lined up in the entrance hall. Even the cook. All except for Lilen. She's probably still at lessons. Saesa's eyes widen when she sees me following Margy. I smile at her, and she shakes her head and grins.

"Thank you for welcoming me, Lady Ganvent," Margy smiles up at Nessa. "Tib has told me so much about your kindness to the children. I wanted to come and meet everyone for myself."

"We're honored, Your Highness," Nessa says. "All of us." She gestures down the line.

"Maiseline!" Margy cries, "I've missed you!"

"Pleased to see you again, Your Highness." Maisie sinks into a curtsy and stays low so Margy can see Errie. She's got a strange look in her eye, Maisie. A hopeful look.

"Oh, look at the sweet baby." Margy offers the baby her finger, and Errie curls his tiny hand around it. "Handsome little one," Margy coos.

"Like his father," Maisie says.

"Will he call her Aunty?" Ruben whispers loudly to Saesa. She claps a hand over his mouth and shushes him. Silence falls over the room. Everyone is holding their breath. Maisie looks white. Finally, Tirie clears her throat. If the princess heard, she doesn't say anything. Instead, she moves down the line.

"You must be Raefe!" Margy declares as Raefe bows to her. "And, let's see. Saesa, Ruben, Emmie, and Garsi." She nods to each of them. "Oh, but Lilen isn't here?" she asks Saesa, who cautiously slides her hand from Ruben's mouth.

"She's at the Academy, Your Highness," Saesa replies. "She'll be disappointed she missed you."

"May I take your cloak, Your Highness?" Nessa asks. "Would you care for some tea?"

"No, thank you." Margy turns to me. "I'd like to see your room, Tib." She gives me a secret look. Her eyes trail to the lump under her cloak.

"Oh," I say. I glance at Tirie, who is as disapproving as ever. "It's there." I point up the stairs. Dumfrey's there, just inside my door. He steps out. His orange sleeve flops around as he waves at us.

"Everything's clear up here," he says.

"Very well," Finn grumbles.

"Come, Tib!" Margy runs up the steps and pauses at the top. I turn to Saesa, who grins at me again. "She can come, too, if she wants," the princess calls over her shoulder and disappears into my room.

"Taken away by the city guard before breakfast, and you come home with a princess after lunch." Saesa laughs, and most of the others do, too. She throws her arms around me and whispers, "I'm so glad you're okay." My insides warm. I hug her back.

"Come on," she says, and we take the stairs together two at a time.

Inside, Margy has taken off her cloak and piled it on my floor like a nest. She kneels beside it, hands on either side. "Close the door," she whispers.

I go and peek downstairs first. Tirie is fussing over Maisie's baby. Two guards are posted inside the front door. Dumfrey is showing Raefe and the others a sleight of hand. I close the door and go back to the girls. Saesa is kneeling beside Margy, peering at the pile of cloak.

"I don't see anything," Saesa says.

"You have to be open to it," Margy whispers. "Tib, come here."

I kneel between the two of them.

"He's sick," Margy says. I peer into the cloak-nest. The creature nestled there is white and bony. Frail. Completely still, like he's dead. My heart aches. I reach for him. I know him, somehow. "I forgive you for not telling me, Tib. I know we have to protect them, the fairies."

"Fairies?" Saesa leans closer. Looks harder. Laughs merrily. "Is that what you were doing all morning, Tib? Playing fairies? We were all so worried about you! You should have seen Nessa when I told her about Bren. She's put him on her blacklist. He won't be doing much business after turning you in, when she gets through with him. I had to tell her about Feat, too, but she's okay with it…" Saesa goes on and on, but I don't hear her. The creature turns its head weakly. Opens its black eyes to look right at me.

I remember. Roots. Trees. Fighting. Running. Climbing. Burning. Swimming. He's been with me through all of it. I remember the Mage in Nessa's sitting room. I remember our conversation at the arches. I think of Dumfrey just now under the canopy. How his ward struck us. The voice in my head saying no. The feeling that something had been ripped from me. It was him. Mevyn. Mevyn. He looks so much worse now. Thin, like a ghost. Fading. Almost nonexistent.

"What happened?" I whisper. Saesa stops talking. Watches me.

"Mage. Ward. Draining."

"Oh, Dumfrey," Margy whines softly. "He's so bumbling. He means well, though." Margy reaches out to the skeletal figure. She almost touches him, but stops herself. "Please, what can we do?"

Mevyn doesn't answer. His eyes drift closed. I know he's barely hanging on. I remember the empty pool in Sunteri, near the trees. How he wept. I remember the important thing I had to do. Go to Kythshire. Ask for help in restoring the Wellspring. It's Mevyn's quest. I can't do it without him.

"He needs a Mage," I say reluctantly. I hate them so much. I hate that there's nothing I can do myself. "He needs magic."

"I still don't see him," Saesa says. She's confused. She still doesn't see Mevyn, but she's starting to believe us. "I'll go get that orange Mage. He can help."

"No," the princess says as Saesa starts to get up. "Fairies are secret. No one else can know."

Mevyn moans. Reaches out to the princess. Points to her with one finger. Margy stiffens. Glances at the closed door. Nods slowly.

"All right," she whispers to Mevyn. "But you have to keep my secret, too. All of you. Nobody can know."

I glance at Saesa. Remember what she told me once. There aren't really any secrets, there's just information with a higher value. I wonder whether she'd sell the princess's secrets.

"I promise," she says convincingly. I nod, too.

Margy places her fingertip in Mevyn's palm. It glows with a

soft, pink light that streams from the princess to the weakened fairy. Slowly, Mevyn's form becomes more solid. The flesh on his bones thickens to muscles. His skin deepens to a healthy bronze color. His hair brightens to yellow. Wings of gold unfurl from his back.

"I see a light," Saesa gasps. "A golden light. Is that him?"

I can't answer. I'm mesmerized by Mevyn's transformation. Margy seems different, too. Her eyes are brighter. She's happier. Relieved, like a heavy weight has been lifted from her. She giggles beside me as the fairy zooms past her. He darts around the room and then dives quickly behind my pillow as a knock comes and Tirie pokes her head in.

"At the very least," Tirie says shrilly, "I must insist upon an open door." All of us nod at her, wide-eyed. When she leaves, Mevyn comes to sit on my knee. I've never seen him looking so whole and healthy. His skin glows with winding golden lines. His hair waves on its own. His shining, spiky wings are twice as large as he is. A spear is slung over his shoulder. As I watch, his tattered pants are replaced with armor of leaves and bark that look like they've been dipped in gold.

"You're a warrior," Margy gasps.

"And you, Princess, are not supposed to have magic, are you?" His voice is stronger now than it has been in my head. Deeper. Commanding. It echoes over us and in my thoughts, too.

"I can't help it," Margy whispers. "It just comes to me. It fills me up and weighs me down and makes me cry. I can't let it go or I'll start a war. That's my secret. Nobody can know."

"You'll start a war?" I ask.

"Oh, yes. Royalty isn't allowed magic in Cerion," the princess says gravely. "It isn't like Sunteri."

"Why not?" I ask. When I think about it, it's a good rule. Sunteri would be a lot different with that rule. More equal. Like here.

"Because of the Sorcerer King. Diovicus?" she asks, a little surprised by my ignorance. I shake my head. Stories and history. A boy in the dye fields has no reason to hear about those things. Margy goes on.

"King Diovicus was the King of Cerion a very long time ago. He didn't care about our kingdom or its people. He was cruel and selfish. He burned people who disagreed with him. He controlled people to do his will, and he made armies to march on Kythshire. He wanted to destroy all of the fairies there to claim their power for his own. My great-great-great grandfather rallied an army to stop him. The elves helped him. They won, and that began the Plethore Dynasty. He made a pact with the fairies who survived, that there would be peace in Cerion as long as the Plethore line ruled. With two promises: One, we would keep the fairies' existence a secret and two, the ruling family would swear to never wield magic again."

Margy's eyes well with tears and she shakes her head. "I can't help it, though. It just comes. It comes, and I give it to Twig. He helps me with it. He understands, but now he's gone. Nobody else knows. Not even Paba. I've kept it a secret all this time."

"Give it to me then," Mevyn says. "All of it. And then you will be rid of it for now." He settles in her hand. She closes her eyes and the pink glow returns. Mevyn soaks it all up. Basks in it. Radiates with magic so strong I can feel it myself, in my bones. The golden curls on his skin burst with light. Beside her, Saesa seems to be staring off at the wall over my shoulder. Dazed. I wonder if it's Mevyn doing it. I don't like it. When the magic is finally absorbed, Margy slumps against me.

"What about Twig?" she whispers sleepily. "I need him. He's my friend, and I'm so worried something's happened to him. Please, can you search for him or his tether?"

"Of course you're worried," says Mevyn softly. He drifts up to her face. Places a gentle hand on her cheek. Gazes into her eyes. She smiles peacefully. Drifts to sleep. Mevyn turns to me.

"It's nearly time," his voice echoes in my mind. *"You remember our journey? Our adventure?"*

I nod.

"You did well, Tib. Now that I'm restored, I'm certain we can find your sister."

"My sister?" I whisper. I think back to Nan beneath the tree. Zhilee. "But, she was killed."

"Zhilee, yes. But your other sister. You wanted to find her, remember?"

I'm confused at first, but then I remember her. Older sister, sitting in the red blooms, her nose buried in a book. Riding off with the Sorcerer who later terrorized us, held us with roots. Rage wells inside of me, and with it, longing. Yes. I want to find her. I want her to see me. The brother she abandoned. I want to see her, the last of my family. The family she destroyed with her greed for power. Sunset. Sunset, and she didn't come through for us. Sunset, and she let Zhilee die. I hate her. I love her. I'm confused. How can I feel both so strongly?

"I want to find her," I say. Maybe seeing her will help me

understand.

"*Good*," says Mevyn. "*Then for now, my friend, it is best that you don't remember. As I always do with your permission, for your protection and my own, I will make you forget.*"

I nod, and my eyes slowly drift closed. When I open them, Margy is standing and stretching. Yawning. Saesa blinks rapidly as she comes out of her own trance.

"I'll be going now," Margy says airily. I pick up her cloak. Hand it to her. "I want to be back at the palace in time to dress for dinner. I had a wonderful time." She tilts her head at me and smiles. "Would you come to visit again? I'll send an invitation. And you, Saesa. It would be lovely to have new friends to show around."

"I'd be honored, Your Highness," Saesa grins.

"Please, just call me Margy." She smiles and skips out into the hallway, where Tirie is waiting at the top of the stairs.

"It was awfully quiet in there, Your Highness," Tirie says suspiciously.

"We were playing the whisper game," Margy says without missing a beat. "I'm sleepy now."

"The litter," Tirie calls down the stairs as she fusses with Margy's cloak.

"No, I'll walk," Margy says cheerfully. "It isn't far."

At the door, everyone makes their bows and curtseys. The guards file into their lines. Margy waves at us from beneath the canopy. We watch them go until they disappear around a distant corner, and then Nessa pulls me into the sitting room. Asks me what happened. The others lounge on the floor, listening. My memories are foggy, like I have to fight through something more important to get to them. I answer their questions until my head tips to the arm of the sofa and keeping my eyes open is a battle. Nessa sends everyone off. Helps me to my room. Puts me to bed. Tucks the blankets around me. Smoothes my hair. Kisses my forehead. Stays with me until I drift to sleep.

"*Wake up. Get dressed.*"

It's dark. Silent. The whole house is sleeping. I pull on my shirt from yesterday, yank my rumpled pants over my boots. Grab my belt with the knife on it that I thought Finn took from me yesterday. I don't remember getting it back, but here it is. I yawn. Wipe the sleep from my eyes. Slump onto the bed again. Wonder why I woke so early. There's no light coming in through the shutters. It's not even morning yet.

"Out the window."

Yes, out the window. I push it open and shiver as a gust of wind nearly blows me back inside. Back where my bed is still warm.

"Climb."

Yes, climb. My teeth chatter. I straddle the sill. Pull on my gloves. Wish I had my cloak. Doesn't matter. I climb down the side of the manse. I know the footing well. It's familiar now. Second nature. The snow on the street below is thick. Up to my knees. It finally stopped falling, though. Now there's just the frigid wind.

I creep close to the walls of houses and shops as I make my way into the heart of the city. I don't know where I'm going, but I know the way. Not sure why, but I know I have to. Something in my mind nudges me. Pushes me along. Northward. Westward. I vaguely remember the promise of an adventure. I wonder if this is it. No, Saesa was supposed to come with me. This must be something smaller. Never been this deep into the city. It feels different here. More serious. I stop in an alley and crouch in the shadows. Peer across the street at a low building. There's no moon tonight, but my eyes have adjusted to the darkness.

"Get inside."

Yes, get inside. Five men mill around outside the small stone building. Not guards, thugs. It's one story. A shed, or a shack. Not even as big as our house back home. I have to get in. I creep toward it in the shadows and hide against the side wall. Watch. Listen. No windows on this side to climb through. No chimney on top. There's only one door, and they're all in front of it. Smoking herbs. I creep closer. Slide along the wall to the back, then around to the other side. No windows at all. It's all stone. I come around toward the front again. Peek around the corner.

The men are supposed to be watching, but they're not. They're distracted. Talking.

"Who cares what it is? Doesn't matter, long as we get paid," the biggest one says. He's got a hood on. A broadsword. Chain mail. Wolf's head cloak. Its empty eye sockets stare at me. I creep closer. Press myself against the wall. Wait in shadows. Move slowly. Toward the door. Toward the men. I'm not afraid, just determined.

"If it's worth more than they're payin' us, we could sell it ourselves. Split it four ways," another man says. He's got a club. Fists the size of a horse's head. I try to make myself smaller. Hide in the dark. Hold my breath.

"Five ways," another says. Dressed in dark leather. Decked all over with knives and daggers. He throws a knife into the hitching post nearby. It's already peppered with blades. He throws another.

"Yeah, five ways." The horse-fisted one says, after counting all of them again and remembering himself this time. I glance at the door. It's ajar. There's a big enough space. I'm small enough. I could slip between the broad sword man and the knife-throwing man. I'm right here. They haven't noticed me yet.

"Brilliant plan, Muster. Would be, if our client wasn't so terrifying." I didn't realize one was a woman until she speaks. She's too covered up in her cloak.

"You scared of him, Stone?" The knife one says.

"You didn't meet him," the woman replies. "You'd be, too. Leave it alone. It's an easy job. Just wait here until he comes to pick it up. Then he pays us money. A lot of money. Trust me."

"Do it now."

Yes, now. Now, before I can think too much. Before I lose my courage. I slip behind the big one. Past the one with the knives. Push the door open slowly, carefully. It squeaks. I freeze.

"You're getting soft—" the one nearest me stands straighter. Turns his head toward me. Reaches for one of his many knives. Around me, the air shimmers. He looks right at me. I hold my breath, brace for the knife. He doesn't do anything. He can't see me. I slip inside, where it's even darker.

"Dub?"

"Thought I heard something," says the knife one. They keep talking but I don't stay to listen. I slide along the wall, feeling my way deeper into the darkness. The stone is cold. Wet. The floor is wood, half-rotted. Creaky. Dub comes in, too. The one with the knives. He creeps around looking for me, but I evade him easily.

"Find the hatch."

Yes, find the hatch. Quickly. I sink to my knees. Search the floor with my hands. Find a raised board, a metal ring. It clanks loudly. A knife whizzes past my ear. I don't think. I roll to the side. The blade thuds into the floor beside me. The door slams shut. Outside, the thugs pound on it. Shouting. Rattling it.

"Roll left!"

Roll left. My body acts without thinking. Another knife misses me by a hair, striking the floor where I just was. I grab my own knife from my belt. A flash of golden light blinds me. I see a glimpse of a figure, tiny and golden beside my ear. It darts away from me in a streak. Charges the knife man. Throws a golden spear right into his eye. He doubles over, screaming. Outside, they slam against the door. It splinters.

"Into the hatch!"

Yes, into the hatch. I grasp the ring with both hands. Yank it open. Lower myself inside. Down the rungs of a ladder. Deeper into darkness. Away from the chaos above. The golden figure is gone. The hatch slams shut.

Down, down, until my arms and feet ache. Down until I feel the pressure in my ears and have to open my mouth wide to relieve it. I think about the trees. The roots. The darkness. This shaft is small. Suffocating. I start to panic. Wrap my arms around the rungs. Pant. Shake. Cling.

"Keep going."

Yes, keep going. No, I can't. I can't. My feet won't let me. My eyes strain in the darkness. I can't see. I'm blind. I'm trapped.

"I can't," I whisper.

"You can. You will."

Yes, I will. I forget my fear. Don't remember it now. Keep going down. Like up above, my body moves without me thinking. My boots find the bottom. Packed dirt. It smells here, like mold and decay. A golden light builds slowly above me, glowing just bright enough to show me the small space without hurting my eyes.

"There. The box."

Yes, the box. I see it in the center of the room. A metal chest encrusted with jewels. Sapphire and emerald and ruby. I pick it up. Turn it in the light. Watch the gems flash and glow.

"Open it."

I turn it over and over. It's molded shut. I can't find the lid. I press on the gems. Nothing happens.

"It can't open," I say.

"Be quiet."

Yes, be quiet.

The golden figure appears again. Lands on the box. Places his hands on it. Makes it glow. The top of it slides open. The figure moves away. Its golden wings flutter as I stare at it. It looks up at me, into my eyes.

"Mevyn." I whisper.

"*Quiet,*" Mevyn says again. He looks into the box. So do I.

Inside is a filthy pile of rags and yarn. A button eye. A frayed, stitched-on smile. A doll, a ruined doll. Beside it, pale and sickly, is another tiny figure. Another fairy, like Mevyn. His clothes are rumpled and frayed, his skin smudged with dirt. His wings are sticks of wood that poke out of his back. He turns his head slowly toward us.

"The princess," he says. I blink. Fight through the fog in my head. Remember Margy and her grief over the lost doll. Her secret in my room.

"Twig?" I whisper.

"Tell her," he says weakly, "I'm safe. Tell her."

"Yes," says Mevyn.

"Burn the tether. I'll send a new one. Find me in Kythshire."

"Wait," Mevyn says, but he's too late. Twig fades away. Disappears. Mevyn growls. Kicks the box. "Take the tether," he says to me. "Take it and leave the box. Let's go."

Chapter Nine:

DREAMWALKER

Tib

I do as I'm told. Scoop the tattered doll from the box. Stuff it into my trouser pocket. Turn to Mevyn. Behind him, the shadows seep together. Swirl. Form into a dark figure. Terror grips me. Worse than my fear of the roots. Worse than my fear of anything else. I can't breathe. I can't think.

"This is your champion?" The shadow laughs cruelly. "This boy? This pile of crumpled fear?"

My knees quake. I collapse to the floor, trembling. Whimpering. This shadow will destroy me. This shadow will overcome everything.

"Get up."

Yes, get up. I push myself to my feet. My legs wobble like jelly. The shadow moves closer.

"Stand your ground."

Yes, stand my ground. I square my shoulders. Take a deep breath. Try to be brave. My instincts tell me otherwise. They tell me to run. Run far away. Up the ladder. Back to Nessa's. Back to where I'll be safe. Never come here again.

"Mevyn, Mevyn…" the shadow laughs. "I thought you were smarter. More resourceful. Is this really all it took to lure you in? All it took to trap you? I'm disappointed."

Mevyn doesn't say anything. He puts himself between me and the shadow. Raises his spear. I honestly don't think the weapon will do anything against it. It makes me feel better, though. Protected.

"Don't listen to him. Stand with me. He can't harm us."

"Ha! But I can."

"You know that you can't touch him, or me. We're leaving. We did what we came to do." Mevyn flies to the ladder. Lights the way into the shaft.

"Climb."

Yes, climb. I start to follow, wary of the swirling darkness that watches me with no eyes.

"He cannot. His legs are bound."

I look down. My ankles snap together. I try to walk but I stumble forward.

"Bound with what? Look closer, Tib." Mevyn says. "Don't listen to him."

"Tib, is it?" The shadow asks as I realize Mevyn is right. There are no bindings. I'm free to move. I rush to the ladder. Start to climb. "Tib, wait a moment. Listen to me." Every time he says my name, I feel a stronger connection to him. Like he's my friend. Like he has power over me. His voice is soothing. It lures me. Makes me want to stay, to hear what he has to say to me. "Listen." I pause with my hand on the wrung.

"Climb," says Mevyn both aloud and in my head. His voice is booming. Earsplitting. It courses through my body, commanding. Pleading.

"Wait." The shadow demands.

Yes, wait. No, climb. Somehow I'm compelled to do both. My head starts to pound. My body fights itself. Hands cling, feet climb. Arms shake.

"What do you know of Mevyn?" the shadow asks. "What do you really know? Only what he has revealed to you. Only what he wants you to know, hm? And even that, he takes away until he needs you to know it again. Over and over. What do you think that does to a young boy's mind?"

I look up at Mevyn. I do know him. We're friends. We help each other. But the shadow is right. My memories have holes. Not holes, chasms. Dark places that are difficult to get to. I think of Zhilee. Try to remember, but I can't. The shadow is right. What else has Mevyn taken from me? What harm has he done to my mind?

"I've given you things, Tib. Knowledge. Gold. Safety. Freedom. We need each other. Close him out. Don't listen." I remember how I somehow knew to tie the sails, to impress Cap. I remember the gold coins I tucked under Saesa's pillow, the excitement on her face when Feat was finally hers. *"Friends, I've given you friends. Nessa, Saesa, Raefe, Lilen, Ruben, Emme. Margary. Climb. Climb back to them."*

I will my hands to move. I'm a fair climber. I'm a third of the way up when the shadow closes in around me. I can't see a thing. Not

Mevyn, not even my hands in front of me.

"Keep climbing."

I quicken my pace, scrambling to get to the top, but the darkness follows. Halfway up, images swim through my thoughts. Dreams. Red blooms and laughter. Chasing Zhilee in the sunshine. The pages of a book fluttering in the breeze. Nan, not stooped and aching but tall and strong, standing in the doorway, smiling at us. Viala reading aloud from a storybook. No work to do. No picking or hauling. No whips or deadlines. Just happiness. Playing. Love. It's so real, so real I can smell the flowers. So wonderful that the laughter bubbles in my throat. I feel Zhilee's hand in mine. I'm not here, in the shaft. I'm there. There, in the field with my family. This is how it should have been. My childhood. What would I have become, if it had been like this? Red petals float in the air around us, drifting in the warm breeze. Zhilee wants me to catch them. I reach out. My hands leave the rung. I turn to chase the petals. I'm falling, falling.

"Tib!"

Pain. Pain as my head cracks hard against the floor. Pain splinters from my ankle to my knee. My chest aches. I gasp for the breath that was knocked out of me. I blink into Mevyn's dim light. My vision is closing up, blurring and blackening.

Someone is laughing. Laughing hard. Mocking. Not Mevyn. The shadow. The darkness.

"Can't hurt him. That's what you said, isn't it?" The laughing echoes. "Don't underestimate me, Mevyn. You will fail. You and your pathetic champion. I'll leave you now, to watch him die."

Something in the air shifts, and even through my pain I can feel it. Heaviness lifted. Darkness brighter. The shadow has gone. I try to look to make sure, but my range is too narrow, like I'm looking through a tunnel. My head won't turn. My neck aches. My leg. I close my eyes. I want to die. Death would be better than this pain.

"Tib. Stay awake. Talk to me." Mevyn says silently. Like one of his commands. My head feels like it will split open. I try to obey.

"What?" my whisper rattles. It hurts to breathe.

"Talk to me," Mevyn orders. "Don't fall asleep."

"Talk?"

"Yes," he says desperately. "Ask me a question. Any question."

"Who was that?"

"Dreamwalker," he seethes.

"Who is—?" I cough painfully. Taste something on my lips.

Something sticky. Lick it away. It tastes like metal. Like blood. My lungs are burning. Filling up.

"That's not his name, it's what he is. A Dreamwalker. We are old rivals. It's a long story," Mevyn says. He starts to tell me. I try hard to follow but I can't focus. His voice is too far away. The pain is too much. My leg is broken, I know it. I can't move my neck. My chest is rattling.

"Stay with me."

Nobody knows I'm here. Nobody except the thugs. They'll find me. I'll die here. I'll die, like the shadow said. Nobody will know. Nobody will care.

"Stay with me!"

Stay. I can't. I'm fading away. Falling away. I can't help it. I drift off.

When I wake up, I don't know where I am. Don't remember how I got here. I can't move except to open my eyes. Everything else is too painful. There's a shaft above me with rungs going up. Someone was with me, but now they're gone. Something twinkles beside me. Something small and jeweled. A box, I think. Otherwise, I'm alone. Utterly. In the dark. In the dirt. My breath comes in short gasps. My mouth is dry. My tongue is crusted. Stuck to my teeth. I need water. It's like the roots all over again. What roots, I wonder, and then I remember. I try to calm myself, but the panic takes me over. My head feels light. The room spins. My eyes close. I black out.

The sound of wood scraping on wood wakes me. Creaking. A beam of light splashes down the shaft. I squint into it. My heart races. Someone from up there will hurt me if they find me. Could they really? I'm already in more pain than anyone should be. Maybe they'll kill me. Relieve me. I hear a pair of feet on rungs. Another. Whispers.

"How can you be sure?" a male voice asks. It sounds familiar.

"Trust me, okay? I just have a feeling." A girl. My heart thumps. Saesa.

"We shouldn't be in here, it's private property!" Another girl.

"Then wait outside, Lilen, for crying out loud." The boy again. I know him. Raefe.

"By myself? No way. Look. Look at this." The other girl. Lilen.

"Saesa, wait for us. Whoa, is that blood? Look at all of it." Raefe.

"I'm not going down there. You shouldn't, either. We should get the guard." Lilen.

"No, he's down here, I know it. He's alive." Saesa's voice is nearing. I hear her feet on the rugs, coming closer. I remember being up there. Remember something else. The shadow. I try to shout up to her to warn her, but my voice is too weak. It comes out as a croak. My throat is too dry. My chest aches. My tongue is hard and dry, like a desert stone.

"How do you know? What if this is his blood? What if he's—?"

"Shut up, Lilen," Raefe interrupts, annoyed. "Just wait here." I hear his feet on the rungs. They don't talk on their way down. They just climb.

"They're coming. Don't move. You're safe now."

Yes, they'll be here soon. I'm safe now. I'm safe. I close my eyes. My head hurts too much to keep them open. They finally make it to the bottom. Saesa cries out. Drops to her knees beside me. I'm too afraid to open my eyes. Too afraid that something got her.

"Oh, Tib," she whispers. Liquid is poured into my mouth, cool and soothing. Cleansing. I feel it go all the way down. It takes the edge off of my pain.

"Water," I whisper, and Saesa cries out with relief.

"Water, Raefe, can he have it with this potion?"

"Yeah, it's just a pain draught. The other one's the healing one. He can drink all he wants. But look at him, Saesa. Potions aren't going to do much. He's going to need a real healer. He's a mess. Tib, can you hear me?"

I open my eyes. Try to nod. My neck is stiff but the pain is going away. I feel like I'm floating. "Ugh," I manage.

"I'll stay here with him," Saesa says. "Go get someone. We can't move him, he's too hurt."

I want to warn them. Tell her no, that the shadow could come back, that she could be in danger if she stays, but I can't. The draught has made my eyelids heavy. My mouth won't form the words. But the pain, the pain is gone. Gone. The two have a discussion, and they're all the way down the tunnel again. Echoes of voices all run together. Feet on rungs again, going up. Saesa's hand gingerly on my shoulder.

"What was he doing down here, Mevyn? How did he fall?" she asks after the hatch closes above us and we're alone. Mevyn. I remember him.

"Dark magic," Mevyn replies. "Deception. Now that you have found him, I will ask, for my protection and yours, that you allow me to make you forget. You will not remember me. You will not see me again. You will go with Tib, if he asks you to. Do you understand why, Saesa?"

"Of course," Saesa says. Her voice is distant. Strange. I wonder if mine sounds like that when Mevyn asks me to agree to forget. I open my eyes and watch. Mevyn has his hands on her face. He looks deep into her eyes. Streams of golden light curl from them like smoke from a campfire into his. Like he's collecting memories. I close my eyes before he sees me watching. I drift back to sleep.

When I wake up, I'm tucked comfortably into my bed at the Ganvent Manse. I scoot up a little stiffly against my pillows. Take a drink from the water cup on my bedside table. Saesa's curled in the chair beside me, sound asleep. I look outside. Midday. Snowing again. I sit cross-legged. Think back. Remember. Surprisingly, I remember all of it. Even Mevyn. I shrug my shoulders. Bend my knees. Wriggle my toes inside my boots. I slept in my boots. I always do. Everything is sore, but nothing's broken. I'm hurting, but not like before. Was it a dream, all of it? Was it real?

"It was real."

Yes, it was real. I pat my pockets. Search for the doll. Margy's baby. Twig's tether. I made a promise.

"*I burned it already,*" Mevyn says.

In the chair beside me, Saesa stirs. Opens her eyes. Flashes of green. Jungle green. Jewel green. They warm me.

"You're awake," she says with relief. "How are you feeling?"

I tell her I'm okay, and she tells me Lilen spelled me with levitate to get me out. Raefe brought a healer to weave my insides back together. They bound me to Raefe's back to carry me home. I slept for a whole day. Nessa thinks I fell out of an icy tree. Princess Margy sent us an invitation. By the time she's finished, I'm exhausted again. I sleep through the afternoon, until I'm roused by a gentle touch on my cheek. A soft hand. It smoothes my hair back. Rests gently on my chest.

"Tib," the voice is pretty. Soft. Concerned. I know this voice. Nessa. I open my eyes. Look at her.

"You're crying," I say. She nods. Smiles through her tears. I wonder what's made her cry. She's usually so strong. I think of ships. Her husband. Something must have happened to him. "The Admiral?" At first she looks puzzled, then she laughs softly.

"No word on him, Tib, but I was certainly worried for you. What in seven stars were you thinking, out in the middle of the night, climbing trees?"

I shrug. Wince a little. Still sore. She watches me.

"Boys." She rolls her eyes. Shakes her head. "Come here." She holds her arms open like I've seen her do with the others. I sit up. Let her hug me. It feels nice. Warm. I let her hug me for a while. Hug her back a little. She sniffles. "Promise me no more climbing in the middle of the night. Okay?"

"Okay, Nessa," I say. It feels nice, but strange to have someone care about me. Cry over me. She just keeps hugging, and eventually I wriggle away.

Garsi calls for her, and Nessa gives me one last squeeze before she goes out to get her. I sit back against my pillows. My head is clearer now. For the first time in a while, I feel like my thoughts are my own.

I look around the room. My room. I never really looked at it before. The furniture is fine, and the walls are sturdy and safe. It's almost as big as our whole house in the dye fields. Higher up, too. No bugs. No sand. I'm used to the bed now. I like it. I don't know how I slept on the mats for so long. I don't think I could go back to that. This could be my home now.

The vision that the shadow, no, Dreamwalker gave me is still vibrant in my memory. Looking back on it, I realize how foolish it was for me to think it could be real. It can never be. Nan is dead. Zhilee is dead. Viala is gone. She's forgotten us. Forsaken us. Got herself into trouble. Stripped, Saesa said. Disappeared.

A shimmer on my down covers catches my eye. I watch it as it flashes and brightens and Mevyn emerges, broad and strong.

"I remember you," I whisper.

"I know I can trust you now. You passed the test."

I sit up. Drink some water. Think.

"Test?" I ask.

"Of sorts," Mevyn says. "It needed to be done, and I couldn't have done it without you, but you've proved your courage and your loyalty. Your trustworthiness."

"I don't understand."

"You and I are paired by circumstance. Forced together. Bonded by our strife. That connection bears power. It's how we were able to leave Sunteri. How I was able to aid you in our journey so that you could carry me here. You are my champion, and I am your guide. We chose each other, and we were chosen for each other. And after our encounter with the Dreamwalker, I have faith in you. You were strong."

"Strong?" I scoff and sink back against my pillows. "I wasn't strong. I believed what he showed me. I thought it was real. I let go. I could have died. I wanted to."

"If you had any idea," Mevyn settles in my palm, "just how powerful he is, just how wicked, you would not be ashamed. You would be proud of yourself. As proud as I am."

I don't say anything. I'm not sure what to say. Between him and Nessa, it's too much. Too much kindness. It makes me uncomfortable. Happy, but I feel undeserving.

"You have an invitation from the princess." Mevyn drifts over to my bedside table and lands beside a folded page sealed with purple wax and a gold ribbon.

"Yeah."

"Go," Mevyn says. "Tell her about Twig. Ask her for help. We must go to Kythshire and find him, like you promised."

"By myself?" I push myself out of bed. I'm a little stiff, a little weak, but the pain is gone. I cross to my cabinet. Look for something fancy to wear.

"I cannot enter the palace grounds," Mevyn explains as he flies to hover beside me. "They're too protected. It would reveal me. I must remain a secret."

"But what about Twig? He goes around the palace. Nobody sees him." I find a white shirt with lace on the cuffs. Wrinkle my nose. Put it on. Cover it with a deep blue jacket. Shove the ridiculous lace up into the sleeves.

"He must have found a way around it, for the princess," Mevyn says. "Or perhaps it allows for the Kythshire fae. Sunteri magic is different."

"How did you know," I ask, "that he was trapped down there? How did you know where to find him?"

"Once I knew what to look for, it wasn't difficult. A stolen tether, a doll. Tethers hold strong magic. They're always calling out. If you're quiet enough, you can hear them. We can, that is. Fairies."

"How did you open it?" I search through a folded stack of pants for a pair that hasn't been torn from my climbing and patched up by Maisie or Nessa. I find some in the bottom of the pile. Pull them on.

"It was locked on the outside by magic. Wards bolstered by riches. Man's magic. Magework. Twig couldn't get it open, he's a fairy."

"But you're a fairy, and you could open it."

"Because I had you, a man. You wanted it open, with good intention. See? We worked together. Alone, I couldn't have done it. Neither could you, unless you were a Mage. It required a pairing."

I still don't understand, but I'm shaking and sweaty from the effort of dressing and trying to make sense of Mevyn's explanations. My stomach growls. It's been empty for over a day. There was a time when I was used to that. I could go a couple of days without a scrap. Now I have three meals and snacks between, if I want them. I wonder how I used to survive.

Nessa's happy to see me downstairs, dressed and eating. She's not happy when I tell her I'm going to the palace. She doesn't think I'm well enough yet. She convinces me to wait for Saesa. I'm not sure if that's okay.

"It's fine," Mevyn says, so I wait for her to get back from training, and we go together to the palace as the sun sets.

At the gate I show them the invitation. They nod us through with no trouble. Collect our weapons for safekeeping. This time, I feel Mevyn's absence as soon as I cross through the gate. I walk nearer to Saesa as a page escorts us to the indoor garden, just to fill that empty gap. Saesa's eyes are wide as dinner plates. She doesn't sit where we're invited to. She walks around, sniffing flowers and touching things she probably shouldn't. Taking it all in. Examining things in a way I wouldn't think to. We don't have to wait long. Margy runs to us. I try to bow, but she dives at me. Hugs me. Hugs Saesa. Cerion is big on hugs.

There's a different guard watching us today. Sterner. His name is Thurle. He takes his duties seriously. Posts himself no farther than an arm's length from the princess. That makes it hard to talk, but Margy is clever. More clever than I am.

"Let's play pretend," she says. "I am a fairy princess, and I'm asleep. You are brave explorers, and you come and wake me." I don't like this. I'm no good at pretend. There was no time for it in the field. It makes me feel awkward.

Margy lies down on the grass and plays at sleeping. Saesa and I kneel beside her.

"Look, we've found a fairy!" Saesa declares. "Wake up, little fairy." Margy sits up. Stretches.

"Oh, I was dreaming," the princess gives an elegant yawn. "What a lovely dream. It was about my dear friend, Twig."

Margy nods at me. I shift uncomfortably and glance at Thurle.

He doesn't show any signs of hearing, but I know he's listening.

"I dreamed he was safe in his home," Margy goes on. "I was so happy. You see, he was lost, and I was so very worried. But now I know that he's safe, and I'm so very happy. Now, we shall dance!" She takes Saesa's hand and mine, and dances around in a circle. Tirie snaps her fingers in the doorway, and two musicians appear from who knows where and start to play.

"Princess," I whisper as we twirl, "you're right. He is safe. He told me—"

"Play louder!" Margy shouts happily. The musicians do. Thurle and Tirie watch on, glad to see their princess in such good spirits. My weak limbs and aching head protest, but I keep on letting her pull me along. "Go on," she whispers.

"He told me to come and find him," I say. "In Kythshire."

"I know," says Margy. "He told me in my dream. I made arrangements already. I have them waiting for you." She lets go of my hand and falls back into the grass, laughing. Saesa and I tumble down, too.

"And now," the princess says dramatically, "I shall send you on a quest! Go and seek out Twig, who wishes to repay you for your kindness. Bring him this." She reaches into her pocket and produces a bracelet woven of ribbons and pearls. Gives it to me. "Go now, brave adventurers." She leans in closer to me and whispers, "I'll send along the rest of the things later. You'll go, won't you? To Kythshire?" I glance at Saesa, who's just as wide-eyed as before.

"Yes," I whisper.

"Do you need men?" she asks. "Horses?"

"I don't know," I whisper. I think of Mevyn. Wish he was here. He could tell me yes or no.

"I'll send them. You can send them back if you wish." She leans closer.

"You can do that?" I stare at her. Can't believe that a child has the power to order men and steeds. Saesa sits up. Brushes grass from her vest.

"Yes. Watch," the princess whispers, then speaks louder for the benefit of Tirie and Thurle. "Tib, I have decided that I will help you. You've been kind to me, so I shall grant your request." The music quiets. Tirie raises a brow. Listens.

"Thank you, Your Highness," I say. Try to sound convincing even though I don't know what she's talking about.

"I shall arrange an escort for you to the Southern Crossroads of Ceras'lain. There, you can follow the road to your uncle's."

"You have an--?" Saesa stops herself. "Oh, right, your uncle."

"Yes," I say, catching on to the lie. "He's old. I want to go see him. Her Highness said she'd help."

"I'll come, too." Saesa pushes herself to her feet.

"It's settled, then," I say. "We'll leave in the morning."

Chapter Ten:

THE SPAR

Azi

Rian, Mya, and Elliot bend over the lists spread across the table, sorting through what needs to be done and deciding which one of us should do it. I try to offer my help, but I'm too distracted by the fox impostor that greeted us at the border. Who was it? Was it the same person who tried to steal Flitt's diamond? I feel uneasy. Between that and Princess Amei's pains, Flitt's nearly stolen tether, and our encounter with Iren and Viala, I find it difficult to concentrate on anything else.

"Sir Hammerfel," a page calls from the doorway that leads out to the courtyard. I look up expecting Mum or Da to answer him, but they're not here. Mum is upstairs keeping vigil with Amei, and Da went to see the village smith. "Sir Hammerfel," the page says again, and I realize he's addressing me. "His Highness requests a spar," he says, and my insides fill with dread. The others look up from their lists, and Rian tries hard to hide his scowl.

"I'll come watch," he says, but Mya shakes her head.

"You need to do this," she taps the pile of parchment, "especially if we're losing Azi to the practice yard. There's a lot here, Rian. We need to get through it if we're to stay on track once the princess is feeling better." Rian agrees. He's smart. Arguing with the guild leader is a bad idea, especially when she's also your mother. He beckons me and I bend down for a kiss.

"Be careful," he whispers, and kisses my earlobe.

The courtyard is open to the sky, but closed in on all sides. It's clean, but run down. The ground is packed dirt and the fountain in the center is cracked and empty. Several royal guards line the peeling stone walls, and two lords Eron's age lounge in an alcove to one side. The lords are his cousins, Fresi and Kris. They met up with us in the last village, right on schedule.

The prince himself is waiting for me across the yard. He makes a show of his footwork as I approach, demonstrating a fancy combination that seems a little too flowery to have any practical use in battle. I try to look impressed anyway, just to cover up my nerves. The lords call out to Eron, telling him how formidable he looks, applauding his sword dance. When they see me, one of them whistles low.

I bend my knee and bow my head as the prince turns to face me. He lets the tip of his sword drag in the dirt as he comes to stand over me. I curse my heart, which is thumping so loudly that I'm sure he can hear it. He stays there awhile, as if he's making sure I'm well aware of my place: in the dirt, kneeling to him. Finally, he addresses me.

"Sir Azaeli," his tone is merry, but his words are slightly slurred. I can smell the drink on him. "Armed and ready, I see."

"Yes, Your Highness." I keep my head bowed. I can almost feel his sneer.

"Stand up, then, and show me your skills. I wish to spar with the legend," he laughs, and the lords in the alcove echo him.

"If it pleases Your Highness," I say, mustering my patience as I stand up and take my sword from the sheath on my back. One of the lords makes a crude remark, but I ignore it. I've trained for this. Thanks to Dacva and his crew, I know how to keep a level head even when my opponent is spitting venom and insults and doing everything he can to rattle me.

I try not to think of how ungrateful Eron has been since Rian and I lifted Viala's enchantments on him. I try not to let it bother me that he treats me this way, despite all we've done and all we continue to do to ensure his comfort and clear his name. He's my prince. The heir of Cerion. The son of my liege. It's my duty to respect and obey him, even if he doesn't return that respect.

We face each other and raise our blades in salute. He eyes me with a hunger that makes me uncomfortable, but I try to ignore it and concentrate on the bout instead. I'm growing used to my new sword, which Da forged for me in the weeks after the battle at Kythshire. It's lighter than my old one, but the grip is still too new. I miss the one I lost. It was a good friend to me. Still, this one is well made, with a broad blade and a long, slender handle that requires two hands, like my last one.

Lord Kris calls out to start the spar, and Eron advances immediately. His sword is two-handed as well. It's similar to mine, but richly encrusted with deep red jewels that glisten like fresh blood. Our bout starts smoothly. We're evenly matched as we swing and parry against each other.

We go on for a while, easily driving one another back and forth across the yard. His style is much showier than mine. I ease up, since he obviously feels like he has something to prove to his cousins. He performs the dance again and arcs the blade in a quick and complicated combination that drives me backwards across the courtyard.

"I'm disappointed," he announces loudly. "All that talk about your skill, and I've got you backed into a corner already." I raise my sword to block his, and our blades meet at my chest. He presses closer, and I shove him back with all of my strength to gain some ground. He stumbles a little but quickly regains his footing. We clash together again, driving each other back and forth across the space while the young lords call out to Eron, congratulating him for every small advantage he gains over me. Finally, right beside the alcove, I pin him against the wall with my sword.

"You're as good as they say," he says through clenched teeth. "Would you be so skilled with my sword?" He thrusts his hips lewdly. Lord Kris laughs at the prince's banter. Lord Fresi gives a halfhearted chuckle. Eron keeps his sword up and reaches with one hand to grope my chest plate. I dodge his hand and skip backwards and he comes at me with a new fury that leaves me breathless in my defense. I gain some advantage again and touch him with my blade once, twice, three times. Every time I do, his rage grows. The lords go silent as the spar grows more furious, more dangerous. Eron doesn't hold back, and neither do I. The clash of our swords rings out loud and fierce over the courtyard. A storm cloud drifts overhead, casting a shadow over us.

My mood shifts. I don't care if he's my prince, I want to see him bleed. I want him to hurt. I want him to know that he can't do what he does anymore. Not to me. Not to anyone. Not with his wife suffering in her room, heavy with his child. This isn't a game. This is life. His cruelty, his unseemly behavior needs to stop.

He advances and I drive him back with an elbow to his nose. Slash at him with fury, with rage. I know I'm screaming battle cries. I don't care. I don't even see his face anymore, I only see the enemy. He has to learn, and I'll be the one to teach him. My sword is swift and true. It meets its mark again and again. One touch after another, and at first the lords stay silent. The prince stumbles backwards, and when I don't let up, the guards close in on me, shouting. I drop my sword and start punching. I don't stop until a heavy hand clamps over my shoulder and drags me back. I blink back to my senses to see Eron kneeling in the dirt, cowering.

When he realizes that I've stopped he jumps to his feet, adjusts his chest plate, and raises his chin dubiously. His lip is bleeding and he taps it with his fingertip and looks at the blood with anger.

"I'm bored of dueling," he says petulantly. "Let's go for a hunt. My horse!"

He storms off with the lords and the guards trailing after him. The lords look over their shoulders at me as they go with a mixture of awe and fear. The hand on my shoulder loosens a little.

"Great guts, Azi, what's gotten into you?" I turn to see Bryse looking down at me, his stony gray brow deeply furrowed with concern.

"You really laid into him," Cort says from behind him.

"I just…I guess I got carried away," I retrieve my sword and slide it into its sheath with a little trouble, my hands are shaking so hard. I flex my fingers. My knuckles ache.

"Serves him right," Bryse mutters, "maybe he'll keep his eyes to himself from now on."

"Mya won't like it," Cort says. "We're supposed to be protecting him, not killing him in the sparring pitch."

"I wasn't trying to kill him," I say, scowling.

"*You sure looked like you were,*" Flitt says at the same time Bryse speaks.

"Come on, let's have a drink. Forget about it for now. No harm done."

"I'm going to go change," I say. I need to get out of my armor and clear my head. Too much has happened. It isn't like me to lose control that way, especially around the prince. Cort is right. We're here to protect him, and if they hadn't stopped me, I'm sure I would have kept going. I might have really hurt him, or worse. I think of the guards and wonder why they didn't stop me. It was very strange how they just stood there watching. Like they knew he had it coming. It jars me a little.

Rian and the others are gone when we go back in. The table has been cleared of papers. I leave Cort and Bryse behind and break into a jog. I'll feel better when I get back to my room, I think. When I'm alone.

"*Wish I could have seen the whole thing,*" Flitt says. "*You were really impressive. What got you so angry?"*

"He tried to put his hands on me," I push the thought to her without much effort. *"Again."*

"Creep."

I pause outside of my door. At the end of the corridor, Dacva is sitting in a chair outside of Amei's door, dozing. Mum is standing beside him, chatting quietly with a guard. I worry that he's telling her what happened, but I don't remember him being in the courtyard. Mum sees me and waves. Even from this distance I can tell she's relieved to see me. I put off changing and go to her instead. I need to feel her peace. She puts her arms around me, and I instantly feel better.

"Where'd you disappear to?" she asks me.

"I'll tell you later." I glance at the door. "How is she?"

"She'll be fine. She's resting."

"What happened to her?"

"She says she had a nightmare that upset her," Mum whispers, "and then she started to feel pains. She was worried for the baby, but Donal and the physician have both assured her that the babe is perfectly healthy. We'll ride tomorrow, I'm certain."

I lean back against the wall beside her. It's strange, I think, that all of us had nightmares last night. Dreams that caused very real problems the next day.

"Did you have any odd dreams last night?" I ask Mum.

"No, Sweeting. I haven't dreamed of anything but Kythshire, since we left."

"Really?"

"Yes. I long for it, sometimes. It's a part of me now, somehow." I study her for a moment, look at her as others might. Her face is older when I look at her so differently. A little wrinkled and careworn. I've never thought of her as anyone but my mum, but I'm starting to realize that she's a person, like anyone else. Not just Mum, but Lisabella, too. It's strange to think of her this way. She smiles at me with a twinkle in her eye. She always looks at me like that now. With a deep pride in me. I know I should tell her about what just happened with the prince, but I can't bring myself to say the words.

"I'm going to go change," I say instead. I kiss her cheek before I go back to our room.

Flitt is there, rooting through my packs.

"Left pocket," I say. "I reorganized."

"Oh, thank goodness. I thought we were out. You need to buy

more." She pries open the pocket with a little difficulty and pulls out her favorite treat: a sugar cube. "So." She says as she crunches into it, watching me.

"So?" I ask. I haven't forgotten what she said earlier at the Maker's tree. I'm still a little annoyed. I don't appreciate being called stupid.

"You beat him good. How did it feel?" She licks her fingers and smacks her lips.

"I shouldn't have done it." I pull at the pauldrons that cover my shoulders and they slide off easily. One of many advantages of the armor that Iren gifted me is that it's ridiculously easy to get into and out of by myself.

"Well," Flitt says haughtily, "he shouldn't have done lots of things. I still can't believe they're not going to burn him. I thought humans burned bad people. Even princes."

"What? No they don't. Not in Cerion, anyway. Not anymore." I stow my armor near the bed and dress in a loose, billowy shirt and baggy trousers.

"Oh, that's very becoming," Flitt says sarcastically.

"Hush, it's comfortable."

"Well, I just came for a sweet and to check in. I'm going to go back now if you're not riding 'til tomorrow. Lots going on at home and I don't want to miss it."

"What's going on?" I tie a sash around my waist and tuck my purse into it.

"I'll tell you later, okay? See you."

"Okay, be safe." I watch her blink away and sink down to sit on my bed. My head is still spinning from everything that's happened, and Flitt's quick visit hasn't helped matters much. I wish she wasn't so infuriatingly vague sometimes.

The sound of hoof beats thunders outside as the prince leaves on his hunt. Part of me is proud that I finally stood up to him, but I know it will have consequences. I made him look weak in front of his guards and his lords. That isn't something someone like Eron will put behind him. I'll have to be on guard around him even more, now.

I should probably tell the guild. Even if I don't, I'm pretty sure Bryse and Cort will. I'm grateful Bryse was there to pull me away. I shudder to think of how far I might have gone. It isn't like me, I think, to be so violent. Certainly I'm a warrior. I've trained for most of my life to be skilled at swordplay. My intention has never been to cause pain or suffering, though. I am a protector. A guardian.

Between the nightmare last night and all of the action today, I feel like I could burrow myself into bed and sleep until supper. Instead I force myself to get up. I don't really know where I'm going until I arrive at the stables, where Pearl is munching happily on her oats. The creamy-white mare is new to me, a gift for my Knighting. She's been brushed already, her hooves picked, her mane and tail braided. Someone has taken great care with her. I stroke her neck and lean against her, and she blinks at me. Something about the way she looks at me makes me feel like she knows everything, and she's perfectly fine with it. I smile.

"Good fight," the voice makes me jump, and I turn toward it. "Good day, Lady Knight."

"Good day…" I say. I lean back against Pearl, who leans into me just as much as I scratch her shoulder.

"Jac." He bows, and then straightens and smiles at me. He's my age or a little older. Broad-shouldered, with dark hair that curls loosely at his shoulders. His eyes glint handsomely in the sunlight. It takes me a moment to realize that he's dressed in the uniform of the Royal Guard. That seems to snap me back to my senses. I think of Rian and feel a little guilty for being so taken in.

"Good day, Jac." I turn back to Pearl and go through the motions of checking her for injuries. "Shouldn't you be with the prince?" I ask.

"I'm off duty."

"I see."

"Do you think you might…" he trails off awkwardly and I look back at him over my shoulder. His face is bright red, his thick arms crossed uncomfortably over his chest. There's a dimple in his chin, and his jaw is strong and square. "Sorry," he shakes his head, "It's too forward of me. Never mind." He turns to leave.

"No, it's all right. What is it?" I'm curious now. I've never really known a guard as anything but a guard. Usually they're very disciplined. They keep to themselves when they're off duty. They're always respectful. Royal guards have to go through years of conditioning and grueling training. When they come out of it, their one goal in life is simple: Serve the palace. Protect the royal family. I feel a little guilty that I've never considered any of them as individuals who have an identity outside of guard before.

"I was hoping you might show me that move. The one with the

pivot of the blade that nearly disarmed His Highness. And perhaps the counter? My strength is with the shield and short sword, you see, but I'm trying to move up to broad." He sees my hesitation and steps toward me. "With trainers, of course. No need to don armor."

I nod, and we go to the courtyard together and pick up a pair of wooden swords meant for training. He's a quick learner, and soon has me fighting to keep hold of my own weapon.

"There, you have it!" I laugh as my sword goes flying. He picks it up for me and hands it back with a smile that makes my heart skip. We spend half of the afternoon in a lighthearted spar. He's a formidable partner, and I find myself learning from him as much as he learns from me, if not more. When it's finally time to go in, I'm a little disappointed to have to stop. It's refreshing to have an equal to spar with, someone who isn't older than I am or better, or trying to prove something or make a move on me. Jac is very respectful. He's careful not to touch me or look at me the way men sometimes do. On their own time guards are usually bawdy, but he isn't. He's a gentleman.

"Thank you," he bows to me as he did in the stable, "I learned quite a lot."

"So did I," I grin. "Perhaps we can spar again."

"I would very much like that, Lady Knight," he smiles at me and tips his sword up in salute, then rests it on his shoulder. I watch him until he disappears through the door that leads back to the stables.

"I said be careful, not hey, Azi, try to kill Eron," Rian materializes beside me and I jump back and nearly fall into the empty fountain.

"Will you stop doing that!" I smack him with each word, and he raises his arms up to shield his face.

"All right, all right, ow!" He winces and rubs his arm. "Take it easy, bruiser!"

I roll my eyes and shake my head, and he pulls me close and kisses me tenderly. He starts to pull me into the Half Realm with him, but it makes me uneasy. After Eron's lewdness I'm not in the mood for romance, and after Iren's warning I'm wary of the Half Realm. I take his hand from my hair and hold it as I step back a little.

"What's wrong?" he asks.

"I'm all sweaty," I say. It's a lame excuse. Sweat never bothered either of us before. "I want to wash up."

"I'll come with you," he wriggles his eyebrows.

"Stop," I swat at him playfully.

"Again with the hitting?" He ducks away. "Fine, fine. Have you seen Flitt at all?" he asks as we walk to the washing room.

"She popped in for a quick visit just after the spar," I say. "Why?"

"I'm sorry I missed her," he says as we pause in front of the door. "I wanted to play the question game."

"You *wanted* to play?" I blink at him in disbelief. Flitt's question game has long been a source of annoyance for Rian. I'm shocked that he'd be actively seeking to play it.

"I've been thinking some things over," he shrugs, "and I have a lot of questions that I'm sure she could answer."

"She said she'd be back later," I hug him and he kisses me. "See you at supper."

"Love you, Azi," he whispers softly in my ear. As always, it sends tingles through me to hear him say it. I close my eyes, and for some reason Jac comes to mind.

"Love you too," I say. I go inside and close the door behind me.

Chapter Eleven:
THE LAST LEG

Azi

Supper has a festive feel to it. The tables are laid with steaming hot venison and boar, and the cousins make sure to regale everyone with tales of the hunt, where Prince Eron was clearly the champion. They lay it on thickly, and Eron is pleased. He puffs out his chest like a proud cock and goes on and on about the chase, and the hunt, and the struggle with his prey. With Amei beside him, back to her usual smiling glow, the mood is optimistic.

Mya, on the other hand, is not quite so happy. The Elite have been moved from our usual place of honor beside the royal table to a smaller, more cramped setting toward the back of the dining room in order to make space for the young lords and their traveling companions.

I know that my actions contributed to it, and I know everyone else is blaming me. It's a tiny guild. News travels fast. I was relieved when there was no time for Mya to give me a talking-to about it, but this is worse. I wish I could take back my actions. It wasn't worth embarrassing my family over. To make it worse, Rian is giving me the cold shoulder, too. After my bath, he and I argued over who the impostor fox might have been, and that turned into another discussion about Viala…or Ki, and whether or not we should ask to bring her back to Cerion with us.

When those arguments calmed down, he kept trying to pull me away into the Half Realm with him and getting increasingly annoyed when I refused. We should heed Iren's warning, I said, but as all men do at times, he's got other things on his mind. The Half Realm is our one place to be alone together, and now that's been taken away. Here with everyone else, there are too many eyes on us. The guild is tolerant of our affection for one another, but everyone's watchful that we don't take it too far. Our parents are actually quite pleased. Mum has even mentioned marriage more than she probably should, but I keep telling her I'm still young. I'm only seventeen. Rian and I don't want to rush into anything.

Not that it matters. Things between us now are lukewarm anyway. I'm starting to get irritated by things about him that never bothered me before, like how perfectly straight he sits when he eats, and how he always has to be right about everything. Like now. He and Bryse are arguing over the border between Cerion and Hywilkin. Hywilkin is Bryse's homeland. Of course he would know that the border is called Haigh, and that it stretches across the mountain. Rian is arguing that the west border touches the sea, while Bryse insists that it touches the Outlands. Of course Rian has a map which he unfurls across his plate and mine. Of course the map proves Bryse wrong. He starts to roll it up again and tips my dish into my lap, covering my trousers in a mess of gravy and roast.

"Sorry!" he cries as I jump up and curse. The room around us goes quiet. Mum stares at me, her mouth covered in disbelief. It's unseemly for a Knight to use words like the ones I just shouted. I don't even know where they came from.

"Sorry," I mutter as Rian casts a spell to clean up the stains and mess. "Thank you," I whisper, feeling everyone's eyes on me. Conversations slowly resume, but I excuse myself from the table. Rian moves to follow me, but I tell him I want to be alone. I'm surprised when he doesn't argue. Honestly, I'm relieved.

Outside, the night air cools my reddened cheeks. I look up at the stars and let their peace blanket me.

"Beautiful night," a familiar voice calls. I look over my shoulder at the guard posted at the far corner of the inn building and realize it's Jac.

"The sky is so clear." I join him at his post and lean back on the wall a respectable distance away. Out here in the fresh air, away from Eron's boasting and the shame I put on my family, I feel better.

"Ready to ride tomorrow?" he asks me.

"Very much so." I'm looking forward to the last leg of the trip. I feel like the journey lately has been cloaked in darkness. Once we see Eron and Amei to the safety of Kordelya Keep, I'm hoping things will settle down some. We should reach the crossroads tomorrow. Then I'll go to Kythshire to see about Ki. Hopefully Rian will come, too. If not, then I'll just have to do it on my own. I stand there in silence for a long time, thinking about the journey ahead and all that has happened recently. Jac stands beside me, watching into the darkness, silent and steady. I realize that between Rian and Flitt, I don't get a lot of quiet anymore. Not like this. It's nice.

"*New friend?*" Flitt asks. I close my eyes. So much for that.

"Well, goodnight," I say to Jac.

"Goodnight, m'lady."

The guards at the rear entrance to the inn nod me through, and I listen to the supper revelries as I make my way back to my room. As soon as I close my door, Flitt bursts forth in a flash of light.

"Hello!" she says, her multicolored ponytails swaying excitedly. "Want to play?"

"Not really," I say wearily. I sit on my bed and tuck my knees under my chin. "Rian wanted to, though."

"Oh, yeah?" she chirps. "Okay! I'll go get him."

Before I can say anything, she blinks away. I wait a while for her to return, but she's gone for so long that eventually the sleep I've been battling against for hours wins out.

I'm woken hastily in the morning by Mum, who is already dressed, packed up, and halfway through doing mine, too. I feel a pang of guilt. She's the knight, I was the squire. I'm the one who should be packing her things up, not the other way around. That pang is followed by another. I never said goodnight to Rian last night.

Thanks to my laziness and the barking commands of Baron Stenneler's Captain of the Guard, breakfast consists of cold bread on horseback, and I don't even get to eat until we're through the throngs of well-wishers who've come to see their prince and princess out of the small village. A cold wind has blown into the valley. It blows the horses sideways and snaps the banner hard against my helm as we quicken our pace. Rian gets whipped by it several times before he decides to slow his own horse and ride a few paces behind me. Flitt tucks herself into the space between my shoulder armor and my neck and chatters endlessly into my ear.

"*...and then Crocus said maybe we should just put a block on all of the tethers, and Scree said 'Yes, that would be best, until we can determine the threat.'*" She deepens her usually squeaky voice in a fairly accurate impression of Scree, the stony companion to Crocus, both of whom lead the Ring in decisions made concerning the wellbeing of the fairies of Kythshire. "*And then Ember said that tethers are a bad idea anyway, and that we should all just stay inside of the borders from now on and let the men fend for themselves. And* *then Shush said that we should be free to go where we want, and he said remember Azi? She's trustworthy. Not all people are bad."*

"You haven't gotten to the part about why you have to stay with us, yet." Rian reminds her. The two of them have been playing the question game since we left, all in Half-Realm talking. I feel like my head will split open.

"I'm getting there," Flitt says. *"So then Twig showed up, and he looked terrible, like he'd been drained out for a week! And he told us that his tether was stolen, too! And when he woke up, he was trapped in a box! And some strange fae and a boy from Sunteri let him out. So then everyone started to argue about the Sunteri fae, and how stupid they were to lose control of their Mages, and how they should have been more careful with their Wellspring. And then that turned into an argument about whether they deserved to lose their magic, and whether they should be allowed to try and restore it, because you know, we still have that pebble with Emris's magic inside, and nobody knows what to do with it."*

"Can't you just put it in your Wellspring?" Rian asks. My head throbs with every word.

"I'm still answering your other question, Greedy. Typical."

"Sorry, go on."

A horse approaches my other side, a white steed five hands taller than mine. Mum sits tall in the saddle, her armor sparkling in the sunlight that dances through the bare branches of the trees.

"It's terribly quiet up here," she says, glancing at Rian and me. "Everything all right?"

"Sure," I say, thankful for the break from the chatter in my head.

"Your father and I were talking," Mum goes on, lowering her voice. "Perhaps you should take a day in Kordelya before you go on to Kythshire, Azi. We all deserve a rest. It's been a long journey."

"I had a break from riding yesterday," I reply, a little annoyed by her coddling. "I'm fine, Mum."

"It wasn't much of a break, was it?" Mum presses. She knows what we were up to yesterday. Rian must have told her about our jaunt to Kythshire. I glance back at him, but he and Flitt are too deep in conversation to notice.

"I was talking to some of the escort," Mum goes on. "It seems there may be a candidate or two for squire at the keep. Eager to serve in Cerion. You could interview them, if you'd like."

Ever since I was knighted, Mum and Da have been on me to choose a squire or a hopeful. I don't see the point. I manage fine on my own.

"It couldn't hurt," I agree, simply to keep her from pressing on the subject.

"Think about it, Sweeting. And you're falling behind again." I look ahead at the carriage and quicken my pace to close the gap. Behind me, Rian catches up.

By the time we arrive at the keep, I'm chilled through to my bones and exhausted. My thoughts are swimming with new information from Flitt and Rian's incessant conversation. Apparently, the use of tethers has been suspended by the fairies of Kythshire. Flitt was forced to make a choice: travel to me and stay until we're ready to return to her land, or remain in Kythshire and wait for us to arrive. She chose to come to me one last time and stay as long as it takes. I'm touched that she'd make such a choice. It softens my mood to know that she'd rather stay with me. I want nothing more than a hot bath and a warm bed, but as soon as I reach the rooms that were assigned to us, a Page knocks on the door.

"His Highness wishes to see you," he says with a bow. In my mind, Flitt groans.

"*Creep,*" she says.

"*Stay with Rian,*" I push to her.

"Of course," I say wearily to the Page. I haven't even had time to pull a brush through my unraveled braid. I follow him through the keep, which is vastly different from the small inns we've had to squeeze into for the larger part of our journey. This keep is a stronghold, the last defense before the Kordelya Castle where Eron and Amei will spend the final weeks of her pregnancy.

The keep is very well protected, with sturdy walls of thick stone and parapets where trebuchets and catapults stand oiled and ready for battle. Its custodian is Baron Stenneler, one of King Tirnon's most trusted subjects. He is a stout bachelor with a stern brow and an even less hospitable disposition. It's obvious that he believes his keep is a structure that's meant for battle, and not for entertaining. I find that interesting, considering that Cerion hasn't seen a war for a century and a half now.

Still, it's warm and safe, and the corridors that lead to the prince and princess's temporary rooms are far from plain. Tapestries and crests line the rough stone walls, all well cared-for. Portraits of the royal family dot the walls closer to the Royal rooms, and I wonder if they're always here or if they were just put up on display for Eron's benefit. The page stops at a door, and two guards reach to open them. I look at both of them, hoping one might be Jac, but they're not familiar to me. My heart sinks a little as the page ushers me inside.

"Sir Azaeli Hammerfel," he announces, and I dip to my knee at Eron's feet.

"Thank you, Page," Eron says with a condescending tone. I wonder if the prince has even bothered to learn the boy's name.

Just like in the courtyard, Eron doesn't relieve me from my bow as the page goes out. Instead he lets me kneel in my armor, weary from my ride, with my head bowed low.

"I have heard," he begins coldly, "that you'll be making a little side journey on your way home. Is that true?" His voice is so thick with disdain that the hairs on my arms raise up with chills.

"Yes, Your Highness." I try to keep my own voice steady. My orders came from the King. He told me to keep them to myself. No one was supposed to know, least of all Eron. It was better this way, His Majesty said. He didn't want to burden his son with such things. He wanted him to be able to focus on his impending fatherhood. His princess.

"And where will you be going, Azaeli?" His boots come into view, and the smell of mead is strong on his breath. If he knows I'm going on a journey, I'm certain he knows where. "Kythshire?" he guesses before I can reply. I close my eyes. I don't want to answer. He takes my chin and raises it roughly. Reluctantly I look into his face. He smirks. "I thought so. You're going to fetch her, aren't you?"

"Yes, Your Highness."

"Good," he says, tightening his grip on my jaw. "Bring her back here, and I will deal with her myself."

"Your Highness, I'm sorry, but—"

"You will bring her here, Azaeli," he says angrily. "Or I will have you hunted down and arrested for treason for that stunt you pulled in the courtyard. I have twelve witnesses who will attest to your actions. You will bring her here to me, or you might as well say goodbye to your perfectly untarnished reputation. Do you understand?"

"I would be disobeying a direct order from the King." I try to pull my chin away, but he grips me tighter and forces me to my feet. He leans closer to me, speaks through clenched teeth, his voice low and gritty.

"Whose wrath would you rather suffer?" he asks, his eyes wild.

"You forget that when Tirnon is dead, and I will be king."

When I don't agree, he gets even more heated.

"I hope it's sooner than later," he hisses. "The man's a weak, damn fool. You will do as I say. Bring her to me."

He yanks me up by the arm, opens the door himself, and shoves me out of it. I wince as it slams shut behind me with a crash that echoes down the hallway. The guards flanking the doors slide their eyes to look at me. My hands are shaking, my knees feel like jelly. It takes me a moment to compose myself enough to be able to walk. When I finally can, I rush back toward our side of the keep.

Rian. I need to tell Rian. Tears blind me as I quicken my pace to a jog. He'll know a way out of it. He'll be able to figure out what to do.

I round a corner and nearly crash into someone. A royal guard, a palace guard. He reaches out to steady me, but drops his hands before they touch me.

"Lady Knight," Jac says. "Forgive me, I was in my thoughts and didn't see you."

"Of course." I try to blink my tears away before he notices. "No, it's my fault, I came around the bend too fast." I feel my cheeks grow hot and hope he doesn't notice that either, but he's a royal guard. It's his job to be observant.

"Something's happened," he says. "What can I do?" I look up at him, into his eyes. They're so dark and rich, so sincere in their concern. For a moment, they make me forget what I was running from, or running to. When I look away again, I remember.

"No, nothing. Thank you," I say. "I'm sorry. I have to go."

"Of course," he says, and steps aside for me to pass, but I'm reluctant. Something about him makes me want to confide in him, to give him my trust. Perhaps he could help. No, I can't put him in that position. He's sworn to protect the prince. Of course he'd tell me to do what Eron wants.

"I'm sorry," I repeat before breaking into a jog again. Even in my desperation to find Rian, I secretly hope that it isn't the last time I speak to Jac.

I find Rian in the sitting room that connects all of our quarters. His head is tipped back against the chair and his eyes are closed while Flitt bobs around and around him. Mya and Elliot are stretched out on cushions near the hearth, chatting with Mum and Da. Cort and Bryse are in the far corner, bent together, throwing dice and betting with

Dacva. Nobody seems to notice my arrival or care that I was gone at all.

"You're not even changed yet?" Rian spies me with one eye. He looks like he's resisting the urge to swat Flitt away. Apparently, she's finally getting on his nerves. "Dinner's soon."

"I need to talk to you," I say. The others stop what they're doing and look up curiously.

"Don't you want to take a bath first?" Rian asks. "You couldn't stop talking about it all the way here." His tone is tinged with annoyance. I guess I deserve it. I did complain a lot about the cold. Still, I don't appreciate him talking to me this way in front of everyone.

"Fine," I say. "Later, then." I shove the door open and stomp to my room. I'll figure something out without him. Maybe I should have asked Jac for help after all. I shake my head to clear my dark mood. A bath will help me think.

The water is lukewarm and does little to raise my spirits. Annoyed, I barely stay in long enough to wash myself. Etiquette says that as a knight, I should wear my armor to dine with a Baron, or at least a gown. I don't care. It's too cold. I dress in three warm layers with my teeth still chattering. I've just stepped into my slippers when Flitt appears out of nowhere, right in front of my face. Her light is so bright that I have to look away, but not before I glimpse the panic in her shimmering eyes.

"Azi," she says urgently, "you have to come quick! It's Rian. Something's happened."

My heart skips and then starts racing as Flitt darts straight through the thick wooden door out into the hallway. Rian. Something's happened. If he's hurt, I'll never forgive myself. I've been so callous toward him these past two days, ever since the nightmare. I think of Jac, and it makes me feel even worse as I follow Flitt's light along the hallway. *Please,* I pray, *please, let him be okay.*

Flitt is quick and determined. I almost lose sight of her once or twice. I remember Rian's globe of light which had me jumping into a ravine. This time, I'm a little more careful. There's no need, though. She leads me straight to an open door.

"In here," she says, *"hurry!"*

I race through the door, skid to a stop, and look around at the room. There's a bed, a writing table, a chair near the fireplace. Rian's there, sitting with a pile of parchment in his lap. He isn't reading though, he's looking at something in his hand instead. It looks like a ring. The metal glints in the firelight. He looks up at me with surprise as I rush in, and tucks the shining object away. There's nothing wrong with him. He's perfectly fine.

"What's wrong?" he asks as he sets the pages on the arm of the chair. "You all right?"

"Well, that's a cruel ruse," I say, and cross my arms. "What are you playing at, Rian?"

Rian's eyes go innocently wide. His mouth hangs open as he looks from me to Flitt. "I don't…what are you talking about?"

"Forget it. I'm going to dinner." I turn to leave, and I'm met with Flitt's finger jabbing harshly at the tip of my nose.

"You're not going anywhere!" she says. "Not until you make up with Rian." She grabs two handfuls of my bangs and uses them like a horse's reins to steer me toward him. He stands up, watching with thinly veiled amusement.

"Flitt, you said something had happened. You scared me." I tug away from her grip, but for such a tiny little thing, she's quite strong. When we're close enough together, she keeps a firm hold on my hair with one hand and tugs at Rian's side lock with the other until our noses are almost touching.

"Well something has, and you need to fix it right now. Look at him. And Rian, you look at her! Don't you love each other?"

I'm reluctant at first, but then I glance up into his face. He doesn't meet my eyes, but I don't need him to. The pain I've caused him with my dark moods is written there like words on a page. I've been unkind to him, I know. I've been acting strangely. He's tried to help me, and I've pushed him away. I've been cold. I've made things change between us. I'm not sure what's gotten into me.

"Rian," I step closer until I'm leaning against him. It's difficult to speak around the lump in my throat. I don't need to, though. When he finally looks into my eyes, I know he understands. When he bends to kiss me, the gesture is filled with forgiveness that spreads through me slow and warm. It melts away the chill better than any hot bath ever could.

"That's better!" Flitt claps her hands beside us, and Rian swats at her without breaking our embrace.

Chapter Twelve:
THE LURE

Azi

Following Flitt's little trick, Rian and I are inseparable again. We reluctantly detach ourselves from each other for long enough to show ourselves for dinner, but then as soon as we're able to make our excuses, we do. Mya has called a guild meeting for the morning, but tonight is ours. We sneak away to a quiet corner of the keep and get back to making up for lost time.

"*All right, all right, you two,*" Flitt pesters, "*you're starting to make me wish I never tried to help! We have things to discuss, don't we Rian?*"

"I have something to tell you both," I say, thinking of Eron. The last few hours with Rian have been blissful, but now it's time to get back to reality.

"Right," Rian says. "Come on."

He takes my hand and leads me to the room where Flitt had brought me earlier. Each of us has a room of our own here in the keep. It's a nice luxury after having had to share with Mum and Mya the past few nights. As I settle onto a sofa, he crosses to the door and casts a ward of silence over it so no one will be able to listen in. He does the same at the window, even though the room is three stories up. I'm a little disappointed when he takes the chair across from me, but I suppose it's probably best if we're not close enough to touch each other and get distracted again.

"Eron threatened me with treason if I don't bring Ki to him," I say, and at the same time, Rian says:

"The fae have closed Kythshire's border and temporarily suspended the use of all tethers."

"What?" We both reply in unison, each of us shocked by the others' news.

"He's right," Flitt says. "Nobody can get in or out."

"Because of what happened to Twig?" I ask. I vaguely remember the story from earlier when she was talking to Rian as we rode. I wish I had paid better attention.

"Uh huh." Flitt comes to perch on my knee. "Until they can figure out who's behind the theft of the tethers."

"Do they have any ideas—?" I stop as Flitt raises her chin and one finger.

"My turn," she says. I didn't realize we'd already started playing. "Why have you been in such a mood lately?"

"I haven't been…" I trail off at their looks of disbelief. "I guess after I had that dream. The nightmare about Viala and the undead army. Ever since then, every little thing seems to annoy me. It's hard to brush off even the smallest slight." Flitt nods. My turn. "Do they have any ideas about who's trying to steal tethers?"

"Sort of," Flitt says, "but they need your help. The diamond. Dabble says that he might be able to figure out who tried to steal it if we can get it to him. He needs to do some magic to it. I don't really understand it, so don't waste a question asking me to explain. It's Maker stuff, really advanced." She pulls her knees to her chest and her wings sparkle brightly as they lazily dip down and up, down and up. "What did you say about His Royal Creep?" I shake my head at her. Rian laughs. "His Highness, Creepy creep?" I press my lips together. It isn't right to mock him. "Oh! Prince Creepy. That's good. Short and sweet."

"Flitt, you shouldn't…" I try, but I can't help but laugh.

"I'm a fairy. I can do what I like. Anyway, what was that you said?"

"He's demanding that I bring Ki to him. He knew somehow that we were planning to bring her back to Cerion for His Majesty, but he wants her instead. He wants to make her pay for what she did to him." I shiver. "He's threatened me with treason if I refuse. Because of what I did in the courtyard yesterday."

Rian lets out a long sigh and tips his head back against the chair. He closes his eyes and I wait to ask my question in order to give him time to think. He's brilliant. I know he can figure out what to do. Flitt huffs impatiently after a long pause, and so I take my turn.

"How can we get back into Kythshire to give Dabble the diamond if the border is closed?" I ask.

"Through the Half-Realm," Flitt replies matter-of-factly. "Are you going to bring Ki to Eron, then? Even though she's not Viala anymore?"

"No," I say firmly, glancing at Rian. His presence alone is enough to clear my mind and help me make the right decision. "Our loyalty is to His Majesty, not to Eron. We'll bring her to the king. We'll tell His Majesty the truth. When it comes down to it, what I did was treasonous. There's no running from it. Perhaps he'll show me mercy." I think about my next question and ask, "Iren warned us against going into the Half-Realm. Isn't there another way?"

"Nope," Flit answers simply. "Who is that new friend of yours?"

"His name is Jac. He's a Royal Guard. Couldn't Iren let us in?"

"Nope. Are you sure he's who he says he is?"

Her question brings me up short. My heart starts to race at the mention of Jac's name. Across from us, Rian watches me. I look away, ashamed, and try to think. Why would I have any reason to doubt that he's who he says? He wears the uniform, he keeps to his stations…But then a bit of doubt creeps in. Maybe Flitt has a point.

"Are you saying he isn't?" I ask.

"You can't answer a question with a question." Flitt says.

"But my question is my answer."

"You can't answer a question with a question, even if your question is your answer. Answer the question first. Not with a question, with an answer."

"You hurt my head sometimes," I say, pressing my temples with my fingertips. Rian laughs.

"Tell me about it," he says, "she never stopped talking today. All. Day. Long."

"I haven't had any reason to think otherwise." I say in regards to Jac. "Are you saying he isn't?"

"I'm just saying be careful. Mage magic and Sorcery isn't always flashy. Sometimes it's quiet. Sometimes it's really sneaky. Like the impostor fox. So, do we have a plan, then?" She looks across at Rian, who rubs his eyes.

"We'll have to go like you say," he shrugs at her and looks at me.

He's weary, I can tell. His eyes have dark circles under them. I wonder if he's been sleeping well, and I feel bad that this is the first time I've noticed. I've been too wrapped up in my own emotions and troubles lately to care about him or anyone else, really.

"Through the Half-Realm," Rian goes on. "It'll be quick, like the last time you brought us, Azi. Then we can give Dabble the Diamond and hopefully he can figure out from it exactly who's behind all of this, and what to do next." He closes his eyes again. "I don't know what to ask. Azi, you can have my question."

"Why are you so concerned about Jac?" I ask her.

"Something about him buzzes my wings," Flitt shrugs. "Plus, I don't think it's very nice to Rian for you to be sneaking around with other boys."

"Aw, that's kind of touching, actually," Rian smiles.

"I'm not sneaking!" I say defensively. "We just had a spar and I bumped into him a couple of times after that, that's all."

"It's all right, Azi. Really." Rian waves a hand dismissively.

"Well, aren't you jealous?" Flitt says. "I've heard that people get really jealous. So much that sometimes it sends them into fits! That'd be fun to see."

"No, I'm not jealous. I trust Azi." He looks across to me, meeting my eyes. I feel my cheeks grow warm, and I cross the room to sit in his lap. He pulls me close and we kiss slowly and deeply.

"Not again, come on, you two! I don't know what's worse!" She places a tiny hand on my cheek and pushes me away from him. "Come on, we still don't know what to do about Prince Creepy."

"She's right," Rian murmurs between kisses. "How could Eron threaten you with treason? It would be treason to ignore the King's orders. He's got to see that."

"He's angry that I bested him during the spar at Mare's Head." I snuggle into him, and he tightens his arms around me.

"What made you lose your head?" Rian asks me. "Bryse said you were half-wild." I consider telling him what the prince said and what he did, but I know it will only make him angry. He'll insist I tell the others, and I really just want to put the whole thing behind me. Tomorrow, we'll part ways with the royal party. I won't have to see Eron again for a while, hopefully.

"Nothing." I lie.

"It wasn't nothing," Flitt says. "He was being his usual creepy self. And the other ones, the lords, they thought it was funny. Azi was just defending herself."

"Flitt…" I try to stop her, but Rian won't let me. She tells him everything. I didn't realize she'd seen so much. When she's finished, Rian's jaw is clenched so hard I fear he'll crack his teeth.

"You need to tell someone," he says. "Your father."

"My father?" I scoff. "Can you imagine? No, it's not that big of a deal."

"So, you're going to just let everyone think you lost your head and attacked the prince for no good reason?" Rian asks angrily. "It wasn't your fault, Azi. If I was there, I'd have…"

"Stop," I say. "You weren't there. I'm glad you weren't." I push away from him and get up. "I can take care of myself, and now that Eron knows it he's trying to find other ways to intimidate me. I won't play into it. We'll go get Ki, we'll bring her to Cerion. Like I said before, if there are consequences for that, I'll face them when the time comes."

Rian doesn't say a word. He simply shakes his head and drums his fingers on the arm of his chair. Little sparks of magic pop and fizzle where his fingertips meet the fabric. He's losing control, probably because he's so tired. I lean down and kiss him softly.

"Go to bed," I say. "We have to be downstairs early tomorrow."

On the way back to my room, I pass by my parents' quarters. The door is closed, and inside I can hear raised voices. Not just Mum and Da's, but Mya's and Bryse's, too. Part of me wants to listen in, and another part already knows why they're fighting. It's about me, I'm sure, and my inappropriate behavior these past two days. Cursing in front of the prince, fighting with the prince, being short and disrespectful with more than one member of the Elite, slowing the procession with my absentmindedness… No, I don't have to listen in. I already know the trouble I'm facing.

I'm not wrong, either. In the morning Mum and Da meet me at my door. Mum takes my hand and we walk in silence. Da is just as quiet. When we arrive at the guild meeting, Mya is already there. Elliot sits beside her, and Rian beside him. The mood is somber, even after Bryse and Cort come in laughing together and start filling their plates with breakfast. At the end of the table, Donal and Dacva are bent together praying. I take a seat between Mum and Da. With everyone assembled, Rian places the wards on the doors.

The table is set with an amazing breakfast spread, but my stomach feels like I've swallowed a lead ball. I put a few things on my plate but don't touch them. When Mya rises to speak, I can't seem to meet her eyes.

"Firstly, congratulations to everyone on a successful journey. We've seen His Highness and Her Highness safely to Kordelya, which was our first mission. Well done."

"Well done," everyone agrees in unison. Bryse and Cort, as always, are raucous in their reply, but the rest of us are more subdued.

"And now, as was planned, we will return to Valleyside while Rian and Azaeli journey to Kythshire. We'll await them there and ride back to Cerion together when their task is done. Are we agreed?"

"Agreed," we all say together.

"First, though, there is a small matter." I feel her eyes on me, but I still can't look up. "Azi, stand please."

I do, but my knees are shaky with nerves. I put a hand on Da's shoulder to steady myself, and a glance at both him and Mum shows them masking their frowns. Across the table, Rian's jaw is clenched again. He catches my eye and his gaze gives me strength.

"Azi," Mya sighs. "Your actions lately have cast a shadow on us all. You've acted in a way that's unbecoming of a guild of our station." She lists the same transgressions I'm already aware of and she tells me what I already know, that my behavior was unacceptable for a knight, and for the standards of the Elite. I stare at the table in front of me. "If you aren't able to check yourself, Azi, and if you continue to allow yourself to lose control, you'll be stripped of blue and gold and cast from the guild. Do you understand?"

I nod as I feel the blood drain from my face and my fingertips go numb on my father's shoulder. On the other side of Da, Bryse is protesting loudly but I can't make out what he's saying. My ears are ringing. Never would I have imagined I'd be facing disbandment from the guild. Never in all of my life.

"*Tell them,*" Rian pushes to me. "*Tell them why. If you don't, I will.*" My eyes snap to his again and I shake my head slightly. He waits for a moment and then he gets to his feet. He tells them everything. Not just what happened in the courtyard, but before that, too. How Eron is always eyeing me with that hunger, and how he made advances at me in the palace just before the King's Quest last Highsummer. By the time he's finished, you could hear a cricket sneeze, as Flitt would say. Then the room erupts into chaos.

Da is on his feet and halfway to the door before Mum can stop him. I feel her wave of peace strike me full on in an attempt to calm Bryse who reaches it first and nearly rips the door right off its hinge.

"I told you," Elliot is saying to Mya from beneath his foxlike-fringe of orange hair as he tips his chair back on two legs. "I knew she had to have a good reason."

"He put his hands on her?" Bryse seethes. Mum's peace is doing little to placate him, but it seems to have calmed Da enough for him to see some sense. He's holding Bryse back, hanging on one of his arms with both hands while Cort has the other. "I'll make sure it doesn't happen again. Rip his hands right off, I will."

"Bryse!" Mum cries as she slams the door closed again. Rian is right behind her to set the ward again. "Enough! Someone will hear." We all stand holding our breaths while Bryse works to calm himself. The giant's temper is useful on a battlefield, but not so welcome when you're meant to behave as an honored guest in the home of a Baron.

"So what, we're not going to do anything? You heard Rian! You heard what he said!" Bryse growls in frustration. He picks up a statuette from a nearby table and rips off its head. "Azi, I swear, if you'da told me why you went after him that way, I'da let you finish what you started."

I nod slowly. I've seen Bryse's fury before, but this time it's different. This time it's in defense of me, of my honor. It's very touching. He's always been protective of me, much like a second father in many ways. Still, I never expected a reaction like this. Beside him, despite Mum's efforts, Da's own rage seems to be building again.

"With that considered," Mya keeps her tone soothing and gestures to the vacated chairs, "Azi, your actions were mostly justified. Gentlemen, please. Sit." Her voice blends well with Mum's peace, so much so that Da and Bryse manage to calm themselves enough to return to the table. "But I hope that next time, you'll come to one of us so we're aware of any…"

"Assaults," Bryse spits out.

"Assaults, yes," Mya says with a sigh. She looks around at everyone to make certain they're suitably in order before continuing. "Moving on," she starts, but Da interrupts.

"That's it? Moving on?" he says angrily. I'm shocked by his tone. He barely ever raises his voice to Mya this way.

"Yeah, what?" Bryse growls. "Just because he's a prince, we're going to let him do that to our Azi? No. What are we going to do about it?"

Mya sits back and closes her eyes. She takes a deep breath, and when she opens them again, they meet across the table with my mother's. They exchange a knowing glance before she looks away again.

"What do you propose?" Mya asks, and glances from the door

to Rian, who nods to assure her that whatever she says will remain in this room. Still, she lowers her voice. "Eron is a lecher. Azi is not the only member of this guild he's made advances on. But all of us," she looks at my mother again, "are strong. And after Mare's Head, Eron knows that he's met his match in Azi as well. I'm ending the discussion there. Someday, if fate is just, he'll get his due. It's not our place to dish it. Are we in agreement?"

Elliot snores softly beside her as Cort shakes his head in disbelief to his left. Bryse and Da are both staring, slack-jawed, at Mum. Brother Donal's eyes are closed, his lips moving in silent prayer. Beside him Dacva is staring at Mya with a mix of respect and disbelief. Rian's eyes are locked on her as well. Honestly, I'm not surprised. I wouldn't be surprised if I heard that Eron had laid his hands on every woman in the country. I shake my head and cross my arms over my chest. It may not be our place to dish it, but I certainly hope I'm there when it finally comes back to him.

"Are we in agreement?" Mya asks again, more firmly.

"Aye," everyone says in unison.

After the meeting each of us is eager to ride and put as much distance between ourselves and the prince as we can for as long as we can. Flitt is eager as well. She clings to the edge of the pauldron on my right shoulder as I jog down the stairs. The horses are already packed and waiting as we leave the keep, and I start to rush to Pearl when Rian takes my arm.

"Look," he says. "There are too many horses." I count them. He's right. There are nine of us and ten steeds.

"Excellent," the prince calls out from behind us. The others turn and bend a knee and Rian and I exchange glances before we do the same. Eron stands at the top of the staircase, gazing down over us. Beside him, Princess Amei looks radiant in deep purple gowns that set off her burnished brown skin perfectly. Eron's lips curl into something between a smile and a sneer. "Sir Hammerfel," he casts his eyes on me and a shadow from behind me creeps across as Bryse comes to tower over us both. "I've gifted you one of my best to accompany you on your journey. I've given him orders to report to me if anything goes awry," he eyes the others. "Should you need any assistance, of course." He snaps his fingers and a guard in a barrel helm steps forward from the shadows of the keep door.

"Of course," I say. "Thank you, Highness."

"May you find what you seek," he says to us. "And may you

have a safe journey."

I glance at the guard. His helm covers most of his face, but dark curls peek out from beneath it and I have a good idea of who it might be. Flitt's warning from the night before causes the hair on the back of my neck to prickle. *Are you sure he's who he says he is?* Jac's dark eyes glint in my direction and I turn to Rian and take his arm. In the meeting, everyone agreed it would be best to go on with our plan. Rian and I would ignore the prince's threats and return to Cerion with Ki.

"This complicates things," he pushes to me, and I give a slight nod in response as Amei steps down to thank us for our service and say her farewells.

Chapter Thirteen:

JOURNEYS ENDED AND BEGUN

Tib

We fight the wind all the way home from the palace. It bites us and tears at our cloaks. I have a new one now. Deep brown, like Mevyn's. Lined with fur. Still, it's not warm enough against this awful wind. We stumble inside together and Saesa takes a deep breath through her nose.

"Stag stew," she sighs with a smile. "I'm starved. We're home!" she calls to no one in particular, and Nessa is the first to appear from the sitting room. My muscles ache. I'm so tired. I could go back to bed and sleep for a week. I should find Mevyn, I think. Tell him that the princess will help us.

"How was the princess?" Nessa asks as she hugs Saesa, then me.

"Good," Saesa says. "I'm hungry now."

"Me too," I say. "Tired, though." I lean back against the door. Saesa reaches to steady me.

"You see? You ought to have waited. Poor Tib." Nessa slips an arm around my shoulders. "Go to bed. I'll send up a tray."

"But we have to tell you," Saesa starts, but Nessa holds up one hand.

"Plenty of excitement for today, Saesa," she says. "Whatever you have to tell me can wait."

"But you always say to tell you when it's fresh. So we don't forget." Saesa starts to follow us as Nessa guides me gently up the stairs.

"Tomorrow," Nessa says. "It can wait."

She leaves me alone in my room to undress. I don't, though. I'm too tired. I just take off my jacket and my ruffled shirt and sit on the bed. I think about taking my boots off this once, but decide not to.

They're dry enough now. I stomped them out good on the mat.

"What did the princess say?" Mevyn's voice startles me. I can't see him, but he speaks aloud, not in my head this time. I lean back against my pillows. Pull the warm blankets up to my chin. "May I look?"

"What do you mean?" I murmur sleepily. I sit up straighter. Try to stay awake. Supper is coming.

"Into your memories," he explains. "You've let me before. Remember?"

He floats in front of me. I can see him now. I look into his eyes. See flashes of the past. He's right. I've shown him before. He saw lots of things. Where I lived, how I worked. My family. The moment Viala rode away with the Sorcerer. The night we were taken. It didn't hurt, I remember, when he looked. It felt nice. Like a connection. Like friendship.

"Okay," I agree. I get comfortable against the pillows and he gazes at me. Watches us playing with the princess. Sees the plan she's woven for us. When he's through and he breaks the connection, I'm disappointed. A little sad. But then Nessa comes with stew and hot bread with gobs of melted butter, and Mevyn fades away before she sees him.

Saesa is in my room the next morning before the sun comes up. She sits across from me on the bed and we whisper plans. She thinks we need to pack all sorts of things, but Mevyn tells me secretly not to worry about that. I try to explain to her why, but she doesn't know about Mevyn. He made her forget. It complicates things. I want to ask him to make her remember, but he's supposed to be secret. How can I ask him while she's here?

"Not yet."

Fine, not yet. Maybe later. When we're on the road.

"Will Nessa let you come?" I ask her.

"Sure." Saesa says brightly. "We can leave anytime. She tells us often. This is our home and we're always welcome, but we're free to go, too. She just likes taking care of us, and honestly, why would we want to go anywhere else? You see how it is here."

"Yeah," I say. She's right. If I didn't have to go with Mevyn, I'd want to stay.

Downstairs, someone knocks on the door.

"That'll be the page, maybe!" Saesa says excitedly.

"This early?" I ask.

"Well," says Saesa, "Her Highness might have sent one to check before she sends everyone else. Remember? She said we could send them away if we don't need them after all."

"We didn't tell Nessa yet, though."

"I know!" Saesa says. She jumps from the bed and runs downstairs. I go a little more slowly. I'm still a bit weak. Others in the house start to stir. It's unusual for anyone to knock this early in the morning. Even a page.

"I'll answer," Nessa calls. She looks different in her night gown, not all done up. Younger. Her brown curls bounce lightly on her back as she rushes down the stairs, tying her robe. Raefe goes down with her. Lilen and Emme and Ruben join me at the railing. Mevyn is here, too. Watching. I can feel him. Nessa opens the door. A man in uniform stands straight and tall. I've seen the uniform before, in a painting of the Admiral that hangs over the fireplace. I wonder if that's him.

"Dorian!" Nessa cries excitedly. "Come in out of the cold." She reaches for the man's arm and pulls him inside. "What word have you? What word?"

"The fleet is a day's sail behind us," Dorian says. He brushes the snow from his shoulders. Stomps his boots on the mat. Hands Nessa a stack of letters.

"Who's that?" I whisper.

"Dorian. Captain of the scout ship," Lilen says. "The first ship to arrive from the Admiral's fleet."

The house erupts into celebration. The Admiral is coming home. There are letters for everyone, even me. I'm surprised by that, until Saesa explains that Nessa writes to her husband every day. The letters talk of faraway places and promise gifts for each of us. The children take turns reading them aloud. Ruben can't wait to see what a mouth harp is. He hopes it shoots things. Lilen is getting books. She hopes they're exotic spell books. Saesa is promised a vest of studded leather. Raefe, a new kind of spyglass that has two barrels that can be looked through side by side. I'm getting one of those, too. Nessa does a lot of crying and laughing. Dorian stays for breakfast.

The others go on and on about the journey. They pester Dorian with questions until Nessa tells them to hush and let him eat. Saesa glances at me. Now's the time to tell her about our plans to leave. I open my mouth to speak, and another knock comes on the door.

"I'll go," Maisie hitches Errie up on her hip and rushes out. She comes back with another letter. "For you, Tib." She sets it on the table beside me. Everyone stops eating and stares. They know I have no one to write me. I've told them before that I'm orphaned now.

"It's from your uncle."

"It's from my uncle," I say as I pick it up and open it. The words written there don't make sense to me. I never really learned to read. Mevyn helps me. "Dear Tib," I repeat after the words that echo in my head, "I'm delighted to hear that you are in Cerion. A visit would be most welcome. I'm sending an escort to accompany you to Ceras'lain. They should arrive shortly after you receive this letter. Please offer your hostess my sincerest thanks for keeping you warm and safe. I look forward to seeing you. Yours, Uncle Filbery."

"You have an uncle, and he's an elf?" Ruben asks.

"Don't be ridiculous, Ruben," Lilen says. "Of course he isn't."

"He studies with them."

"I do. I wrote him when I got here. He studies with them," I say, my mouth going dry. I hate lying to them. "The elves."

"I'd like to go with Tib," Saesa says. "Do you think I could, Tib?"

"Sure," I say. "Uncle's got lots of room."

"So he's a Mage, then?" Lilen asks, a little skeptically.

"A cartographer."

"He makes maps," I explain. "He's mapping the roads there."

"Don't elaborate."

Right. Don't elaborate.

"Saesa, you won't be here when Gaga comes?" Emme looks at her sadly.

"I'll see him when we get back," she says. "Just think, Emme, what an adventure! To go to Ceras'lain and see the elves!" On the other side of her, Raefe scowls.

"I don't like it," he says. "We don't know this uncle of his. He could be anyone."

"Of course you don't like it," Saesa frowns. She stabs a piece of potato with her knife. "You never let me do anything, Raefe."

"Your brother is only looking out for you, Saesa. Why don't you go with them, Raefe? Between you and the escort, you'll certainly be safe. It could be your coming-of-age tour. You've always talked about Ceras'lain."

Saesa and I exchange glances. She presses her lips together. Her nostrils flare out. She doesn't want him there.

"It's fine."

"It's fine," I say. "Raefe can come, too."

"What was his name again?" Lilen asks.

"Filbery," I reply after a quick reminder from Mevyn.

"Oh, I know of him. He has several maps archived at the Academy. He's a fine artist, too. He does all of his drawings himself. I thought he was working in Vermina Isles now, though. Yes, I'm certain of it. He's quite renowned for his records of the local flora. Why, just last week, he…" Lilen trails off. Her eyelids flutter a little. Beside her, the air shimmers. Unseen by anyone else, Mevyn gazes into her eyes. "Oh wait, no, I'm mistaken," she says distantly. "That's Folbury, not Filbery. Never mind." She tucks back into her porridge. Stays quiet for the rest of the meal.

After breakfast, Saesa pulls me aside while Nessa says her farewells to Captain Dorian.

"Tib," she whispers. "One problem with your story, and by the way, how'd you do that with the letter?" When I don't answer right away, she waves her hand dismissively. "Forget it. Anyway, I was saying, the princess is sending a royal escort. A cartographer in Ceras'lain wouldn't be able to do that."

"It's taken care of."

"Don't worry about it," I say. I'm more concerned that there will be horses involved. I've never ridden a horse before. I hope I don't fall off.

The morning is a blur. Nessa spends it in the drawing room, writing. I'm not sure what. Raefe is packing, too. Maisie and the others are cleaning for the Admiral.

"I wish I could have my vest that Admiral is bringing." Saesa says in whispers as she sits cross-legged on my bed. "It would be good to have on the journey."

A knock downstairs has us both jumping up to run and answer the door. Saesa is fastest. She gets there first and throws it open. A man dressed in chain mail with a great sword strapped to his back gives Saesa a friendly nod.

"I'm here for Tib and Saesa?" He peers inside. Nessa rushes out of the drawing room.

"They're here already?" She looks out into the street, where a carriage is waiting. "You're not even packed yet!"

"Oh, a carriage!" Saesa cries. "I thought we'd be riding! A carriage, how exciting!"

"I want to go on a carriage," Ruben whines.

I'm not so excited. The last time, the only time I was on a carriage was when we were stolen in the night by the Sorcerer. I remember the sound of it being crushed and swallowed by the roots of trees. I shiver.

"Come in out of the cold," Nessa says, but the guard shakes his head.

"We'll wait out here for their things," he says. "Take your time, m'lady. No rush."

Raefe brings a large sack downstairs with him. He says he packed for Saesa, too. I don't need much. I have my cloak, my boots. My knife, if I need it. We say farewell to Nessa, who gives Raefe a letter of reference.

"This is for Evelei, in Felescue. She's a friend," Nessa says, sounding a little hesitant. She smiles at us a sadly. "I do wish I could go with you. What an adventure you'll have."

"We'll come back and tell you all about it!" Saesa cries tearfully as she throws her arms around Nessa.

"Thank you for everything," I murmur. I don't want to drag out goodbyes. I just want to go, so I do. I jog down the stairs and climb into the carriage and wait for the other two.

Inside it's warm. There are bundles on the seats. One for each of us. Even for Raefe. I lift mine onto my lap and open it up. It's got a leather vest and bracers, a padded shirt, and a bandolier full of throwing knives and tiny, colorful vials filled with powders and liquids.

"Are these from you?" I whisper to Mevyn, who I somehow know is hovering beside me. I take one of the vials. Hold it to the light.

"Yes. Keep them safe. Don't play with that."

Saesa climbs in as I'm buckling the bandolier across my chest. Her eyes are still wet. She sees the bundle with her name and pulls it close as she sits beside me.

"You don't have to go, you know," I say.

"Don't be silly. If course I know that. I want to come. I've dreamed of leaving Cerion for as long as I can remember."

"But why?" I can't imagine. Cerion is a good place. A place you want to stay. It's safe. Kind. Clean. Peaceful.

"Adventure," Saesa grins. "It's boring here. I want to see what's outside of the gates, Tib! And now we're going to!" She starts pulling things out of her own pack. Leggings of green leather dotted with brass studs. A sturdy vest of the same. Sleeves and bracers. Leg guards. With each item she pulls out, she gasps. "Where did all this come from? The princess?"

Raefe climbs in before I can answer, and the carriage starts moving. I reach over and pull up the shade so it doesn't feel so closed. Try not to picture Nan sitting across from me or the terror on Zhilee's face as we bump along the cobbles. Instead I watch Raefe open his pack.

"I needed one of these..." he murmurs as he pulls out a chain mail shirt. "These, too," he says in awe as he turns a pair of well-made studded gloves in his hands. "Who are these from?"

"A friend."

"A friend," I repeat. Outside, the gates of the city streak past us. We're moving fast. Faster than a carriage like this should be able to.

"So, are you two going to tell me the big secret?" Raefe asks as he pulls on one of the gloves. "I'm pretty sure I've figured out there isn't any uncle in Ceras'lain."

"Not yet."

In the time it takes me to glance at Saesa, something shimmers over Raefe. His eyes close slowly. He falls asleep. Then Mevyn does something that surprises me. He shows himself to Saesa. Sits right on her knee and reveals himself. Saesa gasps. Looks into his eyes.

"I remember you," she says. "I do! You're the one who told me where to find Tib!"

"I am," says Mevyn.

"Did you just make Raefe go to sleep?" She looks across at her brother, a little concerned.

"I did," Mevyn says. "He isn't ready yet."

"Ready for what?" Saesa whispers.

"To know the truth," Mevyn replies.

"Oh."

"He will sleep as far as the mountains," Mevyn says. "When we reach the White Wall, I will wake him again."

"What's that?" I ask. "The White Wall?"

"It's the border between Cerion and Ceras'lain, where the elves live." Saesa explains. Lilen says it's made of the grandest white-barked trees you've ever seen, all grown to take the shape of past elf kings. They line the wall for leagues and leagues. Inside of them it's hollow. The White Line lives there. They're the elves that keep watch over the border to make sure that anyone who enters is worthy. Lilen says they have ways of seeing your darkest secrets. Only those with good intentions can enter."

I shiver as I look out the window. I have secrets. Dark ones. I wonder if they'll let me through.

"Don't worry."

No, don't worry. Mevyn is right. Somehow, I know he has a plan that will make sure we get to Kythshire. Too much depends on it. Margary. Twig. The Sunteri Wellspring. My sister. We make our plan. We'll get Raefe to Evelei in Felescue. Then we'll slip away in the night to Kythshire. Make the rest of our journey on foot. Mevyn says they might not even let me and Saesa in. The fewer in our party, he says, the better. Besides, Ceras'lain is safe. The elves are peaceful. We won't have trouble traveling alone.

"Look at the road," I say to Saesa. We've been following on the map. As we race past the village called Valleyside, the road gets smoother. It's made of flat stone that glitters in the sunlight. Saesa slides nearer to me to watch out the window. The air is warmer here, even as we climb into the mountains. We shed our cloaks and tuck them under the bench.

Saesa makes me turn around so she can put on her new armor while we climb the winding mountain road. I watch Raefe sleeping. He's scowling. Fighting. Having a nightmare.

"Get your hands off her!" he shouts in his sleep. He throws his fist to the side so hard that he dents the metal wall of the carriage. Saesa rushes to him. Takes his arm. He throws her off. Growls. Kicks.

"Raefe!" she cries. The carriage slows. Stops. I hear our guard climbing down from the seat on top. His name is Gruss. Mevyn ducks behind me as he peers into the window.

"Everything all right in here?" he asks. Saesa nods.

"My brother's just having a nightmare." She shakes him. "Raefe, wake up."

"All right, well, you can't be jumping around in there. You could turn the carriage. These mountain roads are treacherous. Sit still." He glances over his shoulder. "Not a good place to stop."

As soon as he utters the words, I see them. Eyes in the deep green forest, peering out at us. Dozens of them. Watching.

"Drive, Edsin," Gruss grips the handle beside the door. "Drive, dammit!" The carriage picks up speed. Something hits the sides. Lots of things. One of them pierces through the wall right beside me. Arrows.

"Cease your attack, in the name of the Throne of Cerion!" A voice booms from above us.

"Get ready."

Yes, get ready. I pull on my new bracers. Take a throwing knife in each hand. I've never thrown knives before. I wonder what Mevyn was thinking.

"The blue vial. Put it on the blades."

I do as he says. The arrows keep coming. Saesa draws Feat. Crouches beside the door, ready. Raefe wakes slowly. Above him, Mevyn fades from view. When he hears the chaos, Raefe's alert. He sees Saesa at the ready and draws his rapier.

"What is it?" he peers past her.

"Brigands, I think," Saesa whispers. "Lots of them."

Outside, the escort is shouting. Faster, faster. The driver pushes the horses. The trees streak past in blurs of green and yellow. The arrow strikes slow down, but we don't. We fly over the smooth road. Then the darkness creeps in, chilling us. The shadows. I know this threat right away. Dreamwalker. The horses slow. One of them screams. I never heard a horse scream before. I hope I never do again. The carriage stops.

"Cut it loose," one of our men is saying. "Quickly."

"I give the orders here, Gruss," says Edsin angrily. "You cut it loose."

"Bah, what difference does it make?" Someone jumps down. Gruss, I think. "We gotta keep moving."

"Hitch yours up, Dev. Move it!"

Saesa risks it. Pokes her head out of the door. Her eyes go wide.

"One of the horses is down," she whispers. "Shot. They're hooking up one of the other ones now."

"Get your head in!" Raefe hisses. She does just as an arrow sinks into the wood of the door frame where she had just been looking.

"They're coming," she whispers. She isn't afraid. She's ready to charge outside. Fight. Oddly, I am too. I feel brave. Confident.

"Hold, there!" Gruss shouts. "In the name of Cerion, hold!" Arrows screech. Thud into flesh. Another horse screams. "Your actions are treasonous! You will stop in the name of the King!"

"Is that who you have in there, pretty little man? King? Princess? No, something else. We can smell it." A voice drifts from the underbrush. "Something with great magic."

"Give to us, and you shall pass."

"Yes, give. Give to us."

The voices echo in whispers through the leaves. Wild. Feral.

"Give to us."

"Not something. Someone."

"Fae. Fae. Fae."

"Sunteri fae."

The whispers give me chills. Shrill and desperate. Hungry.

"Give to us or die."

"How do they know?" I whisper to Mevyn, who is hidden beside my ear.

"The Dreamwalker told them."

Saesa looks at me, her green eyes determined. All secrets have a price. Some are worth more than others. This one could be worth our lives.

Chapter Fourteen:

THE WHITE LINE

Tib

"What are they talking about?" Raefe whispers. "We don't have anything like that."

Saesa turns to look at me over her shoulder. Waits for me to say something. Outside, the whispering continues. I watch her. Wonder what she'll do. She shakes her head. Her lips press into a thin line. Her fingers flex on her sword.

"They'll see my blade first," she whispers to me.

"Give to us. Give, and you shall pass."

"No need to fight. Give to us."

Outside, the men keep working. There are four of them. Three guards and a driver. Two on horseback, and Gruss who was riding on the carriage. He comes to the door now. Opens it a crack.

"Don't worry," he whispers. "We don't give in to brigs. Stay inside." The whispering stops. They're waiting for Gruss's reply.

"Send out your leader," Gruss calls. Laughing erupts from the forest.

"We are the Wildwood. We are not fools. Give to us. Pay your passage."

"This road belongs to Cerion," Gruss shouts. "You have no right—"

An arrow whizzes through the air. Strikes just outside with a clang. Gruss curses loudly.

"Dented my chest plate!" he shouts angrily.

"Hold on to something, Gruss," one of the other guards calls.

Reins crack. The carriage jolts and rolls forward. We make our escape. The forest shrieks. We race off. Take a corner too fast. The carriage tips with a crash that throws Saesa and Raefe onto me, pinning me. Like the trees. The roots. Her blade glances my bracer. I scream and kick and try to shove them both away. My breath comes in quick gasps. I can't think. Under us, the carriage is being dragged. Grinding along the road with a deafening screech. The trees will grow around us. The roots will swallow us up.

"Calm down. Be ready."

Outside, more arrows. More horses' screams. Scrabbling feet across the stone road. Throaty battle cries. Hisses. Saesa and Raefe push themselves off of me. We roll onto our bellies and slide the driver's window open to watch. The horses are dead, and one guard already. More frightening are the creatures. Scores of them, rushing us. Wild-eyed, filthy. Stringy looking, like the drained fairies of Sunteri. Bony. Fierce. Larger, though. As tall as Emme, maybe. Twigs and leaves sprout from their heads and backs. Vines wrap their arms and creep into their hair. They fire their bows and raise their spears. There are too many. We won't survive.

The storm cloud creeps over us, but it isn't a storm cloud. I know. It's Dreamwalker. It blots out the sun so that it could be midnight. The Wildwood clash into the last three of our guards. Gruss has a dozen on him. As soon as one falls, another takes its place. More of them scramble to the overturned carriage. They climb on top of it. Rip open the door that's now above us.

"Your blades."

Yes, my blades. My gloved fingers fumble for the blue-crusted knives as black eyes bear down on us. Saesa is the first to attack. She growls and arcs her sword way over her head as they spill inside. Hits two of them. The metal sizzles as it slices through their woody flesh. Their screeching pierces through me. My head pounds. The two climb out, but more come. Saesa and Raefe hold them off. They crawl in from above. They try to shoot through the little driver's window.

"Throw it."

I flick my wrist and the knife leaves my hand. I watch its path. It hits one easily, turns impossibly. Hits another. The gashes it leaves sizzle, too, but it's different. The blue makes sparks that turn to flames. The flames turn their woody flesh to charcoal. The two creatures are engulfed. They drop inside, nearly missing Saesa. The others on Saesa and Raefe stop fighting. The creatures watch in horror, and then lunge at me. I'm ready, though. I have the other blade. I throw it and it catches them. Lights them up. They have no time to climb out. They crumble to ash.

Saesa turns to me, wide-eyed. Raefe looks at me in disbelief.

"Get out," he says as he comes to his senses. "Get out or we'll all burn!"

"Stay."

Yes, stay. I shake my head at them. Raefe clings to Saesa. We watch the flames flicker, fade, and die out. I sift through the ashes for my knives. Wipe them clean. Coat the blades again. Outside, the battle is fierce. One of our guard is down. Edsin, the driver, is down. Gruss is still up, fighting. So is the other guard. They flank the carriage, trying to fend off the Wildwood. The creatures keep coming, though. Swarming from the woods. Outnumbering us a hundred to one.

"There's no way we're getting out of this," Saesa whispers. Raefe and I exchange glances. We know she's right. The storm cloud seems to sink closer. I feel it pressing in on us.

"Whatever they want, just give it, Tib. You have it. Give it to them." Raefe says.

"Tib, no," Saesa whispers. "You can't."

Give him up, a voice presses in on me. Not Mevyn. *Give him up and be free.* Dreamwalker.

"Leave me alone!" I scream.

"Good. Have faith. Throw again." Mevyn.

Yes, throw. I move away from the others and climb up through the window. Aim at the group on the guard below. Throw. My knife arcs strangely, hitting one after another. Sparking. Opening black, charred wounds. Ten fall. Ten more. Hundreds to go. The rest see it, though. They pause in their charge. They look at me with fear. I raise my arm. My second knife flashes. They cower. Some creep backwards, into the safety of the forest. Others bare their teeth at me.

"Give to us," they hiss, but the sound is weaker now.

"Leave us alone!" I shout. "You can't have him! You can never have him, you filthy, disgusting, horrible—"

"Tib, no…"

"Oh, no," I whisper. Shouting at them is a mistake. It bolsters them, somehow. Enrages them. They surge out of the forest again. Swarm us. Take down another guard. Only Gruss is left. Saesa and Raefe pull me back inside. We ready ourselves at the windows. I coat another blade. Outside, Gruss grunts. We watch through the window as he slides down, lifeless. With him out of the way, the Wildwood spill in toward us. We fight them off. My blades do their work, but coating them again takes time. Too much time. Saesa tries to cover me, but they overcome her. They slash at her face. They drive sharp spears through her shoulder. Beside her, Raefe suffers too. He fights fiercely, but we're outnumbered.

We crowd together into a corner as the carriage fills with them. They bear down on us, their wood-like teeth glistening. Saesa is panting. Trying to be brave. I think she can't lift her sword arm anymore. It's up to me. The Wildwood stink, like decay. Like the musty water that dripped into my mouth. I hate them. I fling my knife and they light up. More come.

Outside, another sound mixes with the whispering and screeching. A lower sound. Like wind catching in a sail, but more rhythmic. Steadier. The sun creeps out again. The storm cloud has broken. The Dreamwalker is gone. The Wildwood in the carriage pause. They look to the sky. The sound comes louder, and with it an odd clicking. Bird-like. Hissing. Snake-like. I creep back to Saesa. She's holding on.

"The pink vial. Give it to her."

I search in my bandolier. Find the vial. Give it to her. She drinks it and looks better. An eerie silence falls over the carriage. All around us, the Wildwood crouch down. Hide their heads. They're like mounds of earth, dotted with seedlings and mushrooms. The three of us peer up out of the window. A great feathered wing sweeps across our view. As Saesa passes the vial to Raefe, I pull myself up to look.

There are three of them. Strange creatures, with bird-like, feathered white bodies. Bigger than horses. At their chests, the feathers fade to scales of blue, green, purple. Their heads are proud. Like swans, with pointed beaks and yellow eyes. On their backs, each has a person. No, an elf. I know what they are, even though these are the first I've seen. Sister always wanted to meet one. She read stories and stories about them. Now I understand why. There are two men and one woman, and even the men are beautiful. All dressed in white. Slender and elegant, with pale faces that smile even though now they're stern. I think these must be kings and a queen, the way sit with their backs so straight and their shoulders so square.

"Go," one of the men says. All around us, the rest of the Wildwood hop up and skitter away. Back to the woods. Back to shelter.

"What is it, Tib?" Saesa asks weakly.

"Elves," I reply. "Riding bird-lizards."

"The White Line," she whispers. "On cygnets. Oh, I want to see." I drop down beside them. Raefe's arms are around her. He's shivering even though it's not cold. Pale. Saesa is slumped against him.

She looks a little better after the potion. Not much, but she's stopped bleeding. I wonder how I got through it without getting hurt. I'm sure Mevyn has something to do with that.

Outside, the elves speak quietly to one another. I don't understand the words. It sounds like Mage talk. The hair on my arms prickles up. I don't like magic. It isn't a spell, though. Just talking. I hear them dismount lightly. Their feet barely make a sound as they walk among the fallen.

"Go and greet them."

I don't want to leave the other two, but Mevyn tells me he'll stay with them. Don't worry, he says. But I am, a little. Something nags at me. A thought that I try hard to push away. He should have fought more. He should have, but he just hid and ordered instead. Saesa fought. Raefe fought. Mevyn hid. I climb up out of the window. Look at the bodies all around. Dozens of Wildwood. Our three guards and driver. Four horses. Five, if I count the first one we lost. My anger grows. Mevyn has magic. Magic powerful enough that those Wildwood creatures wanted him. He could have done more. He could have prevented these deaths.

"Begone from here," the lady elf says. Her hair is long and white. It shines yellow in the sunlight that comes through the trees. She carries a bow that's almost as tall as she is. The carvings on it are detailed. I want to see them closer. Instinct tells me to look away, but I can't stop staring. I creep forward. "You are not welcome." At first I think she means me, but then a voice echoes through my thoughts.

"*I go where I like*," it says.

"You shall fail," one of the men declares. His hair is long, too, and just as white. His armor is white. His sword and shield are white. "You shall be destroyed."

"Go, Dreamwalker. While you are still able." This one is the same as the other two. Too beautiful to look at. So white he gleams and I have to squint, but I can't look away. As he walks toward me, I can feel the weight of the Dreamwalker lifted. It's almost like the elf has a cloud following him. A bright cloud. Full of hope. It settles over me as he raises a fist to his chest to greet me.

Even through the elf's fog of false-hope, I hear the Dreamwalker's reply. "*It has only begun*." Then, nothing.

"He's gone," I whisper, relieved.

"He can hold no sway over us," the elf explains. "The Dreaming cannot touch the elves." He smiles down at me. He's tall, very tall. The other two brush past us, checking the fallen. I watch one of them pause at Gruss. I hold my breath. She whispers something to him. He sputters. Coughs. Curses. Moves to grab his sword. She holds him down. Murmurs soothing words in elven. He settles. She raises her head, tips it to the side. Stares at the carriage. Says something in their language.

"*I see now, what had the Wildwood so interested*," Mevyn translates her words in my mind.

"Oh, that is clever." Her laugh is melodic. It makes me smile. She turns to me. "I shall speak in your language then, my child. Come with us to the wall. There, we can discuss things more openly. All of us." She helps Gruss to his feet. The men help Saesa and Raefe from the overturned carriage. Saesa gapes at the cygnets. Raefe stares at the road strewn with bodies. The elves help us onto the mounts. They secure us in the front of the saddles. Saesa and I sit together, side by side with the lady elf behind us. The cygnet's wings stretch out, and we slowly rise.

Up we go, higher than the tree tops. Higher than the ship's tallest mast. Higher than the tallest burning tower. Higher than the cliffs of Cerion. I can see everything from here. All of the world. I want to stay in the sky forever, with the wind blowing my hair and the sun shining on my face. No one can touch me here. Up here, I'm safe. Up here, I'm free. Beside me, Saesa whoops and throws her fist up.

"Saesa, hold on! Both hands!" Raefe shouts from the cygnet beside us. He isn't enjoying the ride as much. His shoulders are hunched, his knuckles white. He says something to the elf behind him who laughs. Raefe leans over and loses his breakfast. On the cygnet on the other side of us, Gruss clings to the seat. He looks like he'll be ill, too.

"Go higher! Faster!" Saesa shouts, and our rider pulls the reins to make the cygnet surge upward. We laugh together as we glide on the wind until I can see the line of white stretching through the forest below us. The cygnets dip low and my stomach jumps up as we glide along the White Wall. It's just like Saesa described. The trees are tall, bold, and white. They're shaped like kings, with branches sprouting from their heads like crowns. When we get closer, I can see platforms along the branches. Some are lined with sentinels and others are empty. We land on one of the empty ones with an easy grace that surprises me.

My heart races as the lady elf helps me and Saesa down. This place is nothing like Sunteri's desert or Cerion's snow-covered streets.

Everywhere is green. It smells like flowers and sounds like rushing water. It reminds me of the atrium in the castle, where Margy offered me nectar and cakes. Other elves rush to take care of the cygnets while our three lead us away from them. Raefe still looks a little green. He leans on Saesa for support. Something about this place makes me feel lighter. I can see it in the others, too. Even Gruss looks better.

"Where are we going?" he asks. "What about my fallen comrades? We can't just leave them in the road."

"They are being retrieved, even now," the elf who was Raefe's driver says. "We shall respectfully return their bodies to Cerion."

He turns to face us as we pause in a small room with a high, domed ceiling. There's a hole at the top to let the light in. It shines over carvings in the wood. Leaves and fairies. Wildwoods and flowers. Winding vines. Animals great and small. They seem to dance along the wall. I don't realize the elf is talking to me until I feel Mevyn nudge my jaw. I blink. Everyone is staring. Waiting for me to answer whatever his question was.

"Sorry, what?" I ask.

"I said, you are the bonded one?" I glance at the others. Remember what Mevyn told me. We're a pair. We're bonded now. We work together. Belong together. I nod. Saesa looks at me, confused. "Very well. The two of you shall join me, please. The other three shall go with Julini and Zevlain." He makes a graceful gesture with his hands at the other elves and bows his head. Raefe scowls and counts us.

"Um, there's only four of us," Raefe says. Julini and Zevlain laugh softly.

"Doesn't matter, we're not splitting up." Gruss crosses his arms. "I'm sworn to protect these. All of them. Can't do it if some are one place and some are another."

"And I'm not going anywhere without Tib." Saesa steps to me. Takes my hand. My face gets hot.

"Nor I, without Saesa." Raefe puts a hand on Saesa's shoulder and she rolls her eyes slightly.

"*Adorable*," Julini says in the elf tongue. Thanks to Mevyn, I understand her. "*Still they don't trust us.*"

"*What do you expect?*" Zevlain shakes his head. "*Especially from that one. The guard.*"

"Their language is so beautiful," Saesa whispers. "Like a song without music."

"We shall go together, then," the first one says. "But if you wish our help, we will need to speak with the one who needs it most."

"I've heard the elves were cryptic," Raefe whispers as we follow them through bright archways. "Guess that wasn't an exaggeration."

Once, when I was young, I found a wasps' nest that had been abandoned. I pulled it apart and discovered all of the little chambers where the wasps made their homes. The White Wall reminds me of that nest. One side is closed off, with rows and rows of doors that go all the way to the treetops and down to the roots, too. The other side is arches grown from the wood of the trees. It overlooks a sunlit valley far below. Mists from waterfalls float in places along our path. It's sort of the same as my root prison, but it feels too different here. Peaceful. Safe. Bright.

They bring us to a high platform that has comfortable chairs and a table set with food and drink. Above us cygnets roost in the towering branches of the tree. Below, a little stream trickles down along ferns and moss. It's a nice sound. I like it. It's pleasant here.

"Well, perhaps we should start at the beginning," my rider puts his fist to his chest again. "I am Shoel. This is Julini, and that is Zevlain. We are three of the White Line. Our station is *Kueles'ke*, the Mountain Road, as you call it. Our cygnets heard your struggle while we were out on patrol. I regret our timing. Perhaps many Wildwood would have been spared, had we arrived sooner."

"What about our men?" Gruss demands. "Our horses? Those rabble attacked us, and you mourn for them? Then you wonder why we don't trust you." Gruss glares at the elves. "I lost three good men out there and some fine horses, too. If your job is to keep those creatures in check, you're doing a poor one."

"*Adorable,*" Julini smiles. "*Look how his face goes so red.*"

"*Don't laugh, Juli. See how upset he is?*" Zevlain murmurs beside her.

"And you don't even have the courtesy to speak Common!" Gruss barks. Saesa, Raefe, and I move closer to each other. We stay quiet, like children are supposed to when adults are fighting.

"Forgive my contradiction," Shoel's tone is calm. Peaceful. Like he and Gruss are having a cordial conversation about the weather. "It is not our job to keep the Wildwood in check. They are creatures of their own mind, as you and I are. Also, they do not fall within our borders so, as far as elfkind is concerned, they are free to do as they wish."

"So you're saying since they're in Cerion and not Ceras'lain, they're not your problem?" Gruss crosses his arms.

"Indeed." Shoel nods. "Still, it is unusual for the Wildwood to disturb travelers. They are peaceful creatures. They keep to themselves."

"Well, something got into these," Gruss says. "Never saw anything like it."

"Yes, you are most right," Zevlain says. He looks at me. "Something did."

Gruss doesn't miss it. He puts himself between me and the elf. Rests a hand on his sword.

"Friend," Julini smiles at Gruss, "tell me, what was your vow regarding these young ones?"

"To see them safely to the gates of Ceras'lain."

"And so you have," says Julini softly. "Your vow is met. Your task is done. Leave them in our care. We shall give you a meal and a horse for your return. Come." She rests a hand on his shoulder. Smiles. Slowly, his knit-together brow smoothes out. He turns to us.

"Thank him. Tell him you'll be safe."

"Thank you, Gruss. We'll be all right here. Right, Saesa? Right, Raefe?" The other two nod slowly. They don't seem as sure as I do. Raefe gives Julini a lazy smile. I think he likes her.

"Thank you, Gruss." Saesa echoes me and then rushes to him and hugs him. "We thought you'd been killed. I'm so glad you weren't!"

Gruss returns her hug. He looks at me over her disheveled red curls. "You sure?" he asks.

I nod, but he still hesitates.

"We shall keep them safe. We have no reason to harm children here. Please, go with a light heart. You have fought bravely. May your journey home be quick and without peril," Shoel bows to him.

"Right…" Gruss shrugs one shoulder uncomfortably. "And I guess I should thank you. For saving my life and all."

"Of course," Julini smiles.

"Well, you lot be careful," he says, pointing at the three of us. Then he glances at the elves again, and follows Julini out.

2015

Chapter Fifteen:

BOUNDARIES BREACHED

Tib

The elves are generous and kind. They bring healers to look at Saesa and Raefe, and they fix them up right there on the platform. The healers are just as impressive as the warriors. Not like the ones in Cerion who wear brown robes all of the time. These are dressed in bright blues, greens and purples. They're just as tall as Julini and Zevlain and Shoel. Their skin is just as pale. Their hair just as white. One of them, a lady, has colorful feathers tied in her hair and bells that chime as she moves. Saesa loves her. She stares and grins and talks and talks to her about everything.

Raefe gets his own healer. He isn't as talkative with his, though. He lies back in the chair that has a long end to put his feet up on. My own healer comes to me. Gets me comfortable. Tells me his name is Celorin. Checks my eyes and teeth and nose. Doesn't touch, just runs his hands above me. He starts at my head and goes all the way to my feet. He stops there at my boots, like there's something interesting there.

"*This child has lli'luvrie,*" he says to the others, in their language. They all pause.

"*Yes. He is paired.*" Shoel comes to stand beside him. He says something else, but Mevyn doesn't translate it for me.

"What's lli'luvrie?" I ask. The two elves look at each other.

"It is a special word," Shoel explains. "The closest meaning it has in your language is…" he looks to Celorin for help.

"Mm…" Celorin taps his lips thoughtfully. "Tether, I believe."

"Yes, that's it." Shoel nods. He looks over his shoulder at the others. Raefe has fallen asleep. Saesa is chatting away with her healer. They're well distracted. He sits down next to me. "Why have you come here," he keeps his voice low, "all the way from Sunteri? And why have you brought," he nods at my boots, "that which you have brought?"

"Tell him we must talk alone. Go with him."

"We must talk alone," I say before I can even think. The words are elven. They're strange to say. I look across at Saesa and Raefe. They're safe, but I'm uneasy leaving them. This place is too big. We would never find each other if we got separated. Shoel nods and gets up. He gestures for me to follow him. I don't want to. I try to stay, but my legs slide off the chair and I'm on my feet before I know it.

"I'm not leaving them," I say firmly. I plant my feet. It makes me feel dizzy but I do it anyway.

Shoel turns. I think he realizes that I'm not talking to him. I cross my arms. Wait for Mevyn. He says nothing. Still, I don't budge.

"What is it you fear in stepping away for a moment?" Shoel asks gently. It makes me feel childish.

"I don't want any of us to get lost," I explain.

"Zevlain." Shoel says to the remaining White Line. He straightens a little in response. "Wait here with the young ones until we return."

Zevlain nods. Saesa looks up from her conversation. She starts to get up, but her healer says something and she sits again. I wave to her. Try to tell her it's all right. I hope I'm right. I still feel uneasy as I walk away from them. I'm starting to resent Mevyn. His orders. His demands. Protecting him while he hides away. But then I remember how he saved me from the roots.

How we were able to help each other through the desert to Zhaghen. We needed each other. We still do. I think of the word Celorin used. Lli'luvrie. Tether. My boots. Think of my reluctance to take them off. Wonder why Mevyn didn't just tell me what they were, or why I never figured it out on my own. Now that I know, it's so obvious.

And where does he go? Why does he even need a tether, if Sunteri's Wellspring is dry and there's no one left there? I remember the long stretches of time in our recent past when he seemed to be gone. I felt so alone. He went someplace. He left me. But where? Why haven't I ever wondered about this before? Because he took my memories away? Maybe it has to do with Ceras'lain. I feel different here. Clearer. I'm so absorbed in my thoughts that I bump into Shoel when he pauses at a door. He turns and looks at me over his shoulder. He's amused.

"Sorry," I murmur. He nods.

"Please," he says as he sweeps his hand through the open door. As soon as it closes behind him, Mevyn emerges. He looks paler. Not as gold as before. A little battered looking. Tired, like he's trying hard. What's the phrase Nessa uses? Keeping up appearances.

"It is customary," Shoel starts without any formality, "for a fae to bring himself to our size when visiting Ceras'lain, that we might look each other in the eye." Suddenly I'm afraid, and I don't know why. A glance at Mevyn explains it. This is his fear, not mine. "But I see that you are weak, and so I shall not ask it of you."

"Well, that's very accommodating of you," Mevyn's long hair curls and waves as he speaks. His tone is sarcastic, I think. I stare at him. The gold lines on his skin glow and fade and glow again. I want to ask him things. Lots of things. I want to be like Saesa and think of all the best questions. Instead I sit quietly in a chair, out of the way. I don't interrupt. I listen. I'm only here because Mevyn wants me to be. I'm not meant to be part of the conversation.

That's made even clearer when they start speaking in the elf language. Without Mevyn translating, I don't understand. Saesa says it sounds like a song with no music. Not to me. To me it's frustrating. Rude, even. I can't do anything but listen and try to figure out what they're saying and why they don't want me to know. They talk for a long time. All I can get from it is Mevyn is hiding things and Shoel is suspicious. Finally, Mevyn turns to me.

"The elf would like to ask you questions. Be honest. I'll wait elsewhere." He disappears, leaving me alone with Shoel. He comes closer to me. Sits in a chair close by. Even when he sits, his posture is perfect. Like he's always on watch. Always alert. I sit straighter, too. It makes me feel stronger. He smiles.

"Tell me, friend," he says warmly, like he really is a friend, "how do you feel?"

I don't understand the question. It's too broad. I'm not sure how he wants me to answer it. Suddenly I wish Mevyn was still here. He'd know. He'd tell me the right thing to say. Shoel tilts his head slightly. Watches me. I feel like he can see my struggle.

"Fine," I say. It's a good answer. A safe answer.

"You look well enough." He drums his slender fingers on the arm of the chair. They don't look like warrior's fingers. They're too smooth. Too elegant. All of him is. "Fed and clean, outside of your battle grime. You throw, I see?" He nods to the knives on my bandolier. They're all still there. I wonder why he and the other elves didn't try to take them away.

"I just started." I think of the battle. Remember how the blades spun and hit more than one mark. How did I do that?

"You're a fair mark," he nods. "You felled many of the Wildwood with your faerie fire." The blue liquid Mevyn told me to use was faerie fire. Interesting.

"Is that what this is about?" I forget to sit straight. I slump back against the cushion. My heart starts to race. I killed a lot of them. Twenty, maybe thirty. "Am I in trouble?"

"We do not take it upon ourselves to dole justice outside our own kind, young one. We leave that to your own conscience. No, you are not in trouble. I speak to you now out of concern for your safety."

"What do you mean?" My leg starts to bounce nervously. He eyes it. I stop.

"Did you enter into this partnership with Mevyn of your own free will?" he asks.

"I don't know," I answer slowly, thinking back. "It just sort of happened. We were in trouble. We needed each other to survive." The question annoys me. It's not his business.

"Do you wish to remain with him?" He watches me closely. I try to keep my face even while I think about it. I never really considered that, the possibility of going on by myself. It never entered my mind. I wonder why. Did Mevyn keep me from thinking about it? Or was I just happy to go along with him? The idea bothers me. I don't like it. I don't like Shoel for asking me such a thing. He has no right.

"Yeah, I do," I say. "I want to stay with him. We've got stuff to do." I stand up. "I want to go back to Saesa now."

"Of course. In a moment," he says, but he doesn't get up. "Tib, you must understand. I am offering you assistance. I wish to help you. Do you feel safe? Please remember that Mevyn asked you to be honest."

I scowl and cross my arms. I can't help it. I'm too uneasy. He's looking at me. He sees. Sees something I can't, maybe. The truth is that ever since Mevyn and I teamed up, I've done a lot of things I never would have before. Exciting things. Dangerous things. Climbed towers. Burned them. Swam in the ocean, to a ship. Left home forever. These are good things, I tell myself. Adventurous things. These things got me out of there. Away from the dye fields. Helped me start a new life. But then I remember the fear as Dreamwalker attacked me in the pit. The pain as I fell. How I wanted to die. How as soon as I got up again, I was ready to do whatever Mevyn said. He protected me. Saved me. But if it wasn't for him, I wouldn't have been there in the first place.

"He gave me things. Friends. Other things." I finger the soft leather of my new bandolier. Wiggle my toes in my boots. My good, new boots. I thought they were a gift, and they were. The first thing Mevyn gave to me. They were something more, though. Something Mevyn needed more than I did. *A gift is a trick*. I swallow the lump in my throat. "We're friends," I say, but I'm more confused now than ever. I hide it well enough, though. Shoel believes me. He gets up.

"Very well," he says. "We shall bring you to the border of Kythshire tomorrow. From there, you must go alone. We respect our neighbors' border, but we shall take you as far as we can by cygnet."

"But Raefe," I keep my arms crossed. "He doesn't know we're going there."

"I advise you to tell him," Shoel opens the door. "For Saesa's safety."

His words ring in my ears as we walk together back to the platform. Not just the part about Saesa. The other parts, too. I was so sure before. I was on an important quest. I had to do this. It never felt like a choice. But now, with all of Shoel's questions, I'm doubting it. Doubting Mevyn. Doubting myself.

It doesn't feel the same as when the Dreamwalker made me think bad things. This is different. It comes from a good place. It feels more like the truth. Or maybe it isn't. Maybe this *is* the Dreamwalker all over again. This place feels as nice as my vision while I was climbing the rungs, the one that made me fall. Maybe this place is a trick. I stop walking. Reach out. Touch the wall. It feels real, but so did the sunshine. So did the flower petals that brushed my fingers.

"Tib?" Shoel turns. Comes back to me.

"Is this place real?" I ask him. "Are you?"

He puts his hands on my shoulders. Kneels. Looks into my eyes. His are silvery blue. Honest. There's no magic there. Not like when Mevyn looks at me and everything feels like a spell.

"Yes," he says firmly. "This place is real."

"I thought maybe the Dreamwalker…" I trail off. Look away.

"His kind cannot enter here," Shoel explains. "We are protected, as is all of Ceras'lain. He cannot reach your mind within our borders."

"How do I know you're telling the truth, and not just part of the illusion?" I look at him again. His honest eyes hold something else now. Pity.

"You don't," he sighs. "You have nothing to go on but instinct and your own heart. You must learn to trust both. Trust in yourself, Tib, above all others. Only you know what is best."

I sit right beside Saesa when we get back. She's laughing. Happy. I smile, too, but inside I'm still confused. When Mevyn returns to me I don't feel much better. The elves show us to a room with three beds. They tell us to rest, and that we'll leave on cygnets in the morning.

Saesa gasps and pulls me around, showing me the view from the balcony, and pointing out the fairies carved into the pillars of the beds. The beds have curtains on them. I never saw that before. They're soft. So are the mattresses. I climb on and sink into it. When I do, I don't want to get up again. It feels like a cloud. But I have to. I struggle out of the bed.

"Tomorrow, did you hear? We get to ride the cygnet again. Julini said I can ride with her. I bet we'll go even higher." Saesa's curls bounce as she hops up beside me. Across from her, Raefe has the letter Nessa gave him out. He turns it in his hands.

"Hopefully, this Evelei in Felescue is easy to find," he says.

"We're not going to Felescue," I cross the room to his bed. Lean on the post.

"*Tib, no.*" Mevyn's voice rushes into my head. *"It'll be just you, me, and Saesa. Remember?"*

"What do you mean?" Raefe asks. He looks up from the letter. I feel Mevyn's warning, but I ignore it. Shoel was right. If something happens to Mevyn and me, someone needs to be with Saesa.

"You were right, back in the carriage," I admit. "There's no uncle in Ceras'lain. We're going to Kythshire," I say. "All four of us."

Raefe looks around. Counts three. Shakes his head.

"Why does everyone keep counting wrong?" he asks. "There's three of us. You, me, Saesa."

"No, there are four. Mevyn's here." My heart is racing. I remember Shoel's advice. *Trust in yourself.* It's easier here. Easier to be myself. To ignore Mevyn's directions. It feels daring to ignore his anger and his commands.

"Why are you betraying me?"

"I'm not betraying you. I'm making sure my friends are safe. I've trusted you, now you need to trust me, too. Raefe is my friend. He loves his sister. He's good. He'll keep our secret."

"Outside. Now."

Saesa looks from me to Raefe, who is sitting up in the downy cloud of his mattress, staring at me. I shake my head.

"No more orders," I say. Raefe's eyes widen. He looks at Saesa. Mouths something about me being mad. I glare and cross my arms again. My feet start to shuffle away and I will them to stop. "I mean it." I plant them to the spot. It takes a lot of effort. My head starts to hurt.

"I need to speak to you alone," Mevyn says a little more gently, but his will is just as strong as ever. *"Please come onto the balcony."*

"That's better," I say. I excuse myself and go outside. I can hear them whispering about me back in the room. It makes me angry that Raefe said I was mad. I'm not. Maybe I shouldn't have told him after all. I hope Saesa's defending me. I'm sure she is.

On the balcony, Mevyn is fiery gold and bright. Strong-looking. Not how he was in front of Shoel. It makes me even angrier. My arms are crossed so hard I feel like I'm holding my chest together.

"You have no right," he flies toward me. Hovers in my face. Our eyes meet briefly, but I look away. "No right to reveal me to anyone. Ever." He drifts around my head. Tries to catch my gaze. I duck away.

"Stop it." I know what he wants. To make me forget. All he has to do is look into my eyes. In the past he always asks me first, but I won't take a chance this time. I won't even let him look. I won't even let him try.

"What did that elf say to you?" he demands. "What has changed between us?" He stops trying to catch my eye. He droops onto the railing and stands there. "I need you, Tib. Please."

"What difference does it make if Raefe knows? You told Shoel. You told Saesa. You let her remember, too."

"Saesa has been tested. I know she'll keep me safe now."

"How?" I ask angrily. "How was she tested? When?"

"The carriage ride," Mevyn explains. "Even in the face of danger, she didn't reveal me. She didn't betray me."

"That was a test?" I pace. Shake my head. Remember the danger, the fear. The creatures pouring in through the windows. Saesa being stabbed. The storm cloud. The darkness that fell over us. The road littered with dead. "That was you?"

"Oh no, no. That was not me, Tib. It was the Dreamwalker. You heard the elves. He cannot touch us here. No need to be afraid."

I close my eyes. Press my palms to them. Try to think. He said the same thing in the pit. It was my test, but it was the Dreamwalker.

"Who is it?" I ask. "Who is this Dreamwalker? If not you, then who is he? Why is he so interested in you?"

"Look at me," Mevyn says soothingly, "and I will tell you. Look at me, so you know that I am telling the truth."

Reluctantly, I let my hands drop and open my eyes slowly. He's right there, waiting. He puts a hand on my cheek. The gold swirls dance. Suddenly, I feel foolish. It doesn't matter who the Dreamwalker is. Not really. All that matters is getting to Kythshire. Getting help to restore the Wellspring. Everything else is unimportant. I feel bad. I shouldn't have questioned.

"Tib, I'm sorry. I must. I will ask you as I always do, for my protection and your own…"

In the morning, Saesa wakes me. We're all excited. Ready for adventure. Saesa jumps on Raefe's bed. Shakes him awake. Hurries him to get dressed. Julini comes to walk us to breakfast. She and Saesa chatter away together. Raefe and I walk more slowly. We're both still trying to wake up. Nobody says anything about the night before. None of us remembers.

At breakfast, we go over our plans with Shoel. Raefe will deliver Nessa's letter to Evelei in Felescue. Saesa and I will go with Shoel. Shoel glances at Raefe and then looks at me. He's disappointed that I didn't tell Raefe the secret. I'm not sure what the secret was now. It must not have been too important. I just have to go with Shoel. I know that much.

I'm excited to ride the cygnet again. Saesa is, too. Raefe isn't, though.

"You be careful," he says to Saesa. "Hold on with both hands, all right?"

"I will," she says, and hugs him. "Don't get sick again."

He hugs her back. Seeing them together reminds me of someone from my past. Someone I miss. I think of red blooms and a fan of black hair. I wonder if I'll see her again.

"Take care of her, Tib," Raefe smiles at me. Gives me a hand to shake. I do.

"I will," I promise. "Don't worry."

Saesa slips her hand into mine as the cygnet carrying Raefe and Zevlain opens its feathery wings. With a loud cry and a puff of wind, the mount lifts up from the platform and dives away. We watch it go until it's a tiny white dot in the distance. Saesa's the first one to break the silence.

"Our turn!" she laughs and runs to Julini, who's waiting to help her onto her cygnet. Shoel turns to me.

"Are you certain about this, Tib? It isn't too late. We can bring Raefe back. For Saesa."

"Say you're sure."

Yes, say I'm sure. I am. I say it. Shoel eyes me. I smile at him.

"Very well," he sighs. "Up you go." He boosts me onto the cygnet's back and climbs into the seat behind me. Next to us Saesa is stroking the soft feathers, waiting to go. She waves at me, grinning. White wings spread gracefully and take us up. Soon we're so high that even the wall is just a thin line. I close my eyes and feel the wind in my hair. I could stay up here, soaring, forever. Up here, I'm safe. Up here, I'm free.

Chapter Sixteen:
THE FALLEN
Azi

Rian takes the banner for the ride back to Valleyside. It's a much quicker journey without the Royal Carriage and the columns of guards to slow our pace. Mya sings a song of speed, and her song gives our horses strength and stamina. We ride hard and cover twice the ground in half of the time. Thankfully, we're spared Flitt's constant banter. She sleeps through most of the day tucked under my collar. When we finally stop for the night, we've made it all the way to Sorlen River Crossing. The streets are quiet as we ride through the village, which is mostly closed up for the night. I'm relieved that we'll have no fanfare to welcome us. All of us are hungry for our supper, and we just want to get in where it's warm.

"That's half the distance to Valleyside," Rian says as he helps me down from my horse. "If we ride as hard tomorrow, we can make it there. We could get to Ceras'lain in two days' time if we end up having to ride. From there, the ride to the other border shouldn't take long. Another day, maybe." He rubs a splash of dried mud from my cheek with his finger and draws me for a quick kiss as the stable boy leads our horses away. Behind us, Da clears his throat.

"Oh Benen, let them be," Mum whispers. "Young love…" she lowers her voice further and I don't quite catch the rest. They laugh, and Rian takes it as permission to kiss me even longer. I don't mind.

"In the middle of the street? Really, you two?" Mya calls.

"Clearly, your mother needs to teach mine a thing or two," Rian murmurs in between kisses.

"Yours is right, though." I look around. Jac is milling by the door. Everyone else has gone in. The streets are empty and dark. A cold wind whips my hair around my face and I shiver. "Jac's watching. Let's go in."

Rian looks over his shoulder at Jac and then turns back to me. He draws me in even closer and kisses me with such passion that I'm left blushing. Warmth and happiness surge through me from head to toe. I love being this close to Rian, I truly do. I've missed it since we've been avoiding the Half-Realm. I don't care that we're in the middle of the street or who's watching. When he pulls away, Rian's eyes dance with mischief.

"Think he caught that one?" he asks with a wink.

"He'd have to be blind not to," I laugh and take his hand and we try to slip past Jac into the inn, but he nods to us as we near and it's obvious he wants to talk.

"Master Mage, Lady Knight," he salutes us casually. "A word?"

"I'm not a Master," Rian says. "Just Rian is fine."

"Yes, and Azaeli. Of course." Jac pulls off his helm and tucks it under his arm.

"No, Lady Knight is good for Azi." Rian nods matter-of-factly and I nudge him with my elbow and roll my eyes. "What can we do for you, Jac?" Rian asks.

"Oh, no, sir. I'm to serve you, remember?" he says smoothly. He's careful to keep his attention on Rian and not look at me. I can tell it's an effort for him.

"Right," says Rian, entirely unconvinced. His demeanor shifts slightly. He raises his chin in a very uncharacteristic way. Uncle does that, when he's trying to be stern. I look away to hide my amusement. It's very unlike Rian to act the way Mages tend to: Haughty and self-important. "Right now, you can help by allowing us to go in and eat our supper before it gets cold."

"*See?*" Flitt says through a yawn at my shoulder. "*There it is, that jealousy I was talking about. Hmm. What will Stinky do? Will they fight now?*"

'Certainly." Jac's eyes catch mine as I turn back to them. My heart skips and I offer him an apologetic smile. When I look away, I'm slightly annoyed at myself. Why do I allow him to affect me that way?

"Come on, Rian…" I tug his hand.

"Oh, go in and rest, Jac," Rian sighs. "None of us needs a guard." He pulls me inside without waiting for an answer.

The tavern is richly decorated, warm and welcoming. The great hearth takes up half of the far wall, and the guild has already made themselves at home among its patrons. In the short time since we've arrived, Mya has drawn a small crowd with her lute. At a long table beside her, Elliot nods off in his chair. His red hair seems to dance in the firelight as he dozes. Cort and Bryse have found the gamblers. Brother Donal is whispering with the barkeep while Dacva leans half-asleep against the bar with his chin in his hand.

The tavern is surprisingly occupied despite the late hour. The other patrons sprinkled around the dark room look up as we enter. Their interest isn't on me, but on Rian. It's rare to see a Mage outside of the city, especially with such a small party. When we had been traveling with the prince and princess, the inns where we stayed had been cleared out for us in advance. Now that our guild is on its own, there's no need for such measures. Rian and I cross to the others with strangers' eyes on us the entire time. Even after we sit, they watch us.

The tavern girls are busy laying out a spread for us. At the sight of the food and drink, I realize how famished I am. I drop into a chair beside Mum and Da, who are bent together with their hands twined, whispering. I pour some cider into Rian's goblet and my own, and I'm so thirsty that I drain it before Rian has a chance to do his spell. As I refill it, he brushes a finger over the lip of his own cup and whispers the spell. The table top rattles softly, and Mum's goblet tips over. Red wine seeps across the worn wood. She looks at Rian, wide-eyed.

"Did you drink any of that yet, Lisabella?" Rian asks my mum, who shakes her head slowly.

"Good," Rian says. He reaches across to his mother's goblet and looks inside. Mya stops playing. The tavern goes quiet as everyone turns to watch our table, which has started up again. It rumbles steadily and my cup tips and spills amber across the wood. Rian catches the flagon and his own cup before they do the same. The lingering taste of the cider I've already swallowed goes sour on my tongue. A barmaid rushes to us with rags to mop up Mum's wine and my cider, which are pooling together along the crevices in the wood and dancing like Elliot's hair in the firelight.

Rian says something, but his voice is far away. The light is beautiful. It flashes like the orange and yellow flecks in Flit's diamond. The barmaid wipes it away with her rag like a storm cloud blotting away the sun. I try to fight the strange sensation that spreads through me. It's like ants, thousands of ants that crawl on my skin. As they crawl I feel light, like I'm floating away. I try to shake it off, try to blink, even, but my body won't respond.

All around me I'm vaguely aware of my guild mates panicking. Rian is shaking my shoulders. Flitt's tiny hands bat at my cheek and tug my hair.

"Look at me, Sweeting," Mum is saying. Da's voice booms beside her. Flitt is talking, too. Her voice echoes in a faraway part of my mind. I try to reach it, but I can't. It's too far away. Brother Donal comes. I feel his healing spread through me. It isn't working, though. I push myself through the tingling, trying to fight back to them, but my eyes close slowly. I'm drifting away through the Half-Realm. Straight into the Dreaming.

It's dark until I become aware of the trees. They stretch up into the black sky all around me, their trunks so close together that I have to squeeze myself between them. I push through and I'm aware that I have no armor. Instead, I'm dressed in a scarlet gown that cinches my waist uncomfortably and swirls around my feet, threatening to trip me. I wander, clinging to the rough tree trunks while my eyes grow accustomed to the dark. I'm not afraid. I know if I can just find my way back to the tavern, I'll be safe. I find the beginning of a path where the brush is worn away and the trees have parted for me, and I follow it. Something compels me forward. I know this is the way I'm meant to go. All around me, the forest is silent. Watching ominously. I'd feel so much better in my armor, with my sword. I wonder if this place is like Kythshire. I wish for my sword and my armor, but they don't come to me. Ahead, I see a figure on the path. She's a woman, wearing the same gown as me and running toward me but making little progress. I speed my pace toward her, and as I near I realize that she's a Mage. Her golden hair is swept up on top of her head, and her high collar frames her face perfectly before it plunges daringly low. Her skin isn't pale like a Mage's, but bronzed by the sun. When I try to call to her, I have no voice. She's still running toward me, though, looking frightened. I skid to a stop right in front of her, and she mirrors the action. Her blue eyes meet mine, and that's when I realize it isn't another woman on the path. It's my reflection.

I press my hands to the glass and she stares at me. Her lips are painted red, her eyes lined with black. She says something to me. Something desperate and pleading.

"I can't hear you," I try to say, but my own voice is mute. A strange notion comes to me. I realize that somehow I'm the reflection and she's the real me. The true Azaeli. The thought makes me dizzy. She raises a hand and presses it against the glass on her side, against mine. Her lips move again. I pick out certain words, Mage's words. She's casting a spell. Between our hands, the mirror cracks. Her eyes flick to the space behind me, and in the mirror's reflection I see it, a moving shadow. Its shape changes. First it's the shadow of a man, then a fox-impostor. My reflection pushes against the glass and I pull my hand away just in time to avoid the shards as they shatter and fall to the ground.

Her hand closes around my wrist and she pulls me through to her side.

"Run," she says, "Go!"

Hearing my own voice this way is very disorienting. I can't seem to make my feet obey her command until she shoves me and tells me again. I run away from her and risk a glance over my shoulder to see her raise her hands and shout a spell. Lightning shoots from her fingertips toward the shadow. The lightning crashes again and I run faster, away from myself and the shadow, deep into the forest.

The trees twist and move around me, guiding my way as they had before. I know I shouldn't trust anything here, but I must. I have no choice. There's nowhere else to go but down the path that they create for me. Behind me the lightning fades away until all I can see are the black forms of tree trunks and the even blacker sky.

I run for what feels like hours down the never-changing, narrow path. Countless times I wish for my armor and my sword. The soft fabric of my gown feels foreign to me as it swirls around my legs; foolish and unprotected. I run as though I'm trying to get someplace. After a while I forget where I'm running to, or what I'm running from. The harder I try to remember, the more my memories elude me.

I slow my pace as dawn breaks in the distance, washing the distant trees in dull lavender. With the light comes clarity. I don't know where I am or where I'm going, but I know I don't belong here. I have to find a way out.

The path branches off and I pause at the fork. To my left it's just trees forever, as it has been. To my right I see my reflection again in the distance through the mist of morning. I start toward it and pause again. It's an obvious choice. If someone was trying to lure me, to trick me, that's the choice they'd expect me to make. But if they knew I was clever, they'd anticipate that choice and expect me to go down the other path. I shake my head. Logic was never my strength. I always leave the puzzles to him. His name has slipped my mind for now. I'll remember it later.

Besides, why do I assume someone is trying to trick me? There's a reason. A good one. I can't remember that either, though. Still, deep down I'm cautious and I trust my instincts. I take the left path, away from my reflection. An eerie quiet settles over me as I walk. There are no birds in this forest, no small creatures rustling in the underbrush.

The dim light of dawn lingers. With it comes a thick mist that settles over me. Droplets soak my hair and my gown and weigh me down. I walk endlessly until the woods begin to have a familiar feel to them. I've seen this tree with two low branches before, and I've passed this one with a knot that looks like a face. That's when I realize I've been going in circles, but for how long?

Exhausted and hopeless, I sink to the ground and hug my knees. I could go back. Back to the other path, to the mirror. Perhaps it wasn't a trick. Perhaps my reflection could help me again and I could escape this never ending path. But I've convinced myself that that way is a trap, and so I sit and think instead. In the quiet, I start to remember things beyond this nightmare.

"Rian!" I whisper. That's his name. And Flitt. Their faces swirl into my memory and I cling to them. I remember the tavern and the cider, and then some movement in the forest nearby steals away my attention. I turn and squint and see through the mist a flash of red fur and the swish of a white-tipped tail. A fox. He looks at me. His eyes are familiar and bright, not milky like the impostor.

"Elliot!" I jump up and squeeze between the tree trunks. The fox ambles toward me playfully and then bounds away again through gaps between trees so narrow that I have to shimmy between them.

"Wait!" I cry as my gown snags and tears against the rough bark. "I'm coming! Wait!" I yank at the caught fabric and curse. "Let go," I whisper. "Please!" I stumble forward as the fabric is freed and glance back at the tree in disbelief. I could swear that it leans toward me just slightly, as though bowing. I shake my head and spin, searching for the fox, and see it up ahead through another gap too narrow for me to squeeze through.

"Move, please?" I put a hand on each trunk and the trees bend apart. A rush of power surges through me at the discovery that I can manipulate the forest this way. "Thank you," I whisper as I pass through the gap.

Elliot is not as accommodating. I call for him to slow down, to wait for me, but he's in too much of a hurry. As I chase after him, I wish aloud again for my armor and my sword. My gown is cold and wet and too revealing. I feel foreign in it, and I long for the protection and comfort of my own things.

"You don't need them," the forest whispers around me.

"Don't need them."

"Don't need them."

"Not here."

I spin around to find the source of them, but there are only trees. Even the fox is gone, and everything is still again.

"Please," I whisper. "Who's there?"

"We all are. We're here." I can pick out the voices. Dozens of tiny whispers that echo in the forest around me and also in my mind.

"Who?" I cry, and my voice is snuffed out by their hisses.

"Shh! He'll hear! Hurry!" they cry.

"Hurry!"

"Hurry!"

Red fur streaks along the edge of my vision and I spin and chase after it. A touch from my fingers and a whisper bends the tree trunks to my will. Knowing this secret makes the chase much easier. This new power surges through me with such a rush that I can't help but laugh as I amble through the forest. I can see where the fox is leading me now. All around me the forest is bare and gray except for a curtain of willow fronds that shimmer gold and green ahead. Elliot disappears through them and I crash in behind him.

Everything goes dark again, heavy and desolate. At first I think I've made a grave mistake. I turn to leave, but there are no willow fronds. Something grabs at my skirts and chaos erupts.

"*Help us*," a hundred voices assault my mind, and then I see them. One by one, tiny faces appear in the darkness. They might be fairies if they weren't so horrid looking. I can see only glimpses. Their eyes are dark and wide, pleading and desperate. Their skin hangs off of their emaciated little bodies. Their wings are stubs at their backs. Still, they hold hope when they look at me, and I understand that I'm all that they have. I'm their only way.

"Please," they whisper, and my heart bends to them like the tree trunks that parted beneath my fingertips. "Please, help us."

"She was right behind me. I had her," a familiar voice echoes through the darkness. "Azi?" it calls. The fox. Elliot.

Cold little hands grip my fingertips, my arms, and my hair.

"Please don't go. Please help us. Please."

I don't belong here. I belong there, out there with the fox. But these creatures need me. They're desperate. I have to do something.

"How?" I ask them. "How can I help you?" The fox calls me

again, but it's slipping farther away. I can barely hear it anymore. "Who are you?"

"We are the fallen."

"The fallen."

"Forgotten."

"The last."

"Homeless."

"Helpless."

"Nowhere to go."

"Help us."

"Help us."

"How?" I ask as Elliot's voice fades away, and somehow I know I've made my choice. For now, I'm staying here. The fallen creatures cling to me desperately, stroking my hair, whispering their thanks. As my eyes adjust to the darkness I can see them more clearly and I realize that I've seen them before. If not these, then similar fae, dancing among the roots of trees, crouched over a red tablet, taking orders from Sorcerers.

I watched them from Elliot's back as he brought me on a tour of Sunteri to show me the desolation there, just before our battle at the Keep. I remember the Wellspring, nearly drained of its magic.

"Yes. You see," they whisper all around me.

"Our home."

"Our life."

"Drained."

"*Stolen.*"

"Destroyed."

"Desolated."

"*Dying.*"

"Help us."

"Help us."

"*Help us.*"

"I will," I say. "I am. I'll help. Tell me how."

More of them flock to me, surrounding me. They're timid and shaken at first, but I stay still and they come and cling to me. I have such pity for them that my heart feels like it might shatter into a thousand pieces. I can feel their fear like a wound in my soul. They remind me so much of Flitt that my eyes sting with tears. I can't imagine her this way, so broken and drained.

"Who did this to you?" I whisper.

"Not one. Many," comes the answer. "Many and slow."

"Dark ones."

"*Sorcerers.*"

"Not to be trusted."

"What can I do?" I ask. One of them nuzzles my neck and I pat it gently. Again I'm reminded of Flit.

"Speak for us."

"Speak for us."

"In Kythshire. Speak for us."

"In Kythshire."

"Help us."

"Help us restore it."

"Help us go home."

"I will," I whisper. "I'm going there soon. I'll ask them if they can help. I promise."

"She promises. She said it."

"Go now, quickly."

"Back to the fox."

"Away, he comes."

"Dreamwalker."

They pull me to my feet in the direction Elliot disappeared, and I let them guide me. The darkness grows impossibly darker as I move through it, and I feel something bearing down on us, closer and closer. One by one the drained creatures fade away. I can't see or feel anything. Just when I fear I'll be swallowed up by the darkness and suffocated, something shifts. The light blinds me and I gasp for air.

Chapter Seventeen:
HERE AND THERE
Azi

I come to on the floor of the inn with the faces of half of my guild swimming over me, almost as though I'm seeing them from beneath some glassy surface. I feel the pressure of it on my chest and try again to breathe. My lungs burn painfully and my head is pounding.

"Give her space," Brother Donal says, and everyone except for Mum and Da backs away. They're holding my hands but I can still feel the tiny, cool fingers around my fingertips even though I know they aren't here. I left them behind, trapped someplace awful, threatened by some nightmarish shadow. I made a promise. I'll save them. I'll help them. I meet Mum's eyes.

"We have to go. Me and Rian. Now. It can't wait. They need help." I try to sit up but Brother Donal pushes me down again gently. My chest aches and I fall into a fit of coughing that makes my head throb with pain as I fight for breath.

"Slow down, Azaeli," Donal says. "Slow down and breathe. Water, Dacva." His tone is so peaceful and quiet it's almost disinterested. It infuriates me. I try to get up again and he presses his hands to my shoulders and looks at Mum and Da. "She needs to lie still."

I close my eyes until Dacva comes back with a pitcher. Rian is right behind him asking questions. At the sound of his voice, I fight to sit up again.

"Rian," I try to reach for him but they're still holding my hands, keeping me down. He takes the cup from Dacva and helps me drink it, and it cools the burn in my throat. His eyes linger for a moment on my neck and then he and Mum exchange a worried glance.

"What did you find?" Brother Donal asks Rian as he helps me sip.

"Nothing," Rian scowls. "Nothing unusual at all."

"Curious," Donal sighs. "Well, at least she's coming to, now." He brushes a hand over my head and whispers, and the tingling sensation of healing washes my headache away.

"I told you," Rian murmurs, "you should've just let me sip it. I could have had her back with us much sooner."

As the two argue, I become aware of other voices farther away. Mya speaking with the barkeep. Bryse and Da shouting at someone outside. Cort trying to quiet them. Others whispering.

"Look, she thinks she's back."

"Back with her friends."

"Back in the smoky place."

"She isn't?"

"No, she isn't."

"No, she isn't. Not all the way."

"She can't be."

"She promised."

"But she left."

"Not really."

"She's in both places."

"Yes, clever girl."

The whispers come from far away, from that place beyond the darkness, a vast distance from the tavern. The forest with the fallen fairies. The Dreaming. My eyes drift closed as it pulls at me.

"Oh, no, Azi! She's fading again," Mum says from what sounds like the far end of a long tunnel. Her hand is heavy on mine, more solid.

"Azi, look at me. Open your eyes," Rian says. I try to, but my eyelids don't seem to want to do as I bid them. When I force them, I feel a lurch forward. I'm the rope in a game of tug of war. One side is reality, where my parents grip me tightly and Rian calls my name, and the other side is the Dreaming, where the whispering of fallen fairies lures me back.

"Promised, she did."

"Do you remember it, girl? The promise?"

"Speak for us!"

"Speak for us."

"Yes, in Kythshire," I whisper aloud.

Rian calls my name and holds me, but I don't feel him. Just like they said, I'm not there. Not really. I'm looking at all of them now, kneeling on the wood floor, holding me. Mum, Da, Rian, Donal. I see them from another perspective, as though I'm watching through the glass again at myself and the scene playing out around me. My body there fades away until Rian's hands are pressed to the wood floor and Mum and Da kneel staring at their empty palms.

"*I understand*," Rian pushes to me, and then it all goes black again.

"What just happened?" I whisper into the darkness.

"You sent your message, and now we must go, quickly!" the voices answer.

"No." I blink into the darkness. My heart is racing with anger and confusion. "Not until you tell me exactly what's happening. Am I really here, or am I there? Is this a dream, or isn't it? If it's not, then why am I dressed like this? I'll help you, but I need to have my things. My armor, my sword." My hand flies to my neck to feel for the cord that holds the pouch with Flitt's diamond. It's gone. I sink to my knees onto the soft, mossy ground. I wish I could see. "Why is it so dark?" I whisper mostly to myself, since the voices have gone silent.

"He's coming. You must go. Quickly," one brave whisper warns me.

I'm aware of someone running toward me with quick, light footsteps. At first I imagine the fox, but whatever it is sounds bigger. As it nears, I push myself to my feet. Aside from the quickened breath of my approacher and its footsteps, everything is silent. As it nears I'm aware of something else. Not something I can see or hear, but I can feel it like a fog creeping toward me. A dark energy, strong and confident. The softer footsteps quicken and I try to duck away from whoever it is, but we collide and she cries out as we tumble to the ground together.

"Who's there?" we whisper in unison. The voice is familiar. I try to place it.

"It doesn't matter. It's coming. We have to run. Now!" She grabs my arm and pulls me up, and we crash through the dark forest together. My eyes have adjusted now, but it's still too dark to make out anything but vague forms. I risk a glance at the woman beside me, half expecting to see myself again, but her hair is too dark and her figure too lithe. Her fur cloak spreads out behind her as she runs, and her bow is gripped tightly in her other hand.

"Ki?" I whisper.

"Not now," she answers breathlessly. "Just run!"

Far ahead of us I can make out a golden glow between the trees, warm and inviting. Lovely sounds echo from within: laughter, music, birds chirping. It reminds me of the Ring in Kythshire. I push my legs harder in my effort to reach it. The faster I run, the farther away it seems.

"Here, quick!" Ki takes my arm again and points to a different escape as we skid to a halt. This one is a tiny cave mouth, dank and dark. Before I can argue she shimmies into it. I watch as her black hair is the last thing to be swallowed up by the darkness, and I glance again at the welcoming golden light through the trees ahead.

"Whatever you see up there, it isn't real," she calls from the cave. "Don't trust it!"

With the darkness creeping ever closer, I'm close to panic. I can't let it reach me, but my instinct screams at me not to trust Ki, even though she isn't who she used to be. The golden light seems the best choice, but it's too obvious. She's right. It's probably a trap. Tendrils of the darkness lick toward me as it nears. There's little time to think. I dive into the cave mouth and I'm instantly assaulted by bright light.

It's as though I've emerged in the midst of a deep blue summer sky. I cover my eyes as the effect makes them water and burn.

"Step in a little closer," she whispers. When I do, the light dims.

"What—?" I start, but she hushes me. She's pressed against the rocky wall of the cave. At her throat, a dainty blue stone shines brightly. It casts a beam of light across to the opposite wall where the cave mouth we just passed through stands gaping. The light from her necklace cascades like a waterfall over it, concealing us from the outside. I'm reminded of my own necklace and Flitt, and my heart aches with remorse and fear. How could I have lost it again? Is Flitt safe? Ki's wide eyes are fixed on on the blue wall, her finger pressed to her lips. I turn and watch. Beyond the wall, I can see the darkness creeping. Even though it's formless, I get the sense of a man within it. Someone powerful and dangerous. Someone not to be trifled with.

Ki steps closer, placing herself between me and the darkness as it creeps past the cave mouth. Her bow is loaded, pointed at the glowing wall. To me it feels pointless. I doubt an arrow would do anything at all to the powerful force searching for us. Still, I find myself wishing for my sword again as it pauses at the cave mouth. I don't like feeling defenseless.

For what seems like hours we stand motionless, pressed against the cold stone, silently on edge as we wait for darkness to pass. When it finally does and sunlight begins to splash and pool against the light from her necklace, Ki turns to me.

"Dawn," she says. "I'll be waking soon." She brushes the stone at her throat with her fingertips and the wall of light that blocks the opening fades away.

"Wait, you're dreaming? You're not really here?" I ask her. She seemed solid when she touched me before. It's all very confusing.

"I am. I'm here, and I'm dreaming. Aren't you?"

"No," I frown and look down at my strange red gown. "I don't know. When I woke in the tavern, I was in my armor. I watched myself fade away. And now I'm here, dressed this way, and all of my things are gone. But if I'm not there, if I watched myself disappear…" I press my fingertips to my brow. "I don't understand."

"Confusion is a way of life here in the dreaming." Ki slides her arrow back into the sheath at her hip and pushes her long, loose hair over her shoulder.

"They said I was in both places," I sink back against the wall. "They said it was clever of me."

"Who did?" she creeps close to the opening and looks out cautiously.

"The little ones. I think they were fairies once." I answer and follow her gaze. It's bright and cheerful outside now. The threat is gone.

"The fallen, from Sunteri?" she asks. She turns to me and I catch the sadness in her eyes before she looks away again.

"You know them?" I ask. She nods. "Where did they go?"

"Into hiding. They fear him. The darkness. I imagine it's even more frightening to them than it is to us. I can't know for certain, though. They won't speak to me. They fear me, too."

"Oh," I frown. It makes sense that they wouldn't trust her. I was a witness to Viala's cruelty to Flit and the other fairies she encountered. Still, I have to remind myself that this is Ki, not Viala. Viala is gone. "Why are you here?"

"Nightmares," she looks away. "Iren says they're of a time long past, but still they punish me. Things I did. People I forsook. In waking they're forgotten, but in Dreaming, they plague me. He plagues me." She lifts her chin toward the outside. "Dreamwalker."

"Who is he?" I ask.

"Someone wicked. Someone who wants to cause pain. He's so

consumed by his own darkness that he wants nothing else but to inflict it on others and watch them suffer."

"But who is he, really?"

"I don't know." She closes her fingers around the stone necklace. "I wish I did. I've been trying to figure it out, but I can't get close enough to him. Iren tells me if I'm discovered here, it could destroy me. My fealty is to the Crag, so I have to tread carefully in this place. I'm learning how to keep myself hidden from him and watch. To gather information for Iren and Kythshire." She tips her head to the side, as if listening for something. "I'm waking now. Be safe, Lady Azaeli. Travel only by day. Iren says the border is open to you if you seek it."

"Can't I go with you?" I ask her. "You could guide me, couldn't you? To Kythshire?"

"I wish I could, but it doesn't work like that. Our paths can cross in Dreaming, but we have to find our own way out. Your way is different than mine. I'm sorry. I'll seek you out tonight, if you're still here. Good-bye." She fades slowly away, leaving me alone in the cave.

My first thought is to try to get to Kythshire through the Half-Realm. It's easy enough to do it in waking, and so I imagine it will be just as easy in Dreaming. I start to doubt myself, though, when I begin. Rian is usually the one to lift the Revealer and settle us completely into the Half-Realm. I wish I knew how he pulled us back in so easily.

Come to think of it, now that I'm without him, I wish I knew many of the things Rian knows. His shield wards would be useful here, as would his offensive spells. We could survive together without my armor and my sword because of his magic. He has a spell of direction that would certainly guide me to Kythshire. The more I think about it, the more my heart aches for him. I need him by my side. We belong together.

"Rian," I whisper and I wait, half-expecting him to come to me somehow. He doesn't, though. No one does. The cave is damp and cold, and the darkness reminds me of the Dreamwalker. I squeeze myself out into the sunlight with no regard for the delicate fabric of my gown that catches and tears on the jagged rocks. When I emerge, I gasp in wonder at the sight that greets me.

A sunlit meadow stretches out from the mouth of the cave, sprinkled with flowers of red, orange, yellow, and purple. The trees, so close and ominous last night are wondrous in the daylight. The scene is so vibrant and lush that I can almost taste the color on my tongue. I'm greeted by a flock of blue and gold finches that dive and rise playfully before they settle in the flowers to drink their nectar. Their song fills the air around me, lifting my spirits and urging me forward, away from the cave. I close my eyes and drink in the lovely scent of blossoms kissed by sunlight as the soft breeze plays in my hair. Out here, Kythshire seems possible. Anything does.

Kythshire. I imagine Flitt's grotto, with its sparkling clear water and bubbling waterfall. I picture Rian standing knee-deep in the pool and chuckle. When that doesn't work, I think of the Ring, with its perfect circle of whitecap mushrooms and the gathering of fairies who dance and discuss. I whisper the names of places as I think of them in my effort to get there.

"The Ring. The Grotto. The Crag. The field, the Wel—"

"Shh!"

I'm startled to my senses as the shushing drags out to a low hiss. My eyes fly open and search the meadow and the trees, but I see no one. Not even a shadow. At my feet, the flowers rustle and the ground starts to shift. I stumble backwards as a lump of earth stands on two feet and a curious creature looks up at me.

"Not too smart, is she? But she is pretty, yes. I've seen her before, but no, no, she isn't the same one. This one's got more to her. Come down here, girl." I sink to my knees in the tall grass and come to his eye level. We look each other over carefully, cautiously. His face is flat and dirt-covered, with a wide mouth and big, amber eyes. He wears a shell-like chest plate, and on his back lush fronds of grass and bright orange flowers grow from a hump that reminds me of a turtle's shell. In fact, he could be a turtle, were it not for his human-like hands and feet and his size. If the two of us were both standing, he'd come to my waist.

"What is her name?" he asks me.

"Azi," I answer, a little confused.

"Oh, no," he says. "Her full name. With titles. She has titles, I can tell."

"Azaeli Hammerfel," I start, and he waits for the rest. I don't like spouting off my titles. It makes me feel conceited. But he asked for them, and somehow I feel obliged. "Sir Azaeli Hammerfel, Knight of His Majesty's Elite," I take a deep breath and try to remember all of the titles Crocus bestowed on me, "The Temperate, Pure of Heart, Reviver of Iren, The Great Protector, and Cerion's Ambassador to Kythshire." I let out a long breath and press my fingertips to my cheeks, which I'm sure are as red as they are hot. "And, you are?"

"Stubs." He grins and bows.

"Sorry? Just Stubs?" I blink in disbelief.

"She doesn't need to rub it in," he says, sounding dejected. "Yes, just Stubs. I'm only a field knoll, after all. Nothing special. No grand titles, like she has." He peers up at me and looks me over carefully.

"Hm, something else about her," he says. "She bears the Mage seal. Apprentice?" He points to my forehead with a stubby finger, where Rian touched me at the moment I agreed to become his student.

"No," I shake my head. "Not really." Becoming Rian's student was a quick and necessary decision, and I never pursued it. Mages are only allowed one student at a time. In choosing me as his, he was able to share secrets with me that were necessary for the protection of Kythshire against the Sorcerers. It also prevented Viala from coercing him into her plots to perhaps begin secretly teaching magic to Prince Eron. That seems like a lifetime ago, though. I had forgotten all about it since. Rian knows I have no interest in learning magic. I have a healthy respect for the Arcane arts and prefer to leave them to those more suited to learn.

"She's been accepted, though. Claimed by a teacher. Why not pursue it?" He blinks at me slowly.

"I have no interest. I'm a knight. A swordswoman."

"A swordswoman, no sword," he reaches up and scratches at his nose.

"No. I left my sword behind, and my armor." I try not to make a face as little clumps of soil tumble from his nostrils.

"Behind where? Wasn't very fitting of a swordswoman."

"Where I fell asleep. In the tavern, with my family. Please, do you know how I can leave here? I need to get to—"

"Kythshire. Yes, I heard her shouting all about it. The Grotto. The Crag. Shouting all over the meadow. Even almost said the one thing she oughtn't, didn't she?"

He's right, I did. I almost mentioned the Wellspring aloud. I was careless.

"I thought I was alone," I scowl.

"Never. She is never alone here," he warns. The grass on his humpback sways as he shakes his head. "She'd be wise to remember that."

"Please," I say desperately. "Can you tell me how to find my way?"

"Same way to find anything," he says with a shrug. "By looking. Sometimes we must look in places we don't want to, hm? Use methods we don't like?" He scratches at his soil-covered head and squints as he pushes his finger in and digs out a grub, which he holds up between two fingers. "No biting!" he scolds, and tosses it to the ground before turning his slow-blinking attention back to me.

"I'm not sure I follow," I say as I watch the grub burrow into the earth near the toe of my boot.

"Magic," he says. "I can teach it to her. Then she can find her way, hm? Yes?"

"How will learning spells help me leave here?"

"Magic," he corrects me. "Not spells. It's different. Everything here is made of it. Even me. Learn it, and she will find her way." He leans closer to me and clasps his hands, his amber eyes hopeful as he anticipates my response.

"Why?" I ask. His eagerness only makes me more wary. I'm not a Mage. Not here, not anywhere. I'm a knight. I wield steel, not magic. "Why do you want to help me?"

"Because we share a common enemy, we do," he says, and lowers his voice. "He walks in the shadows. Tampers. Frightens. He thinks all of this belongs to him, and it doesn't. It doesn't. It is ours and theirs. It is to be shared but he snuffs it with darkness and makes us hide away in the night. He reaches across into the waking and plucks his strings and makes them dance, and their dreams become dark and twisted, and so does their waking. And we can do nothing. Then, she comes with her titles. She who can walk in both realms and in-between. She who is loved and brings love. She will need her sword and her magic together to stop him. He's her enemy, too." He looks up at me with his deep amber eyes. "The Dreamwalker."

M. Sheldrake
2016

Chapter Eighteen:

MENTALISM

Azi

Stubs proves a strange but welcome guide in this new world that I feel so trapped in. He leads me through the tall grasses and shows me where to step in order to avoid hurting anything or disturbing creatures that are best left undisturbed. With the sunlight warm on my skin, the place doesn't seem nearly as daunting or threatening. In fact, it's very pleasant here. Almost as much as Kythshire. Almost enough to make me want to stay and forget about all the things that seemed so important to me only yesterday. I recognize the magic of this place, though. It's meant to do just that: to make me forget, to make me want to stay and never leave. I remember Iren's words to me only days ago: *Memory is a most precious commodity. It empowers us. It makes us who we are.* I can't forget, or I will lose myself to this place.

"Here now, will she sit?" Stubs gestures to a soft, grassy spot in the middle of the meadow and I gather my skirts and have a seat.

"All right," I say, still a little wary of his lessons. "How do we start?"

"First, we practice See What I See. She will do to me, yes? Look through my eyes. Go on."

"What? How? I can't—"

"No saying "can't!' Do it. Imagine it. What I must see. Go on," he taps his cheek just below his eye with a grubby finger. "Look."

It takes me a while of staring at him before I get it. First, I see myself reflected in his great amber eyes, looking back at him with my blue ones. When I lean in closer and peer a little deeper, the space between us starts to shift. My eyes start to tingle pleasantly, and the sensation spreads through me slowly as my perspective changes. It's very disorienting at first when I look up at myself through Stubs's eyes.

The meadow is more golden from his perspective, larger and far more beautiful. I take myself in as well, this woman before me. The red of my gown is so bright that it's jarring, and my blonde hair seems to glow in the sunlight. With the sight of myself comes emotions that aren't my own: curiosity, admiration.

Part of me wants to look away. It's too imposing, too personal to be inside of someone else's view this way. As I withdraw, I become more aware of my own body and the sensation of pure delight and power that charges through me. Magic. My toes and fingertips are pleasantly numb, my head is oddly, wonderfully light.

I dip my attention to Stubs again and the euphoria rises in me as I look back at my own face once more. My lips are plump and red, my eyes such bright blue that they rival the sky. My skin shimmers soft and bronze in the sun. Elegant golden lines curl slowly from my chest onto my neck. They remind me of the Mark, but these aren't wicked. They shine with light, and are elegant as filigree on the frame of a fine painting. They enhance me.

"Good, good!" Stubs says. "She's got it! Now, try another."

"Another?" I ask a little vacantly as I slide my perspective back to my own eyes again. The lovely sensation of magic flowing through me fades slowly, and with it comes a desire to fill myself up again with it. Restraint, I often heard Uncle telling Rian, is the most important aspect of training in magic. Now I understand why. This feeling is so delicious that the need for it could easily consume me. "I don't understand, Stubs. How is this going to help me? I need to get to Kythshire and I don't see—"

"Knowing." Stubs raises a finger to his temple and taps it, causing a cascade of soil to tumble down his flat cheek. "Knowing this way, what others see, it is a boon. She will understand in time. Now, this time, look deeper. See my past. Hm?"

He blinks up at me and I'm incredibly tempted to do it again, but I stop myself and shake my head.

"I won't, Stubs," I say firmly. "I'm not a Mage. Besides, I have questions. Things here don't make sense. If I'm truly here, why were my armor and sword left behind? And my necklace, too? Why did I see another of myself when I arrived? Was she really me? Why can't I travel as I have in the past, to all of the places I know of in Kythshire? How do I find my way? Sitting here isn't accomplishing anything."

"Look and see. I will show her. Look. Just once more. Come." He takes my hand and gazes up at me. "Look, Lady Knight." My curiosity in the face of all these questions wins out over my attempt at restraint. Against my better judgment, I want to feel that rush again. I look at him and see myself, and then he widens his eyes and I tumble away, far away, into Stubs' memories of a time long past.

I'm alone in the same meadow, but my viewpoint is much lower as though I'm peering up through a hole dug in the earth. The night is falling quickly, and somehow I know that with the darkness come other things. Wicked things. My view is obscured by tall grass, but I don't dare move. Robes rustle through the grass nearby and three figures approach: a woman, a man, and a younger man perhaps a little older than I am.

"See now, my child, how lovely? You will be safe here. This place will protect you," the woman pauses and takes the younger man gently by the shoulders. In the waning sunlight, I can see the Mark on the woman's face, curling up from her jaw to her brow. She wipes a tear from his eye and he looks away.

"I don't care. I don't like it. I want to stay with you, Mother!" he cries.

"Enough, Jacek. You know we're only doing what's best for you," the man with them says sternly. His cold, distant demeanor is a stark contrast to the woman's. The Mark on him is so prominent that only a hint of his yellowish skin peeks out between the blue-black lines. Instead of covering them up, he wears a rich, sleeveless red robe that ties loosely at his waist and displays them proudly, like a trophy.

"You know what we've had to do to bring you here," the older man says. "This place will keep you safe. You are to remain until we return for you. You can do what you like until then. Anything you like. Do you understand? Stop sniveling. You should be grateful." His tone tells me he's the sort of man who doesn't tolerate being challenged.

"Yes, Father," Jacek looks down shamefully. As the sunlight fades and the meadow goes gray, the woman holds him close and sings a sweet song to him. I've heard it before. Mya used to sing it to Rian and me sometimes. We called it the Sunteri song.

"Dineae. Say goodbye," the man says impatiently.

"Just a moment longer, Corbin. Perhaps we can stay through the night?" Dinaea presses her face into Jacek's hair and the boy looks straight at me. His eyes are dark, his hair long and black. He and the other two are vaguely familiar, but I can't quite place them.

"We've gone over this. Don't be weak. We can't linger. Come." Corbin takes her by the arm and lifts her to her feet. Her eyes lock with

Jacek's as she and Corbin fade away. When they're gone, Jacek sinks to his knees in the grass and weeps.

The scene before me shimmers and I'm in a memory of the meadow again. This time it's night, but I have a sense that quite a lot of time has passed. Years, perhaps. A figure moves among the tall grass, dark and ominous. His robes billow out behind him like a storm cloud. He flicks a finger and several nearby lumps of earth rumble and rise and shake themselves off. They're creatures, like Stubs, and it's clear that they're under this man's control. He turns toward me and his dark eyes flash with mischief as the corner of his mouth curves into a smile. Again he gestures and I feel Stubs' limbs move under his direction.

What follows sends chills through me. I can hardly bear to watch as Jacek makes his commands and the hatred that surges through Stubs is so strong I can taste it. All around me, the other field knolls bare their teeth and charge each other, gnashing and snarling and sending tufts of grass flying. As Stubs joins in the fray, Jacek's laughter echoes over the meadow. There's no way for them to fight it. Pain surges through me as one of them yanks a handful of grass from my back. I whirl and lash out and bite off its stubby finger and it screams in agony.

This is wrong, I think to myself as I pommel my opponent with my knobby fist. We are peaceful. We are kind. This is not our way. The thought brings clarity with it. I push away the hate. I fight it. I find my heart and cling to it until my fist is my own again, but it's too late. My opponent, my friend, it's too late for him. Jacek's laughter creeps over all of us like a dense fog, but it can't touch me now. I'm too aware. He has no power over me. I should fight him, try to stop him, for my brothers' sake, but I don't. I'm too confused, too frightened by this young man and the power he wields over us. I sink into the earth and bury myself. I grieve for my brothers and wait the evil to pass.

With a gasp, I'm jolted back to the present. I fall back into grass and gaze up into the deep blue sky. My limbs feel so light that I could be floating, and my head is spinning, tingling pleasantly. Despite what I just saw, I'm smiling. The sensation of magic surging through me is too wonderful to ignore. As the feeling slowly fades, I'm assaulted by the information I've learned. It horrifies and angers me, and it makes me want to do more, to wield more magic and push the uneasiness away. I want to fill myself up with that power again, so I don't have to think about anything else.

"Lady Knight?" Stubs's cautious whisper brings me to my

senses. My thoughts are of Dineae, Corbin, and Jacek. I remember now.

"The Sorcerers." I close my eyes. "The mother and father. They were at the keep. The battle in Kythshire. They were the first ones we encountered." I remember Iren blowing flecks of golden dust at Dinaea and Corbin on the balcony. I remember watching them thrown against the keep wall, seeing them slide lifelessly to the rubble below. "They didn't survive." I prop myself up on one elbow and look at Stubs. "That first memory. How long ago was it?"

"In her time, years," he answers. "Our time moves differently. Days are slower." He watches me and I start to slide into his great amber eyes again. This time, I ache to go there. My skin prickles with the need to feel that floating again. I want to soar in my own skin, to lose myself. Instead I stop myself and look away.

"So this man, Jacek, he has been here for years?"

"Such a long time. Every day he grows stronger, and every night he creeps and brings his fear. He is king here now. He rules the Dreaming. We are all too terrorized by him to stop him. All of us who are left."

"But, why? To what end?"

"It started as boredom. Loneliness, we imagine. We were his playthings. It was his way of keeping occupied. But as he grew in power and discovered how much he could own, he didn't stop. As the son of two Sorcerers, is she surprised by this? He has no regard for our world, or any world. He walks in dreams and reaches through to the Waking and tweaks and pulls and manipulates. He touches things that oughtn't be touched. He makes his plans. He holds his sway. He grows, and none here are brave enough to stand against him. He is no longer Jacek now. All of us call him something else."

"Dreamwalker," I whisper. The sensation of magic coursing through me is fading, and creeping over me in its place are depression and exhaustion. My arms and legs are heavy. I can barely keep my eyes open.

"Yes," Stubs sighs. "Dreamwalker. I know she is tired now. It is to be expected. But there is one last thing she must learn, and she is such a fast learner, hm?" He smiles apologetically and blinks his wide eyes, and despite my weariness, I agree once more and gaze into them.

"Good," he says, sounding rather tired himself. "This time," his voice is distant and coaxing, "she will do what Jacek did. She will move me herself. Make me do something, I won't say what, so she will believe it was her own doing. Think about it and do it, Lady Knight."

I don't know if it's my exhaustion or my repulsion to the idea of controlling someone else that keeps me from picking this bit of magic up as quickly. It takes me a long time to achieve the effect Stubs is so keen on teaching me. He doesn't want me to sink into him this time, as I do when I see through his eyes. I have to do it from the outside, so that I can remain within myself.

The sun slowly climbs into noon and then starts to dip lower. It's hours before I finally make his arm raise up. Magic surges through me, prickling my skin, charging me with its power. I push harder as it courses over me. I imagine strings that flow from my fingertips to his arms and legs. I make him walk, I make him run until he's breathless and stumbling over his own feet. It's difficult for me to stop, as filled with elation as I am, but when he blurs past me I see the fear in his eyes, the pleading, and I let go.

He stumbles and rolls to a stop in the grass before me, panting. The tantalizing sensation caused by magic drains away, and in its place I'm filled with an awful sense of dread and exhaustion. My first instinct is to do more, more magic to fill me up again, but I fight the urge. Stubs' gasping for breath on the grass before me frightens me. I did this to him, and he had no way of stopping me. The notion makes me sick to my stomach. Why did I agree to such a thing? This isn't me. I'm a swordswoman, not a Mage. Not a Sorcerer.

"Stubs, I'm so sorry." I crawl to him and stroke a frond of grass from his face as he shakes his head at me and brushes my hand away.

"She did what I taught her," he says breathlessly. "She learned it well." His eyes drift closed as he continues. "Now she must rest, while she is safe in the light. Tonight, she will see into the Dreamwalker. She will learn things. She will stop him."

"What? No, Stubs…" I shake his arm gently. "How can I manage to see inside him without him suspecting? What good will it do? He's a Sorcerer, isn't he? Wouldn't it be better to learn how to defend myself against him? What you've taught me isn't enough to defeat him. I need my sword at least. Tell me how to arm myself."

"Not defeat, only look. She must believe in herself," he says sleepily. "She is already armed. Rest now. Rest, Lady Knight. While it is still light." He curls up with his head tucked beneath his grassy hump so that he looks like a small hillock in the rolling meadow, and snores.

The absence of magic leaves me feeling bleak and empty. It

sends me to dark places, even as exhausted as I am. What if I never leave this place? What if I'm like Jacek, trapped until someone comes to release me? Trapped forever because my captors have died? Will I ever see Rian or Flitt again? Or my own parents?

I gaze at the golden Mark that curls down my arm and into my palm. What am I now? What forbidden rules have I broken? What will Uncle say? What will Rian say? Will I lose him? Despair washes over me. They will cast me out. Even if I am able to leave the Dreaming, things won't ever be the same. I've Marked myself, and the worst part of all of it is even as I lie here lamenting about it, I want more. Just a little more, to feel that wonderful vibration again.

A flock of birds dips and rises across the meadow, and I fix my attention on just one of them. I push myself to it easily and see the ground far below, speeding past in a blur. Magic charges through me, relieving the gloom, filling me up with its bliss. Reluctantly I pull myself away after a while of soaring and immediately I regret my decision to try one last push. My head drops back into the grass, and I pass out straight away.

I wake to darkness and a sense of foreboding. There is no twittering flock of birds now, no gentle breeze to carry the scent of blooms to me. Something lurks nearby, something heavy and grim. Slowly I reach out to Stubs to rouse him, but he isn't there. There's just a mound of earth covered in tall grasses, so convincingly still that I begin to wonder whether he had ever been here with me at all.

That's when panic sets in. I'm not ready to face the Dreamwalker alone. I don't know enough. I'm too weak, I don't have my sword. I see him now, creeping ever closer across the meadow, his black cloak spreading out behind him like a shroud of darkness that smothers everything in its wake. I try to scramble away but the grass is too noisy, so I freeze where I am and hold my breath.

The little sound I've made has given me away, and though I try my hardest to lie flat in the grass, he approaches. I hold my breath as I watch him near. He's older now than the boy whose parents left him in the meadow. Older than I am by ten years or so. His face is narrow and gaunt, his dark eyes circled and blackened by the Mark.

I try to imagine the strings as he approaches, like I did with Stubs. It's my only hope of keeping him away. I envision them like golden lines that curl around his feet in the tall grass. I try to make him turn and leave. He laughs, and I'm surprised by the pleasant tone of his voice.

"Have you been amusing yourself all day in the meadow, then?" he asks with amusement. "I enjoyed it here as well, when I first arrived. So many playthings. But they grow dull after a while."

I don't answer. I hold my breath and try again, willing him to move away, to leave. I'm bolstered by the magic that courses through me. It makes me feel alive. Confident. Again, he laughs.

"Oh, my darling," he says. "I'm so pleased by all you've learned, and in such a short amount of time. Stubs is a fine teacher. We shall do well together, you and I. Come now, let me see you."

I glance at the lump of earth in front of me, where one amber eye watches from the soil beneath the grasses. I don't know what to think. The only way Jacek could know it was Stubs who taught me is if he was in on it. The eye closes quickly when I meet it with my own, and disappears into the earth again.

Shaken, I slide back to put distance between myself and Jacek, who is slowly closing in on me. My heart is racing. I don't know what to think anymore. I trusted Stubs, but why? Should I have? The golden curls of the Mark on my arms and legs glow softly in the starlight.

"What have I done?" I whisper to myself.

"You did what you thought to be right, Azaeli," Jacek soothes. "It took me some time to figure you out. Once I did, you were quite simple to manipulate. You see, my dear, you have a strong drive to save people. Or creatures, as the case may be. And you are trusting, but you trust in yourself more than others. So I had you greet yourself at the mirror. I had you coax yourself in. Once the promise was made, the wheels were set in motion. Now you have the drive, you see. Now, you will go to Kythshire to speak for them. I knew those pathetic whelps would come in handy, Azaeli, and they did. Most certainly. Come and look, my sweet. I know you have questions. I have the answers for you right here."

His voice is so alluring, and the temptation along with it to use magic again and feel it coursing through me is difficult to resist. He can tell me what I need to know, everything I want to know. He can give me answers. Maybe I can find out how to leave this place, how to get back to Rian and Flitt.

I'm worried about them. It must be difficult to reach me here, or I'm certain they would be by my side by now. Maybe he knows how I can reach them. Still, some small part of me screams out in warning. Run away. Run and don't look back. I stand up and turn away, and his voice is sweet in my ear just as I start to run.

"Where will you run? Everything here belongs to me. Come and look, Azaeli. See my kingdom and all of its little pleasures. I have things, you see. Many things. Some forgotten, some thought to be lost forever. Come, my sweet, beautiful lady. Come with me and see." His cloak flutters near my shoulder and gives me pause. His words invoke a strange memory. My sword, a gift from my father, forged by his hand. My sword, slipping from my grip into a powerful vortex, in the midst of our battle with the Sorcerers. My sword, spinning away from me.

"It's here?" I whisper, dazed. I had thought it lost forever. If it really is here, I could claim it. I could use it against him. I slow my pace and look at him over my shoulder. His cloak is dark as starless night. It floats around him far and wide, like ink spilled into the sea.

"Let me show you," he whispers, beckoning to me. Starlight dances in his dark eyes as I turn toward him. I'm drawn to him by some unknown force. Before I can think, I step closer and fall into his open arms.

We tumble together into nothing and he holds me closer. His touch is cold and confident, and it makes me want to trust him and fight him away all at once.

"This world is as vast as one's imagination," he whispers to me as we fall. My heart is racing. I squeeze my eyes shut. I have always feared heights and falling. It's even worse when everything around is dark and there's no way of telling when the impact will come.

"Master it," he goes on, "and you own it, Azaeli. That, I have done. Open your eyes," he says as I feel his cloak flutter around us and my feet touch the ground gently. "Behold my kingdom."

Chapter Nineteen:

THE BORDER

Tib

The trees and water are a blur below us as we soar over the countryside. It looks different from up here. Smaller. It makes me feel small, too, to see the whole world stretched out beneath us. The wind whips my hair around and I laugh. I have never felt this free. We fly through the morning and into noon. Behind me in his high-backed seat, Shoel flicks the reins. The cygnet circles lower. We're nearing our destination.

"*The border.*"

Yes, the border. Kythshire. I look out to the west, but I can't see a wall or a marking. All that's there is ocean and sky and bright green land. The leaves shimmer brightly in the sunlight and make me look away. I feel a strange sensation. Something repels me. I don't belong here. Turn around, it says to me. Find another way.

The cygnets slow. We dip beneath the canopy and weave between tree trunks. The forest is thick. There are no paths or clearings. No markings for travelers. No way to know where you are or where you've been. We glide low along the ground and land gently. The space is small. The cygnets barely have room to spread their wings. The elves climb out and then help Saesa and me down, too. Julini takes Saesa aside and speaks quietly to her. Gives her something.

"Tib," Shoel says quietly. I look up at him. He smiles at me, but there's worry in his eyes. "You're certain of this?"

"*Yes.*"

"Yes," I nod. I'm certain. This is where I should be right now. Shoel still doesn't look too convinced. He shakes his head. Reaches into his vest. Hands me a square of cloth. I turn it in my hands and look it over. It's a white scrap, just the size of my palm. There's elf writing on it, and the head of a cygnet sketched in black.

"What is it?" I ask.

"It is a Sigil. If you are ever in trouble," he explains, "whisper to it, and I shall hear." I fold it and tuck it into my bandolier.

"Thank you for everything!" Saesa throws her arms around Julini. The woman smiles and looks at Shoel. She says something in their language as she pats Saesa kindly. Shoel sighs and replies to her, and she nods reluctantly.

"We cannot linger here," Shoel says. "I ask you once more, Tib, are you certain this is your choice?"

"Say you're certain."

"I'm sure," I say with more confidence than I feel. Really, I want to go back on the cygnet. I want to fly again. Shoel puts a hand on my shoulder.

"Be safe, then, friend. Do not hesitate to call on me. Trust in yourself, Tib. You have a strength I have not seen in one so young for many years."

Julini eyes me and says something in their language to Shoel. Their discussion goes on for a few minutes. She seems like she's worried. He does, too. But he shakes his head and says something else, and she nods a little sadly and climbs up onto her cygnet. Saesa comes to my side and takes my hand. The cygnets spring up with a mighty flap of their wings. We watch them rise through the canopy and into the sky beyond until they're gone.

"Well, that was an adventure! Imagine, Tib! Wildwoods and elves and cygnets. We spent the night at the White Wall, even! Wait until I tell Nessa and the others. Lilen will be so jealous! So, now where?" She looks off to the east.

It's a good question. I know we're in the right place. The border of Kythshire. Still, I can't remember why we're here. Just beyond these trees, I think. Just there is where we need to go. But I get that feeling again, like something is pushing me away. Telling me to get out, that I don't belong. It makes me want to turn around and leave and never come back. I wonder if Saesa feels the same way.

"Through there," I say, and point through the forest to the west. Saesa turns to look.

"Are you sure?" she asks a little hesitantly. She crosses her arms and takes a small step back. "I don't know. It seems like we shouldn't. Where were we going again?"

"Just walk."

Yes, just walk. I take the lead. There is no path. I have to step over brush and climb through thorny vines that catch my skin. Toward the place that warns me. Into the danger. I feel like I'm being pulled in two directions at once. One part of me wants to run far away. The other part knows the importance of going forward. Lives depend on it. Worlds depend on it. I push myself against my judgment. I keep going. Behind me, Saesa grumbles at the thorns.

"Are you sure this is the right way, Tib? It feels wrong. Maybe we should turn around."

"Keep going."

Yes, keep going. I reassure Saesa. I push through the thick forest. I change directions without realizing it. Southward. I feel better. It's not as daunting.

"This way."

Yes, this way. I turn westward again even though I don't want to. The warning feeling is so strong that my heart races. I don't like it. I don't want to go further.

"Tib, we can't," Saesa whispers frantically, tugging on my arm. "We shouldn't."

I can feel it now. A force along my right side. A great, invisible wall. It tells me to go away. To leave. I don't belong here. I'm not welcome. I crouch for a stick and toss it through the trees. The air shimmers white and silver and gold. The stick passes through.

It happens all at once. On the other side of the unseen border, the trees twist together. The ground rumbles. Roots. Roots and earth. Bark. Vines. They curl together. They'll get me, I know. They'll bind me. Trap me. I turn away. I start to run. Saesa does, too. The trunks lash together. The cracking of wood is as loud as thunder. I stumble and fall, and Saesa trips over me.

"Wait."

Yes, wait. I lie there, panting in the underbrush. I watch in terror. The trees aren't trees. They're men. Giants, made of twigs and branches and roots and earth. There are two of them. They look identical, down to the single eye on each of their foreheads. They tower over us. Menacing. Fierce. Still. They don't need to move. Just looking at them is enough to terrify me. Saesa clings to my arm.

"Show yourself," they say together. Their red eyes pulse with each word. Saesa and I look at each other. We're right out in the open. They can see us. Still, I push myself to my feet and she stands beside me. I take a shaky step forward. "Show yourself," they command a second time.

The air shimmers beside me. A tiny winged man emerges. He hovers at my shoulder. He's dressed in gold armor from head to toe. I stare at him and he gives me a quick glance. As soon as he meets my eye, I remember him. I know him. Mevyn. We've been through things together. Many things. We're a pair. We protect each other. There are holes, but I remember. We've traveled a long way together. We're nearly there now. Kythshire. We've come so far. We're almost done.

"We are Oren," the voices boom over us. "We are the Great Forest embodied. The Arbor Keepers. The Fallen and the Risen. Esteemed Guardians of the Eastern Border. Watchers of the East."

Mevyn's wings blur as he darts up to face the Guardians. They're tall. So tall that their giant heads tower over the tree tops. When he reaches them, he's so far away that I can barely hear him speak.

"I am Mevyn. Mason Evret Valor Yester Numinous. Last of the Sunteri Fae. Keeper of the Wellspring. Guide to Valenor. Sworn Sage of the Known. Keeper of Songs. Spear-Bearer. Warden of Sands. Second to Demsin. Second to Valenor. Second to Cintigra. WindCaller. Weaver of Threads. Mindspinner. If you allow it, Lifebringer."

One of the Orens holds out its palm and Mevyn settles onto it. A stream of red filled with golden tendrils of light flicks from the giant's enormous eye. It beams into Mevyn and Saesa moves closer to me.

"What's happening?" she whispers. "They aren't hurting him, are they?" Her hand moves slowly to Feat's hilt, but she seems to think twice about that and lets it drop.

"No," I watch the golden tendrils curl and flick. "Oren is looking at him. At his memories." I don't know how I know it, I just do. I can see them too, a little. Pieces of our journey together flash and fade in my mind. As I watch them, they become clearer.

"What is he showing them?" The golden light reflects brightly in her green eyes as she gazes up.

"Everything," I say. "Everything he can remember."

"How do you know?"

"I see it, too. Like a play. Like a show in my mind."

"What do you see?" she whispers.

"I see our time together, and then I see before that, too." I say quietly. The words come as quick as the images. "Back to when I didn't know Mevyn. What it was like before. Back when the Sunteri Wellspring was thriving. It wasn't always a desert around it. It used to be a deep green jungle. Then they came, the Mages.

"They weren't careful. They built their cities. They became Sorcerers. They sucked the Wellspring dry. Everything died and crumbled. All around it turned to sand and dust. Then the fae started dying, too. They couldn't survive on this plane. They passed what they knew and what they were to each other. Passed it down, before they went. Left their empty bodies behind in the sand. Soon there were only a few left.

"Those few were a collection of all those past. Mevyn is one of them. No, many. He is so many of them now. The last of them. That's why he has all those titles. He's holding them for when the Wellspring is restored. For when they can all come back. If he fails, he'll be alone. They can never come back."

"Oh, Tib…" Saesa hugs me and I'm suddenly aware of the tears rolling down my face. I brush them away angrily. This isn't my sadness. It's his. I don't need it. I have enough of my own.

The other Oren dips its head beneath the canopy to peer at Saesa and me. It blinks its red eye and nods, and I know it's my turn. I square my shoulders and I let it look at me. The golden tendrils swirl and weave between us. They draw out all kinds of things. Memories from a long time ago that I forgot. Memories too old to cling to. My mother tries to hold me on her lap, but her belly is so round with Zhilee that I kept falling off. Before that, my father. My father working with me strapped to his back. I can only see his neck but I know it's him. I've tried to remember him before, but I never could. I try to see his face, but he fades away. Next comes Nan, walking me in the field. Someone screaming in the house. Mother. And then mother is gone, and Zhilee is here, and Mother is never coming back. Picking red, red, red. Petal after petal into the basket, for years and years. Hauling. Loading. Starving. Filth. Toil. Sorrow. Sister.

Viala. My sister, reading her books. Telling stories. Getting lashed for not filling her basket.

"This we have seen before," one of the Orens says.

"Yes, we are aware of this," the one with Mevyn replies.

Oren skips ahead past my older sister. It looks further. I can't stop it. It sees the trees, the roots, the fighting. It watches me climb and burn and swim and sail. It sees Nessa and my friends in Cerion. It sees Margy and Twig. It sees the pit and the Dreamwalker and my fall. It sees our journey, and the Wildwood and the elves. Through it, I can see, too. I see everything Mevyn has hidden from me. I realize how very many holes there were.

I see his giving and taking of my memories. I see his commands and his control. By the time the tendrils fade and I'm left to my own mind again, I'm fuming. Shaking. Close to raging. How could I be so unaware of how strongly he held me in his grip? How could I let him control me that way? He told me things were my idea when they weren't. He made me see things his way when I never would have on my own. He used me, like a tool. Used me to do things he couldn't do himself.

"Tib," Saesa whispers, but even her concerned hand on my arm does little to soothe me. I'm furious with Mevyn. I hate him. I want to lash out at him, but he's still way up, eye to eye with the other Oren. Unaware. I turn to Saesa and shake my head. Oren turns its eye to her and looks. It's her turn now. It isn't like with Mevyn, though. I can't see any of it. I put my hand over hers. I don't let go. She's all I have now. My only friend. She stood by me. She was lured in, too, and it's my fault. I'll protect her now, until I can get her back home. I won't let anything happen to her.

She whispers things while Oren looks. Words, here and there. Mother. Cold. Please. Raefe. I squeeze her hand. Her time with Oren is shorter than mine and Mevyn's. When it's finished, the giant blinks slowly. Saesa closes her eyes and takes a deep breath.

"You have an object which you have vowed to deliver, Tibreseli Nullen and Saesa of the house of Ganvent. We grant you passage into Kythshire. You shall find Twig at the Ring. Doe will accompany you. In the name of the East, welcome."

Saesa and I cling to each other as we cross over the unseen barrier into Kythshire. As soon as we do, everything changes. Colors are brighter. Melodies of birds' songs delight my ears. The air feels different here, too. Like it's full of magic. I can feel it all around me, almost like I could reach out and take it and mold it in my hands. Orbs of light float around lazily, all different colors.

"Oh, it's more beautiful than I ever could have imagined, Tib. Look!" She points at the trees. "So many of them…" She's right. I can see them, their eyes all watching us. Hundreds of fairies laughing and pointing and watching curiously. They flutter back and forth from one branch to another. Whisper. Giggle. I have decided I don't really like them, even though Saesa is dazzled. After everything with Mevyn, fairies give me the creeps.

One of the orbs drifts close and starts to grow until it's my size.

A pretty lady emerges from it. Her hair is as long as she is tall, and her wings are like a dragonfly's, long and slender. Her gown is all leaves and flower petals that sparkle with dew. Her large eyes are framed with dark lashes, but the rest of her face is more animal-like. Sort of like a baby deer's, with a black nose and velvety fur. She's very strange looking, but beautiful.

"Hello," she says with a smile. "I'm Doe. I'm pleased to be your guide." Her voice is soft, like a breeze through leaves.

"Hi, Doe! I'm Saesa, and this is Tib. Oh, you're so beautiful! May I touch your wings?'

I look up at the other Oren while Saesa chatters with Doe. It's still streaming memories from Mevyn. He must be old, I think. He has a lot to share.

"Will he come, too?" I ask the Oren who let us in.

"If he is worthy." Oren replies. I gaze up. I don't know whether to hope he is or isn't. I want to make him pay for what he did to me, but I don't want to lose him. It's confusing to feel both things at the same time, and so strongly, too.

"This way," Doe says gently. "They are expecting you."

She leads us away down a winding path. It meets with a brook that sparkles and babbles beside us. Saesa and I are quiet. I'm too caught up in the memories that Oren showed me. I imagine she is, too. I wonder what she saw that she had forgotten. For me, it was my mother and my father. Did I always have those memories before I met Mevyn? When were they taken from me? Why would he hide them that way? Beside me, Saesa pauses. She's staring into the water. Doe stops, too, and watches her.

"What's wrong?" I ask.

"Jewels," she whispers. "Look at them, Tib. The whole stream bed is filled with them." She steps off of the path toward the water and I follow her gaze. She's right. Beneath the rushing water, I can see them. Flickers of green emeralds and red rubies. Blue sapphires. Nuggets of gold. Just a handful of these riches would make us wealthy for a lifetime. I glance at Doe. A curious smile plays on her face. She blinks slowly. Calmly. Watches us.

"Saesa," I try to stop her from going to the stream, but Doe presses a finger to her lips to quiet me. I can tell she wants to see what Saesa will do.

Saesa is too fixated on the jewels to notice. I can see her struggling with herself. I can imagine what she's thinking. It would be wrong to take them, but there are so many. And they're just lying there, like any other useless stone. Still, it's wrong. Especially right in front of Doe, who's watching so closely.

"Come on, Saesa," I say and step toward her, but she ignores me and wades further into the stream.

When she bends toward it, reflections of the water's surface splash across her face. She pauses with her hand in the water. She's still considering it.

"Saesa," I say again. This time, I'm a little more worried. What will happen if she takes some? What will Doe do? All around us, the chattering and giggling of fairies hushes. The drifting orbs of light dim out. I creep closer, ready to stop her if she tries.

She doesn't, though. She scoops the crystal clear water into her hand and turns to Doe and asks, "Is it safe to drink?"

"Of course, child." Doe smiles.

We drink until our thirst is quenched, and then continue along the path. Every once in a while, I notice Saesa looking at the jewel-encrusted stream bed with longing, but she resists it. When Doe finally pauses beside a huge willow tree, it's past noon.

"Here is our entrance," she says dreamily. "But you cannot attend the Ring at your size. May I?" She nods to us both and reaches toward us.

"What?" we ask together. I back away from her.

"I shall shrink you down to their size, so you do not trample them. There are many, and you are too large."

"Can you put us back to normal after?" I ask her.

"Of course," she laughs softly, and Saesa and I exchange glances before we agree.

It's a strange feeling, shrinking. It makes my skin tingle and my stomach flip. Otherwise, it's more like everything around us is growing and we're staying the same. Doe shrinks, too. She ducks into a hole at the base of the tree. Into the darkness of the twisting roots.

"This way," Doe beckons. Saesa looks around. She tugs on a tall blade of grass with amazement and laughs, then follows Doe into the roots.

"Tib!" she calls from the darkness. "Oh, it's beautiful!"

This close to the ground, the scent of the earth is heavy in the air. The smell brings me back to the desert, to the roots. It's musty, like the water that dripped into my mouth. The ones before me seem to curl and dance strangely. They taunt me. They laugh. I can't go in there.

I can't follow, and the roots know it. They know it and they mock me for it. Saesa pokes her head out and grabs my hand. I fight her, but she pulls me through into the darkness.

"It's all right, Tib, see?" she says. "It's just a door. Open your eyes. Look. Look what's on the other side!"

I don't want to, but I do as she coaxes. I open one eye first, then the other. We're not in the roots. We're outside. I can see why they call it the Ring now. It's a wide circle of grass, all surrounded by trees. White mushrooms dot the outside of the circle, and it's surrounded by crowds of fairies. All different kinds, all different colors. Some are bright and cheerful like flowers, and some are dark and dirty like mushrooms. Some are like Doe, and look like animals. Others look like beetles and bugs. There are dozens of them, and they're all completely silent. None of them turn to look at us when we approach them. They're all too fixed on something in the center of the circle.

Saesa and I follow Doe as she creeps closer to the crowd. Doe gasps and covers her mouth, and Saesa cranes to see over a tall, skinny fairy who looks like a broken stick. I crouch on the other side of him until I find a gap to peek through.

In the center of the Ring, there is a tiny, frail looking child standing on a dark stone. Her skirts look like long pink flower petals, and her hair is a greenish yellow puff on top of her head. A tall, slender man kneels in front of her. I don't think he's a fairy. He doesn't have wings. He's dressed in blue and gold Mage robes, and he looks vaguely familiar. Beside him in the grass, there's an arrangement of deep blue armor. It sparkles in the sunlight like polished stone. A white cloak is spread out beneath it. I shift to try to see it better, since that's what everyone seems to be interested in.

"Is that…?" Saesa whispers.

"That's Crocus," Doe whispers.

"No, not her," Saesa says under breath as she cranes her neck to see better. She moves closer to me. Peeks through my gap. Claps her hands over her mouth. Her eyes go wide and she turns to me in disbelief. "Sir Azaeli," she breathes. I look again and see the blonde braid draped over the shoulder of the armor. I can't see her face. It's covered by her visor.

"Is she dead?" I whisper to Saesa. One of the fairies in front of us turns around and hisses angrily. Doe places a hand on him to settle him, and then presses a finger to her lips at me. I understand. Saesa and I crouch together and watch in silence, waiting to see what happens.

Chapter Twenty:

RIAN'S SIDE

Tib

Crocus gazes down. Not at the knight and the Mage, but at her own feet. I'm not sure why, but I get the sense that everyone's waiting for her to say something. She looks up and around the circle of mushrooms slowly. She's so calm and peaceful, and blurred at the edges like a dream. It makes me feel lazy just watching her. When she starts to speak, her voice is sweet and warm. Something about it makes me want to rush to her. I want to protect her. Keep her safe. Do anything she says. It reminds me of Mevyn. At first I don't know why, then I realize. Fairy magic. I scowl.

"Rian Eldinae," Crocus says a little wearily. "Windsaver. Oathkeeper. Arcane Guardian. Steward of the Wellspring." She pauses and the Mage tears his gaze from Azaeli. He grips her hand in his, though, like he's afraid of letting go. Magic crackles from his fingertips. Beside me, Saesa moves closer. She links her arm through mine.

"We are certain," she continues, "that the Makers will find answers now that Flitt has gone to deliver Azaeli's tether to them. At the very least, they will determine who has been meddling with our traveling fae. Perhaps we shall find out why, as well. While we await her return, tell us from the beginning. What has become of our ambassador?"

"We had just arrived in Sorlen River Crossing," Rian presses Azaeli's fingertips to his cheek while he talks. His gaze rests on her face. All around, the fairies are silent. Listening. There's a power to his voice. The kind of power that always seems to shine from a Mage. Makes you like them and fear them all at once. He goes on.

"Azi and I had been out in the street, and then we went into the Inn. The others of our party were already settled."

"Oh, tell us about the Inn," someone in the gathering of fairies calls out.

"Yes, what was it like?" another fairy asks.

"Was there dancing?" says a third.

"Was there singing?" Their interruption gathers momentum, and soon everyone is chattering excitedly. Saesa looks at me with amusement. In the center of the Ring, Rian scowls. The rock beneath Crocus starts rumbling. It shakes the ground beneath our feet. The fairies slow their chatter until it's silent again.

"What was that?" Saesa whispers.

"Shh!" The group around us hisses. Doe shakes her head and presses her finger to her lips. Rian continues.

"The table was already set with drinks. Azi poured herself a cider. I usually check everything first, but she must have been too thirsty to wait. She drank while I was casting the Detection." He shakes his head. Kisses her fingertips. "It didn't take long for whatever it was to take effect. She faded. Slipped away. We couldn't wake her. We tried everything. Brother Donal, our Cleric, he tried purging her of poison. Lisabella tried with her auras to wake her. My mum, Mya, even tried a Song of Resurgence. Nothing worked. Then came the blame. Bryse needed someone to blame. Someone had to have put something in the cider. First he thought it was the barkeep, but that was proved false. Then, the tavern girls. With every person we disproved, Bryse and Azi's father grew more furious. They stormed outside and confronted Jac. He's a guard assigned to us by Eron. Everyone's suspicious of him, but that's another story. In the meantime, I was trying to figure out what it was that was in the cider, not who put it there, and how to get her back. I even thought to drink some, but the others refused to allow it.

"Then, something that Donal did worked. Azi woke up just for a moment. They called for water. She looked right at me. She looked and she said, 'In Kythshire,' and then she was gone again. As soon as she passed out, Lisabella, it was so strange," he shakes his head, "she lost her temper. I've never seen her like that. She shook Azi. Tried to wake her. Screamed at her. When that didn't work, she grabbed the cider from me and drank it. Nothing happened, though. It didn't have an effect on her. Then my mum started. She was furious. She accused Lisabella of acting irresponsibly. What if she had been poisoned, too? But Lisabella wouldn't hear it.

"It was all so irrational. Mum and Lisabella never fight. Mum has such a level head. Brother Donal tried to get them to see reason, but he got drawn into the heat of it, too. To top it off, the conflict in the street was escalating. Bryse and Benen had Jac by the collar. They were dragging him inside. They would have started a brawl. A brawl with a palace guard! It's unthinkable. And all of this, with Azi lying there on the filthy floor of the tavern, unresponsive. Helpless. If there had been a fight…" His voice trails off. He shakes his head. "I had to do something. I had no choice." His fingertips crackle with energy. He lowers Azaeli's hand tenderly. Puts it on her chest. Makes a fist and closes his eyes. The crackling stops. He repeats at a whisper, "I had no choice."

The Ring stays silent. It's like everyone is holding their breath, waiting for the rest of the story. Next to me, Saesa has her hand clapped over her mouth. Her eyes are wide. She's just as caught up in it as the rest of them. It takes a while for Rian to calm down enough to go on. When he does, I can barely hear him, his voice is so low.

"It was Flitt's idea. Not that I'm blaming her, of course. It was brilliant. It had to be done. There was no other way, was there?"

"I imagine not, Rian. I'm certain you acted as you saw best fit. What was it you did?" Crocus tilts her head slowly to the side, waiting.

"I slept them. All of them. The entire tavern." As he says it, his voice thins out. He looks tired. Drained. I didn't notice it before. "I put them all to sleep, and I locked the Inn doors and warded it with everything I know. I made a golem to watch over them. Then Flitt and I brought Azi here through the Half-Realm." He presses his hands to his face. Rubs his eyes. His hands are shaking. A spark from his fingertips startles him, and he moves closer to Azaeli and grips her hand again.

"Something's happening," he whispers. "Something bigger than cider, poisoned or not. A darkness has been affecting us. I noticed it early on our journey. It was slow and subtle, but it was there. Nuances. Feelings. It affected all of us on some level, but Azi was particularly taxed. Our guild is usually so temperate. Amiable. We're like family. We all love each other. But our journey has been fraught with spats and shadowed by anger and annoyance. It isn't like us. The Elite is renowned for its good temperament."

After another long silence, Rian tears his gaze from Azi and says to Crocus, "Ah, it's my turn to ask a question, isn't it?"

Crocus laughs softly and nods. "Yes, and there it was. Now it is our turn. What do you suspect is the cause of this darkness which spreads within your ranks?"

"Something powerful. It feels like Sorcery to me. It started with nightmares. Suggestions to our minds. It toyed with our emotions and our perceptions." He shakes his head, "It even had Azi attacking the Prince. I should have realized it then, that some force was at work. I should have seen it. I don't know what it could be. I've never encountered anything like this before. Have you?"

"We are just now learning of it, as you are, though it does ring true with songs our muses have sung for generations. We have not encountered it, but we have been aware of it. Anticipating it."

"Are you saying that you knew this was going to happen?" His palms crack loudly. Overhead, thunder rumbles. "You knew and you didn't warn us? Or do anything to stop it?"

"We understand a man's tendency to temper, and so we forgive your tone. But it was not your turn, and you asked three questions of us. Therefore, the game is done." Before Rian can argue, she turns her attention to the rest of the Ring. Rian gapes at her and then closes his eyes. It's obvious he's trying to control himself. He clasps his hands in his lap. His jaw is clenched tight. Crocus pays no attention. She calls out over the rest of us.

"We call Soren Hasten Udi Swiftish Haven," she nods to a mushroom across from us. A tall, green fairy dashes down from the cap. He looks like a large mantis, with spindle legs and long, sleek wings. He's covered in a shell of green armor except for his head, where his blonde-green hair is swept back like he's been flying into the wind. "Shush," Crocus nods to him and smiles.

"Crocus," Shush whispers rapidly. "Thank you for choosing me. I'll help in any way I can." His voice is like a gust of wind. Crocus smiles. Tilts her head.

"*Fly swiftly to the Avenside, fetch a crystal. From there, to Iste. Then Shest Cove. Speak to the Oracle.*"

Shush nods and shoots up into the sky.

"That was strange," Saesa whispers to me, "She didn't even say anything."

"Yes she did—" I start, but the fairies in front of us turn and glare. Crocus speaks again.

"We recognize Ki of the Shadow Crag," she sweeps a hand northward and the gathering of fairies erupts into whispers.

A little ways along the circle, a group parts to allow her to pass. Saesa and I shift our view to try and see, but everyone is moving around too much, changing our gaps. The stone that Crocus stands on rumbles again. Everyone mostly settles. When we can finally see into the circle again, Ki is already bent in a kneeling bow just on the edge of it. She's very humble looking, with a bow slung across her chest and a quiver of arrows at her hip. Compared to everyone else here, she's nothing special. Her armor is dull gray cloth studded with the same color studs. Her cloak is gray, too, just a shade darker. She wears her hood up, so all I can see is her nose. A Sunteri nose.

There's something else about her. Something different. Saesa notices it, too. She leans toward me and whispers, "She has no wings. I think she's human."

I nod. I can tell. She's got no magic. Not even a little. It's almost like she repels it. I wonder why.

Closer to Crocus, Rian looks up. He looks like he's calmed down some. His magic is still ready to burst out, though. When he sees Ki, he shifts himself so he's blocking her view of the knight. Protecting Azaeli, which makes no sense to me. Ki is just an archer. Rian could obliterate her with a wiggle of his finger. Especially here.

"What news have you from the North, Ki?" Crocus's question settles the crowd into a hush. Everyone seems to lean forward to hear Ki speak.

Ki keeps her head bowed respectfully. Her voice brings flashes of red blossoms. Black hair fanned out in the breeze. Book pages rustling. Whips cracking. Viala, riding away in a carriage, tucked beside the Sorcerer. Waving back at us for the last time. I shake my head. Try to focus. Next to me, Saesa grips my arm. I'm shaking. My whole body is. I can't stop staring at the woman they call Ki. She is nothing like my sister. My sister was a girl. Frail. Thin. Bent. Defiant. Focused. This woman is strong but humble. Capable but distant.

"I come bearing a message from Iren, the Shadow Crag embodied. The Mountain Keeper. Esteemed Guardian of the Northern Border. Watcher of the North."

"What message does he send?" Crocus asks. Her smile is different with Ki. More careful.

"Tib?" Saesa tugs my arm. She's not watching the circle. She's looking at me with concern. I take a deep breath. Try to calm my shaking. Unclench my hands and teeth. Wriggle my shoulders. Long for Mevyn. He would tell me what to do. He'd make this confusion go away. He'd keep me safe from it. We should have waited for him. She's my sister, but she can't be. My hand slides to a knife handle on my bandolier. The feel of metal wrapped with leather bolsters me. I want to charge Ki. Rip that hood from her. Tell everyone who she really is.

What she did to her family. Make her hurt the way she left us to hurt.

I can't, though. Some unseen thing is keeping me here, stuck to the grass. I look at Doe. She gives me an apologetic smile. Presses her finger to her lips. She's the one holding me. I can feel the roots around my legs. I look down, but nothing is there. Still, I start to panic. I try to shift my knees and I can't. They won't move. It's like the desert all over again. Roots climbing up over me. Encasing me. Squeezing me. I can't breathe. I can't think. Saesa is shaking my arm. Trying to snap me out of my panic. It's just making it worse. I need to run. Need to get away, but I can't.

"Tib, what's happening, what's wrong?" Saesa hisses at me. No one shushes her now. They're all too fixated on whatever is going on in the circle. I reach back. Claw at my calves. Try to free myself from the unseen bonds.

"Roots," I gasp, and Saesa's eyes widen. "Doe. Holding me. Roots." I pant. My breath quickens and then stops altogether. Tiny dots of gray prickle my vision. Close in around me. I need air, but I'm too gripped by panic to suck it in.

"Tib, breathe!" Saesa cries. "Stop it, whatever you're doing to him, stop! You can't hold him! He's too frightened! Can't you see?"

"I shan't. He meant to enter the Ring with violent intent." Doe's voice is far away. Saesa's too. The murmurs of all of the fairies around us echo in my ears. The gray dots close in. I tip forward into the broken stick fairy. Saesa catches me. Tells me to breathe again. Tilts my head until I can see her eyes through the dots of gray. Green. Bright, but scared. I focus on them. The grip of panic loosens a little. I gasp. Let the air fill my lungs. Let it out again. Take another deep breath. My vision starts to come back.

"Just breathe," she whispers. Strokes my hair back.

"We call Doe of the East," Crocus's sweet voice drifts over the disrupted crowd to us, "and her charges."

Doe closes her eyes slowly. Shakes her head. Looks at me and Saesa. Her lips are pressed into a thin line. Her black nose is flared out. She's angry. Embarrassed. I don't care. She releases the bonds and beckons for us to follow. I spring to my feet. Shove my way forward. Charge toward the Ring. To Viala. To my sister.

Behind me, Saesa cries for me to stop. I ignore her. I don't care. I want to hurt this Ki, this whoever she is. I reach for my knives. Sneer. Scream. Charge. No one tries to stop me. No one needs to. As soon as I step into the pristine circle, my mood changes.

Peace washes over me. By the time I reach Ki my knives are discarded in the grass, forgotten. I dive at her. Throw my arms around her. Sink against her. Her shining black hair tumbles down her shoulder into my face. Somehow, she still smells like Viala.

She kneels there rigid for a moment, and then her arms encircle me. Hold me. I break into sobs. Ugly, wracking, mournful sobs that fill the Ring. Everything is silent. I don't care about the eyes on me. I'm not ashamed of my emotion. My sister is here. She's hugging me. She knows me. We're together again. My family, the last of my family. I didn't realize how much I needed her until this moment. Now that we're together, I'm never leaving her again.

"What is this?" Crocus's sweet voice drifts to us. "Doe, who have you brought to us?"

"This is Tibreseli Nullen, a wanderer from Sunteri, and Saesa of the House of Ganvent of Cerion." Doe bends a knee to Crocus.

"And why have they been allowed to enter and disrupt our gathering? I question the judgment of the Eastern Oren. Why have you come here, Tibreseli Nullen?"

In the arms of my sister, it's hard to remember why I did come. This seems like it should be the reason, after all. To find her, and I did. But then I remember Margy and her bracelet. And Twig. Crocus watches me from across the circle. Turns her attention to Ki.

"Ki of the Shadow Crag, do you know this boy?" she asks.

"Should I?" Ki holds me an arm's length from her. Looks me over. Into my eyes. Hers have changed. They're peaceful. Empty. Joyful. Not creased with pain and determination like they used to be. I wonder what she sees when she looks at me. Have I changed as much as she has? Slowly, she shakes her head. "I do not."

Those three words stab through my heart. I search her eyes. Try to see her hint, some sign that it's a ruse. That she's lying to them to protect me, maybe. She has to know me. She has to.

"I'm sorry," she whispers. She's sincere. She really doesn't. I push away from her. Stand up. I need Mevyn. He made me forget before. He can make me forget this. Or maybe he can make her remember me. My hands are shaking. I pace the grass. Pick up my knives. Shove them into my bandolier. At the edge of the Ring, Saesa is watching me in silence. Everyone is. They're all watching. Even Rian. He's the first to break the silence.

"You're the boy," he says quietly. "The one they were holding in Sunteri." His eyes slide to Ki. He seems to be thinking carefully how to phrase what he says next. "You're alive. Azi will be relieved. She's been fretting over you and the others since the battle. Regretting she didn't do more to help. We both have. We should have tried to find you, but other things kept getting in the way. I'm sorry."

I pause. Look at him. He means it. He would have helped.

"When I took the red tablet," he says, "and wrote to the Sunteri fae to tell them to release you, I hoped you'd be safe. Where are the others? There were three of you, weren't there?"

"Dead." I say coldly. I don't care if he feels bad. I don't care how concerned he was. They're dead, and I'm all that's left. Me and Viala. And she's Ki now. She doesn't even remember me. They might as well have killed her, too. "They killed them. Starved and tormented them. Fought around them. Destroyed them. Nan and Zhilee were too weak to withstand it. They got caught up in it. Didn't make it out." I turn to Ki. "Do you hear me? They're dead!" I shout at her. She winces. Shakes her head. Looks to Crocus for direction. The stone rumbles. Quakes. I stumble into Saesa. We fall to the ground on our knees.

"Enough." A deep voice thunders over the Ring.

"Scree!" The fairies around us yelp and cheer and start to dance around. Music and singing fill the air. Colors start to blur around the edge of the mushroom caps as the fairies erupt into dancing. They twirl and spin and dart around and around. One of them reaches out for Saesa as he passes, but I grip her arm too tightly. I won't let them pull her into it. She's already enamored, grinning and clapping and bobbing her head. Not me, though. I resist it. I've had enough of fairy magic. I've had enough of all of this.

"Shut up!" I scream. "Stop dancing! Stop it!"

"Tibreseli," Crocus's calm voice just infuriates me more. She beckons to me, and I storm across the grass to her. Past Rian. Past the knight. Saesa trails behind. She slows at Azaeli. The fairies keep dancing. They're caught up in it. None of them cares about what's going on in the Ring anymore. When I get closer, I can smell her flowery perfume. It makes me feel slow and lazy. I scowl and step back until it's not as strong. Glare at her.

"What?" I snap.

"Why have you come here?" she asks again. I shove my hand into my vest and pull out Margy's woven bracelet. The one I promised to deliver. I hold it out. Let it dangle from my finger.

"The princess sent me to deliver this. For Twig." I'm

compelled to throw it at her, but I control myself. She'll take it, give it to Twig for whatever reason, and then I'll leave Kythshire. Leave and never come back. Get away from magic and fairies and Mages and Sorcerers. Find a place where they can't touch me. I hate magic. Hate its power. Wish it didn't exist.

"Place it on the stone, please, Tibreseli." Her soft voice grates on me.

"No. I won't come any closer to you." I plant my feet. Stand my ground. Beside me, Saesa stares in disbelief. She slips the bracelet from my fingertips and delivers it to the stone. I watch her pause and breathe in the scent of Crocus's perfume. She sighs and blinks lazily. I grab her arm and pull her away from it. "Don't get too close," I warn her. "She'll get you."

"We don't intend to harm you," Crocus laughs.

"Bet you didn't intend to hurt her, either. Or her." I stab my finger toward Azaeli and Ki.

"That was not our doing," Crocus says quietly.

"Maybe not you, but your kind. All of your kind. You did this. Magic did this. All of it. Magic and Wellsprings and greed and power and selfishness." The dancing slows. Some of the fairies stop. Watch. Listen. When they do, more follow. Soon, they're all standing quiet again. Waiting. My words have power. No one would dare speak this way. Not to Crocus. Not to the thunder voice. I feel the rush of it. Feel the awe and the fear of me and my words.

"Only those with a respect for our ways are welcome here," Scree booms.

"Then I'll be going." I turn on my heel. Turn my back on them. I'm aware right away of the insult. The crowd gasps. Cries out. Doe claps her hands over her mouth. Shakes her head. Ki ducks low, bowing so much that her nose brushes the blades of grass. Rian is pale. He grips Azi's hand. Winces.

"Forgive the boy." Mevyn says. "He has endured more in his short life than anyone should be made to suffer."

I spin again. Crocus is looking out over the audience, seeking the speaker. I do, too. Search for him. I see a flash of gold armor as the crowd parts. He comes to the edge of the Ring and pauses there.

"Who speaks? We do not recognize you," Crocus says.

"I am Mevyn. Mason Evret Valor Yester Numinous. Last of the Sunteri Fae. Keeper of the Wellspring. Guide to Valenor. Sworn Sage of the Known. Keeper of Songs. Spear-Bearer. Warden of Sands.

Second to Demsin. Second to Valenor. Second to Cintigra. WindCaller. Weaver of Threads. Mindspinner. If you allow it, Lifebringer.

"This boy is my Champion," he says as he raises his chin. "He has carried me through the deserts of Sunteri, the vastest seas, and the deep jungles of Elespen. He has guarded me against threats known and unknown. He has kept me safe in Cerion and fought for me along the roads of Ceras'lain. He is steadfast, courageous, and strong. I name him Truest Infallible Bastion. Steward of the Last. Knifethrower. Dreamstalker."

Chapter Twenty-One:

A FAIRY BARGAIN

Tib

All around me, they're whispering. Scandalized. Curious. Saddened. Shocked. Two voices, though, draw my attention. They're not speaking aloud. They're in my head like Mevyn used to be. It isn't him, though. It's them. Crocus and the thundering voice of Scree. I turn to them slowly. Watch them. Her lips aren't moving. She's gazing down at the rock. Silent. Still, her voice is in my head. His, too. Scree. Having a secret conversation they think I can't hear.

"Did he say Last of the Sunteri Fae?" Scree asks. His voice is just as thunderous in my head as it is out loud.

"He did," Crocus replies.

"That means…"

"Yes."

"And what was that last title for the boy? Dreamwalker?" I shudder at Scree's mention of the name.

"Dreamstalker. Stalker." Crocus corrects him.

"Ah, that's his direction, then."

"It would seem so," Crocus smiles at the murmuring crowd and looks at me before resting her eyes on her skirts again. *"Quite young for a Champion. Rough, too. It's interesting. But then who do you suppose the red haired girl is?"*

"I have my suspicions," Scree says.

"I did not expect the songs to come to pass so quickly in succession. The Muses have been quiet for so long, and now this."

"Yes. When they have something to offer, it certainly transpires quickly."

"What of Azaeli, though? She was never mentioned," Crocus's eyes rest on the knight.

"Not in a way we would suspect, no. But she has her part."

"It certainly has come together neatly, hasn't it? So to speak."

"It certainly has. Let the Sunteri fae make his request. We shall grant it of course, as a trade." The stone rumbles a little.

"Of course," Crocus smiles.

"Make him wiggle a little first, though. For fun."

"Oh, indeed." Crocus turns her attention to Mevyn and smiles sweetly. "We recognize you, Mevyn of Sunteri. Please join us in the Ring, which is getting terribly crowded, isn't it?"

She giggles softly and covers her mouth, and the fairies all around giggle, too. Mevyn comes to stand beside me. I edge away from him. I'm still confused. Still angry. What was the meaning of him giving me all of those titles? A gift is a trick. And why could I hear Crocus and Scree when nobody else could? What did all of that mean? I look at Mevyn. I wonder if he could hear it, too. It doesn't seem like it to me.

"Why have you come, Mevyn?" Scree rumbles. The ground beneath me trembles. I glance at Saesa, who's kneeling in the grass opposite Rian, beside Azaeli. Mevyn steps closer. He's got Rian's attention. The Mage is staring at him, taking in every detail.

It's strange to see Mevyn this way, taller than I am. He looks much more like a man. His golden armor gleams brightly. The curling gold lines on his tanned skin seem to shine on their own. They even let him keep his golden spear. I remember how he plunged it through the eye of the man in the shack to protect me. I wonder if that memory just came to me on its own, or if he sent it to remind me that we fight together.

How much of what I've done would I have chosen to do on my own if he hadn't been there? None of it. I'd have been a beggar in Zhaghen. Suffering. Half-starved with the masses of other orphans. I never would have been capable of working a ship's sail, or smart enough to talk my way into passage out of Sunteri. I need Mevyn as much as he needs me. I stare at him in disbelief. Push his influence off of me.

"Stop it," I growl. "Stop." I want to lunge at him. Punch him. Drive his blasted spear into his own eye. I'm sick of his controlling, his manipulation. I'd rather be picking blooms. I'd rather work knowing I'm a slave the rest of my life than constantly wondering whether my mind is my own. I turn to Crocus.

"I'm leaving," I say. "You can have whatever this is. I don't need any of you, and you don't need me. I'm taking my sister, and we're going."

"Oh my, he does have spirit, doesn't he?" Crocus tips her head to one

side.

"Pity that he still considers her his sister."

"Oh yes, quite." Crocus smiles sadly at me. "You are free to leave whenever you care to, friend. But I am afraid that Ki is bound to the Crag. She belongs in service to Iren, the Shadow Crag Embodied. The Moun—"

"Mountain Keeper, yeah, yeah!" I interrupt. "I don't care about your stupid titles! I don't care! She's my sister. She's all I have left." I storm across the grass to Ki. I take her hand. Look into her eyes. Different but the same.

"Why can't you remember?" I ask, choking back tears. "What have they done to you?"

Ki shakes her head apologetically.

"I'm happy here," she says. She actually sounds sincere.

"Because they make you happy," I say angrily. "They make you. Can't you see that? This isn't you." I tug at her hand. "Come with me."

"She cannot," Crocus says. "But you may remain with her, if you'd like. Please, sit and listen to the gathering for a time. Think on it. Try to calm your mind. Do not make a rash decision you may regret later. We understand your emotions. You have a right to them. For now, though, there is much to be discussed."

I look at my sister who isn't my sister. She nods at me. Across the circle, still kneeling beside the knight, Saesa meets my eye. She nods too. Sit and listen. Knowing I can leave makes me feel a little better. I'm free. I can go where I like. They have no rights to me.

"Fine." I cross my arms and drop to the grass next to Ki.

I work to calm myself. As I do, I'm aware of how tangible the magic is here. I feel as though I can reach out and scoop it from the air. I glance at Rian, who has Azaeli's hand pressed to his cheek again. He's still staring at Mevyn. The knight seems to help him keep it under control, even though she's not conscious. Even though he's surrounded by it. He could draw it in, I know. He could take this magic and mold it into anything. He could probably destroy the entire Ring if he wanted to, with one stroke of his finger. Instead, he sits and tries to be calm. He's respectful. He frets for the girl he loves. I've never seen a noble Mage before. Not really. It's nice to know they exist. I still don't trust him, though.

"Please go on," Crocus says to Mevyn. "Why have you come?"

"I have come," Mevyn bows his head respectfully. His words are well-rehearsed. I imagine he's gone over them a hundred times in his head on our long journey here. "To beg for my family, my friends, my people. Our Wellspring has been ravaged, drained. It is no more. We are no more. No longer corporeal, the Sunteri fairies are banished to the Dreaming. Until our Wellspring is restored, they shall remain there, too weak even to appear before you. In the meantime, Kythshire thrives. Your conviction in guarding that which is most precious has been enviable in its success. You are brilliant. An inspiration. And so I beg you. I plead with you. Help us restore our Wellspring. Show us how to keep it safe, how to guard it from those who would waste it. Help my people to be reborn."

Crocus folds her hands at her waist as the gallery goes silent waiting to hear her response. She smiles softly, and then her expression goes grave.

"Your carelessness," she shakes her head mournfully, "has birthed some of the most powerful Sorcerers we have seen in a century. Just last season, they came to us. They broke our border. They tried to expand their reach, their power. They nearly succeeded."

Mevyn bows his head. Closes his eyes. Acts ashamed, as he should. He has no response for her. Nothing to say to that.

"With the aid of these humans," she gestures to Rian and Azaeli, "our armies, and Iren of the North, those who would pillage us were destroyed. Still," she looks around at the others, her eyes filled with tears, "we are not free from the threat of Sorcery. Others linger unchecked. One is unlike any Sorcerer we've seen. He moves in the darkness. Lurking. We are safe here, but if any of us crosses the border, we are threatened. Our travelers cannot leave, for this wickedness seeks them out. He twines himself around those most precious to us."

"Our own Champion," she says, gesturing to Azaeli, "is in his grips even now. This threat, this unmatched Sorcerer was born in Sunteri. His mother's milk was your Wellspring."

I think of what Mevyn said in the pit. *We are old rivals. It's a long story.* I'm certain Crocus is talking about the Dreamwalker. And Mevyn knows him. He's fought him before. I watch him now as he keeps his head low. He knows she's right. His people were careless, and the Dreamwalker is the result of their carelessness.

"I could offer excuses," he says quietly. "Tell you of the slow bleed. How concessions were made, one by one, to allow the Mages of Zhagen more power, little by little. Decade by decade. How I was against it from the start. How I fought to keep our magic locked away. None of that matters now. That I was correct, that they ought to have listened to me, it doesn't enter into it. They need me. My people are nothing more than wisps now, trapped in cold and darkness. Threatened and terrified. Our home is drained. That which used to be lush forest is desert. Wasteland. Given a second chance, I know we would make better decisions. I would do anything, anything to right this. To restore my people."

"There it is," Scree says to Crocus, *"bind him to it. Anything, he says."*

"Yes." Crocus rests her gaze on Mevyn. *"Anything, indeed."*

"Come closer," she says to him, "and kneel."

Mevyn does as he's bidden. All around us, the forest is hushed. Not even a breeze dares interrupt the silence. Crocus squares her shoulders a little, like she's preparing to say something very important. She doesn't get a chance, though. All at once, a jarring burst of color fills the Ring. It appears in a bright blur so blinding that I have to shield my eyes and look away. A voice, squeaky and excited, bubbles out from the light.

"Dabble did it!" she cries. "He figured it out! He knows who tried to steal the diamond. You'll never believe who it was, either! Or maybe you will, actually. And oh! Who are you?" I squint toward the voice. All I can see are colors. Every color imaginable, shifting and glittering and splashing over everything. When I can finally focus, I'm not surprised to see a fairy in the midst of it. She stands with her fists on her hips, looking at Mevyn dubiously.

"I am Mevyn, Last of the Sunteri Fae…" as he goes through his titles, this new fairy raises her chin further with every word. Her eyebrows disappear behind her rainbow bangs. Her arms slowly cross over her chest. The tips of her wings droop down a little.

"Well, that's impressive," she mumbles when he's finished. "I'm Flitt. That's with two Ts. Felicity Lumine Instacia Tenacity Teeming." She bobs her head in a quick nod. "Did I interrupt? That was rather rude of me."

"Under the circumstances it's forgiven, Flitt." Crocus smiles. "Tell us, what has Dabble discerned from the diamond?"

"You'll never believe who tried to steal it. Prince Creepy himself!" Her mouth drops open and she looks around for a reaction. "You know, Prince Eron?" That does it. The crowd is scandalized. They gasp and shout and talk amongst themselves. Some of them shout toward Crocus. They're scared. Angry. One of them, a fiery fairy dressed in red and orange lifts off from her mushroom cap. Sparks of yellow crackle behind her as she hovers above everyone.

"Betrayal!" she shouts. "See? They aren't to be trusted. They've broken their agreement. Cerion's crown is supposed to protect us, not threaten. What's happened in Sunteri will happen here, too. They mean to take us over. He'll be king one day, he'll wage war on us!" She's met with cries of agreement from the crowd. They shout and raise their fists and surge toward the Ring.

The ground starts to tremble, then rumble, then shake so violently that I drop to my knees.

"Silence." Scree thunders. "Silence!"

"Ember is right," Crocus says to Scree. *"Too long has the young prince been obsessed with us. His interest in itself is a threat. He will be king. Soon to have an heir."*

"Do not be so quick to condemn him. We must consider this carefully."

"Perhaps it is beyond us," Crocus looks smaller, somehow. More frail. Tired.

"I agree," Scree says after a long pause.

"If I may," Ki ventures. Her voice rises calm and clear over the din. The crowd quiets slowly. Crocus nods to her. She gets up and crosses to stand next to Mevyn. I do, too. Stay by her side.

"What have you to say, Ki? Do you speak on behalf of the Crag?" Crocus blinks at her curiously.

"Not at this time," Ki says. "I have seen this threat, this shadow in the Dreaming. He used to come to me, into my nightmares. His reach was so terrifying that it disturbed my waking, until Iren realized what was happening and drew the darkness out of me. I have been tracking him, this Sorcerer as you call him, ever since, in my dreaming hours. He holds sway over many. He works with subtlety. And once, I did see him with a man with a crown."

"She would speak up for Eron! Remember who she is!" Ember shouts angrily.

"Enough, Ember. We do not recognize you at this time." Crocus dismisses the red fairy with a wave of her hand.

"What else have you seen in the Dreaming?" Crocus asks Ki.

"Sir Azaeli," she gestures to the knight in the grass. "Just last night. Dressed in a red gown. She was running from him. She hid with me in a cavern as we waited for him to pass. She was confused. She asked me to help her leave, but I had no way of bringing her with me."

"You saw her?" Rian whispers, "She's safe?"

Ki turns to him. Nods.

"She was, just last night, Your Excellency," she says. "But she is stalked by the Dreamwalker."

"How do I get to her?" Rian lets go of Azaeli's hand and stands. "How do I find her?"

"You must be drawn into a nightmare." Mevyn says to Rian. "He controls it now, who is allowed to enter and who is barred. I suspect you won't be able to reach her. It's almost certain that he is expecting you."

"No," Rian paces the grass, his fingertips sparking with magic, "there must be a way. Through the Half Realm? Could I enter that way?" He looks desperately from Mevyn to Crocus and Scree.

"Perhaps," Crocus says. "But there are other ways." She looks at Mevyn, "Are there not?"

"Indeed," Mevyn says wearily.

"Mevyn, The Last of the Sunteri Fae, we offer you this bargain. We shall reward you with a means to restore Sunteri's Wellspring, in exchange for your assistance in recovering our Champion from the Dreaming. Together with her, you shall vanquish the Dreamwalker. Only then, when he is defeated, shall we aid in restoring your lands and your people."

Mevyn gapes at Crocus in disbelief. He steps back from her.

"You can't mean that you expect me to…" his voice trails off.

"We do, and you shall. Enter the Dreaming. Recover Azaeli, and seek out the Dreamwalker. Put a stop to him. If you succeed, we shall provide a means to restore your lands."

"It is too much of a risk. If I was to enter and not return, do you not see? It would mean the utter end of my kind." Mevyn is half-panicked. I watch him, take him in. See something there. A dark path. Eyes in the shadows. Hissing and spitting at him. Jeering. Scorning. He is a coward. He hid himself away when he should have fought at the trees, the roots. He should have claimed his titles and instead he ducked in the shelter of a human and gathered them up as they fell. Trees stretch up into the black, starless sky. Hopelessness creeps like smoke along the ground. Dreamwalker is coming. He senses Mevyn, his power. He wants it, wants to draw it out. To own it.

Mevyn lowers his head. Shakes it. "I cannot risk it," he says. "I shall send my own Champion in my place."

"I don't think so!" I shout at him. "Coward! You're afraid of him and ashamed of yourself, so you send me? I refuse. Why should I? Why should I do anything for you? I don't care about any of this!" I don't. I want to go back to the elves. Make a home there, where the Dreamwalker can't touch me. Or even Cerion. Go back to Nessa.

"You have already been Named, Tib, within the Ring. You are bound to this fate." Crocus offers calmly.

"What? I never agreed to that!" I clench my fists. My shoulders rise. I turn to Mevyn. I want to hurt him. Rip out that ever-waving hair. See the color of his blood. I wonder if it's gold like the rest of him.

"Wait," Rian speaks. He takes a deep breath. Presses his fingertips to his brow. Thinks a moment. His reasoning calms me a little. It isn't magic, it's just the way he goes about it. Logically. I can see it. He turns off his emotion to let himself think. It's a trick I'd like to learn. "Mevyn, you have a means of getting there, right? Do you have a way to track Azi once we arrive? Just bring me. I'll go alone and find her. She and I can vanquish this Dreamwalker, whoever he is. There's no need to drag children into it."

"I'll go, too!" Flitt chirps. She drifts to Azi's side and settles next to Saesa, who grins at her. Saesa loves these fairies, I can tell. She watches them with such interest and affection. I, on the other hand, can see around their charms. Into their secret intentions. They can't trick me. They won't lure me into this.

"I have been to the Dreaming many times," Ki says, "I would be honored to lend my guidance, if I would be permitted."

"That is for Iren to decide. You may go and ask." Crocus smiles. After Ki bows and leaves, Crocus turns to me. "I understand your reluctance, Tib. This battle, you believe, is not yours to fight. But Oren has shown us your experience with the Dreamwalker. We have seen it. You know his power. Mevyn has given you a gift with this title. He has given you a means to stop the darkness. To be renowned. To be the Champion he sees in you."

"*Offer him something. A place. He is too important to the cause. We cannot lose the Dreamstalker,*" Scree booms secretly.

"If you were to succeed," Crocus pauses. Looks off into the woods where Ki disappeared. "It would prove to us your allegiance to Kythshire. We would allow you to remain with your sister on the Shadow Crag."

I follow her gaze. Is that what I really want? To stay with Ki, the sister I lost? Even if she never remembers me? I turn back. Meet Saesa's eyes. Green. Calm. Curious. Worried. I look away, to Azaeli. To Rian, who loves her. Who looks to her to calm him. I understand it. It's how Saesa makes me feel. Grounded. Steady.

"Can Saesa come?" My question brings a wave of relief washing over the crowd. At least I'm considering it. They must really need me to go. I don't understand why. What can I do that a Mage can't? What skills do I have that a fairy doesn't?

"Is there any way?" Crocus asks Scree.

"No, there is too much risk. A blood tie such as that, it would open a way for him. We cannot allow the girl to go." Scree says.

"You're certain she's who you think?"

"I have seen what Oren saw. I am certain. She must remain."

Crocus rests her gaze on Saesa. Takes in her closeness to Azaeli.

"You do not know this knight," Crocus says. "Yet you keep vigil over her."

"I do know her," Saesa looks at Azaeli with admiration. "She's why I wanted to take up the sword. I've watched her for a very long time. She's my inspiration. I've looked up to her. I'd do anything to help her."

"Even if that means remaining here beside her, while others go and fight to bring her back?" Crocus blinks her wide eyes slowly. Smoothes her petals with her tiny, breakable hands. Saesa pulls her gaze from Azaeli. Looks at me. Searches my eyes. I plead with her silently. Choose me. Not Azaeli. Me.

"What good would it do for me to remain?" Saesa asks. "If there's a fight, I want to be part of it." She looks from Crocus to Mevyn. "I can be trusted," she says. It's a strange thing to say. I'm not sure what she means by it.

Beside me, Mevyn locks his gaze with Crocus. They seem to communicate to each other somehow, though this time I can't hear them. It's almost as if Mevyn knows what I can do now. He knows, and so he's blocking me. Still, I get the sense that Mevyn has an understanding of Crocus's need to keep Saesa here and send me away. I open my mouth. Try to say something. Try to tell Saesa about the others' conversation. I try, but the words don't come. I can't think of them. Instead, Mevyn speaks.

"I can take only three along with me. No more. Rian, Tib, and Ki. It would be unwise for Flitt to make the journey. Her light would be a beacon to the Dreamwalker. He would devour her without a second thought."

"I'm not afraid of any Sorcerer!" Flitt jabs her fists to her waist. "I know how to handle myself around their kind, don't I, Rian?"

"I have faith in Flitt," Rian says quietly. "I'd be more comfortable with her than with…" He trails off. Looks at me. Mevyn. "I'm sorry. This is important, and we've only just met." He looks down. Doesn't trust us. I'm impressed. He's very smart.

"Iren has allowed it," Ki says from the edge of the Ring. She steps into the grass out of nowhere. I wonder how she was able to come and go so quickly.

"Then it is settled." Crocus says. "Mevyn, Rian, Ki, and Tib shall go together. Flitt, you may bring yourself, if you're determined. I assume you know the way into the Dreaming? But go with caution. We would be devastated to lose you, my dear."

"Wait," I say, "I haven't agreed to any of this." I cross my arms defiantly. Turn to Mevyn. Part of me wants him to explain, but I know I can't trust a word he says. Could I walk away, though, knowing I left them behind? Knowing that I was so needed, that I could have contributed? "You manipulated me. I don't even know who I am anymore. Why should I do anything to help you? To help any of you?"

"I will show you," Mevyn says. "If you allow it, Tib, I will show you, and then you shall see how important it is. How much we need you. If you allow me to show you, I swear here in the Ring, before man and fairy alike, that I will never again meddle with your mind. A promise made here is binding. It cannot be undone. If you wish it, when we return, I'll part ways with you. You'll never have to see me again."

I can see in his eyes that it pains him to say it. As manipulative as Mevyn is, as tricky and conniving, he cares for me. He tries to be my friend. I think on that, and I know it's not him putting ideas in my head. These thoughts are my own.

"Fine," I say after a long moment to think on it. "Show me."

Chapter Twenty-Two:
JACEK'S KINGDOM
Azi

Jacek's kingdom is more wonderful and terrible than any scribe could write about. It summons more fear and awe than any bard's song could muster. His cloak circles around me, ebbing and flowing like the waves of the sea as he watches me take it all in. We're standing on the rise of a boundless mountain peak, looking into an endless valley. The land is black and charred as though victim to a great, ancient fire. Wind sweeps over it in gusts, causing the skeletons of trees to bend to its will. A murky stream winds through marshes of ink. It circles a rise at the center the valley, where the spires of an impressive obsidian castle pierce the reddish sky.

I tear my gaze from it and look up at him, into those dark eyes circled with the blue-black mark. He stares into me as if he owns me, as if I'm his. I try to pull away, but he keeps me close.

"Is it not to your liking?" he asks. His whisper warms me, tells me everything is right. Perfect. Just as it should be. I want to hear more of it. I ache to hear him speak again. "If not, do what you will to it. Make it yours. Imagine it, and it shall be."

The temptation of magic is more than I can resist. I feel it around me, surging from his cloak, prickling the pores of my skin. My hair is on end, dancing in the mountain breeze. I'm filled with a sense of warning, with a sense of daring. Never before has the Mages' world been so open to me, so welcoming. I gaze at the castle across the marshes. I raise my hands slowly and feel the power of this realm seep into them. Numbing and exhilarating all at once, it creeps through me slowly until it consumes me and makes me feel weightless, powerful and unstoppable. I don't need a whisper of a command, nor any complicated spells. I think of what I want, and it happens.

The ground beneath our feet bursts to life with deep green

grass and colorful blossoms. It stretches out before us toward the castle like a ship's wake in a calm sea, and it spreads to cover all of the black with joyous color. The skeletons of trees burst with blooms of white, and lush green leaves.

When my intention reaches the castle, the glistening black stone softens to coral and white. It gleams in the darkness like a beacon of hope, more beautiful than I imagined. In its soft light, precious little creatures begin to emerge: butterflies, fawns, rabbits. Innocent and timid, they hide and peek at first, but as the castle light splashes across them, they become bolder and emerge into the sparkling fields to drink the crystal waters and nibble on clover.

Jacek takes my hand in his and pulls me closer. His cloak slips around me, enclosing us, pressing us together. The rush of power is draining away. I feel it slipping from my head to my shoulders, seeping, fading. With it comes a sense of pure hopelessness and irrevocable loss. I'm empty, spent. My eyelids are too heavy. Keeping them open is an insurmountable task.

I sink back against Jacek, who bends to my ear. He presses his lips to it. It reminds me of a moment in my past, an uncomfortable moment that slips away like a ribbon in the breeze. An unwanted moment, a glimpse of who I was. I try to grasp it, but his whisper sends it drifting out of my reach.

"Impressive," he says, and his breath gives me chills. "So bright and filled with honesty and hope. And now I see you're ready. Shall we go in?"

I'm too exhausted to answer even with a slight bob of my head. The effect of the channeled magic has weakened me so completely that I can barely stand without his help. Jacek whisks me off into the darkness, and we arrive someplace new. He arranges me on a chaise, and I tip my head back and try to take in my surroundings.

Somehow, I know that we're inside the castle now. This room is large and circular, with great arched doors that are open to balconies on almost all sides. Objects line the walls, some ordinary, some unusual, some familiar: A looking glass set on a dais of sapphire, a tablet of polished red stone, a sword, broad and elegant, with a worn grip and my name etched on the crossguard.

My fingers ache for that sword, but I'm too weak even to wiggle them let alone reach for it. It's so close, too. I could reach it if I could just raise my arm. But then Jacek crosses into my view, and I forget my need for it. He tilts his head and smiles at me with an expression somewhere between amusement and curiosity. His eyes flick to the sword and away again.

"Pity," he says quietly as he stops before the mirror and strokes its frame, "It was far too easy getting you here. I was expecting a challenge. Still, it was a fun game to fill the time."

His words are confusing to me. They're a betrayal of trust somehow. I try to think back as to why I'd feel this way, but all I can remember is Jacek and nothing more. He fills my mind like smoke, snuffing out my past, billowing into my present. I'm tired, so tired, but something inside me warns me not to sleep. Stay awake. I want him to come closer, to sit by me. All I want in this world right now is Jacek. He turns away from the mirror and smirks.

"Far too easy," he says again. "Tell me, if you could have anything your heart desires, anything at all, what would it be? Ask me, and I shall grant it."

My sword is forgotten, all that matters is him. My hand drops to the chaise beside me.

"Sit by me," I say. His thin lips press together in a satisfied grin, and to my relief and my elation, he comes to my side and sits. His voice is velvety soft. It comforts me, lulls me.

"So long have I been alone, commanding creatures lower than myself, never having a connection. But with you, it's different. With you, I see an equal, a rival. Not in magic, no, of course not. But in depth of soul. A light to balance the darkness. Now that I have you," he murmurs as he takes my hand, "I'll show you everything. We can be two halves of a perfect whole. Darkness and light, together. Kindness cannot exist without the wicked. Evil cannot exist without purity."

His words are too abstract, and my thoughts still swirl amid his smoke. They tell me something is wrong, they try to warn me. I grasp at them as they whirl past, but it's too difficult. I'm too drained to fight for them, but it doesn't matter. Soon they're pushed away, replaced by other memories that aren't my own. Scenes of another life, of many other lives.

I see a man I once knew, dressed in princely garb, sitting in a dark room while his wife sleeps beside him. Her skin is burnished brown, her belly round and full with the promise of new life. The prince is a perfect specimen. He has been tainted before, so this time it's easy. This time, I can slip into his mind and manipulate him and no one would ever suspect.

It's strange being inside, so close to another. He tries to fight but he cannot. I'm too powerful. His hands are strong and capable, but I have no need for strength now. I place them on her stomach and feel the child within, moving, growing, thriving. With contact, it's easier to slip from one to another. I flick myself toward the child, touch it. Infuse it with myself. Mark it. Slip away.

Something calls me, something filled with light and power. I will the prince away from his bride, into another room where three women sleep. The object is with one of them. She's beautiful, pure of heart. Kind. Even in sleep, it emanates from her. I know her. She's the one who thwarted the first plan, who blocked the path to Kythshire and destroyed my work with a wish.

She is responsible for the death of my mother, my father, and all the rest. Her actions loosened my bonds. Allowed me to venture. Broke the spells which held me here. Not all of them, though. I am still bound. Still, they were my parents, and she destroyed them. I lash out at her, bestow her with discomfort, a taste of wickedness, a hint of distress. A punishment. I stretch it out toward those she loves, give them gifts of darkness, just enough to make them tense and unsure.

The alluring object shines with hope and promise, and the prince's unfamiliar fingers fumble with the pouch that holds it. I glimpse the diamond, glittering and bright, stroke it with my finger, and then it's gone. Stolen away by fairy magic.

I leave the prince in his bed and drift along the streets. I long to walk these roads in my own form, with my own feet, unbound by the Dreaming, but I'm still a prisoner. Locked away from the waking world, I can only slip into others here and there. At first it was difficult, but my time here has not been idle. I constantly test myself. Play. In the streets outside of the Inn, I see a man. A palace guard, dozing at his post. Like the prince's child, I mark him. Place myself inside him. Just a wisp. Just enough to watch, control, and use him to my will. With it, a suggestion, an experiment. Befriend the knight Azaeli. Charm her. Watch her. Do not leave her side.

The scene changes to one even less familiar. Another palace, another prince. This one is tall and strong, with waves of black hair and a neat beard. He stands at a window, watching the night. The air is thick with smoke from towers burning in the distance. The prince is restless. He wants to stop it, but he can't. He's barred in for his own safety, just as they told me I was. But he'll go free, to woo a princess. His thoughts are filled with her. Cerion's princess. He's awake, so I can't touch him, but I can whisper. I tell him to wed her, to make him hers. Then I go to find her, so I can look upon her.

Cerion is too guarded, though. Its castle has wards against me, too strong to slip through. I wait in shadows to find a way. I stretch myself toward it and feel another beacon, like the diamond that was taken by fairy magic. A castle maid passes by. I whisper to her. Bring this item to me. Bring it so I might look upon it. I want to see what it is, to know what it does.

"Azi, you are brave, you are strong. Whatever has you in its grips, fight it. Fight, Azi," a whisper edges into the memory, breaking me apart from Jacek. I watch him walk away from me, on to another place. He doesn't hear it. He doesn't know that someone else has found me.

My name gives me power. I had forgotten it, forgotten myself, but the whisper reminds me. It bolsters me, somehow. When Jacek turns to me in this strange place, I see him differently. The threat I've been feeling is him. He is the danger. The scene around us fades away, and we're once again sitting together on the chaise. I test my arms without moving them. They aren't as heavy now.

"What happened?" Jacek's smoky voice snakes its way toward me again. "I had more to show you." He reaches for me. Traces a finger along my arm. It tingles warmly, and the pleasant sensation spreads through my body. My eyes drift closed again. It's different this time, though. This time, I remember who I was and how I came to be here.

I wonder if he knows what I've recalled. I try to calm my heart, to keep it from racing. I need to get out of here. If Jacek notices that his grip is slipping, he doesn't let on. He brings me to yet another place. This time, it's long ago.

We're at the edge of a Wellspring, but not in Kythshire. I remember this one. It's Sunteri, but it's different from the last time I saw it. It's ringed with enormous ferns and sheltered by a rich canopy of green. Dozens of fairies dart around it playfully. Now and again, golden jets shoot from it, up into the sky. Magic, being called forth by Mages. A toddling boy claps and giggles beside me, and I know immediately that he is Jacek. On his other side, a woman smiles down on him fondly. She's the same woman who brought him here, the one Iren killed in the battle. His mother.

"No, no, darling, you mustn't touch it," she coos at him as the boy crawls toward the golden pool. She's distracted, though, and careless with the child. He creeps closer, dips a tiny fingertip into the pool, and is immediately stopped by a strong warrior fairy decked in rich gold armor. He points his spear at the boy and shouts in a booming voice.

"You have done what is forbidden. You are no longer welcome here, Jacek. You are banished from this place. Leave, and never return." The terrified child wails and his mother scoops him up with a click of her tongue at the fairy.

"He's just a babe," she shouts at the fairy.

"He doesn't belong here, nor do you," the fairy raises his chin.

"And yet I am here whether you like it or not, Mevyn." The woman narrows her eyes at him. "Perhaps I shall visit the Great Circle. Tell them of your insolence."

"You are the insolent one, Mage. Go. You are no longer welcome at the Wellspring." He raises his spear to her. Others of his kind gather behind him, looming, waiting.

"We were just leaving, anyway," Dinaea barks. She tips her forehead to the child's and whispers to him. "One day, it will be yours, my son. You deserve it. You deserve all the world, my beautiful boy."

"Everything leads back to that," Jacek whispers. "I deserve, it, you see. All of it. My mother's words were prophecy. *One day, it will be yours, my son.* And so I help it along. Little puppets in a play, and all of them dancing for me." Jacek's adult voice drifts over me, pulling me away from the rest of it, back to the chaise in the castle.

"Have you ever touched the Spring, my lovely?" he asks. I try to look at him, but my eyes are too heavy. I'm so sedated by him, so tranquil I can barely make sense of his words. His fingertips brush my jaw and I feel the power that surges from them. They are the same fingers that dipped into the golden pool. The magic they hold gives me strength to open my eyes, to look into his. "Have you?" he asks.

I shake my head, "It's forbidden."

"But you have seen Kythshire's? Been to it?" My eyes drift closed again. I let my head bob lazily. Jacek charges me again with his power.

"Look at me," he says with an urgency that brings me to my senses. I force my eyes open and meet his. "You have their trust, their welcome. You will touch it. Just once. Dip your hand into the glittering surface. Feel the power I have felt, then come back to me. Come and tell me what you've seen. You will understand, and we will be joined. Swear it to me."

"*You're strong,*" the other voice echoes. It's a girl, someone I don't know. She's close, though. So close. Jacek's eyes pull me in again.

They're dark as the night sky, with flecks of ash that dance and float within them. I watch the random patterns as they drift close and far. They hold me and guide my thoughts. The Wellspring, yes. Just once, I would like to touch it. Just once feel what's so forbidden, what's so guarded.

"*You can overcome this,*" the girl whispers firmly.

"I will," I whisper, more in reply to the echoing voice. Jacek takes it as my vow, though. His eyes widen with triumph. Then, with a wave of his arm and a rustle of his cloak, he's gone and I'm falling, falling into darkness, falling away from him, tumbling into nothing.

My shoulder hits the ground first hard and without warning, and then my head. It cracks painfully on the cold stone, sending stars bursting across my vision. These injuries, this agony is nothing compared to the loss of Jacek. He left me, he cast me away. Now I'm alone in the darkness, blind and helpless in his vast world. I feel empty, discarded. Finished. I could die.

"*Wake up,*" the girl whispers to me. "*Just wake up.*"

"Who's there?" I cry. I try to see, but it's too dark. I should stand up, but my legs are tangled in my gown and I can't be bothered to fight free. My head pounds so much that I fear it will split open. I press my palms to it as if trying to keep myself from breaking apart.

"Who's there?" I call again, and my voice is wracked with sobs.

"Just wake up," she whispers once more, but I can't. I'm tired now, so tired. So heavy. I press my cheek to the cold stone floor. My eyes close again. This time when I sleep, I don't know for how long.

I dream of strange things and even stranger places. The gold fairy appears to me more than once. He shows me people and places. There is a man, and there are children, and there is Jacek. Faces flash before me. Red hair, black hair. Jacek, the boy who became Dreamwalker. He's angry. Jealous. Dangerous. He lashes out, causes pain. His power is more than they can control.

They have to do it. With Mevyn's help, they send him away. Someplace distant, someplace safe. Guard the others, the other children, the ones who stole his father away. The ones who deserve pain. Ward them and guard them until Mother and Father can stop him. It's confusing, frightening. I can't watch his pain anymore. I turn from it and find myself safe in my bedroom, facing a small, circular hatch. My hatch. Our hatch.

Rian, oh, my Rian. Oh, my Rian. My love, my only love. I reach up and push the door open with a shaking hand. Will he understand?

Will he forgive me? I peer inside at his usually rumpled bedroom, but it's stripped bare. Nothing remains but an undressed bed and a cleared off table. Downstairs, our housekeeper, Mouli, is singing. The aroma of her cooking makes my mouth water. I go to my door, try to open it, but it's locked from the outside. I shake the handle, pound on the door, shout for someone to let me out, but no one comes. The house is empty, the Elite are no more. The smell of her cooking is gone, and so is she. I'm alone, all alone, trapped in my room where they think I'll be safe. Trapped and alone. Alone and forgotten. Rian has left me. They've all left me.

"It isn't real," the girl whispers, *"whatever you're seeing, it's not real. Wake up."*

I spin around to see where the voice is coming from, but there's no one else here. Outside my window, dawn is breaking. I can see the sun peeking up over the horizon of thick green leaves.

Trees tower over me. Their trunks are broader than my shoulders and so close together that there's barely room for the light to shimmer through. I'm not in my room anymore. I'm in the forest where I started. Through the narrow cracks between the tree trunks, I can see the meadow. I'm still in the Dreaming.

As the morning light grows brighter, it pushes my memories of Jacek away. The pain in my head and shoulder fades, too. Instead I think of Rian. I fill my heart with him. I focus on him as I push my way between the trees. I need to get back to him, to the inn where my family is waiting, and away from this strange, confusing place.

I finally reach the meadow and take in its beauty. The newly-risen sun splashes across it, causing the morning dew to sparkle brightly in a vast array of colors. It reminds me of someone else. Someone dear to me.

"Flitt!" I call out, "Flitt, where are you?"

"Azaeli, wake up."

The voice isn't hers, but someone else's. The whispering girl.

"How?" I shout. "How? Help me!"

"Just…open your eyes."

Chapter Twenty-Three:

AWAKENING

Azi

Open your eyes. It seems like such a simple suggestion, and so obvious. Why hasn't it occurred to me until now? I saw myself fade from my mother's arms in the inn. I felt the shift to this realm. I'm so confused. Is it another of the Dreamwalker's tricks? Is he trying to make me believe I'm not really here, that I'm actually asleep somewhere? That all I have to do to escape this strange, confusing place is simply wake up?

I look down at my hands, which are familiar and unfamiliar. Thin golden lines swirl across them, glittering and shining in the sunlight. I turn them over and rub my fingers together. They feel real. I feel real. When I fell, I was in pain. I felt my bones crack. I reach up now and press my head gingerly where it hit the stone. The pain is gone.

I close my eyes. Somewhere in the distance, someone is calling my name. I don't know the voice. It sounds like a boy. A young Jacek, perhaps. I block it out and try to wrap my mind around this new concept that maybe I really am asleep, and all I need to do is wake up. *Wake up,* I tell myself, *wake up.*

Slowly everything around me shifts, and with it comes the feeling that I'm fading out and in again. This time, I'm lying in the grass with the sunlight warm on my face. Someone is beside me, holding my hand. Close by I'm aware of familiar sounds: Dancing, singing, laughter. The air is thick with magic. It seeps into me and settles over me with such a subtle power that my breath shudders from the shock of it. When it touches me, I know in an instant that I'm in Kythshire.

"I think," the one holding my hand announces quietly to the Ring, "I think she's waking." It's the girl, the whisperer. "Sir Azaeli?"

The dancing stops abruptly. Everything is quiet. My eyelids are so heavy, but I force them open. The first thing I see are green eyes framed by a shock of red curls. The girl grins and squeezes my hand.

"She is! She's awake! Oh, I'm so relieved." She pats my shoulder through my armor. My armor. I have it back. My free hand searches in the grass.

"My sword?" I feel for the hilt at my back, but it isn't there. I start to panic.

"It's here," the girl says. She reaches to the grass above my head and pulls my weapon close. The look in her eyes as she holds it is that of awe. With a careful reverence, she lays it beside me and places my hand on the hilt. When she looks at me and smiles, her eyes are glistening with tears.

"What's your name?" I ask her. I feel like I've seen her before. She has a vague familiarity, like a face in passing who I've seen many times but never really met.

"Saesa." She straightens a little and gives me a respectful nod.

"Saesa, you saved me," I say. "I heard your whispers. I thought I was really there, but your words, they made me see another side."

"Good thing you sent me for that crystal, Crocus," Shush's voice comes like a breath of wind from somewhere close by. He zooms to Saesa's side. I smile at the familiar sight of him as he pushes his goggles to his forehead. "It really worked," he whispers, pointing to the orange-colored crystal that bobs over my chest.

"It was foreseen, and so it was," Crocus declares abstractly. All around us the fairies murmur their agreement. Shush leans over me and blows softly on the crystal, and it fades and disappears.

"What was that?" I ask him.

"Just a little something to open up the channels," he replies, always whispering. "Avenside crystal. Always does the trick. Of course, this little one did most of the important work." He points to Saesa. "Couldn't have reached you without her."

"Nessa taught me that words have power," Saesa beams. "I guess she was right."

"Nessa?" I prop myself up on my elbows and she helps me to sit up in the grass.

"She's my mother. Well, foster mother. She takes care of me and my brothers and sisters." She sits back on her heels again and slides my sword to her. While she talks, she buckles the harness around my shoulders. "There were six of us until Tib came. Now I guess that makes seven. She teaches us things." She helps me to my feet and clasps my hilt to the harness.

"Thank you," I say absently. While Saesa fetches my gloves I look across to Crocus, who's watching the scene with interest. As always, a gentle sort of curiosity plays in her smile and her bright eyes.

"We recognize Azaeli Hammerfel, The Temperate, Pure of Heart, Reviver of Iren, The Great Protector, Cerion's Ambassador to Kythshire, Champion of Kythshire, and we are glad to see you restored."

"That last one is new, isn't it?" I ask Crocus. Saesa fastens my cloak to the golden clasps at my shoulder and adjusts its draping as Crocus and I talk.

"It is," Crocus nods slowly.

"I didn't earn it." I shake my head. "I've been foolish, and quick to anger. I've allowed myself to be manipulated. I've…" A pang of guilt stabs my heart. I pull off a glove and look at my hand. The golden swirls have faded, but they're still visible. "I've used magic, Crocus. Selfishly." I hold my hand up to show her. Around the edge of the Ring the fairies lean in, wide-eyed and curious. They whisper among themselves. Crocus beckons me closer and takes my hand.

"Mentalism," she says quietly. She looks up at me curiously. "You learned this in the Dreaming?" I nod apologetically. Her mention of the Dreaming brings a hint of a thought to my mind. A memory of promises made. One in particular, a strong one that I never ought to have bound myself to. I shake my head and push the thoughts away.

"Do not be ashamed," she says brightly, "this magic is rare, but it isn't ours to steward. Kythshire has little dominion over it. It comes from another place."

"Sunteri?" I ask. It seems the next likely source.

"Not Sunteri. We shall tell you another time. Right now, your path lies ahead of you. You must return to the Dreaming and seek those who ventured to rescue you."

"Those who ventured…" I turn around and scan the circle, and my heart starts to race. Rian. Flitt. They're not here. How did I miss that before now? "You mean they went, they're there? They're in the Dreaming? How? Why would you send them there if you had that crystal?"

"The crystal was a failsafe, and Shush retrieved it much more quickly than we anticipated." Crocus says regretfully. "We had to ensure your return, one way or another."

"So you put my friends in danger?" I ask frantically.

"We did what we knew we must," she says. "We did not wish to lose you."

"I have to find them before nightfall, Crocus!" I cry. "You don't understand what they're facing. How can I get to them? Please!" She knits her brow together painfully as I squeeze her hand in my panic, and I drop it right away. "Sorry."

"I'll take her," a voice calls out from across the Ring. It takes me a moment to place it. "I have to go, anyway, to make a delivery."

"We recognize Tufar Woodlish Icsanthius Gent, Steward of Princess Margary, Keeper of the Castle." Crocus beams.

"Twig," I whisper and turn to watch him float toward us with his dirt-encrusted toes brushing the grass. A loop of woven ribbons and pearls is slung over his shoulder, and upon his arrival those outside of the circle erupt into cheers.

"Margy's Twig?" Saesa asks behind me.

"How do you know the Princess?" I ask her.

"We're friends," she grins. "Tib and I. We brought her bracelet here for Twig, see?" She points to the loop that Twig is holding. He nods to her.

"And I thank you for it," he says. "Now the Princess will have a new tether to replace the one which was lost. I'd like to thank Tib as well, for setting me free from that box. Is he here?"

"No, he went with the others," Saesa sighs and looks away. It's obvious she's worried for him, whoever he is.

"Are you certain you're well enough?" Crocus asks Twig cautiously. She reaches out for him and he hugs her. A soft green glow settles around them both, and Crocus seems to grow a little. Her colors brighten. "All right, all right, you've made your point," she giggles. "Don't overdo it. Very well, then, Twig, you may take Azaeli into the Dreaming with you."

"What happened, Twig? Who's Tib?" With the mention of his tether, my hand automatically goes to the pouch where I keep Flitt's. It's empty.

"Well, the long and the short of it," he explains, "is that I tried to visit with the princess and got trapped in a box for a few days until Tib found me and let me out. My tether was destroyed, so I have to bring her another one through the Dreaming."

"Oh, that's horrible, Twig! How frightening."

"It was at the time, but I'm fine now," he shrugs. "Just concerned for the princess. I haven't seen her in several days," Twig looks off toward the east, toward Cerion. His brow is knit with worry.

"Yes, the Dreamwalker is growing bolder by the day. Right

now we are warded against him, but we fear his reach may soon extend into Kythshire if he isn't stopped." Crocus's sweet voice is filled with warning.

"Do you mean to tell me," I turn to him, "that it was the Dreamwalker who held you prisoner?" I remember a moment in the Dreaming, when Jacek showed me how he compelled the maid to bring him the object of power. "It was your tether," I whisper. "That's what he wanted."

"Yes, it was he." Twig watches me closely. "You know the why of it."

"What have you seen, Azaeli?" Crocus asks. All around us the fairies lean closer, encroaching on the ring. Scree rumbles a little and they give a little space before I go on.

I tell them what Jacek showed me, all of the people he touched and manipulated. I tell them about the boy I saw, being left by his parents. How he controlled me and clouded my mind and manipulated me. Finally, I tell them about my vows.

"I promised that I would speak for the fallen Sunteri fae. They're so weak, so hopeless and miserable. They live in fear every moment. They need their place, they need to be restored," I tell Crocus.

"We already made a bargain to that end," Crocus says. "Mevyn was to return you to us, and then we would aid in the restoration of their Wellspring. But he failed. You returned to us on your own. He had no part in it."

"Mevyn." I think back. "He was at the Wellspring when Jacek touched it as a baby. He tried to stop him, and when he couldn't, he sent them away."

"We know this," Crocus says. "Oren has shown us. Mevyn has stumbled along his path more than once, and now he has failed in his agreement with us. He has failed to redeem himself."

"You can see what the Oren has seen?" Saesa interjects, and ducks her head right away. "Sorry, I didn't mean to interrupt."

Crocus looks to me. For a moment I'm not sure why, but then I realize it was my turn for a question.

"It's all right," I say. I'm curious about what Saesa asked, too.

"Yes." Crocus answers. She closes her eyes slowly. "The Guardians watch our borders, gathering information. Each of them is connected to us, to Scree, through the stones and soil and earth. They send their thoughts to us, that we may be aware of incoming threats.

"This way we are always aware of our security, or lack thereof. For example just now, on the Western border coastline, Aren, the Golden Coast embodied, the Sand Keeper, Esteemed Guardian of the Western border, Watcher of the West, Spirit of the Tides, sees a ship passing by. We can see it clearly in our mind's eye. It poses no threat. It respects our sea borders." She looks at me and smiles. "What was your second promise, Azaeli?"

Shame and self-loathing settle in the pit of my stomach like a heavy stone. I don't want to tell them, but I know I have to. I've betrayed them with this promise. I've forsaken myself. When I tell them, I know they'll never see me the same way again. How can I remain their Champion, their Ambassador, when I've promised to defile the one thing they hold sacred?

"I was weak against him," I lower my head and look away from them. "He had such a wicked way of making everything seem right, of making me want to please him. I needed him. I needed him, and nothing else mattered." I shake my head. "He asked me to touch it, just once. To dip my fingers into the Wellspring and see how it feels." I close my eyes against the tears that brim in them. I could be alone in a meadow, it's so quiet. "I agreed." I wait for the eruption of anger and disbelief, but it doesn't come. Instead, Crocus speaks.

"But it was not a binding promise, Azaeli," she says quietly. "He believes it was, but you were not speaking to him at the time, were you? Do not be troubled. Do not be ashamed of your weakness. This threat is unlike any we have seen.

"It has been foreseen that you shall one day touch the Wellspring. That is certain. But not today. Not while the Dreamwalker looms. Today, you must display your bravery, your temperate heart. You must bolster yourself against this evil. You must face him again and this time, overcome. Prove to yourself that you are not weal, that you are the Champion we believe you to be."

I don't know what to say. Crocus's faith in me is obviously stronger than my faith in myself. Behind me, Saesa sniffles. When I turn to her she smiles at me. I take her in, really look at her for the first time. She's nearly as tall as I am, with a finely made sword at her belt. Her armor is new and perfect, though studded leather is meant for a novice.

I realize where I've seen her face before. We passed each other often in the halls of the Arms guild. I see the hope in her eyes and the hunger that comes with the desire to prove oneself. I see all of the things I felt when I was her age, looking ahead to the future, wanting nothing more than to become a squire and one day a knight.

"Stand by me," I say to her. "Unless someone else has already sponsored you. Stand by me and be my squire. Come with me to the Dreaming."

Her eyes widen with shock and disbelief, and then her actions surprise me. She looks at Crocus and the fairies beyond, and then she bows her head and hides her face. At first I think she's crying, but she shakes her head and takes a deep breath. She looks up at me, straight into my eyes, and I fall into hers the way I fell into Stubs's. She shows me the other side of it. Her side, with images and words that rush into my mind.

"When I was very young, three or four years perhaps, my mother fell ill. It came on suddenly one day. She went blank and vacant. She couldn't speak or move. She only sat there, gazing off. Sometimes she would be gripped by terrors that made her scream. Other times, she would sob for hours.

"Our father was traveling when the illness began, and so it fell to my brother Raefe to be our caretaker. He was young, just six years old, but he was capable. He went out into the streets of Cerion and begged. He kept our bellies full. It was then that the nightmares started. They plagued us so much that we would wake nearly every night, screaming.

"I remember always being frightened, always terrorized by these threats and dark thoughts that plagued us. It went on for years, and Father never returned. One day when I was five and Raefe was eight, too sad to go out, we were visited by a creature. A fairy who shined with golden light. He worked magic over us, protecting us. He brought us peace. It was too late for Mother, though. Her suffering had gone on too long. Her madness consumed her, even after Mevyn pulled the darkness out of her.

"And so we went to live with Nessa, who loved us as a mother loves her children, and who provided for us in ways we never would have otherwise been cared for. She kept us safe. She found a safe place for Mother, too."

She shows me shining white warriors, beautiful and lithe, with striking faces and long, pointed ears. Elves.

"I didn't know until I arrived here. I had forgotten about all of it. Even my mother. Her name is Evelie. She lives with the elves. She has red hair, just like me. I didn't know until the Oren showed me, and even then I didn't understand why. What was this darkness that plagued us? Why did our father abandon us?

Oren showed me the truth. The dark threat was my father's son. Not Raefe, no. Father had a child before us, with a different mother. A Sorceress. Her jealousy of my father's new family, her dark thoughts and hatred bled through to her son. He saw how the knowledge of our family destroyed her. He had powers unlike any other, even from a young age.

"He lashed out at us across the miles. He inflicted the same suffering his mother felt on my mother. He was young. He didn't understand. But as he grew, so did his power. Soon, nobody could stop his wicked heart. His mother tried to tame him, and so did his father. My father. They came to realize there was no hope in controlling him, so they sent him away. They trapped him in another realm."

The memory burns bright in my mind's eye, the one Stubs showed me only yesterday. The man and woman covered by the Mark, standing in the meadow. The boy they left behind, sobbing in the tall grass.

"They bound him there with a blood oath," Saesa continues. "Blood of the father and mother. His imprisonment can only be ended when one who shares his bloodline comes to the Dreaming to seek him out. Only then can the bindings be undone. So you see, I can't go with you. If I do, I risk setting my half-brother free."

Her handling of this knowledge surprises and impresses me. I have so many questions for her, but there isn't time now. She's right. She can't come with me. If she did, Jacek would certainly find a way to use her. We have no way of knowing whether Mevyn's protection would extend into Jacek's kingdom.

"Sometimes, the bravest act is restraint," I say to her with a smile. "When I return, I'll have a squire to rival every squire in Cerion." She bows her head again, grinning.

"Azaeli, time is short as you said. Unless you have another question, we suggest that you be on your way." Crocus says.

"Just two more," I think for a moment. "Quickly. You said that Mevyn failed to bring me back, but if he does this time, will that fulfill his end of the bargain?"

"Yes. Is there anything we might provide to you, in order to aid you on your quest?"

"My diamond. Flitt's tether. Do you have it?" My hand goes to the empty pouch again.

"Dabble?" Crocus calls, and Dabble appears right at my feet.

"Here you are. Good as new, with a few improvements as I saw necessary. Flitt knows all about them." He holds the sparkling gem up to me. It's as big as my head in my shrunken state.

"Thank you," I take it carefully and tuck it under my arm, then turn to Saesa, my squire. "Be safe," I say. "I won't be long."

"Oh, Saesa and I shall have a great game of questions together, I think," Crocus smiles. I'm sure she's right. Being one of Nessa Ganvent's charges, I'm certain my new squire will be a fountain of information for those here. I shake my head.

"Be careful," I say to her, and then lean in to whisper, "fairies are tricky."

"I will," she giggles. "You be careful, too."

On my other side, Twig offers me a gentlemanly arm. I slip my hand into the crook of his elbow and he grins at me.

"Ready for adventure?" he winks. The crowd beyond the mushrooms slowly blurs as the gathering of fairies starts to dance again.

"Let's go," I say urgently. The prospect of going back into the Dreaming doesn't appeal to me in the least, but for Rian, for Flitt, I don't hesitate.

"Close your eyes," he places a hand over mine as I do, and the ground beneath our feet falls away. I feel myself bobbing and floating carefree, like an autumn leaf carried by a lazy breeze. It floats us gently away from the Ring. The dancing and singing fade, replaced by a different melody, quiet and slow. An underlying, pleasant hum is flecked with a higher timber, a rustle.

"What is that sound?" I ask him as our feet find the ground again.

"Keep your eyes closed and listen," Twig says. "See if you can figure it out."

"Are we here? In the Dreaming?" The hum fades a little as I speak.

"Yes. Shh. Listen," he whispers.

After a moment of quiet, the strange music grows louder. To me, it sounds like the low thrum of heartbeats, dozens of them, and the higher sound of whispering. I can't make out what the whispers are saying; there are too many of them. Still, the effect is beautiful and peaceful. It's an ancient song, played long before my time and one that will continue into eternity. I feel both a part of it and a stranger to it. It brings me comfort and reassurance. This song has always been here, and it always will be.

"Now, open your eyes." Twig whispers.

We're in the midst of the bright forest, where trees tower over us, thick and strong. In the canopy high above us, leaves rustle and whisper in the breeze. The great trunk beside me seems to vibrate with its own contribution to the hum. I stare in disbelief at Twig.

"The trees are singing?" I whisper.

"They always sing," he laughs. "You just never heard them before." He places a hand on the root in front of him. Pats it lovingly.

"Why can I hear them now?"

"I gave you a gift. I thought it would be helpful," Twig grins. He closes his eyes again. The stick-like wings at his back open and close slowly. "Listen," his whisper is filled with affection. I kneel beside him and rest my hand on the same root.

I don't hear anything, but I imagine Rian and Flitt walking through these very woods, past this very tree. With them are a boy with black hair, a golden fairy, and Ki with her bow out and ready. The group pushes through the underbrush and slowly disappears behind a tree with an oddly bent trunk. The hum of the trees vibrates through me. I wait for something, some words or direction, but I'm too impatient. I want to find them now. They're here, looking for me. They've placed themselves in danger to find me.

"Thank you!" Twig says brightly. "There you go, Azi! They went through there." I look off to the distance, where Twig is pointing. Sure enough, there's the same bent tree that I imagined them walking past.

"So you're saying I can talk to trees now?" I ask incredulously.

"Just for a little while. What else? Oh!" He waves a hand at me and I start to grow. The diamond tucked under my arm remains the same, until it fits neatly in the palm of my hand. Twig flies up to perch beside it. "Better put that away. I think that's everything, right? I've got to get to Margy before she wakes up. She's napping, you see."

"Of course," I say. "Thank you for everything. Really. Are you sure you'll be safe?"

"I think so, as long as I don't linger past nightfall. Good luck!" With little warning at all, he darts off into the trees, leaving me alone in the Dreaming.

M. Sheldrake
2015

Chapter Twenty-Four:

VIALA'S LEGACY

Azi

Perhaps because I've entered on my own terms this time, the Dreaming feels different. I have my sword and my armor, I don't feel defenseless or alone. I keep my wits as I push through the thick woods with a purpose, pausing from time to time to rest my hand on the rough bark of a tree and listen. Their songs are a constant companion to me, guiding me along a path I couldn't see before.

The Dreaming is so much vaster than I had imagined. Now that I'm here without Jacek's influence, I see it differently. It's a beautiful place, filled with many wonders. Tiny fae dragons, bright-colored lizard-like creatures with wings that sparkle in the sun, weave and dart playfully around me as I walk. Unicorns and cygnets graze in distant meadows. I curb my curiosity of these creatures and focus on the trees. The sun is halfway to noon. I need to find the others before nightfall.

The trees guide me to the same meadow where I met Stubs on my previous visit. The grass is taller today, and the breeze too soft to bend it into waves. When I crouch among the blades, they stretch up over my head. I weave a frond around my fingers and try to listen to it, but my listening skills are apparently limited to trees and not grass. Still, the trees did lead me here…

When I stand again, my heart sinks. The meadow is endlessly vast. They could have gone in any direction searching for me. It would take hours to exhaust every option. I don't have that much time. I remember what Stubs told me. Time moves differently here. I hope he meant that it's slower.

"Listen to your heart," someone mutters nearby. A patch of grass rustles just a few steps ahead. I unclasp my sword and slide it from its sheath.

"Who's there?" I raise my weapon at the ready. After last time, I'm not taking any chances.

"But she looks different today, all in her armor, with her sword, too. She's ready for a fight."

"Stubs?" I peer into the grass and catch the flash of an amber eye. With a huff, I turn on my heel and storm past him.

"Where is she going?"

"Away from you," I snap. I don't need his tricks today. I won't let him lure me in.

"Oh, but she is angry. Angry with Stubs?" He follows beside me in the grass, huffing and bobbing to keep up with my quick strides. I try to ignore him as I scan the vast field, but he just keeps talking. "Had to do it, had to. Not just had to, wanted to. Wanted to help her. I did! See? I gave her a gift. She can see minds now, can't she? That was no trick. I helped her. Dreamwalker made it seem like his idea, but no. It was mine. He wanted her not to trust me. He wanted her to be angry with me, so she would leave me and need him more."

"I don't have time to argue with you or figure out the truth," I turn, searching for any small sign of a group passing through. There's nothing. Not even a bent blade of grass. It's useless searching here, so I start back toward the trees.

"She's looking for her friends. She won't find them in the meadow." Stubs blinks up at me and I pause.

"You know where they are?"

"I showed them…"

"What? What did you show them, Stubs?"

"Showed the gold fairy. Mevyn, he's called," he watches me eagerly as he speaks. "They all saw what I saw: Dreamwalker wrapping her in his cloak, taking her away. They went to rescue her. I hoped they would succeed, but now she's back again."

All I can think of is Rian seeing me in that memory, falling into Jacek's arms, gazing up at the Dreamwalker with a hunger that should only ever be reserved for him. My eyes burn with tears.

"He saw, and he still went to search for me?" I whisper.

"Mmm. They went to the castle." He twists his grubby hands, sending a cascade of soil to the ground. "I was trying to help. I didn't want her to be in danger."

"How do I get there, Stubs? Please."

"I already said. Follow your heart. But she should put away her sword first, probably." The grass at his back shivers as he nods.

He looks earnest enough, but I still don't trust him.

"So, what you're telling me is to stow my sword and head straight into the danger unprepared?"

His eyes widen and his jaw drops open. "Oh, that's what it sounds like to her, isn't it? No, no. That isn't my intention at all."

"What is your intention, then, Stubs?" I ask, growing increasingly annoyed.

"Ten years, Lady Knight. Ten years he has terrorized us. We want him stopped, and never have we met someone before who we believed in as much. And her friends are here, too. She can stop him. We would never sabotage that. We want our lands back. Our peace. The previous Dreamwalker, he kept to his own. Never ventured here. This one, he thinks he owns everything he sees. He thinks he can do whatever he likes. All for his pleasure, and we are too weak to stop him."

"The previous Dreamwalker? There was another?" I slide my sword into its scabbard but leave the clasp undone just in case.

"It is a position like any other," he explains. "One can be pushed out by another, more powerful. There cannot be two. Only one can rule the night here."

The sun is at the noon mark already. Time is moving too quickly for more questions. I have to get to the others before nightfall, before the Dreamwalker comes again.

"Follow my heart?" I ask. Stubs nods. I think I understand. It's just like Kythshire. Like traveling through the Half-Realm. I close my eyes and think hard. In my mind, Rian appears before me. His eyes shine with that endearing glint of mischief that belies just how much power is held behind them. His auburn hair is getting longer now. He's growing it out for the winter months. His robes are soft yellow and blue, his arms warm and welcoming. *Rian*, I send the thought out, searching for him.

The ground falls away beneath me and I try not to yelp in surprise as I begin to tumble away from the meadow. Despite the unpredictable plunge, I try hard to keep my focus on my destination: his arms, his smile, his kiss.

I land hard against him, flattening him to the cold stone floor with a crash that knocks the breath out of me. Rian too, from the sound of it. He lies crushed under the weight of my armor, unmoving. I scramble off of him and help him sit up but he does nothing to greet me. Right away my thoughts go to the vision of Jacek and my heart sinks. He hates me.

"Rian," I take his hands in mine, "please forgive me. I shouldn't have gone with him. I was weak. I'm so sorry."

His eyes are wide open, staring but not seeing. Tears stream down his cheeks. He shakes his head slowly and raises his trembling hands to his face.

"He can't see you," a boy says from the shadows. "He can't hear you, either. He's someplace else." I've heard this voice before, only once. It called my name just as I was waking from my last nightmare here. I draw Rian closer to me to protect him. Even if he hates me now, even if he renounces me, I'll keep him safe. I won't let anyone touch him.

"Who's there?" I squint at the source of the voice in shadows, and the boy creeps forward into the dim light. He moves with a graceful purpose, as though every motion is meant to conceal some well-kept secret. He's a slim young lad, with a fringe of tousled blue-black hair that nearly hides his dark slanted eyes. A half-dozen knife hilts slung across his chest glint in the dim light.

"My name's Tib," he says, "And you're her, aren't you? The reason we came here. The knight."

I nod in reply and turn my attention back to Rian, who is still staring blankly at nothing, crying.

"What happened? Rian!" I jostle him again gently. "Where are the others? Flitt, Mevyn and Ki? They came with you, didn't they?"

"We got split up. It was all confusing. I could see shadows and then they were on me. Rian tried to cast a spell but they moved too fast. He grabbed me, and suddenly we were here. Then he started going crazy casting spells. He used up a lot of magic. I had to hide, it almost hit me a few times." His eyes slide warily to him. I'm glad Rian's somewhere else and can't see how afraid Tib is of him. It would break his heart.

"Rian," I whisper to him, pulling him closer. I kiss his cheeks, his lips. His skin is cool and clammy, his eyes glazed and distant. I know what I have to do even though I'm repulsed by the thought of it. I need to look into him. To see what he's seeing. I gaze into his eyes, fall into them, spin away from the stone and the walls.

At first I don't recognize where I am. A steady rain pummels me, drenching me in an instant, sending rivulets of inky runoff spilling over the blackened earth. Melted coal-like stubs protrude from it in a wide circle around us. The sky above is dark and threatening. It rumbles with ear-splitting thunder as it pours down its wrath. I creep forward, trying to figure out where I am.

Beyond the circle drenched in rain and soot lie piles of refuse. As I move closer I realize it isn't refuse at all, it's bodies. Lifeless fairies, as charred and blackened as the ground. My heart races. We're in Kythshire. In the Ring. Crocus' lifeless form, coated in black, withered and twisted, lies slumped over Scree. Shush's body crackles beside them, still smoking. I spin to face Rian, who's kneeling in a pool of mud, crumpled and devastated. Beside him, my armor lies singed and empty on a soot-covered white cloak.

"I couldn't hold it anymore," his whisper is nearly drowned out by the rain. Rather than look up at me, he sinks lower until he's curled into a tight ball in the mud. "I tried, I tried so hard, but I couldn't stop it. It's what I always feared. I wasn't strong enough. I killed them. I killed all of them. I never should have come back here."

I take a deep breath and remind myself that it isn't real. This is his nightmare, his fear come to life. A trick of the mind, designed to destroy him. I rush to his side and kneel. I take his hands in mine just as I had in the room where I found him.

"Look at me," I say. "Rian. Look at me."

He refuses. His body wracks with sobs. I feel my own heart sinking, falling into the pit of darkness that he has already plummeted into. I steel myself and take his face in my hands.

"Look at me, Rian." I say again. His hazel eyes, ringed in red and smeared with black, lock to mine. It takes only a moment for him. He blinks and pulls me close and kisses me so passionately that I'm breathless, and then we're falling away again, back to the stone, back to Tib in the tiny cell.

"Ha! Told you she was here," Flitt squeaks. "Azi, you have a Mage stuck to your face again." Flitt's light shines through my closed eyes as Rian continues to kiss me. This time, I don't care who's watching. To feel his arms around me, his lips on mine again is better than any medicine, more powerful than any spell. By the time we reluctantly pull away from each other, we're both grinning like fools.

"How did you…" Rian trails off and shakes his head as he gazes into my eyes.

"Oh, Flitt!" Flitt says dramatically. "I'm so glad to see you! Thanks for coming to this scary place to help find me. What a great friend you are!" Flitt perches on my knee, hands on hips, scowling up at me. I scoop her gently into my hands and kiss her too, on the side of her beautiful, perfect, multicolor-pony-tailed head.

"I *am* glad to see you," I laugh.

"Ugh, you still have Mage spit on you," she groans and wipes away my kiss. With her nose still wrinkled in disgust, she floats up to the pouch around my neck. "Good," she says. "You got it back. Ooh, and Dabble made it nice and shiny, too."

"Shh," I warn. I don't want to call any attention to it in this place.

"Now that we're all reunited…" The voice is droll and heavy, but it holds a certain power that instantly garners my respect. I turn toward him, the fairy in golden armor who I saw in the vision that Stubs gave me, and who was mentioned at the Ring.

"You must be Mevyn," I bow my head in greeting.

"Glad we found you, Lady Knight," he says abruptly. "Now we should be moving on."

Behind him, just on the edge of the shadows, Tib and Ki stand together. The blue stone of her necklace casts a soothing light over the small space and I get the sense that we are protected. Not only is Ki here, but Iren is too, watching over us. I look from her to Tib and back again. Their features are oddly similar. They could be—

"Oh," I gasp, "You're the boy in the roots." His eyes narrow beneath the black fringe and his lips set in a tight line. "I wanted to go back for you…" I remember my journey with Elliot, when he took me to the sands of Sunteri to show me the devastation there. I cried when he fled the trees where the little bundles were held captive. There wasn't time to help them, though. There were much bigger things at stake.

"It's fine. I got out of it, right?" Tib folds his arms across his bandolier. No thanks to you, his body language seems to say. I don't miss that one hand is resting on a knife hilt. "Are we going, then?" he asks impatiently. "We've got her, haven't we?"

"It's nearly nightfall," Ki says softly. "The shadows are starting to creep."

"Where are we?" I don't know why I feel the need to ask. A part of me already knows. I've been here before.

"We saw the castle and thought for sure that if Dreamwalker had you, this is where you'd be," Rian says. "Mevyn tried to get us in together, but some strange ward separated us. That's how I ended up in here, with Tib."

"Lucky you showed up, Azi," Flitt says with a grin. "We were only split up for a little while, but we had no way of finding Rian. But then I felt you close by and I brought the others to you. You didn't bring any sugar cubes, by any chance?"

"Left pack pocket." I roll my eyes as she dives into my pack.

"Time is passing more quickly now," Ki whispers. "Soon it will be dark."

"Yes," says Mevyn. "We'd best be on our way."

At the back of my mind, something calls to me. An object I thought lost, a beloved old friend begging to be rescued. My sword, propped against the wall in Jacek's tower, just out of reach. I was so close to it, close enough to touch it. Close enough, but my arms were too heavy and then Jacek, he was right there, right beside me. I could get it back again, and maybe I'd see him, too. My heart starts to race and then Tib walks up and strikes me hard across the cheek, snapping me out of my trance.

"Hey!" Rian thrusts a hand out toward him and I see the wave of a spell pass over the boy, but he seems unaffected by it.

"It's okay," I push Rian's arm down and rub my cheek. "He saw it. I was slipping into the Dreamwalker's grasp." I turn to Tib. "How did you know?"

Tib shrugs. His eyes slide sideways to Mevyn just for an instant.

"I could see the shadows in your eyes," Tib says. With his frown, I get the sense that this is a talent he's reluctantly accepted.

"Can we go now?" Tib asks.

"We really should." Ki has her bow out now with an arrow nocked and ready. At the mention of shadows, Flitt shines her light a little brighter, pushing them back until the room is entirely bathed in her prisms.

"Yes, we'd best go quickly." Mevyn beckons us closer and we link arms together.

"I'll do it this time," Flitt says around a mouthful of sugar. "Just say where."

"Back to the meadow?" Ki says thoughtfully. "There, we can keep the shadows at bay and make a plan."

"I have a better place," Mevyn says thoughtfully. "A safer place."

"Where?" I ask.

"I can't say. Not here. The shadows have ears."

"Sorry," says Rian. "I don't know you well enough yet to trust you that much, Mevyn. I have a place. I need to check on them anyway." He looks at Flitt, who nods slowly.

"Yep," she says. "That place is as good as any. It's already all warded up, too."

"Well, how do I know I can trust you, then? Turn those tables, Mage." Mevyn's eyes narrow, his golden hair floats around his head as though he's under water.

"Do you want our help against the Dreamwalker, and with the Wellspring?" Rian asks. "If you do, then you have to trust us, don't you? We're going after him either way, with your help or without it."

"Very well," Mevyn agrees wearily. Beside him, Ki shifts her footing, looking slightly concerned.

"Are you permitted to leave the Dreaming, Ki? To go to the waking realm?" Rian asks.

Ki closes her hand over her necklace and bows her head. When she looks up again, she nods slowly. "Iren consents, and trusts in your wards, Your Excellency."

I think of Eron, how he was so keen to have me bring Viala—Ki—back to him. Bringing her with us outside of the Dreaming would put her in a dangerous position, and she has no idea of the risk. I wonder if Iren does.

"Can I speak to Iren though that?" I nod to her necklace.

"Of course," she says. "But quickly. It's nearly nightfall now."

She takes the stone in her palm and I move closer to look into it. The gem is a chip of Iren's own eye, the Oculus: Midnight blue with flecks of gold that float through it like the stars in the night sky. I focus on it and fall into it the same way I fell into Stubs' amber eyes and Rian's hazel ones. Iren's is far vaster, though. Its thoughts greet me cautiously. I can see its kind, stony face smiling down on me as golden orbs drift lazily around us.

We don't speak to each other. Instead, I recall the meeting with Eron. I send the moment out into the space between us, and Iren watches. When that memory fades, another one emerges slowly. One from the distant past.

Viala and Eron stand together in the annex beside the ballroom of Cerion's palace, their heads bent close together, secretly planning. Beyond the door, the sounds of a ball are muffled and fleeting. I feel myself drawn closer to her until I'm seeing the scene through her own eyes.

"*If we fail in this,*" she's saying, "*if we do not succeed together, then we shall both fall. Swear to me.*" She holds his hand in hers and traces strange runes over it. Black tendrils curl out from the runes and tighten around their clasped hands, binding them. "*If anything happens, swear that you shall stop at nothing to find me, to bring me back to you.*"

"*I swear it, my love,*" Eron says passionately. "*I am yours and you are mine, always. One day, we shall rule together. Our kingdom will be endless, as will our power. I will never lose you. I will always come for you.*"

"*Together, or not at all,*" she whispers. "*This spell seals it. Bound by words, heart, deeds, and darkness, never to be undone, except in death.*" Eron leans closer to her. I feel his lips on hers and pull away, disgusted.

"*Some magic,*" Iren says quietly, "*cannot be undone except by its caster. Your refusal to cooperate with Eron matters little. He will stop at nothing to reach her, no matter who she is now. To him, as long as she is alive, she is Viala, the one who cast the spell to bind them. Even now, only she can sever those bindings. So you see why I must allow her the chance to choose well, should she be faced with it.*"

"*But she has no memory of that time now. How can she possibly undo a spell she can't even remember casting?*"

"*She is no longer clouded by fear, darkness, power, hatred. She has been given a second chance. When the time comes, if she is faced with it, she will remember. This is her final test. I must allow it.*" Iren shows me another memory, this one more recent.

Ki and Tib in the Ring, holding each other. Ki and I in the cave together, guarded by Iren's blue light. Ki, standing at the crest of the Shadow Crag, keeping watch over Kythshire and the lands beyond the border. Ki, resting curled in the protective crook of Iren's elbow. With every scene, I can feel the confidence and peace in her, the sense of purpose and belonging.

"*It would be cruel of me,*" Iren says, "*to conceal this from her. To deny her this chance to redeem her past. Even while making his choice for her, Rian said the same. Everyone deserves a second chance.*"

"*But what if she chooses poorly?*" I ask. "*What if she allows herself to be clouded again and Eron gets his way?*"

There is a long silence before Viala's voice drifts into the space between us once more. As I fall away from Iren and back to the stone room, her words drift through my mind over and over.

"*Bound by words, heart, deeds, and darkness. Never to be undone, except in death. Except in death. In death.*"

I'm aware of my feet on the ground and Rian's hand on my shoulder as I slip away from Iren. Ki is watching me curiously, but I avoid her gaze. I don't want her to see what I've seen.

"All right?" she asks quietly. I nod. Beside her, Tib watches me with suspicion, his eyes narrowed. It makes me feel uneasy, like I've been caught in a lie. I shake it off and turn to Rian.

"We can go," I whisper. "All of us."

With Viala's spell still echoing in my thoughts, I take Rian's hand. The rest of our group comes together, linking arms and holding on, and Rian murmurs the spell that will take us to the Half-Realm, and then on to Sorlen River Crossing.

Chapter Twenty-Five:

PLANS

Tib

It's the third time today I've been lurched through space to someplace new, and I don't like it any more this time than I did the first two. I cling to my sister and squeeze my eyes shut and try hard to concentrate on something else. Like the conversation between Azi and the stone giant, Iren. The things I heard, just like I could hear Rian telling Flitt we were going to Sorlen River Crossing. Just like I could hear Crocus talking to Scree.

I feel like I should tell Ki. Tell her what they said. This is some sort of sick test. He's controlling everything she remembers, just like Mevyn did with me. If she fails, death. How did we both get ourselves into this mess? It's her fault, really. She never should have agreed to go with that Sorcerer. A gift is a trick, Nan told her. If she'd stayed and just picked blooms like she was supposed to, if she'd started filling her basket and stopped reading her stupid books, neither of us would be here.

Maybe she deserves what's coming to her.

Rian whispers something as we spin around, and I feel the magic around us shifting. Preparing for us. Letting us in. I never noticed things like this before the fairy ring. I was never sensitive to magic the way I am now. I know what it's doing before it happens. I can see it and avoid it.

I think back to the stone room when we got split up from the others and Rian was raging. He was flinging spells everywhere and not one of them touched me. I knew where they were going, and I just moved away. Then after I slapped the knight, he tried it again and I didn't even feel it. It's like it split in two and went around me. I don't understand it, but I'm not complaining, either.

We land with a thud on the floorboards loud enough to wake

the village, but it doesn't wake any of the patrons up. I remember the story Rian told back at the Ring, about his guild. I look around at them. They look unharmed. Sleeping in the middle of a fight scene. Chairs and tables turned over. Plates shattered on the ground. Wine and cider spilled everywhere. It stinks in here, too. Rotten food. Burnt meat. Unwashed people.

Azi gasps and rushes to one of the sleepers. A woman. She looks like an older version of Azi with the same blond braid. She's slumped over a bench, her arms draped awkwardly across it like she's passed out from too much drink.

"Oh, Mum," Azi brushes some stray hair away from the woman's face. Arranges her arms a little more comfortably. Looks up at Rian. "Was this you? You put them all to sleep?"

"After you passed out," Rian's shoulders go up apologetically, "they all started fighting. I didn't know what else to do." He starts going on, telling the same story he told us in the Ring. Ki goes to stand by the window and watch out. Mevyn sticks close to me. I want to shove him away.

While Rian's talking, I go from one of the sleeping guild members to the next, looking them over. Last time I saw them, they were riding out of Cerion. I stop next to the biggest one. He's huge. Stone-skinned, with plate armor. He's out cold, snoring loudly.

I look at Rian again. He's not that much older than Raefe. Eighteen, maybe. How does he have so much magic that he can just put all of these people to sleep? I inch away from him and lean against the wall beside the hearth. Close to Ki. I don't like it. Nobody should be so powerful.

"No." Rian whispers as he looks around, suddenly frantic. His hands are in his hair. He rushes across the tavern and drops to his knees before a huge pile of glass shards. "No, no, no."

"What is it?" Azi rushes to him. "Rian, what's happened?"

"My golem," he picks up some shards. Closes his eyes. The glass in his hands glows softly. "Something fought it. A man. In Cerion's livery. They fought, and he smashed it, and then…"

Azaeli goes to his side. Touches his cheek. He looks up at her. Swallows. She gazes into his eyes the way she did in the castle. Falls into them. A golden tendril creeps across her neck. Peeks up over her collar.

"Jac," she describes what she sees quietly. "He woke up somehow. He destroyed the golem. Smashed it. He wanted to kill everyone while they were sleeping. Elliot stopped him. The fox. They fought. The fox wounded him. He wouldn't let up. He chased him out of here."

She tears her eyes away from him. Pushes herself to her feet. Walks across to another snoring man, a much smaller one. His hair is orange and brown. It covers his face with bristly fringe. Dark lines are painted across his cheeks. They look like whiskers. She rests a hand on his arm. Looks at Rian.

"Can you wake him?" she asks. Rian comes to her side. Shakes his head.

"I never slept him. He was already out when I cast the spell. It wouldn't have worked on Da, anyway. Sleep spells don't work on him."

I look from Rian to the man. They have the same nose. The same jaw. The same pointed ears, though Rian's are a little more rounded.

"I'm confused," I say. "He's a fox and he's your father, and he chased someone away, but he's still sleeping, and he's here, but he isn't?"

"That's about right!" Flitt chirps. She's nestled into a bowl of cherries. She nibbles one and red juice drips from her chin.

"Clever one you have there, Mevyn," she says around a mouthful.

"Can't you just wake him up?" I ask. "Nudge him, if it's not a spell?"

"I don't dare," Rian says. "Not if he's still after Jac. If they're fighting and I wake him, it could be bad."

Rian looks away from his father to a woman sprawled beside Azi's mother. She's older, with bright red hair. Not like Saesa's. Sharper. Like the blossoms. It's spiked up in a strange style. Her armor is soft leather. Dark blue. Tight. Her skin is pale and covered with freckles. He stoops to her and puts a hand on her shoulder. Whispers Mage words. She blinks slowly. Sits up. Stretches. Looks around at everyone sleeping.

"What in the seven…?" her eyes rest on Rian. "Did you do this?"

Rian gives a little nod. He's different with her. Younger, somehow.

"I had to. Azi needed help, and everyone was getting out of hand."

She looks around again and shakes her head slowly.

"Did you get Marked?" she asks with a scolding tone.

"No, Mum. It's only Twelfth Circle." Rian replies. He smirks a little, like he's amused he knows more than she does. Still, she reaches for him. Tugs down the collar of his robes. Peeks at his chest. I press my lips together. Try not to laugh as he shrugs away from her. Azi doesn't spare him her amusement. She laughs softly. That's when the woman notices her.

"Oh, Azi, we were so worried!" she cries. She hugs her and takes her face into her hands and looks her over.

"I'm okay, Mya." Azi pats her arm. Offers a reassuring smile.

"Mum, something happened," Rian says. "I was careful. I set wards. I set a guardian, but Jac woke up somehow. He shattered the golem, but Da stopped him." He goes to Elliot again. Puts his hands on his shoulders. Mya goes to Elliot's side. Settles on the bench. Strokes his cheek softly. Closes her eyes. Hums a melody that I can see, somehow. She presses her forehead to his. I watch the magic weave between them.

"Something," she whispers, "something's wrong. A darkness. Tangled. Twisted. Something flicking toward us. Trying to tear us apart."

"Dreamwalker," I say. If Mya hears me, she doesn't react.

"Is he in danger?" Azi asks. "Should we wake him?"

"He's distracting it," Mya puts a little distance between herself and Elliot. "Luring it away. Keeping it occupied. Like a hunt. He's clever," she smiles to himself, "we don't need to worry about him. Not yet."

There's a long stretch of silence while everyone thinks that over. Ki is the first to break it.

"People are walking past like they don't even see this place," she says quietly from her post at the window.

"That'll be the wards," Rian explains to her. "I set a Look-Away, along with several others. I'll take them off once I wake everyone."

Mya looks from Rian to the window. "Who are you talking to?" she asks.

"Oh, right. They're still…" Rian looks at Ki, then me. Mevyn sinks behind me and I scowl. Flitt's bowl of berries is right in front of her on the table, but Mya doesn't seem to notice her, either. "Do you want to come out, or?"

"They probably should," says Azi. "It'd make it easier."

"I don't mind," says Ki. She looks at me. I shrug.

"I guess."

"Mmnope!" Flit says around a mouthful.

"Nor I," says Mevyn.

"Course not," I mutter.

"Tib can speak for me," Mevyn sinks lower. I glare over my shoulder at him.

"We brought some friends," Rian explains to Mya. "This is Ki." He casts a spell to reveal her. Mya's eyes widen. She looks from Ki to Rian in disbelief. "And that's Tib." He says the spell again, sweeping a hand in my direction. The air shifts around me.

"Where?" Mya looks at the hearth and squints.

"The Revealer won't work on the Dreamstalker," Mevyn chuckles. "Tib, just step out."

"Step out?" I scowl at him. "What's that mean?"

"Just imagine stepping out of hiding so they can see you. Then take a step," Mevyn explains.

I wrinkle my nose and look at the rest of them. Mya's still staring over the top of my head at the wall, trying to see me. Beside her Rian and Azi are whispering together, looking impressed and a little concerned. I shrug my shoulders, think about showing myself, and take a step like Mevyn says. The change around me is subtle, like walking through a spider's web. It works, though. Mya sees me.

"Oh, there," she offers me a smile. "Were you there the whole time? I had no idea."

"That's the point," Mevyn mutters dryly at my shoulder.

"Yes m'lady," I reply, ignoring Mevyn. I want to bat at him. Grab his little golden wings and send him flying right into her face so he can't hide behind me anymore.

"Well, it's a pleasure to meet you…both." The hesitation in her voice when she turns to Ki tells me everything. She knew my sister before. When she was Viala. Still, she smiles. A real smile, not a put-on. Then she turns to Rian again.

"What exactly is going on?" she asks him. "Wait. Perhaps we should wake the others before we get into explanations. To save time."

"Perhaps not," Mevyn says. "The truth is not meant for a broad audience."

Rian and Azi exchange glances.

"Mum, there are others here, too," Rian says. "Others who need to be protected. They need our help, but they don't want to show themselves. They can't risk being seen or saying too much in front of too many." He watches her closely. Mya shakes her head. Her smile is full of mirth as it dawns on her who he must be talking about.

"Them again? I ought to have known they'd enlist you both in some new quest. You understand though, Rian, that our fealty is to Cerion and its King? Peace in our kingdom is our duty. You aren't losing sight of that, are you? You haven't forgotten your reason for traveling there in the first place, have you?" She nods pointedly at my sister, who is still watching out the window.

"This is a common enemy," Azi says calmly. "He was involved with those who breeched the border of Kythshire. He's meddled with each of our minds. It's why we've all been so on edge. He's even tampered with the princess's baby. He's shown an interest in Prince Vorance and Princess Sarabel, as well. He's even stolen from Princess Margary. I fear his interest in the throne. There's something about the Plethores that fascinates him."

Mya sighs. Pinches the bridge of her nose. Looks at her husband, then her son.

"Very well," she says. "But the Elite works together. Whatever you tell me, it's their right to know it as well. We've sworn oaths to each other. In times like these, we do not keep secrets from each other. If you seek our aid, then you'll have all of us or none of us."

Rian looks at me. I'm not sure why at first, but then I realize Mevyn has drooped behind my shoulder again. I shift a little so the Mage can see him. To my surprise, he drifts toward Flitt a little. Looks at her.

"What would you do?" he asks. "Would you trust them? All of them?"

Flitt looks at Mevyn, wide-eyed. She opens her mouth to say something, but a crash from outside interrupts her. It's followed by screaming. Panic. People running. More crashing. Doors slamming.

At the window, Ki raises her bow. Her face is pale. Her lips pressed into a thin line. Outside, thunder rumbles. The sky is dark as night. She turns to us. Her necklace flashes blue.

"Something's coming," she whispers.

"What?" Mya rushes to the window. Looks out. "What is that?" She spins to Rian.

"Wake them up," she orders urgently. "Now. The guild. Quickly." She runs past him and grabs her mandolin. Turns to me. "Stay out of sight," she says, "unless you know how to use those." She points to my knives and then rushes the door as the rest of her company stumbles to their feet. She doesn't go out though. Instead she starts to play on her mandolin.

Her song is quick and encouraging. Like stepping out of the Half-Realm, I let the magic of it affect me. It makes me feel brave and strong, like I can succeed in anything. Like nothing can stop me. I watch Rian wake the others, calling them each by name. Bryse, the big one. Cort, the dark-skinned fighter. Lisabella, Azi's mother. Benen, her father. Donal and Dacva, the healers. Everyone except for Elliot.

The members of the Elite seem to recognize what the song means. They don't hesitate or question. They draw their weapons. Prepare for battle. I watch Flitt zoom to Azi. Tuck herself into her collar as the knight pulls her helm on. Behind me, Mevyn clings to my bandolier.

"*Stay here*," he says to my mind, but his words hold no power anymore. Just for the sake of defying him, I charge the door behind the others. Out of the tavern. Into the street, where the dark clouds drop sheets of drenching, freezing rain over us all. Mevyn doesn't follow. I didn't expect him to.

At first it's confusing. People everywhere. Chaos. Rain. Screaming. Darkness. Thunder. The ring of steel on stone and wood. Cries of pain. I can't see. The rain is in my eyes. Something skitters toward me. Something small. Fierce. Teeth. Claws. I draw my knife. Slash at it. Feel the blood wash over my hands as its life drains away. I wipe my eyes. Try to see what it is, but another one is on me. It bites my bracer and I shake it free and kick it away.

There's a flash of light. A sizzle. A hiss. An explosion of magic so powerful that everything around me is thrown back. I can't hear anything, not even the rain. That's because the rain has stopped. I wipe my eyes again and peer up at the sky. Not stopped, shielded. Beside me, Rian lowers his hands. Narrows his eyes. The barrier is just big enough to fit us all. Just tall enough to cover Bryse's head. We huddle together inside of its protection, all ready with our weapons.

Without the rain to blind me, I can make out our attackers now. Dozens of them. Bears. Wolves. Field lions. Foxes. Mixed in with them are strange creatures, small and knobby. Some look like the Wildwood, with spindly legs and mushrooms and grasses sprouting from their backs. Others are uglier. Dog-like men, with patches of shaggy fur and snouts that drip with mucus. All of them pace outside of the barrier, snarling and snapping and watching and growling.

The animals try to charge us and bounce off of the magic. The dog men throw spears and shoot arrows that can't penetrate the field. Bryse guards Cort and Donal behind his shield, which is the size of a large door. Benen stands with his back to the giant, his own shield up, his hammer ready. Azi stands beside him, and on his other side Lisabella mirrors her daughter, holding a long sword ready.

"What in blazes? What a way to wake up!" Bryse booms. "What's all this?"

"Sorcery," Rian calls from beside me. "Look for the source." He squints past the shield, past the chaos of animals snarling and snapping at it.

"Sorcery? Not again," Cort groans.

"And Necromancy, from the looks of it," Benen points into the distance. Skeletons, marching toward us. They grin widely. Remind me of the fallen fairies at the roots.

"I hate those things," Bryse grumbles over his shoulder.

Something else is there, past them. Dark and powerful. Not the Dreamwalker. Something just as strong, though. Just as ruthless. I stare into the space where I can feel it until I see it. Him. A man in a dark robe with a hood that covers his face.

"There!" I point, and he moves away. Toward a house. His gesture rips the door from its hinges. I tug Rian's sleeve. Point again.

"I see it," he says. "I see him."

The others turn. Watch as the Sorcerer beckons. From the darkness of the doorway, three figures emerge. A woman, a man, and a child. Commoners. They're weeping. Begging. Walking with stilted motion. Like Nan. Like Zhilee and me, when he came to take us. I pull a knife from my bandolier. Coat it with blue. Don't care what's blocking me from him. Don't care about the creatures in my way. What he's doing is despicable. Horrible. Unforgivable.

Nobody tries to stop me. I charge. The wild animals tear at my arms and legs. Pain shoots through my wrists, sears into my legs where they bite me. I don't let it stop me. I barely feel it. All I see is the Sorcerer. The innocents. I scream. Not in fear, in rage. It works. I have his attention.

He turns to me. Spreads out his fingers. Casts a spell. It breaks apart around me. Fails. I laugh. Skid. Throw my knife. Watch it plunge into his robes. Watch the flames take hold. Watch his face fall. He grasps the handle. Pulls it out. Laughs at me. The flames die. They barely touched him. Just singed his robes a little.

Behind me everything is chaos again. My charge broke Rian's ward. The Elite are swarmed by skeletons and forest animals and dog-men. The Sorcerer thrusts his hand out again. His spell shoots toward me in a spray of red and yellow sparks. It fizzles as it reaches me. Breaks apart again. My immunity to his power makes me giddy. I laugh in his face.

"The orange. Quickly!"

I sneer at Mevyn's voice in my head. Take another knife. Fumble with an orange vial. The commoners stalk toward me. The man, the commoner, grabs my throat. Closes off my air. I can't breathe. I coat the blade, or hope I do. I can't look down to see. Can't breathe. I hope this works. My vision is going black. I know where the Sorcerer is, the one who's controlling them. I aim. I throw. I pray that it meets its mark and doesn't hit an innocent.

A sizzle. A spark. A flame. A horrible scream. The commoner's hands loosen. He falls on me, pressing me into the ground, into the mud. He's heavy. Crushing. Lifeless. No, still breathing. I try to push him off, but his wife has fallen on me too. They hold me to the ground. Press me into the mud like the roots, like the trees. I will myself to take slow breaths. Not to panic. Someone will see me. Someone will help me.

The sorcerer lies nearby, ash and flame. I did that. My knife. My shot. All around us, the animals scamper away. Freed from their spell, free to hide now that their master is defeated. There's still fighting, though. Skeletons and dog-men and Wildwoods. They're all too busy fighting them. They don't know I need help.

I try again to shove the man off of me. I fight to breathe. I can't, though. He's too heavy. Too heavy, and nobody sees. Nobody knows. I try to keep my eyes open, but I can't. I have no air. No breath. The darkness takes me. I black out.

Chapter Twenty-Six:

FAIRY EMBERS

Tib

"Tib, get up." Weight is lifted. Rolled away. Someone shakes my shoulder. Rough. Frantic. "Tib, hurry!"

I can't move. The breath has been squeezed out of me. I'm dragged away. My throat burns. Rain drenches me. Mud seeps into my pants, my boots. I gasp for air. Cough.

Music. Mandolin music. Beautiful singing. The rain stops. I'm inside on the wood floor. Whoever is dragging me stops. I open my eyes. Push my hair out of my face. Watch Ki run off again. Out of the tavern. Into the rain. Into the fray. Skeletons. Magic. Dogs and creatures.

I push myself to my feet. Start to run back out into it. I can sense another one of them, the source of a spell. This one dark. A Necromancer. Someone grabs my shoulder, though. Pulls me back. Pushes me into a chair. He's young. Azi's age. Dark hair. Serious looking. Dacva, I think Rian said his name was. He puts his hands on my chest. Prays. I feel my throat open up. I can breathe. The pain leaves. I feel much better.

"Thank you," say. I jump up and try to run out again. The action makes me dizzy. He puts an arm out. Blocks my path.

"You need to rest a moment," he says. I hesitate. Outside, the battle is raging fiercely. I want to be out there, not in here.

"Rest, Tib."

"Don't tell me what to do!" I shout at Mevyn, who's tucked safely into a space between the shutter and the frame, watching out the window. I turn to Dacva. "Not you, sorry."

"You have to give your body time, or the healing will be undone," he says. "Sorry. My healing is weak. It takes longer to set than Father Donal's." He shifts himself on the bench so he can see past

Mya, who's standing near the open door, playing. Her song makes my heart drum in my chest. Makes me believe I could take down every last one of those enemies out there. I want to go back to it, but I heed Dacva's advice. I try to be still.

In the street, the fight is fierce. Hard to make out, with so many enemies on so few defenders. I look for the villagers who were under the spell of the Sorcerer, but I don't see them. Their door is back on its hinges, closed tightly. Brightly colored light splashes across the house fronts, dancing erratically. Its source is the center of the fray. It beams from Azaeli, who swings her sword with fury and purpose. At her collar, Flitt's bright hair bounces with Azi's movement. The light is hers.

Creatures who charge her are completely blinded by the fairy's glare. They swing and bite ferociously but miss. She hits their heads with the flat of her blade. Knocks them out cold. Dog-men and Wildwoods are strewn in defeated piles at her feet.

Beside her Rian scans the distance, searching for the source, watching for more Sorcerers. There are three more. I know there are. I can feel them. There's also the storm that hovers. The darkness. Dreamwalker.

Bryse is not as gentle as Azaeli. He slashes at the creatures, slicing them in two as easily as a scythe through fresh grass. The others fight furiously, driving back the throngs of attackers, sending skeletons clattering to the ground.

I look for my sister, but don't see her. I see her arrows, though. Firing into the melee from the roof above us. Hitting their mark every time.

I bounce on the balls of my feet impatiently. I need to be out there. I have to fight. I see another one of them, a Sorceress. She stands in an alley between two houses across the street. Her cloak is deep purple. The wind flaps them open, revealing robes of crimson beneath. Red like the flowers. The petals. The scoop of dye in a barrel. She moves her hands gracefully. Fallen skeletons reassemble. Rise. Stalk forward. I draw my knives and my orange vial. I wet the blades.

"*Be smart,*" Mevyn says, watching me. *"Don't just charge out there again. And add the black, as well."*

I glare at him. Uncork the black. Spread it on. Turn to Dacva.

"Long enough?" I ask him. My heart is racing to Mya's music. I'm confident. Strengthened. Dacva nods and I start out, but stop at the threshold. Close my eyes. Think about it. How I stepped out of hiding before, for Mya. If I stepped out, surely I can step in again. I will it. I take a step. I feel it again. The shift. The spider webs brushing across my skin.

"Good."

"Shut up," I murmur. I stalk away from the tavern. Into the rain. Straight through the battle. Nothing turns to me. No one sees me. Flit's light dances across my vision. My boots squish in the mud. They're not new anymore. Properly broken in. Dirtied. Flecked with blood. I fix my eyes on the Sorceress. Watch her fingers in the air, dancing, conducting. Letting those she manipulates do all of the work.

Mya's song is far away now, but my confidence doesn't fade. I stride into the alley. Right up to the Sorceress. She doesn't see me. She has no idea I'm here. I raise my knives like scissors. They slice through her wards like nothing. Take her pretty hand right off. Her wrist sizzles orange, then the black starts creeping up, up. I stare at it. Watch its slow progress, fascinated. She screams. Writhes. Panics.

Then she collects herself. Speaks a word or two. A spell. The black fades, leaving a stump where her hand was. She waits for more to happen. Nothing does.

She screams again, this time out of rage. Thrusts her good hand forward. A charge of red energy wells at her fingertips and bursts toward me. I brace myself. It strikes me with the force of a pleasant breeze. Passes through me. Shoots up and across the street. I turn in time to see its new mark: Ki, perched on the balcony railing high above the tavern door.

Blue light bursts from her necklace. It absorbs some of the spell, but she didn't see it coming. The force of it throws her off balance. She tries to right herself, but can't. She plummets. Lands with a sickening, muddy thud. Doesn't move.

"No!" I scream. I start to run toward her and the air shifts again. I realize too late that I've revealed myself.

My skin crawls. Bony fingers catch me by the back of the collar. Drag me back to the alley, out of sight of everyone. More hands clamp around me. Disarm me. Throw my knives into the mud. Wide white grins and dark eyes loom over me. Bones. Death. The Sorceress bears down on me, seething. She raises the charred stump of her arm.

"You'll pay," she growls. Snaps the fingers of her remaining hand. A knife of flames stretches from her fingertips. The skeletons press my wrist against the stone of the house. Hold me so I can't struggle. Can't kick. Can't move. Can't do anything but scream until a stinking bony hand clamps over my mouth. It smells awful. Worse than the roots. Like a grave. I gag. The woman's eyes glint in the fire. Her face fades into the darkness of her hood. It's covered with black swirls.

She presses close. Brings the fiery knife up. Holds it to my wrist. One of her bony servants rips off my glove, my bracer.

"Yours will be a suitable replacement," her laugh is wicked. Maniacal. Insane. She presses the spell-made blade to my skin. I feel nothing. No heat, no slice. The spell fizzles. Fades.

"You little freak," she spits furiously. "What are you?"

She screams in frustration. Rips a knife from my bandolier. Raises it to slash. I close my eyes. Brace myself. Focus on the sounds of battle outside of the alley to distract me. Maybe someone heard. Maybe they'll save me. I try to fight, but the skeletons are too strong. Like the roots. I can barely move. I wait for the pain to come.

The blade slices into my skin with searing pain. I fight. I struggle, but they hold me. She's unskilled with the knife. Not strong enough to make the cut cleanly. There's nothing I can do. I try to focus on something other than the pain. Try to distract myself from it so I don't pass out.

I feel my vision closing in on me, like before. See the tunnel that comes right before the darkness. I force my eyes open. Fight to keep myself awake through this. I know, if I let my eyes close, it will be for the last time. She'll take my hand first, then she'll kill me.

I imagine myself as one of her undead servants and push the thought away. Instead I focus instead on her eyes, wild and filled with madness. Determined and filled with blood lust as she makes her cut. She doesn't notice the flutter of gold at her shoulder. Isn't aware of the spear until it plunges into her neck. Twists. Releases a flood of red that spills over her robes. She chokes, sputters. Stumbles.

The knife clatters to the ground as she falls backwards, clutching at her throat. Mevyn hovers over her. Drives his spear into the other side of her throat. Watches her life drain away. Gazes into her eyes. Steals her memories until she's gone and her skeletons crumble to piles of bone. Lifeless, as they should be. Someone in the street cheers.

"Pink vial. Rest. Search her," Mevyn says to me before he fades again. Hides himself away. Leaves me to sink into the filth of the alley and clamp my bleeding wrist to my stomach. The rain makes the blood spread. Makes the wound seem worse than it is.

I fumble a pink vial from its loop. Pull out the stopper with my teeth. Pour it on the jagged slice that would have taken off my hand. Watch the blood stop, the grisly insides knit together, the skin close neatly. Drink the rest of it, just for good measure. Tip my head back against the stone. Breathe. Listen. In the street they're still fighting. Something's off, though. Missing. The music. Mya's playing has stopped.

I push myself to my feet. Sway dizzily. Cling to the wall. Peer out. Try to see Ki. She's gone. Mya's gone. Dacva's outside, kneeling. Healing someone. Donal. Azi's gone. Rian's gone. Bryse and Benen and Cort are fighting dog-men and Wildlings. Keeping them away from Dacva. Not many left. Ten, maybe. They can manage.

I catch my breath. Try to calm my racing heart. Try not to think about what just happened. What could have happened. I crawl toward the lifeless Sorceress. Retrieve my glove, my bracer, my knives. Look at her. She's got a belt of pouches. An amulet.

Search her, Mevyn said. He saved my life. I do it. I take the necklace. The belt. Rings from her fingers. Find the severed hand. Take its rings, too.

For now, I wear it. All of it. It's the easiest way. There are still two Sorcerers out there. I can feel them. One controlling the dog men, one controlling the forest creatures. I step to the mouth of the alley. Stare at the place where my sister landed. Steel myself. Step into hiding again.

Overhead, the clouds rumble and swirl unnaturally. Dark, like a cloak. I can feel him pressing down on us. Dreamwalker. Watching. Laughing. Taunting. I ignore it, and run across the street to where she fell. I can't tell what happened after. Too many soggy footprints all muddled together.

"Ki!" I shout. Light glints in the distance, all the colors of the rainbow. Flitt. I charge toward it. Race toward it. Find them at the edge of the village, fighting the third Sorcerer. Azi is swinging her sword. Rian is casting his shields as fast as his opponent can break them. I sprint. Slide between them. Draw my coated blades. Drive them into the Sorcerer's robes.

They glance off, stopped by a shield that's stronger than I expected. I strike again. The shield weakens. Azi swings her sword. Breaks the shield down completely. I stab again. This time my knives sink into flesh. Blacken it and the robes around it. He starts to cast like the Sorceress did, to stop the spread. Rian counters with a spell that binds his tongue and clamps his lips shut.

Together we watch the black and orange crackle and creep over him, encasing him until he is completely covered. I give him a push and he falls backward and smashes into pieces.

"Whoa," Rian whispers. He stares at me in awe. "How did you…"

"Fairy embers," Flitt says from the safety of Azi's pauldron. "Clever."

Azi pokes at the crumbled remains with her toe. "It's like what Iren did to Emris," she says, somewhere between impressed and disgusted.

"Look out," Rian spins on his heel. Spreads his arms. Casts a shield just in time to block us from the charging dog-men. They don't attack, though. They run past, into the woods. Free now.

"One more left," I whisper, mostly to myself.

"How do you know?" Azi asks.

"He's right," Rian says. "See, all that remains are those grass creatures." Rian points to the creatures in the center of town, fighting with Bryse and Cort and Benen. Donal is up now. Dacva's retreating to the tavern again.

"Oh Rian, they don't stand a chance. They don't know what they're doing." She winces as Bryse slices the last two of them apart with one strike.

"Can you tell where it is, Tib? The last Sorcerer?" Rian asks me.

I close my eyes. Concentrate. Listen. All I can feel are the clouds pressing in. Darkness swirling down from them. Touching everything. Then, Dreamwalker speaks. His ominous voice thunders over us.

"See how they destroy your town, these so-called Elite. They come with their banners and their Mage. Careless. They fight in your streets. They have no concern for any of you. They'll watch you burn. Watch your children die. See them, how they threaten. Stop them."

"Oh, no," I whisper. All around us, villagers open their doors. Look outside. Some of them have weapons. Cooking knives. Cleavers. Axes.

"Stay inside," Lisabella calls to them from beside Benen. "It isn't safe yet."

They don't listen. They charge together, twenty, thirty, forty. A mob of villagers. Furious. Unskilled. Wild and raving. They clash into the defenders: Bryse, Cort, Lisabella, Benen, Donal. They engulf them. They kick and stab and punch.

"No!" Azi cries. "No, oh Rian!" She sobs and starts to run toward the crowd, but Rian pulls her back.

"Just wait," he says. "Your mum is in there. Have faith."

I don't know what he means, but it doesn't take long to figure it out. From the center of the mob I feel it. Peace. Soothing. It radiates toward us, washing over the throng, placating them. Slowly they turn away. Shake their heads. Go back to their homes. Close the doors. Lisabella slumps into Benen, who gathers her close.

"Get inside," Donal says. "Everyone. Quickly!"

Rian grabs my hand and Azi's. We run together through the rain, through the street. Follow the others back into the tavern. Slam the door behind us. Latch it. Inside, we're greeted only by Dacva. The sleeping tavern patrons are still asleep, undisturbed. Mya is gone. Elliot is gone. My heart aches for my sister. I hoped, but no. She isn't here, either.

Rian paces near the door, casting spells. Protections. He looks beat up. Exhausted. Flitt goes to him. Shines her light. He looks a little better. Keeps going. The others slump together near the fire. Donal whispers over them, healing them. Lisabella is the first to speak. She turns to Dacva.

"Mya? Elliot?" she asks wearily.

"He woke up when that spell hit the balcony," Dacva says as he presses one of Cort's wounds closed. "He charged outside and chased after someone. Mya went after them. I didn't see who they were chasing, but whoever it was was carrying someone off."

"Ki," I say quietly. "She was up there, shooting. She fell. I saw her. By the time I was able to go help, she was gone."

"Never saw anything like it," Bryse grumbles. "Try to defend their village and they come stalking out, kicking and punching and stabbing." He rubs his arm with a scowl. "What got into them?"

"Not what," Azi says, gripping her mother's hand, "who."

I know the answer to that. She does, too. We know exactly who.

"How do we stop him, though?" I ask quietly. "How do you fight against that?" I turn to Mevyn, who is only now emerging by my side.

"Stop who?" Cort asks.

"Yeah, someone going to fill us in?" Bryse scowls. Crosses his arms. Looks at me. I remember how he took out two of those creatures with one blow. How he sliced them in two. He could do the same to me. I shiver. Look away. I'm glad he's on my side, at least for now.

"Dreamwalker," I say. My voice is shaky. I lean on the table. Start taking off the dead Sorceress's things. An amulet of teeth and silver. A belt full of pouches that I don't want to look through for fear of what I'll find. Gold and gemstone rings. Cort comes over.

"Good haul," he says, and dumps what he's looted onto the table. Bracelets. Coins. Lumpy pouches of mysterious things. Treasure, I guess. Some magical, some not. I don't care what any of it's worth. I drop it all onto the table. Shove it away from me. Go to the window to watch for my sister.

Mevyn stays, of course. Scavenges through the things. Rian sits. Picks up a ring. Turns it in his fingers.

"He's a Sorcerer," Azi says. "He's not like the others, though. He was just a boy when they locked him in the Dreaming. Younger than Tib."

"What he is, is an abomination," I say. The words are Mevyn's, not mine. Still, I agree with them, so I don't fight him putting words in my head.

I stare out into the street. The storm clouds have lifted. The sun is sinking low. It glares red over puddles of mud. Casts long shadows across the lifeless bodies littered everywhere. He did this. All of this. And I'm the one who's supposed to stop him.

"We should go," Cort says, "search for Mya and Elliot."

"I would advise against it," says Donal. His tone is soothing. Kind and wise, like a grandfather. "We all know that they have means of tracking and traveling that don't suit us. Most likely, any of us would impede their progress. It wouldn't be wise to go after them now. Have faith. They'll return."

The others reluctantly agree. Donal and Dacva leave the tavern to go check on the villagers. Heal them, if they need it. I watch them go from door to door, knocking and going in. I never heard of such a thing, healers, just giving their talents away like that. Helping without being asked. It doesn't happen in Sunteri. Healing is for the rich. If you want it, you pay. Lots.

I pull off my gloves, my bracers. Run my finger across my wrist. There isn't even a scar. Nothing to prove that it really happened. Lisabella is the first to break the thoughtful silence. She comes to my side. Looks out, too. Rests a hand on my shoulder.

"They'll find her," she says. "In the meantime we need to know everything there is to know about this threat. Tell us, so we can help. We'll fight beside you."

"Him? He's just a kid," Bryse grumbles. "Loose cannon, too. He broke Rian's ward. You saw him. Ran right out of it. Left us all out in the open. Everybody knows you don't just plow through a shield ward."

"He did," Benen says, "but then he singlehandedly destroyed that Sorcerer who was on us. You got the Necromancer, too, didn't, you?"

I glance at Mevyn. He bobs his head. He'll let me take the credit for it. He's not planning on coming out any time soon. I nod.

"He defeated the one we chased down, too," Rian says. "There's more to Tib than meets the eye."

"Tell us, then," Lisabella says. I feel the peace around her. I let it touch me. It's helpful. Soft and warm. It reminds me of Saesa, drawing the green cloak over my shoulders in the chill winds of Cerion, the day we met. I look at Mevyn, who's examining the tooth amulet. His eyes meet mine as he sets it down slowly. Did he know then, how strong our enemy was? Did he know what we'd be facing?

"Well?" I ask him. "Are you going to tell them, or not?"

The others stare at me, wide-eyed. I know how it looks. Except for Azi, Rian and Flitt, the others can't see Mevyn. To them, it looks like I'm talking to a table. I don't care. I want this to be over with. It's time to hear the truth. I'll make him tell them. Tell me too. I'm sick of his secrets and manipulations. Sick of wondering whose side he's really on.

"Tell them," I say. "Show them. They want to help."

"*Not yet,*" he says sternly. Forcefully.

"Fine." I turn to the others. "I'll tell you myself, then. What I know."

"*You will do no such thing,*" he seethes.

"I'll do what I want," I say angrily, "and you can't stop me. You swore. You swore you'd stay out of my head. You swore that if I did what you said, you'd never control me again."

"*I made you who you are. I gave you everything. I saved your life more than once, and still you don't trust me? It isn't time yet. You will not speak.*" His last word is a command. I feel it hold me. Furious, I push it off. Shove it away, like a heavy stone. I refuse to let him control me anymore.

"I didn't ask for any of this!" I scream so loud I think I might wake the rest the sleeping patrons. They don't even flutter an eyelid.

"Obviously the boy is a little conflicted," Benen says quietly. "Perhaps—"

"No, I'll tell you. I'll tell you everything I know. I saw you fight. I trust you. It's not my fault that *he* doesn't." I turn to the room. Cross my arms. "You need me more than I need you," I say to him. "And we need them, whether you want to admit it or not."

"Fine."

"Who's he talking to?" Cort whispers to Bryse, who shrugs.

"Boy's slap-mad," Bryse murmurs in reply.

"I'm *not* mad," I half-growl. I look around. The others, the ones who can see Mevyn, are watching with interest or pity. They don't think I'm crazy. They want to help, and I trust them. They fought when they didn't have to. They tried to spare lives when they could. They're honorable. I want to put my faith in them. I need to.

I tell them about the roots. The trees. The fallen fairies. Nan. Zhilee. My nightmares. Mevyn. The towers. The ship. Nessa's. The kids. All of it. All of the truth except for Margary's secret. Everything about Mevyn, too. I'm surprised when he lets me. He seems interested to hear my side of it, almost like he didn't think of my perspective before. Maybe it didn't matter to him, or maybe he was avoiding my perspective so he wouldn't have to be burdened by it.

The others listen quietly. Azi and Rian lean against each other. Benen comes to stand next to Lisabella. Holds her. They look out the window. Bryse and Cort stare into giant half-drained mugs of ale. They're compassionate, but impatient. They want to care, but they're worried about their missing member. Even though I've only gotten to the elves, I feel like it's enough for them to know. They're aware of the Dreamwalker. They're aware of how Mevyn has used me.

I raise my chin. Look at him, a little defiantly.

"You don't want them to see you yet? Fine. But you'll tell them what they need to know to help. Talk through me," I say. "Just this once. Tell me what to say, and I'll repeat it."

Chapter Twenty-Seven:

THE TRUTH

Tib

I lean back against the wall. Cross my arms. Close my eyes. Wait a long time while Mevyn thinks it over. He's angry, I can tell. He doesn't like that I have a mind of my own now. He hates not being in control. Too bad, I think to myself. If he wanted a puppet, he shouldn't have given me that title in the Ring. If he wants my help, our help, then he's got to be more trusting.

As the silence stretches on, I start to think maybe he'll go on being stubborn. The others are getting impatient. I don't blame them. I clench my fists. Fight back my annoyance. Open my eyes and stare at him expectantly. He frowns. Shakes his head. Flitt looks from me to him and back again, her eyes wide. Finally, reluctantly, his words flow through me.

"Over a decade ago, nearly two" he starts, "I was not bound by circumstance as I am now." It's strange to hear my own voice saying words that aren't my own. I don't like it. It makes me dizzy. I close my eyes again. Lean against the window frame. Let him go on.

"Many years ago, I was revered. Honored. I was a Guardian, a keeper of peace. I was a steward of the magic that our lands had to offer. Our source flourished, and with it, so did our people. All was well.

"We were not greedy with our magic, nor were we miserly. We shared willingly with those who came to seek it. We had excellent relations with the Mages of Zhagen, the city to the north. They came to study, and we gladly shared our knowledge with them. I was ever cautious of these creatures, who seemed each time to be more curious than they ought to be. Presumptuous and entitled, some of them were.

"With this new policy of sharing, I was witness to the slow drain of our golden waters, our source. The elders were unconcerned, of course. They would not listen to my pleas to put an end to our new deeper alliance with the Mages. What harm could it do? They argued. Magic is eternal. It has always been, and it will always be. What harm indeed?

"Well, I will tell you. My reservations ought to have been heeded. There was a Sorceress by the name of Dinaea, wed to another, the Sorcerer Corbin. Her lust for power was unmatched. So obsessed was she with our magical source that it destroyed her ability to think of anything else. She wandered round it for days, months. Her belly swelled with her husband's child, but she never rested. I did my best to keep her at bay, but she was wild with the need for it.

"I called upon my ally from the Other Realm, whom I had known for many years. Valenor. He was my charge, and I his guide in our lands. He looked into the woman's mind and showed me the truth. Her interest was not completely selfish. She was an observer, sent to collect and deliver information to the libraries of Zhaghen, the great city to the north. A channeler of our powers, a direct link between us and the city. A drain. A parasite.

"This finally convinced the elders to send her away, to close off our precious source until such time as we could be assured of its safety. It did not last long. The child was born, and years later Dinaea appealed to the elders. Pleaded with them. Made deals. She was allowed to return with the boy, whom she called her little prince. She ignored the appeals of her husband to return to the city. She was too consumed by the power, too addicted now. Her child was curious. He touched the source, and therefore became touched, himself."

"I saw this," Azaeli says quietly. I open my eyes. The others turn to her. "In the Dreaming, I was shown memories. I saw the boy touch the pool. I saw you scolding the child. He was only a little one, barely walking. You defended it as though he was a grown man. He was frightened of you." She looks at me I shake my head and close my eyes. Not me. Mevyn. I won't be scorned for what he did. I listen to his voice echoing through mine.

"As I should have. I sent them away, furious with them for desecrating our sacred waters. By now, though, the elders were too tangled in promises and bargains to truly banish the Sorcerers. Corbin was furious that Dinaea would allow such a thing to happen. He left her. Shattered her world. Neither of them realized at the time what they had created.

"No man should ever touch the golden waters. If he does, he

shall never be the same. If he does, he shall be changed forever. Some might say cursed, others forsaken. Tormented. Forever hungry for it. Driven mad with greed and lust for the power that he can never harness or own. Even at such a young age, especially at such a young age, it devours.

"They returned some time later, when the boy was nearly ten. He was out of control. He was unstoppable. Filled with anger, mistrust, rebellion. His parents appealed to the elders, who wanted him put to death. He was brought before me, for it was my duty as Guardian to carry out the punishment. Dinaea pleaded with me. There must be another way, she said. Corbin, too. As difficult as he was, he was their son. They begged me to save their boy. To help them keep him safe until they could find a way to reverse what had been done.

"Perhaps it was my weariness of the constant battle with the elders. Perhaps I was feeling rebellious myself, or reluctant to have the boy's blood on my hands. Perhaps I am a coward, as my kind has branded me. I do not know, to this day, what possessed me to show him mercy. I called upon Valenor, my friend in Dreaming. My charge.

"Of course he agreed to aid me. Why would he not? He trusted me. We were allies. Friends. He allowed the boy's parents passage into his realm, to make certain their son would be safely hidden away. He had no way of knowing, at the time, what he invited. No way of knowing the boy would be his demise, that the child would continue to draw upon the source, that he would eventually usurp and cast out my dear friend Valenor. That he would steal his mantle and wear his title, Dreamwalker."

"What does it mean, exactly?" Rian asks. "Dreamwalker?" He sets down a ring and picks up the belt of pouches. Closes his eyes. Whispers a spell. I can feel the questions it poses. What's in here? Is it safe?

"It is difficult to explain," Mevyn replies through me. "There can be many Dreamwalkers, or only one. It is a ruler of sorts, but not like your kings. A Dreamwalker is more like a creator. A spirit, usually, who manipulates and shapes the world of Dreaming. They are always powerful in their own realm, nearly omnipotent. But when they try to slip out, to join your realm, they have limited power. They can give suggestions, shift emotions. They can create dreams and plant them."

"So there's more than one of these things?" Bryse grunts. Drains a mug. Cort fills it up again.

"Not precisely. Not anymore, rather. This one snuffed the

others out, as far as I can tell. Certainly Dreamwalkers are powerful, but they almost always remain in the Dreaming. They have no desire to leave or to have dealings with this realm, and so they remain within it and no one here is aware of their existence. The only evidence of them in the past has been in dreams. Jacek, on the other hand, is a special circumstance. He does not wish to be there. The Dreaming is his prison. He wishes to be freed."

"Where are the others?" Rian asks as he spills the contents of a pouch onto the table. It's bones, little ones. Toes, maybe. Or fingers. He pushes them back into the pouch with his fingertip, wrinkling his nose. "The other Dreamwalkers? Why don't they try to fight him and stop him?"

"I do not know," Mevyn replies. I clear my scratchy throat. The talking is making me thirsty. Letting him use me this way is making my head pound.

"How do we stop him?" Rian opens another pouch. Pulls out a flat red stone, no bigger than his palm. Its polished surface flashes in the light from the window. He brushes his finger over it, activating it. It pulses with a golden glow, like the one that sent orders to the fae at the roots. Mevyn doesn't notice it. He's too absorbed with the tooth amulet, still.

"I do not know," Mevyn says in reply to Rian's question, "but I know of someone who does. My old friend, Val—"

"Shh," Rian puts a finger to his lips. Stares at the stone. Holds it up to his ear. Listens. It's making sounds, strange sounds. Like voices seeping in and out. Skipping and fading. Echoing oddly. Difficult to understand. Like spirits, whispering.

"Have her," the voices hiss and fade.

"…lost…others...back…"

"Take her to the lake," another voice comes through more clearly. A man. "Cover your tracks. Do not speak to me again unless spoken to."

"Oh my…" Azi whispers. Her eyes are wide as saucers. Her face drained of color. She meets Rian's gaze and then looks at the others while Rian brushes his hand over the stone. The golden light fades. "Is it me, or did that sound like…"

"Prince Eron," her mother finishes for her. "It did."

"Did he hear us, Rian?" Benen asks. "Could he know what Tib was saying?"

"Mevyn," I correct him.

"Sorry, yes. Mevyn," Benen nods to me.

"I don't think so," Rian turns the stone over. "I think the way it works is by intention, and it wasn't our intention to send a message."

Lisabella offers me a cup while the others discuss this new discovery. Their prince is somehow deeply involved in this. He's the one talking on the stone. I wonder if he sent messages to the fairies at the roots. Was he involved in that, too? I sip and stare out of the window, not really seeing. Some of the villagers have come out. They're peaceful, now. Busy dragging away bodies of dog men and Wildwoods. Cleaning things up.

I look toward the edge of town where I battled the third Sorcerer with Rian and Azi and Flitt. A smudge of color catches my eye. Red hair, spiked up. Mya. Walking hand in hand with Elliot. Both of them look tired. Defeated. I look past them for her. Strain my eyes, but I know already. They've come back without her. Ki is gone. Lost. Taken.

As they near, a flash in Mya's hand catches my eye. Blue light. The cord of a necklace twined around her fingers. She closes them around it as they approach the tavern. Hides it away from the villagers who pause to watch them. I race to the door. Throw it open.

"I'm sorry, Tib," she says to me as soon as she sees me. Steps inside. Hands me the amulet. Ki's necklace. Maybe the last remains of my sister. "We couldn't track them. They just…disappeared." I look down at the stone, glowing blue. The floating golden flecks blur through my tears. I feel myself drawn into it. Feel the blue light washing over me. "Don't lose hope. We'll find her." Mya's voice fades, replaced by another, more commanding one.

"She is alive. With your help, she will be recovered," the voice echoes in my head. *"I am Iren. The Shadow Crag embodied. The Mountain Keeper. Esteemed Guardian of the Northern Border. Watcher of the North. Friend to you, Tib, and friend to your sister, Ki."*

"Great," I whisper under my breath. Just what I wanted. Someone else inside my head, telling me what to do. The others don't notice me talking to Iren. They're busy filling in Mya and Elliot, who have crossed to the hearth. "Where is she?" I whisper into the blue glow, "How do I get to her?" I creep toward the door. Ready to run out. Ready to leave them and find her.

"Keep me safe, for now, and I shall guide you. You cannot go alone, Tib. It is not wise."

I feel it rising in me. The anger. The frustration of knowing something can be done and being held back from it. It's not safe, it says. Does it think I'm weak? Afraid? I'm not. I just killed three Sorcerers. I'm the Dreamstalker. Not just a boy anymore. Not a slave to the fields. I've done things. Bad things and good things. Powerful things. I don't need anyone else. I can find her on my own.

Iren senses my thoughts, I think. Interrupts them.

"*Yes,*" it says. "*You are brave. Strong. Capable. But quick to temper, young one. Quick to act without a thought. Slow yourself. Find your own thoughts, which have often been kept from you of late. Find them. Trust them.*"

I stare at the amulet, considering Iren's words. Look up at Mevyn, who is pulling magic out of the teeth of the Necromancer's necklace. Collecting it. Absorbing it. Glowing brighter as he does. Iren is right. My mind hasn't been my own these past weeks. Months. When Mevyn has allowed me to keep to myself, my thoughts have been clouded with emotion. Anger. Mistrust. Confusion. I don't know who I am. Who I really am, beyond all of that.

It's too much to consider right now. It was easier before, just going along. Now is more difficult. Thinking for myself. Knowing I'm free to make my own decisions. Trying to make sense of all of this. I shake my head. Turn my attention to the others.

"First things first," Mya says decisively. Looks around the tavern at the mess of overturned tables and stale food and spilled pitchers. "How long have we been asleep?" She goes to the table. Picks up a loaf of bread. Knocks it on the wood, like a rock.

"About a day?" Rian looks a little guilty.

"It's time you woke the others," she nods to the sleeping patrons and barkeep. "But if you woke the innkeeper now, can you imagine?" She bends at the hearth beside Bryse, where the fire has burned down to gray ash. A great pot hangs there. She reaches for a spoon and scoops out a crusty black glob. Turns to Rian, eyebrows raised.

"Mum, are you serious? In the middle of all this, after that battle, your concern is cleaning up?" He slumps back against the wall. Crosses his arms.

"Yes, I'm serious, Rian. I don't care what we're facing or how tired you are. You don't just come in and destroy someone's livelihood and walk away. You know better. Fix it up first, and wake them. Put it right, and then we can make a plan."

"But, Mum—!" Rian protests.

"Don't," Mya interrupts, raising a scolding finger, "tell me you're tired. I'll play something."

She goes back to her bench and pulls her mandolin from her back and starts sing a beautiful, slow melody. I didn't realize how tired I was before she started. I didn't notice how exhausted Rian looked, either. But as her song drifts over us, I let it affect me. I feel better. Refreshed.

We all stand a little straighter. Look a little more confident. I feel energized, like I've slept all night and now I can run for leagues. Like I can climb anything. It isn't the annoying sort of imposing magic. It's different. Like a joy that was already there inside, being pulled out to the front.

Rian pushes himself away from the wall. Raises his hands in a graceful gesture. He speaks a spell and wiggles his fingers at the fireplace, and it flares and crackles warmly. Inside the pot, something swells up. I crane toward it and sniff. Fresh stew, rich with meat and vegetables. My stomach growls.

He moves around the room, flicking his wrists at one table and the next. Bread softens and steams. Cheese freshens up. Mugs of ale right themselves and fill again. At the bar, he sweeps his arm and rags polish it to gleaming shine all on their own. Stools straighten. Tables mend and tilt back onto their legs. Broken dishes reform and set themselves neatly on top. Candles in holders overhead grow and light. Barmaids prop against the counter, their trays perfectly balanced in their hands. Skirts smooth out and stains fade away. He even fixes their hair so a strand isn't out of place.

He looks at his mother, who nods her approval. Then he raises his hands again, and I feel the spell seep slowly from his fingers. I can almost see the magic as it flickers to each of those still asleep. It wakes them gently, sweetly. The barmaids shake their heads and pick up mugs filled with ale. The barkeep scowls and rubs his face. The din of the few patrons rises slowly until the place is lively again. Full of conversation and laughter. Mya puts down her mandolin and we file together onto the benches to whisper and plan while the barmaids fill our cups.

"We must seek out Valenor," Mevyn says into my mind while the others trade information about what's already happened. *"Tell them."*

"Tell them yourself," I mumble through a mouthful of hot stew. I have too much to think about. I don't need him in my head right now. Across from me, Azaeli leans toward Flitt. The fairy is perched at the edge of the table, waving away the steam from Azi's plate with a look of disgust. I think of how she shined her light right in the middle of battle instead of hiding away. Wish I'd gotten a brave fairy, like that. Instead I got Mevyn. Flitt and Azi lock gazes, and I overhear their conversation like I heard Crocus and Scree.

"Can you please see what Mevyn needs," she sends to the fairy. *"I think Tib is getting tired."* The colorful fairy nods and hops up. She floats across the tavern to a shelf over the hearth where Mevyn is nestled between some dusty old bottles. He starts to tell her about Valenor. I ignore him and turn my attention to Mya.

"Let's look at this objectively," Mya whispers. "We have little to go on. We have the word of a creature half of us have not met and the other half of us barely trust. We have a magical stone that spoke and possibly sounded like His Highness." Mya rests her hands on the table.

"This is a grave accusation," she says. "I'm sure you all agree. The purpose of this trip was to protect the prince and help to clear him. What you're telling me does exactly the opposite. We should not act without at least notifying His Majesty first. In addition, we know there are other forces at play. Forces we don't quite understand that could possibly be responsible for all of it. We can't act brashly. We must really think this over."

The way she talks, the way her eyes rest on each person confidently, makes me want to follow her. Makes me want to agree with everything she says. I want her to like me. I want to be her friend. It isn't magic. It's not a spell. It's just something about her. I don't care what happens to the prince either way, but she's right. We need a plan. Flitt comes back to Azi. Sits on her shoulder. Whispers to her.

"Mya's right," Benen says with a sigh. Donal nods his agreement. "We must inform the king."

"But it's at least three day's ride to the city from here," Cort argues. "A lot of damage could be done by then, whether or not the prince is behind any of it."

Azi and Rian exchange a look. Between them, Flitt whispers. Rian nods to her. Azi leans forward and whispers. I can barely hear what she says over the noise of the rest of the tavern.

"We could get home quickly," she nods. "Rian and I. We could speak to the king or deliver a letter on the guild's behalf and be back by morning, Mya."

The others don't question her or ask how. They seem to know what she can do. They're fine with this plan. She says they all need to rest, even though most of them have been sleeping. Magic and battles take lots of energy, they explain. When I try to argue, she asks me when I last slept. It feels like days, even though it's only been one. It's late now. Almost midnight.

Morning. My heart sinks. I think of my sister, wherever she is. A lot can happen in one night. I stare past them at the door of the tavern. I could leave. Track her down on my own. Save her. I slip my hand into my pouch. Feel Iren's cool blue stone brush my fingers. I could find her. I need to. Iren would help me.

Chapter Twenty-Eight:

HIS MAJESTY'S EYES

Azi

"Good job. You're really getting the hang of that, Azi!" Flitt pats me on the earlobe proudly as Rian casts the Revealer over us and we rush from the Half-Realm. My skin still crawls, though. Our haven has changed since the first time we stumbled on it so many months ago. It's darker, somehow. Forbidding and creepy.

The forest park outside of the castle is covered in a thick blanket of snow, and the air is so cold that my breath catches and stings my nose. I glance through the thick, silent trees toward the west, where smoke billows from the chimneys of our guild hall. It's just past dusk. I imagine Mouli inside, puttering around the kitchen. Perhaps she's stirring up a stew and hot buns to share with Luca after a busy day. The two of them work hard to keep our guild hall safe, clean, and warm. The place wouldn't be the same without them.

For a moment I long to run to them, just for a soft hug from her and a quick bite of something fresh and delicious. Nobody rivals Mouli's cooking. I've thought of it these past days. I didn't realize how much I missed home until now, being so close.

"Come on," Rian seems just as reluctant as he takes my hand and guides me through the snow. Our cloaks snap in the brisk wind and driving snow as we trudge toward the palace, and Flitt tucks herself into my hood to keep from being blown away. The wind carries the scent of the sea with it, something else I've missed dearly on our journey. Despite the danger ahead, it's a comfort to be back home, in Cerion.

The guards at the gate recognize us immediately and wave us through into the warmth of the entry hall, where we're instructed to wait and given hot mugs of mulled cider. Instead of drinking it, Rian paces. He's agitated, I can tell. Something here is off, and it's bothering him.

"What is it?" I whisper. He shakes his head.

"Something new," he says quietly. "Some different sort of magic here."

"Uh huh," Flitt agrees. "I feel it, too."

"What do you mean?" I ask. "Is it dangerous? The Dreamwalker?" I imagine Jacek in these walls, his cloak billowing behind him, licking out at the finery, casting it into darkness. I shiver.

"On the contrary," Rian comes to my side and looks around the room curiously, as though the magic he's noticed is a force that can be seen as well as sensed. "It's warding magic. Protective and strong, but there's a joy and a purity to it. A sort of…"

"Innocence," Flitt finishes his thought as he trails off.

"Yes, that's it exactly," he smiles at her. "It's like nothing I've felt before, especially not here in the palace."

I try to feel it, too, but it isn't as obvious to me. Instead, when I really concentrate, I'm aware of someone nearby. He's slightly annoyed, I can tell. He was doing something amusing and had to be interrupted. Rian folds his arms around me while we wait, and bends to me for a kiss which I gladly return. Oddly, kissing him magnifies my awareness of whoever it is who's approaching.

When the guard opens the door and we lock eyes just for a quick moment, I see a flash of myself in Rian's arms. My hair is a tousled, half-braided mess. My armor is scuffed and flecked with blood, and my once white cloak hangs wet and gray to my boots. Rian looks just as bad as I do. His deep blue robes are torn and splashed with red. His face is smudged with soot and blood. I blink and shake my head, forcing my perspective to slide back to my own eyes as the guard greets us cordially. That was far too easy. I didn't even have to think about it.

As the guard leads us away down a corridor, I wonder whether Rian did somehow lend me power toward it. It was similar to our fight against the Sorcerer, before Tib intervened. I had seen things that weren't mine: thoughts and memories. It had startled me so much that I lost track of the fight. Had Rian not been there, I would have been in much worse shape coming out of it. I haven't told him yet what Stubs taught me to do yet. I wonder if he'd see me differently if he knew. The thought worries me, so I turn my attention to our passing surroundings instead.

It's just now the end of supper time, and the savory aroma of roast meat lingers beneath the sweeter, stronger scent of baked pie and cakes as we follow the guard through the polished passages. My mouth waters as Rian's hand grips my gauntlet, and at my shoulder Flitt sniffs the air.

"*It smells like Mouli's kitchen in here,*" she pushes to me, and it makes me smile that she'd make that association. It makes me happy to think that she's getting used to us and our culture. As we pass the entrance to the feasting hall, I slow my pace to look inside.

The king's chair at the head of the table is empty. Beside it, Princess Margy lies with her head in the queen's lap. Her Majesty strokes the princess's plump cheek absently while in the space between the tables subjects dance to the merry sound of drums and lutes and clapping. I catch a glimpse of Sarabel at the center of it, dancing alone, her brown curls bouncing, her smile sparkling.

We cross into a quieter passage that runs alongside the dining hall. At the end of the hall is a large, ornately polished door blocked by two stern guards. When we approach, the two men turn to the side at attention and allow us to enter.

His Majesty immediately whirls to face us as we enter and the doors close behind us. Together Rian and I drop into a deep bow, but King Tirnon rushes to us and rests a hand on each of our shoulders. As we straighten, I can tell right away that he's afraid of the news we've come to bear. He takes in the blood on my armor, the smudges on my face.

"Sir Hammerfel, Mentor Eldinae. You've come straight from battle," his voice is strong and commanding despite the fear in his eyes. "What's happened? Eron? Amei? Are they safe? Come, sit. Grenis, bring them food." A servant nods and slips out of the door that connects this room to the dining hall.

"They're safely delivered to Kordelya, Your Majesty," Rian reassures him. "We left them in the capable hands of Baron Stenneler."

"Ah, thank you. Thank you," he gives a sigh of relief, and claps Rian on the shoulder. "Come, then, and tell us of the battle that has left you in such a state."

We turn to the table which is already occupied by several men. One of them is young, with dark hair and eyes and a strong jaw. I've seen him before, in the vision Jacek showed me. He's Vorance, the Prince of Sunteri who stood at his window and watched towers burn. Beside him are two stern-looking men in exotically ornate chain armor draped with tabards bearing the Royal Crest of Zhaghen.

Opposite these men, two Mages are seated side by side to the right of the table's head. The closest to the king is Master Anod, High Master and Advisor to the King. The other one I know very well. He's dressed in deep blue robes trimmed with gold, and his dark hair is tied neatly at the nape of his neck. A permanent furrow is chiseled into his brow. Even now when I see him I feel a rush of dread that I'll be in trouble somehow. He is my uncle: Master Gaethon, the head of the Mage Academy of Cerion.

The two Mages stand and nod to Rian. All three of them press their right fists to their chests and Rian bows low to his seniors.

"Mentor," they say together.

"Masters," Rian says at the same time.

"Please," the king says with concern as he motions to two empty chairs. "Sit. Sit. You've not yet met His Highness Prince Vorance, have you?"

Rian and I bow to the prince midway to sitting down. The young man laughs and flicks his wrist dismissively.

"No need for such formalities," the prince says as I slide in tensely beside my uncle. "My princess has told me much you, Sir Hammerfel, Mentor Eldinae. I feel almost as kin to you." His deep-toned voice is thickly accented. He flashes a smile across the table and I'm instantly charmed by his warmth.

"These are my men," he says with a gesture to them. "Resh Kenalal, Resh Alanso." The two men half-stand and nod. Their demeanor is a stark contrast to that of their prince. They seem gruff and skeptical of both Rian and myself.

The others at the table introduce themselves. There is Myer, Captain of the Guard, and Elmsworth, Captain of Arms, and Ganvent, Admiral of the Naval Fleet. I shift uncomfortably in my seat as each of them make their introductions. I've never been in close company with such esteemed men before. Uncle leans toward me and pats my bracer with a hint of a reassuring smile. The child in me is relieved to know that at the very least, he isn't going to shout at me.

The table is littered with maps and sheaves of writing that are quickly cleared away to make room for supper plates for Rian and me. I pull off my gloves under the table and look at my hands.

The gold swirls that stretch across my palms are barely noticeable in the low light, but when I turn them over the light catches on the lines that weave over the backs of my hands, causing them to shimmer. I glance at Uncle and Anod and pull the long sleeves of my undershirt down to cover as much of them as possible before reaching for my spoon. We ate at the Inn, but between the cold and the Half-Realm, I'm famished again.

Beside me, Rian regales the men with the tale of the battle in Sorlen River Crossing while we eat. When he's through, he reaches into his vest and produces the letter that the Elite drafted for us to give to the king. I pass it to Uncle, who passes it to His Majesty. Given the present company, I'm relieved we decided to go with a note. I couldn't imagine saying the things in that letter aloud in front of Prince Vorance and his men. It would humiliate the king. This is a private matter for him.

"Clearly the threat of Sorcery is more present than we suspected," Uncle says in response to Rian's tale. "A brazen attack on a village as large as Sorlen River Crossing is quite concerning."

"Indeed," Anod says. "Your Majesty, I would advise a post of Mages in each major village, to place wards and offer a defense in the event of such a threat repeating."

"They are rare here, these strikes of Sorcerers?" Prince Vorance asks. "In Sunteri, we have them often. They come without notice and take what they will. It is, sadly, a way of life in our lands."

"All the more reason for you to sign, Highness," Anod taps at a stack of pages between them. The prince eyes the pages and rests his chin in his hand thoughtfully.

"You would aid us in replacing our burned libraries?" he asks, falling back into the negotiations we interrupted easily enough. "That must be added. And the ships."

"If His Majesty agrees," Anod turns to the king, who holds up his free hand to quiet them while he reads the letter.

The room falls silent. When he's through, he looks up and meets my eyes directly. His own are narrowed, calculating. I can almost see the thoughts behind them. Under the table, I reach for Rian's hand.

I need to look away, but I don't want to be disrespectful. His Majesty's eyes are crisp blue, like Midwinter sky on a bright day. They hold so much joy, so much pain, so much responsibility. I feel my consciousness being lured away. He doesn't know what I can do. He can't find out. I'm certain that looking into his thoughts would be treason.

Even though I know it's wrong, I can't stop it. I start to fall into them, tumbling into the beautiful blue. To my great relief, the door behind us opens abruptly and the king looks away, breaking the connection.

"Paba." Princess Margy skips into the room and climbs up on his lap, putting herself between the king and the letter of bad tidings.

"Flitt!" Twig cries. A blur of green and brown shoots past my ear and crashes into Flitt, who had been bobbing beside my shoulder.

"Twig!" Flitt yelps. They link arms and ankles and spin across the room together, laughing delightfully. I look around the table. No one else seems to notice the two fairies besides possibly Uncle Gaethon and Master Anod. Both glance casually in their direction before looking pointedly away.

"I'm so sorry, Your Majesty," says a hassled-looking woman who curtseys hastily before rushing to Margy and bending a knee. "Come, Princess, your father is quite busy right now. We mustn't just barge in."

"But he promised," Margy looks up at King Tirnon with wide, mournful eyes. "You promised tonight we'd dance, Paba, and you haven't even been to dine yet."

"Thank you, Tirie," the king waves the woman away and she rushes off wringing her hands and murmuring apologies.

Happy not to be sent away, Margary curls against the king's chest. He rests his chin on her head absently while he reads the letter again. His mood seems to soften with her there. Margary, on the other hand, is on edge. With her arms around her father, she turns her head slightly to peek at me.

In the past we've been close friends, she and I. She helped me more than once, and I have always been fond of her. She doesn't greet me with her usual excitement tonight, though. Instead she regards me with suspicion and mistrust as she tucks herself closer to the king. I can't imagine why until I look down at my hands, where the tips of golden curls glint in the candlelight. I think of what she ran in on. I was so close to entering the king's mind. Is it possible that she sensed it, somehow? That she came to put a stop to it?

I glance at Rian, who's sitting rigid beside me. His eyes are cast down and to the side, fixed on my hands. Slowly he looks up and meets my gaze.

"*What is that?*" he pushes to me. My heart starts to race.

"*Later,*" I push back and tuck my hands between my knees.

The room remains silent aside from Twig and Flitt whispering together at the edge of the table closest to Margary. The king, who is still looking over the letter, strokes his daughter's shoulder as she rests against him.

"Come and dance, Paba," she whines. "It's been a week of you saying tomorrow, tomorrow. You're always in here," she sniffles and looks away from me, and I feel her rejection like a stab in my gut. She knows what I almost did. She has to. This isn't like her at all. The king sighs, long and low. He hands the letter to a page at his shoulder and nods to the hearth, and the page crosses to it and drops the parchment into the fire.

"We'll adjourn for the night," His Majesty says. "I'll consider the libraries with counsel from Anod and Gaethon, as well as the schooling and ships, and we'll have a new treaty drafted tomorrow."

He tips Margy back and she looks up at him.

"Go and tell them to be ready for our song, hm?" he says softly. "I need to have a word with Sir Hammerfel and Mentor Eldenae and then you and I shall have our dance."

The princess slips from her father's lap and smoothes out the skirt of her gown. As she crosses toward the door she looks over her shoulder at me and shakes her head so slightly that I might have imagined it. While the others at the table gather their things to leave, I pull my gloves back on to conceal the swirls. We bow to Prince Vorance as he slips out behind Margary. The others follow him into the dining hall.

"See me after," Uncle murmurs to Rian before he files out to the hallway leading to the rest of the palace. He closes the door behind him, leaving us alone with the king.

"I want to see the stone," King Tirnon says as soon as we're alone. He holds out his hand. Rian produces it from one of his pouches and rests it in His Majesty's palm. "So my son's voice emanated from this object, and that is your basis to accuse him of dark dealings?"

"Your Majesty, you know everything we know. Based on the information, it's difficult to come up with any other explanation."

"What of this Dreamwalker Mya mentioned?" the king closes his eyes and sets the stone on the table. "What do you know of it?"

"His name is Jacek," I say, "he was born in Sunteri and banished to the Dreaming, where he took the mantle of a Dreamwalker and claimed it for his own. I have seen him, Your Majesty. He has shown me things."

The king beckons me and I cross to him. He rests a hand on my shoulder and looks into my eyes, searching them. Again, I can't look away. I mustn't. I will myself to focus on something else. His lashes, the bridge of his nose. Anything but those welcoming pools of blue.

"Could he have grip on my son?" he asks me pleadingly. "Could it be that Eron's darkness is a result of this Dreamwalker meddling with him?"

"It's possible, Your Majesty," Rian ventures.

"It is possible," I echo, "but Sire, if you'll allow me to speak my mind?"

"Please," King Tirnon nods, and I steel myself. What I'm about to say won't be easy for him to hear, and I've never been good at speaking, especially in situations like this. But I feel I have to say what's been on my mind for so many months now. I take a deep breath.

"I fear the prince's motives. He schemes to own things that should never belong to him. I fear that his actions will allow this darkness into Cerion. Your leadership has made this kingdom great, sire, and I fear that when the throne goes to Eron, the generations of peace that the Plethores have worked for will come to an end." I pause as the king sinks into his chair.

"I have been in the grips of the Dreamwalker myself, Your Majesty," I go on. "I have seen the disturbing way that he thinks and works. He has acted through the prince at least once before. He is interested in Prince Vorance and Princess Sarabel as well. I saw through his own eyes, how he lurked outside the palace. He was unable to enter, though. The wards placed here kept him out. He did manipulate your staff. One of them took something of Princess Margary's."

I rest my hand on the ornately carved wood of His Majesty's chair as Rian comes to stand beside me. The king slumps forward and rubs his temples with one hand as he considers my words.

"I will increase the patrols around the castle and ask Master Anod to strengthen our magical security to the city's outskirts." He sighs and pushes himself out of his chair again, looking first at Rian and then at me.

"You must understand that barring titles and ranks, Eron is my boy. I am king, yes, and he is the heir to my kingdom. He is my son, and I will always love him and try to see the good in him. If his own father cannot have faith in him, then who will? I cannot give up on Eron. Not yet.

"Seek out this Dreamwalker. Do what you will to end him.

Whatever it takes. I will lend you whatever aid you need. If after his demise, Eron keeps his wicked tendencies…" his voice trails off painfully and he looks away into the fire. "I will deal with it."

The music in the dining hall changes, and Margy pushes the door open again.

"Paba, they're playing it!" she calls to him, and the sound of her voice smoothes the worry lines from his face and brings him peace.

"Be safe," he dismisses us with a nod and allows Margy to pull him away by the hand, into the room beyond.

"I've got to stick with her," Twig says to Flitt as the door closes. "Don't forget, okay?"

"Course I won't! See you soon," Flitt grins and waves as Twig hops up from the table and then shoots off, straight through the wall into the dining room. When he's gone, Rian turns to me.

"So," he says quietly. His jaw is clenched as his gaze falls to my hands again. Slowly he takes my right hand, pulls my glove off, and holds it to the light. The fine golden lines catch and flash in the firelight. He draws me closer and I think he might kiss me, but instead he pulls the collar of my gambeson away and strokes a finger along what I'm sure must be more of the lines on my collarbone.

"When were you planning to tell me?" he asks, his voice tinged with pain and anger.

I pull away from him and tug my collar up again. His prickly tone sets me on edge. Standing on the table, Flitt watches our exchange, hands on hips. She's angry, too.

"Oh, I don't know," I say defensively. "When would have been a good time? When we were escaping the dreaming with our lives, or while I was defending you from Sorcerers and Necromancers? Or would later have been better, in front of the whole guild and Tib and Mevyn, in the middle of the tavern?"

Rian doesn't answer. He simply shakes his head and thrusts my glove at me before turning away.

"I don't understand why you're so upset," I say. "I was going to tell you when the time was right."

"You don't understand…" he trails off and sighs and then spins to face me. "You never should have come to the palace. If I had known, I would have refused to allow it."

"Refused to allow it?" My jaw drops. I can't believe what I'm hearing. "So now you decide where I can and can't go? What gives you the right?" Rian scowls and shoves the door open.

"We're going to the guild hall. Quickly. We can't stay here, especially not now." He stands there waiting, holding the door while my ears ring with fury. How dare he? Out of spite, out of pure rebellion to his sudden need to control me, I plant my feet and cross my arms.

"Azi," Rian growls and shuts the door before he comes back to me again. "Think about it. Think about what you can do. Think about the liberties you're afforded by your station and by the trust so many people have in you. Do you think just anyone could show up at the palace and be brought directly in to the king inner chambers? Where he's meeting with his most trusted advisers? You think anyone can simply grace his presence and be welcomed? No, they can't, Azi." He grips my hand and a lump forms in my throat as his what he's saying starts to sink in.

"You're welcome in Kythshire, you're welcome in the palace, and you're trusted by those closest to the king and the king himself. The Dreamwalker knows that. He knows it, and he's given you magic now to link you to him. A way of letting him in where he couldn't get in before. To spy. Do you see? We have to leave. Now."

I nod, too choked up to be able to speak through the tears that burn my eyes and spill down my cheeks. The palace is a blur as Rian pulls me along through the winding polished hallways and finally out of the gates and into the street beyond. How could I be so stupid? How could I not have seen?

When I set foot on the icy cobbled stones of the street, I feel the darkness sink over me. Rian whispers a ward, but not soon enough. My eyes close and I fall to my knees in the street, overcome by the Dreamwalker, who had been lurking just outside. Waiting all along, just for me.

Chapter Twenty-Nine:

TALISMANS AND TRINKETS

Azi

"Do not blame yourself, Rian," Uncle says. "You had no way of knowing. Here, set her in the chair. Yes, good. Make her comfortable. Azaeli. Azi. Try to wake her while I set the wards." His voice is far away, wrapped in a cloak of darkness, snuffed by something powerful and cunning.

Someone's hands are on me, shaking me, pinching me, slapping my face. It feels small to me, like pebbles thrown into the ocean. Unimportant. A distant reality. Still I cling to it and fight myself closer. The darkness is feeding on my rage at being tricked, bleeding it away from me. More builds in its place. How could I be so blind? Why didn't I see?

I'm aware of something sinister at the edge of the cloak, another presence that's working to shuffle through my thoughts like a deck of cards, sifting and watching and searching.

"*Get away from me!*" I scream in my head, trying in vain to fight it.

"Look at it," Rian says with disbelief. "She's covered. How did I miss this?"

"Mentalism originates far beyond our borders, magically speaking," Uncle explains. "It is a rare craft, barely seen anymore. Only the most omniscient of creatures can wield it, and even then they must be discerning. They must act with great caution." Uncle says.

"He means fairies," Flitt pipes up. "It's strictly fairy magic. Everyone else isn't supposed to be allowed. Hey Azi, wake up!"

I push closer to the voices. Fighting the darkness is like crawling uphill through thick mud. Everything hurts. I can barely breathe, and then he's here, in front of me, crushing me with the darkness that swirls around him.

"You're not real," I say to Jacek. He laughs and keeps shuffling through my thoughts. I'm sleeping, I know I am. It's just like before in the tavern and in the fairy ring. It's in my head. It isn't real. All I have to do is open my eyes.

"Okay, here goes," Flitt says from the other side of the darkness, which is thickening now and pushing me back. Something strikes my chest, hard. It knocks the breath out of me and sprays a blinding light of every color across the darkness. Jacek screams in pain and the darkness shrinks back. The light is emanating from my chest, from the pouch that holds Flitt's diamond. I shield my eyes and look away.

"Oh no you don't, Azi. You look at me." Flitt bobs in front of my face and starts to grow. Her eyes are swirling with every color: red, blue, green, purple, yellow, orange. I've noticed them before, but never this way. Never with her face this close to mine, as large as my own. The way the colors swirl and sparkle in her eyes is the most perfect, beautiful thing I've ever seen. I try to catch my breath as she locks her gaze to mine and I fall into her, away from the darkness, away from Jacek, back into myself.

I gasp and cough as my eyes fly open. Someone is looming over me. I shove him away and leap up from my chair. Before I can think, my sword is in my hands, poised to strike.

"Whoa, whoa, whoa!" Flitt says. She's back to her usual tiny self again as she floats in front of me, though most of her color is drained to white. "You're back. Just calm down. He can't get you. You're safe."

At the great hearth Uncle and Rian are standing with their hands up, ready to defend themselves if they need to. I turn and take in my surroundings as I try to calm myself. We're in the guild hall. A merry fire is crackling in the hearth, and the chairs surrounding it have been freshly brushed clean. I walk slowly to the meeting table and run my fingers along the worn wood. It's real. It's all real. I lay my sword on the bench and try to compose myself. Flitt comes to my shoulder and I reach up and press her to my cheek in a careful hug.

"*Thank you,*" I send to her. "*Whatever that was, thank you.*"

"New trick with your diamond. You can thank Dabble. I'm just glad it worked. Oh! Do you think Mouli made sweet rolls? I'll be back!" She's gone before I can come up with a response.

I turn slowly to Rian and Uncle who are still watching me with caution.

"I'm so sorry," I whisper hoarsely to Rian. "Are you all right? I didn't hurt you, did I?"

"I'm fine," he opens his arms and I cross and sink into them.

"I should have seen it," I whisper. "I should have realized. I'm so sorry."

"Me too," Rian murmurs into my hair. "I should have, too."

"Sit down," Gaethon says. "Both of you, and tell me everything from the start."

I take a seat in one of the familiar overstuffed chairs and Rian and Uncle sit beside me. Staring into the fire, I tell them everything I can remember from the moment we left on our journey all the way up to our encounter at the village. Rian interjects from time to time, adding his own side of the story.

The apprentice mark on my forehead tingles softly, and I think of all of the times in the past that Rian and Uncle have slipped away to whisper secrets. There is some magic happening now, I know. Some ancient bond between teacher and student that protects and preserves. Uncle leans toward me as I recount, until his elbows rest on the arm of my chair and he's staring thoughtfully at my face. He has nothing to say for a long stretch once the tale is through, and we sit for a while in pensive silence.

"Were we not facing such a threat," Uncle says to me, "I would have you show me exactly what you've learned. We would categorize it and study it and try our best to replicate it. I would forbid you to use it until we could come to fully understand. But in this case, Azaeli, I shall only say to use it with the greatest discretion. The manner it was taught to you was highly unusual. It's unknown whether what you see can be seen by others. Use care, my niece." He pushes himself to his feet and stretches.

"Had I known this quest would be so threatened by darkness," he says, "I would never have chosen to stay behind. Do not mistake me, Rian. I am impressed with your handling of the challenges that arose. At this time, though, I think it best for me to join you when you return to the others." He crosses to the hearth, takes a long pipe from a box on the mantle, and stuffs it with herbs.

"What about the negotiations with Prince Vorance and His Majesty, Master? Aren't you needed?" Rian asks. He seems to be relieved, though, to hear that his master will be joining us.

"You might think so," Uncle says. "But the king knows my stance and refuses to listen. It would be a welcome reprieve for the both of us, I imagine. I shall send another in my place. Hopefully one who can shed a different light on my side of the argument."

"What is your side?" Rian asks. I'm impressed. He's very bold to ask questions I would never dare pose. I watch the exchange between student and master with mild interest. Uncle takes a long pull from his pipe and blows out a slow stream of bluish smoke.

"That we should tread lightly in this alliance with Sunteri," he explains. "The impending marriage is unwise for many reasons. Take the current state of Zhaghen. It is a place of upheaval. Its citizens are at the brink of rebellion."

"Theirs is a land of greed and excess," he goes on. "It breeds Sorcery. Where we in Cerion teach restraint and reverence, they seek only more and more power. The loss of their Wellspring was their own folly. Lending aid to them now would only reinforce their behavior, like a stamp of approval. It would encourage the greed and contemptuous misuse of magic that seems so ingrained in their way of life.

"Sending our princess, his beloved daughter, to that place at such a time," he shakes his head slowly, staring into the fire.

I think of Sarabel dancing and smiling in the center of everyone tonight, so happy, so carefree. Knowing she's about to wed the man she loves only to face such a future is heartbreaking. Sarabel has been my friend since we were old enough to crawl across the palace gardens together.

"What can we do?" I ask.

"Azaeli," Uncle laughs softly and shakes his head, then steps to me and pulls me up from my seat. He gives me an awkward hug and pats me on the head like he used to when I was still a child. "In time, you will learn that it is impossible to fight every battle you're presented with. Right now, you have a much greater threat to face, remember?"

He turns to Rian, "When will you return to the others?"

"In the morning," Rian says.

"And you warded the Inn before you left?" Uncle asks.

"Yes, Master."

"Then go to bed, both of you, and rest. I shall meet you here at dawn." Uncle nods toward the door.

It's strange to be back inside the guild hall again. Though we've only been gone for a couple of weeks, it feels like it could be a year. Everything seems cleaner, somehow, and smaller.

"He knows about the Half-Realm?" I whisper to Rian as we

walk hand in hand toward the kitchens to find Flitt and say hello to Mouli.

"He knows almost everything," Rian replies. "They wouldn't leave me alone until I told at least one Master every detail." I think of the weeks following our battle at Kythshire, how I barely saw him due to all of the hours he was held at the Academy for questioning and evaluation. It was a grueling time for him, during which I tried to respect his exhaustion by not asking my own questions about what they were doing. "I cleared it first, though. With Flitt."

We pause in the doorway of the kitchen. Mouli is passing sweet rolls to grubby little hands at the half-door, which is open to a small crowd of street children. Flitt darts between them all, diving to catch the bits of icing that drip from each roll as Mouli hands them out.

"Ah, ah," Mouli says. "To the water bucket with you! Only clean hands get a treat. Go on. What's that? Do I get a thank you? Good girl. All right, and one for your brother. You tell him I'm praying for him. Yes, dear."

I grin and lean against Rian as we watch until the tray of rolls is empty, then I clear my throat and Mouli spins around, startled.

"Oh! By the stars! By the stars and moon and seas alive! Azi! Rian!" She tosses the tray onto the table with a clatter and rushes to throw her arms around us. "Look at you. Look at the sight of you both! Filthy! Oh!" she clucks her tongue and fusses over us in a way that I never thought I'd miss as much as I did. "You could have sent a note. I have nothing prepared for you. Oh, my. Oh, dear." She wipes her hands on her apron all a fluster and smoothes her hair.

"Mouli, it's all right. We're only here for tonight. We just came to say hello," Rian tries to calm her while I go to Flitt, who's happily full of icing but still drained of her color. I bend to offer her my shoulder and she flies up and tucks herself into my collar.

"Isn't it a little late at night to be passing out treats to children?" I ask her as I peer out at the last few who are licking icing from their fingers.

"Oh, they know to come after supper so nothing goes to waste," she smiles at me and goes to the door. I chuckle to myself as I look at the empty tray and decide not to voice my doubts about how an entire tray of fresh-baked sweet rolls could possibly be considered supper leftovers.

"Go on home now," Mouli leans out of the door. "Go in pairs, yes. Goodnight." She closes up and looks us over again.

"Baths," she says. "And then to bed, both of you."

Despite the heavy guilt I feel for indulging in something so unnecessary at a time like this, I'm glad to give in to Mouli and soak for a while. It puts my mind at ease after all we've been through, and steels me for what's to come. By the time I wash my armor and braid my hair I feel like I've been reborn.

Rian and I wait until she comes to say goodnight, and then he ducks into the Half-Realm and slips through the wall that separates our rooms. We lie in each other's arms, whispering apologies and plans between kisses, allowing ourselves be as close as we want to be. As close as we can, that is, with Flitt tucked beside my head on my pillow. She's sound asleep, and we're careful not to wake her.

"She's so white," I whisper to Rian, who turns over to look at her.

"She just needs to rest," he says. "That little move took a lot out of her."

"It makes sense, though, fighting darkness with light," I say. "It was a good idea, and it seemed to really cause him pain."

"You're right," Rian says. He turns back to me with a grin and a glint in his eye. "You might say it was…brilliant."

"Ha, ha," I groan and shove him playfully. "Go to sleep, Rian."

"You too," he says between kisses to my shoulder. "I mean it, Azi. It's safe to sleep. Promise."

His words soothe a worry which I never voiced, one that had been nagging at me since Uncle told us we should rest. I haven't slept since I was trapped in the Dreaming. With Rian's arms around me in my own bed, I can't think of a safer place to allow it. I trust in him and eventually I let myself drift to sleep.

The night passes without a dream, and I'm woken before the sun by Rian's lips on mine, soft and warm.

"Wake up, Love," he whispers. "I have something to ask you."

I groan and stretch and roll away in protest, and he pulls me closer to him.

"I can't ask you with your back to me," he laughs softly. I rub my eyes open and catch a glimpse of a much more colorful Flitt still sleeping soundly on my pillow before I turn back to him.

"How long have you been lying awake thinking of questions to ask me?" I ask him, and he shrugs sheepishly and slips out from between the covers to kneel at the bedside.

"This is one I've been thinking about for a while." His

expression goes serious as he lays his fist, palm up, between us. I start to sit up but he stops me. "Don't wake Flitt," he whispers. "This is between us." He takes my hand with his free one and gazes into my eyes as his thumb caresses my palm softly. He's delaying, I can tell. Whatever he's about to ask me, he's nervous.

"What is it?" I ask gently. "You know I'd tell you anything, Rian. Don't be nervous."

"I know," he looks down at his closed hand. "It's just…I've known you all my life, Azi. You've always been by my side. And the more we face together, the more I realize how much you mean to me. When you fell in the tavern, I thought I lost you. I was terrified. I can't imagine my life—"

Screams outside my window interrupt him mid-sentence. Together we leap from the bed to throw open the shutters and are struck by the acrid smell of smoke. In the distance toward the city gates, flames lick toward the sky.

"That's Midmarket," he says.

"Oh, Rian, the low houses!" I peer out into the smoke and flames toward the rooftops where the poorer folks make their home in the city.

"Get dressed," he says to me. "We'll go help."

Hastily, I tuck my night dress into a pair of trousers and dash outside with Rian toward the flames. Closer to them, it's chaos. Children and women are huddled along the street away from the fire coughing and crying, while men hoist buckets from the nearby well. Two Mages stand close to the flames, shouting spells that spray water from their palms to calm the raging fires. I run to the bucket line to help while Rian separates to join the other Mages.

I pass bucket after bucket, my fingers stinging from the bitter cold and icy water that splashes over me, and I fall into the soothing rhythm of it. The sun is just peeking up over the sea wall. It casts long shadows across the cobbles. Shadows that creep toward me, whispering words that make no sense. They slip over my arms, caressing me, luring me. I try to ignore them and focus on the buckets. The fire is nearly out. Thick pillars of smoke billow into the pink morning sky. All around us I hear the cries of those who've lost everything.

"*You shouldn't have hidden from me,*" Jacek's voice echoes in my head and the bucket slips from my numb fingers and crashes to the ground, drenching me and the man beside me.

"All right, lass," he says gruffly. "Keep going, it's almost out."

I get the next bucket and the next as I survey the damage left in the fire's wake. The entire market and a half dozen low houses beyond are reduced to charcoal and soot. The Mages manage to snuff out the remaining flames, and by the time the buckets stop coming my entire body is trembling. This is my fault, all of it. Somehow, Jacek caused this because of me. I find Rian working with a group of Mages to try to restore what they can.

"It's a complete loss," he says to me. "Smashed or broken we can easily restore, but burned?" he shakes his head. "There's nothing we can do. Thankfully no one was hurt." I stretch my arms around him and hold him and try not to lose my composure in the middle of the street. "They can rebuild. Don't worry. The king has reserves for matters like this, and the Mages can easily…" he trails off as I look up at him. "It was him, wasn't it?"

I nod, and his eyes go wide as he takes my hand and starts to run. We weave past displaced families and splash through sooty puddles toward home, to the safety of the guild hall. He pushes me through the door first and as soon as he does I feel the shift of the wards that Uncle placed here last night. Wards to hide me, to protect me. To keep Jacek out.

It makes sense that Rian would want me to be here and safe, but Jacek's words echo in my mind. If hiding from him means another attack on innocents, I'd rather be out in the open. I turn to Rian to tell him so, but a light at the top of the stairs distracts me. It glitters and splashes colors all along the wall as Flitt emerges looking much like herself again.

"What happened? I woke up and you were gone," she wrinkles her nose at us. "You smell like smoke, ugh. How'd you get all dirty? And what are you wearing, Azi?"

"There was a fire," Rian answers her absently before turning to me. "He was trying to draw you out. He knows you're a hero, he knows you'd rush to help."

"What am I going to do?" I ask him. "If I stay hidden, I risk more of that." I point toward the outside. "But if I'm out in the open, he'll be able to see anything I've seen."

"Not so," Flitt says matter-of-factly. "He just did that to scare you last night. I've been thinking it over. The Dreamwalker may seem powerful, but he has limits. For example, he can't reach across planes to gather memories. You know yourself that he has to look into your eyes. He can only make suggestions. Last night he didn't see anything. He just suggested to you that he was looking in order to trick you into being scared. That made it easier for him to lure you away. Just like when he made you think you'd drunk some poisoned cider. It was only a thought he put into your head to make you vulnerable. There wasn't anything in the cup, really. Well, aside from cider, obviously."

While she chatters on, she plays idly with a silver band. Its blue stones flash and glint in her light as she twirls it over her wrist like an acrobat's hoop. When she realizes it has caught my eye, she shoves it behind her back and slowly floats backward toward Rian, who plucks it away with annoyance.

"You shouldn't play with that," he says under his breath.

"Well, *you* shouldn't have left it lying around in the bed where she could find it," she whispers back, blows a raspberry, and shoots through the window, probably on her way to the kitchen to see what Mouli is cooking up.

Before Rian can bring up the ring and his unfinished question, I give him a quick kiss and excuse myself to go upstairs and dress. My heart is racing, and I'm not sure whether it's from the firefight or Jacek or what came before that. I imagine the ring around Flitt's wrist. I wish I had gotten a better look at it. Still, if he had asked me…

I shake my head and don my armor, taking care to fasten my sword tightly in its harness. The action reminds me of the girl we left in Kythshire, Saesa. Jacek's sister. The blood tie who could possibly set him free. What if he saw her in my memories? What if he knows she's hiding there? Could he find her? Could he use me to get to her?

Thoughts of him make my blood boil. He's attacked my city now, he's set fire to innocent people's homes. I know that Tib has been given the title of Dreamstalker, but here in the quiet of my room, all alone, I vow to myself that my sword will be the last to drive through him, and my eyes will be the last he looks into as his life drains away.

Rian raps on the hatch between our rooms and I nearly jump out of my skin. I slide open the little door and peer into the mess of his room.

"Didn't Mouli straighten up for you?" I ask him, eyeing the piles of clothes on the floor and the disheveled bedcovers. He grins and shrugs.

"It doesn't feel like home if it's not a mess," he laughs. "Actually, I was looking for something."

"Did you find it?" I ask him.

"Yes." He holds up an elegant looking dagger that I'm sure is of elvish make. He swishes it from side to side rather amateurishly. "Just in case."

I narrow my eyes. "Do you even know how to use that?"

"What's there to know? Stab, stab." He thrusts it forward with a flourish and accidentally drops it.

"Rian…" I shake my head and laugh as he ducks down to retrieve it.

"Relax, Azi," he chuckles. "It's for Tib. I noticed he had a fondness for sharp things, and this one has a kick to it. Ready?"

"Where did you get it?" I ask him later in the corridor as we walk together to the hall.

"Da gave it to me a long time ago, back before Master Gaethon chose me for the Academy. I think he was hoping I'd be a scout like him one day. I never could get the hang of the bow, though. And you know I'm not so fond of the sight of blood."

"No, you're much more comfortable exploding things," I say as we enter the hall together. Uncle is waiting for us at the table, where Mouli has laid a spread of breakfast fit for a king. Flitt is there too, half-buried in a bowl of sweetnuts.

"Hi Azi!" she says brightly. She waves to me and glances at my finger and turns to Rian with a pout. He shakes his head at her and presses a finger to his lips. "Typical," she mumbles.

"*What?*" I push to both of them.

"*Nothing!*" they reply in unison.

"I feel bad letting it go to waste," I say of the breakfast after a moment watching the two of them exchange a heated, silent conversation, "but I don't want to wait. Can we just go?" I look from Rian to Uncle, who nods.

"After the events of this morning, I heartily agree," he says. "But first," he turns to me, "Take this, Azaeli. It was carved of the stone of Gelvindan, of the peaks of Hesta, the mountains of Hywilkin. It's said to have been dipped in the golden waters of the North and imbued with warding powers."

He lowers the talisman into my waiting hand and I immediately feel the shift of protection around me. I look it over curiously. Flitt comes to perch on my wrist and look it over, too. The stone is deep green marbled with streaks of cream white and flecks of coral. It's carved into the shape of an open mouth, with a tongue that curls out over sharpened teeth.

"Yep," she says, "Definitely powerful." She wrinkles her nose and darts back to her bowl of nuts.

"Thank you," I say to Uncle, who gives a cordial nod before turning to Rian.

"And now," Uncle says, "the Mentor will enlighten the Master." There's a glint of amused interest in his eye as he takes Rian's offered elbow. I link my arm through Rian's free one.

"Azi's better at it, actually," Rian says. "Do you want to?"

"Is that so?" Uncle asks, turning to me with a look of utter surprise.

"I don't think I should this time," I say to Rian. "You have better focus." To be honest, I'm nervous about drawing too much attention to myself in the Half-Realm. If Jacek found us because of me, I don't think I could live with myself.

"Alright. We're going fast, then," Rian says. "Brace yourselves." He speaks the words that pull us away into the Half-Realm and then I feel the ground fall away beneath my feet.

"Meet you there," Flitt calls after us as we plummet, and I cling to Rian's arm with both hands. It's not long at all, only a breath or two, before we land with a thud in the darkness.

Chapter Thirty:
ICE AND SHADOW
Azi

At first I'm half-panicked thinking we took a wrong turn or got pulled into Jacek's nightmare, but then Rian pushes aside a heavy curtain and the early morning sun splashes over Bryse, Cort, Elliot, and Tib, who groan in protest.

"Still sleeping. Can you believe that?" Rian says, ducking away from a pillow thrown by Bryse.

"Not at all surprised," Uncle says in his usual droll tone. He flicks his finger and the pillow plunges back to Bryse and smacks him right in the face.

"Hey," he grumbles and jumps up to exact his revenge, but when he sees Uncle he stands down. "Sorry, Gaethon. Didn't expect it was you." His shoulders slump slightly and he scratches his head and yawns.

"Good," says Tib with a strange level of authority to his voice as he sits up in bed. "You're all here. It's time to go. We'll need everyone's help to reach Valenor." He scowls and glares into an unoccupied corner of the room. "Cut it out," he says under his breath, "I'm through talking for you."

"First things first," Uncle says with a suspicious eye on Tib. "Azaeli, go and fetch the others so we can inform them of His Majesty's wishes."

I do as Uncle asks, and return with Mum and Mya to find that my father has joined them along with Donal and Dacva. In the previously unoccupied corner, Uncle is standing against the wall. His eyes are half-closed and glowing with a familiar golden light.

"Uncle Gaethon?" I whisper and start to go to him, but Rian stops me.

"He's getting Mevyn to trust him," he explains. "He's showing him."

"Showing him what?" I ask.

"Everything," Rian says. He closes the doors and windows and sets the wards. Once everything is secure, Rian and I recount the meeting with the king and the events that happened afterward while Uncle keeps on in his quiet exchange with Mevyn.

"I'm glad His Majesty said as much," Mya looks at each of us in turn as she speaks. "It seems the King has set his priorities. Our first course will be to put a stop to this Dreamwalker. Once he's out of the way, we'll be able to determine for sure how much the prince has acted of his own accord. Agreed?

"Agreed," says everyone except for Tib, who seems to be having an internal struggle.

"Do what you want," he heads for the door. "I'm going to find my sister." His fists are clenched at his sides, and he glances at Mevyn and Uncle's corner. His feet shuffle a little oddly and then he winces and steps out.

"He's a spitfire, that one," says Bryse after the door closes with a soft click. "Touched in the head, I still say."

"It's not his fault. I'll go after him," I say. "I know Mevyn needs him."

The boy moves quickly, I'll give him that. He's already out of the inn and halfway down the main village street before I catch up with him. It makes me nervous being outside of the warded tavern. I pray that Jacek doesn't find me.

When I call after him, Tib quickens his pace until we both break into a full-out run. He's faster than I am in my armor, and he gains twice as much ground. Just when I start to worry I might lose him, he starts to slow. His feet drag heavily as we reach the outskirts of the village. At first I think perhaps he's tiring, but then he stops and grasps one leg as though trying to pry his foot out of the mud. When he's unable to, he folds himself in two and drops to his knees in the middle of the street.

I rush to him. His hands are pressing the sides of his head painfully, and his breath comes out in short puffs of white in the chilled morning air.

"Tib!" I cry as I kneel beside him. "What's wrong? What happened? Are you hurt?"

"He won't let me," he whispers as he slumps against me. "It's just like the roots. He won't let me go. I should have told the truth," he says, holding out a scrap of silk with an elvish mark on it. "In Ceras'lain. They would have helped me. They could have kept me safe." His skinny little body wracks with sobs as he presses his face into the crook of my arm. I try to take the scrap to get a better look at it, but he tucks it away protectively.

"Mevyn?" I ask him. "Is that who? He won't let you go?"

"He won't let me find her," he sobs. "She's all I have. All I have left."

"Shh. Listen," I stroke his hair away from his face. It's stringy and greasy and caked with blood from yesterday, but that doesn't matter to me. This close, I see him for who he really is. A boy, alone, small, and confused.

A boy who's been through things that would have broken grown men, and despite everything he's faced, his concern is not for himself, but for the sister he lost twice. I want to tell him everything will turn out for the best, that he'll be safe and so will she. I can't be sure, though, and I won't make him promises I can't keep.

"Tib," I say, clearing the lump in my throat, "I realize how important she is to you. We're concerned for her, too."

I dry his tears and look into his eyes. They're brown, rich brown, and as welcoming as warm steeped tea on a snowy day. Without trying, I'm drawn into them. It's almost as if he knows what I can do and he's inviting me. I fall quickly into fields of red blossoms, where a young Viala sits with a book on her knee. He shows me her innocent days before she became a Sorceress. Shows me how kind she was, how tender to her brother and younger sister.

Despite the grueling work and the cruelty of those who drove them, they had each other. I watch her promise him in the darkness that she'll come back for him one day. I see her waving hopefully from the window of a carriage driven by…Emris. I pull myself away. The face of the Sorcerer comes as a shock to me.

"I swear," I say to him after taking a moment to catch my breath, "I'll help you find her. I'll do everything I can to make sure you're together. I promise. Okay?"

He nods, "okay."

"Let's go back into the inn," I say. "I'll talk to the others. We'll make a plan."

"He swore he'd never meddle with my mind again," Tib rubs his eyes as I help him to his feet. "And then he wouldn't let me leave. He lied to me. I hate him."

"From what I understand," I rub his back reassuringly as we walk back to the inn, "you're justified in that." With one vow made to Tib, I make another to myself in secret. I will find a way to make certain the two are separated. When this is over, Tib will be allowed to choose his own path.

We're met with a surprising scene as we return to the gathering. Mevyn is floating in the center of a circle of the Elite with Flitt perched on Rian's shoulder, scowling at the golden fairy. When she sees me, she darts across the room and tucks herself into my collar.

"Ah, there," Mevyn says. "As I was saying, he can't have gone far."

I feel Tib's shoulders tense beneath my hand at the fairy's words, and I squeeze them reassuringly.

"Is there any way that some of us," I turn to Elliot pointedly, "could search for Ki while the rest of us go with Mevyn to Valenor?"

"Tib must remain with me," Mevyn flies to Tib, who bats him away.

"Yes, that's been established," I try not to scowl. I understand now why Tib always seems so angry.

"*And you think I'm annoying,*" Flitt chuckles in my head.

"If nothing else," Uncle says, "it is obvious that the prince has a dangerous interest in that woman. Perhaps it would be wise after all to seek her out and keep her safe."

It's hard to miss the distaste in his tone. Before she became Ki, Viala was the Academy's prize student. She betrayed the Academy by plotting right under Uncle's nose. Since then his mistrust of the Sunteri has grown tenfold. He seems to have pity for Tib, though. Like the rest of us, he has no respect for those who would enslave others. Still, Mevyn's plight is partnered with our own. Jacek is a direct threat to Cerion now, and without Mevyn's direction, we don't know how to fight him.

"I'll search for her," Elliot says. "Alone would be best. I can cover more ground that way." He goes to Tib. "Do you have something of hers I could use? For reference?"

I can see the reluctance in his eyes as he pulls out the necklace with the blue stone. He looks at it for a moment and then hands it over to Elliot. In the half-elf's hands, it pulses softly. Elliot's eyes go dim and bright again, and I know that Iren is talking to him.

"Don't worry," Elliot says to Tib as he presses the cord to his nose. "I'll find her." He gives the amulet back to the boy and rushes out without another word.

"That's settled, then. Who of the rest of you is coming along?" Mevyn asks. "We really must be going."

"Dunno," Bryse says with a scowl, turning his back on Mevyn to face Mya. "What does our *leader* say?"

"We don't know what we'll be facing," Mya says quietly. "As long as we're in agreement, I think it would be best if we all stayed together."

"I can tell you to prepare yourselves for battle. It will not be easy to get through into Valenor's lair," Mevyn says. "It is likely to be guarded by fiends the likes of which you have never before encountered."

"I'm sold," Bryse says, running a thick finger along his blade. "How do we get there?"

"As am I," Cort grins. "Dark lairs and fiendish guards? Sounds like treasure to me."

"Wait," I say. "Mevyn, if Valenor is an old friend as you've said, then why must we fight our way to him? Wouldn't he just let you in if he knew you were coming to call?"

"If only it were so simple, my dear." Mevyn floats toward me, pausing to hover before my eyes. "They are not guarding to keep us out. Oh, no. They are there to keep him in. You see," he turns to the others. "Valenor is a prisoner, cast out by Jacek. The boy stole his titles and his mantle and shut him away in a place so dark that none would dare venture to seek him. That is why I need you, Tib. That is why I need all of you."

"It seems we're all in agreement, Mevyn," says Uncle. "Where then, is this lair?"

"Deep in the mountains of the ancient lands that my kind calls Sevtis Vailsh," Mevyn replies.

"That's Long Arm," Bryse says. "That's a two week ride from here in summer months. Uphill. Mostly mountains and cliffs and in Midwinter it's all ice. Pass is closed, little man. Probably have to take a ship." Beside me, Rian rifles through his pack and pulls out his map case. He tugs a parchment free from the roll and flattens it out on the bed. Mya and my parents peer over his shoulder as he traces his finger along the route.

"He's right," he says. "No way we could make it there this deep into the season." I follow his finger on the map. Long Arm Pass is a thin stretch of land that acts as a bridge between Haigh and Hywilkin, far to the north. It connects two unlikely allies, the Northern Caste, a hearty culture of men and women who make their homes in cold and unforgiving lands, and the Stone Giants, who are exactly as one might imagine. Bryse would be our expert here, as he is half of each.

"Of course not," Mevyn says. "Not with traditional means of travel. But you," he grins at me and scoops a lock of my bangs into his hand, "you, my beautiful dear, have other means of getting there. Do you not?"

I look across at Rian, whose jaw drops open slightly as his eyes widen.

"Well, Rian and I can… and we've brought others before, but…" I look around at the group as I brush the lock aside. There are fourteen of us all together. Rian and I taking Uncle through the Half-Realm was barely any trouble at all, but attempting so many others… "It's too risky. We've never taken more than one or two with us."

"I wasn't even sure bringing Gaethon would work, to be honest," Rian says.

"Wait a minute, now," Flitt pipes up. She's still safely hidden away from the others, who are oblivious to her rant. "That's supposed to be a secret, you two! What do you mean, spouting it in front of everyone? The Half-Realm is one step closer to our realm. Would you really just let him in?" She points at Bryse with a scowl. "And him?" She points at my father.

While she's going on, the others are discussing what I've said. It's too difficult to keep track of everyone talking at once. I sink onto a nearby bed and press my palms to my head to try and focus.

"Enough," Mevyn says. "Enough. Fine. If it means less chattering, then I can bring you each there, but it must be one at a time. And when I am through, I shall need to replenish." He looks pointedly at Uncle, who slowly closes his eyes.

"Very well," he says. "Who shall go first?"

"Me," says Bryse. "I'll stand guard. Haven't been home in a while."

Once everyone has agreed, the journey to Long Arm Pass is not difficult at all. I take Tib and Flitt with me and focus on Bryse, and I have no trouble falling through the frigid air into the icy peaks of the place that Mevyn called Sevtis Vailsh. Rian brings Mya and Mum with him, and Mevyn takes a few more trips to bring the rest. By the time he's through and everyone is huddled against the wind in an inlet of stone, Mevyn looks ragged and pale. He goes to my uncle, who tucks him into the folds of his robes.

Snow billows around us so thickly that we can barely see our hands in front of our faces. My cheeks are immediately frozen by the bitter wind that whips through the pass. The mountainside is slick and treacherous: a sheer drop on one side of us and nothing but ice-coated wall to cling to on the other.

"This is madness," Da says through chattering teeth. "Are you certain we need this Valenor's help? Perhaps there's another way," he goes on, but the wind roars through and carries his voice away.

"This way," Uncle calls, and we follow his voice blindly. I cling to Rian who creeps ahead of me, careful not to slip to his demise from the icy ledge. This is my worst nightmare. I try hard to put the thought of plummeting to my death out of my mind.

We creep together along the perilous mountain's edge for what seems like hours. My fingers are as numb as my toes, and my cloak drags me down, heavy with ice and snow. Just when I'm about to lose hope, I look ahead to see Uncle and the others disappear into an opening in the cliff face. I slip into it after them, grateful for the reprieve from the harsh wind and snow.

There's no time to rest and warm ourselves, though. The crevice we entered opens immediately to a spacious ice cavern that glitters with Flitt's colorful light. It splashes over a face frozen within the walls, and at first I think it must be Valenor, but I'm mistaken.

The ice begins to crack with an eerie echo that booms through the cavern. The crack spreads and the ice wall shatters, sending glass-like shards shooting toward us. A quick word from Uncle and Rian throws a shield between our group and the shards, which strike it hard and clatter to the ground with a horrendous crash.

When the shards settle the face pushes outward, grisly and awkward. It was once a man, but his eyes are milky white and his mouth open in a wide red grimace. He stalks forward to strike at Uncle, who is at point, and Bryse charges forward to block the attack.

All around us the ice crackles and shatters, and I spin to see several more of the dead figures emerge from their frozen caskets. They growl with a fierce, cold fury as they drag themselves in our direction, striking out with claws and rusted, blunt weapons. One of them sets its sights on me.

He was young when he died, perhaps my age. His hair is long and blonde and glazed with ice. He lunges for me and I swing my sword and he falls to the ground without a sound. I know I've severed his head. I can't bear to look.

"Necromancy," Rian says with his back pressed against mine. "I'm not surprised." Fire shoots from his palms, melting the ice in front of him, burning the dead men who struggle toward us. Between the group of us, the risen are barely a challenge. In fact, when the fight is through, Bryse and Cort look a little disappointed.

"Four," Bryse mumbles to Cort.

"Two," Cort shrugs.

"This way," Mevyn calls from deeper within the cavern. We all follow, careful with our footing on the ice-coated stone.

The deeper we go into the mountainside, the more fiendish our foes become. We battle ice goblins with sharp teeth that drip poison and fury sprites who enrage us so that we can barely swing our weapons and hobnubs who confuse us and try to get us to turn away.

We creep into the winding depths until the only light is Flitt's colorful beam emanating from my collar, and Mevyn's golden glow streaming from Uncle's robes. I keep close to Tib, who has his dagger out and ready. It glows with a greenish light that seems to turn his foes to stone when it meets its mark. He's fought bravely until now, but I fear we still have far to go.

The shadows encroach on us as we continue into the darkness, stifling our vision, filling us with dread.

"Not much further now," Mevyn whispers from his hiding place. "He's here, just here in the next chamber."

"Why should we listen to him?" Dacva calls from the back of the tunnel. "He's done nothing but lead us into danger since we arrived."

"Don't be insolent, Dacva," Donal hisses. "It's unbecoming."

"You're unbecoming," Dacva replies.

"Quiet, both of you," Da says, "I'd sooner suffer those risen again than have to listen to your constant bickering."

"All of you shut up," Bryse growls. "I don't need to hear it. I mean it, I'll throw you down the mountain, every last one."

"Try it, you great oaf," Da says.

"Yeah, I'd like to see you find your way out." Dacva says.

"Probably couldn't find his way out of his own shirt," Donal murmurs to Dacva.

"I heard that!" Bryse plows through half of us to get to the rear of the line where the clerics are catcalling and taunting him. As I watch in disbelief, my vision shifts oddly around them. Tendrils of shadows stretch across Dacva, Donal, and Bryse, creeping across their skin, seeping into their minds. Bryse raises his sword and readies to swing it at Donal, his friend, his guild mate. It's not them. It's the darkness. I try to think of a way to stop it.

I remember Stubs running through fields of grass and panting as I willed him to stop. I reach out to the shadowy tendrils with my thoughts. I imagine strings on them. Like inky puppets, I pull them away from my friends one by one and hold them in place. Bryse blinks. So do Dacva and my father and Donal.

"Don't know what got into me," Bryse says, shaking his head. Dacva looks horrified as he does the same.

"Me neither. I didn't mean it," he says.

"Course not," Bryse says. He looks ahead to Cort, who's just standing there watching. "Why didn't you stop me?" he asks.

"I'm sick of it," Cort sneers at Bryse. "Always being the one to keep your temper at bay. You need to be a man. Take responsibility for yourself. I'm through being your pacifier."

I look closely and see more of the shadows. They creep over Cort, binding him, holding him in their sway. I concentrate on them and push them from him and he closes his eyes.

"Sorry," he says. "I don't..."

"Perhaps a song," Mya whispers as Rian stares at me in disbelief. I've pulled the shadows away and they cling to my arms like a shroud, but they don't affect me. I remember Uncle's talisman. I'm sure that must be why. Mya's soft music fills the passage with sweet echoes. The song soothes us all but angers the shadows, which swirl wickedly around me. They break free of my strings and combine into towering creatures that hover over us wickedly, plucking and poking and taunting.

There's one shadow for each of us, and despite Mya's song they have the upper hand. Half of our group sinks to their knees and drops their weapons to clutch their heads.

"*Shadow wraiths,*" Flitt sends to me. "*Don't let them hold you.*" She shines her light brighter but the shadows aren't affected.

They wrap themselves around my friends and family, binding them, seeping into their eyes and noses and mouths. Rian, Uncle, and I are unaffected. Tib stands watching in disbelief as he's completely ignored by them. The others, though, all of them, lie helpless and writhing on the ice.

I try to concentrate on the one that holds Mum, imagining the strings and pulling them away, but it fights me. It's too strong and I'm too unskilled in this magic. There's nothing we can do. If I tried to stab them it would harm the people they're holding, too.

I drop to my knees between my mother and father and rest a hand on each of them, but my talisman does nothing to protect them. Uncle and Rian try several spells, but nothing seems to work.

"We're getting closer," Mevyn whispers. "This is the last defense. Tib, the yellow."

Desperately, I keep trying to move the wraiths away with my mind, but have no success. Beside me, Tib pulls a yellow vial from his bandolier and coats the blade of Rian's dagger with it.

"Good, now, slowly. Carefully," Mevyn whispers. The wraiths on Mum and Da are too occupied by their prey to notice Tib creeping up to them. He raises the blade and thrusts it. It takes every bit of my will to keep from blocking the attack aimed for my mother. It strikes the shadow, which screeches with the most ear-splitting, unholy sound. Immediately the others spring up. As the shadow on Mum is absorbed into the darkness, the rest of them charge Tib in a savage fury.

Mum and Da, Bryse and Cort, Mya, Donal, and Dacva all jump to their feet and retrieve their weapons to charge. They do little damage to the shadows that swirl around Tib, trying to strike him. The boy is somehow immune to them, though. As he stabs at the shadows with a fury, whispers fill the huddled space.

"Dreamstalker," they say over and over in a chorus that makes the hair on my arms prickle. We stand watching in awe as Tib, with a courage and determination that surprises all of us, drives the wraiths away with nothing but a single dagger coated in yellow.

"Well done, Tib," Mevyn says as the rest of us gather our wits. He turns to us.

"A little warning next time please, Mevyn," Mya says with a shiver. We huddle together in the small passage, and Mum's peace fills us. Mya hums softly, and her song soothes us.

"Of course," Mevyn says. "My apologies, I didn't expect the wraiths so soon. It isn't far, now. Tib, I will ask you to do one last thing for me in this place. Clear the way for the others." He nods into the darkness ahead. "I shall be beside you."

"Sounds more like a command to me," Flitt mumbles in my ear with annoyance. "He's so bossy."

"So will I," I say to Tib. "I can't do much, but I won't let you go alone."

When he looks up at me, his smile is filled with gratitude. He turns to Mevyn.

"I'm ready," he says.

"I'm with you, too," Rian says. He casts a shield that settles over us.

"Your spells will have little effect," Mevyn says. "The shadows follow different rules."

"I won't leave Azi," says Rian.

"We shall remain here," Uncle says, "Until we have your word that the way is clear."

"Very well, then," Mevyn hovers just behind Tib's shoulder. "Onward, Tib, into shadow."

Chapter Thirty-One:

VALENOR'S PRISON

Tib

Ice. Cold. Creeping. Silence. Puffs of breath. Darkness.

My fingers are numb with the cold, but my feet are warm and sure on the ice. I could run in here. I would never fall. Right now, I'm not annoyed with Mevyn. I'm grateful for him. All of those warriors fell. They couldn't fight. They couldn't do anything, but I could. I saved them. The shadows couldn't touch me. They didn't even see me. It gives me courage. It makes me want to use my new dagger again.

A gift is a trick. As we sneak through the black, I think of what Rian said when he gave me the weapon. This will give you courage. It will give you strength and clarity. As soon as I took it I could feel the change. With my dagger and my yellow vial, I'm the only one who can beat these wraiths. Everyone is counting on me. Still, Nan's words nag at me. I don't know what the trick is, yet. I have to be careful. Keep an eye on that Mage.

Wraiths. Shadows. Stabbing. Screeching. Silence. Three. Five. Seven. Ten.

I keep count as they fall, just like Bryse and Cort always do. The wraiths keep coming, but they're no match for me and my new dagger. I thrust and creep and the others follow me until Mevyn stops us at the edge of a deep chasm where the tunnel ends.

"There," he says with awe. "There he is. My dear old friend, Valenor. Azaeli, you may tell the others the way is clear."

I don't know what I expected to see when I peer into the darkness. A wise old man in tattered robes, maybe. A Mage or even a Sorcerer trapped in a cage, reading old books. Or maybe a fairy like Mevyn or Crocus or Flitt. Not this, though. Never in my life would I have imagined this.

"Quiet. Mustn't wake him yet."

Yes, quiet. I stare in disbelief at the creature as my eyes adjust to even deeper darkness. At first he's hard to see, black against black, but then I catch glimpses.

Long, leathery wings cracked with age and frosted with ice. Scales and claws and horns, and a twisted, broken tail. He's cramped at the bottom of the chasm with no room to stretch or move, and even from this distance I can tell he's enormous. Bigger than Cap's ship. Bigger than Nessa's manse.

Shadows stretch across his bony frame, pinning him. Binding him like they bound the others. He's been asleep so long that the ice has crept up over his haunches. He's alive, though. Once in a while I see him shiver.

"Carefully," Mevyn whispers to the others as they approach. "Quietly." Mya is the first to reach the edge. She clings to the wall and peers down.

"Is that?" she whispers.

"Mevyn," Rian breathes the words, barely daring to make a sound. "You never told us Valenor was a dragon."

"You never asked." Mevyn whispers matter-of-factly.

"Typical," Flitt smirks inside Azi's collar. Mevyn goes to Gaethon and I can tell he's saying something silently to the Mage. Gaethon nods and whispers a spell, and the ward of silence stretches out over all of us.

"There," Mevyn says. "Now, Tib and I must get to the eye. I have things that I must show Valenor. You see, when Jacek took his mantle, with it came his most powerful memories. I share some of those memories." He goes to the edge again and looks down at Valenor sadly. "At this time," he says, "my friend doesn't even known his own name."

"That happened to me," Azi says. "When Jacek held me in the Dreaming, I forgot many things. I didn't know who I was. I even forgot…" she looks up at Rian and moves closer to him. Clings to his arm like she's afraid he'll disappear.

"We can't all fit down there," Mya says. "And the climb will be treacherous. What do you propose, Mevyn?"

"The Mages have a means to lower Tib and I, do they not?" Mevyn asks. Gaethon and Rian exchange worried glances.

"Indeed," Gaethon says.

"Do you also have a way to send teams there?" Mevyn points across to an opening in the sheer wall of the chasm across from us, and another to the left. "We shall need coverage against any onslaught that might try to stop us from freeing him."

"Yes, there are levitations and movement spells at our disposal." Gaethon says.

"I don't like it," Benen says. "I think we should stick together."

"Discuss it amongst yourselves," Mevyn says. "I must have a private word with Tib." He turns to me. "If you will allow it," he says with a strange sort of humility.

I shrug, and he flies away from the others and beckons me to follow.

"I have things to show you, if you will let me do so," he says. His tone is slightly urgent but somber, too. I feel his emotion leaking into me. He isn't afraid. It's something else. He's prepared. He knows what he has to do. I focus on his strangely floating golden hair. Avoid his eyes as he goes on. "I could not have gotten this far without you. I owe you a great debt, Tib. Your courage has given you victory in many battles up until now."

"No," I say. "That was you. You and your vials and your knives."

"Perhaps," he says, "perhaps not." He glances at the others and then turns back to me. "I have something to give you. It is the last thing I shall ask of you, Tib. Hold it for me. Keep it safe. When the time comes, return it. Do you agree?"

"I don't know," I say. "I don't understand." I remember all the times he asked me to trust him and then erased my memories. I take a little step back.

"You shall, when you see what it is. Please. It is a burden for me, and you are the only one I trust enough to ease it."

I look at him, really look. He's tired. Not bright like he was in Cerion after his meeting with the princess, or after Kythshire. His skin is paler. Gaethon helped him some, but his glow is fading. Something about him tells me this time is different. I trust my judgment. I nod slowly. With a little hesitation, I look into his golden eyes.

The memories rise and fall between us like waves in the ocean, like a sand storm spinning and billowing and fading again in streams of golden threads. With them come the titles that Mevyn listed in the Ring at Kythshire.

Mindspinner. The image of a beautiful winged woman emerges from the golden threads. She raises her arms as they form from the light. Blows me a kiss. Flies into my chest. I feel a warmth as her light enters me. Fuller, somehow.

Weaver of Threads. Another fairy's image emerges from the threads. This one is a man with a long fabric draped over one arm and a needle and thread in his hand. He plunges the needle into the fabric and pulls the thread through, and then slowly he seeps into my chest just like the woman did.

WindCaller, Second to Cintigra, Second to Demsin, Warden of Sands, Spear-Bearer, Keeper of Songs, and Sworn Sage of the Known all do the same. One by one they form from the golden light and show themselves to me. One by one they fly to me and let me hold them inside me. When Mevyn is through, he looks relieved and also very sad.

"Keep them close," he says, "take care of them."

I don't know what to say. I wasn't expecting that. Around us, everything is silent. I close my eyes and the golden light goes away. I look inside myself. Try to feel all of these fairies that I'm carrying now. I don't feel anything, though. I wonder whether I'm supposed to. Maybe it went wrong.

"Keep them safe," Mevyn says to me as Mya comes to our side.

"We're ready," she says. Rian has agreed to bring us down the chasm. Azi is coming with us, too. Gaethon will help the others into the openings. We decide to rest before we act. The Mages are taxed after the battle and the clerics insist, so we sit against the wall and wait. I spend the time going through my bandolier. My vials are almost empty, the yellow especially. When I show it to Mevyn, he waves a hand dismissively.

"You shan't be needing them much longer, anyway," he says. I wonder what he means as I peer down at the dragon and the massive shadows stretched across him, shackling him. What's left in my vial would be enough for one of them. Maybe two.

"But," I start, and he interrupts me.

"Have faith in yourself, Tib," Mevyn says. "That is all you need."

He goes to Rian, who's poised at the edge of the opening. Gaethon is already moving the others across. Mya, Lisabella, Benen, and Dacva go together. He whispers a spell and they walk across thin air, like there's an invisible bridge supporting them. Bryse, Cort, and Donal go next. Gaethon stays with them at the mouth of the tunnel.

"When you're ready," Mevyn says to Rian. His way is different. We have to hold onto him so he can float us down. I wrap my arms around his middle and Azi holds him around the shoulders. I watch the jagged wall slip past us as we float down. I could have climbed this. I wish I had. I don't like depending on magic this way. He could stop his spell any time, and we could crash to the ground or worse, land on the dragon.

He doesn't, though. He sees us safely to the bottom. Settles us into a small space by the dragon's face.

Valenor's head rests on his enormous cramped foot. The claws of his toes are as long as I am tall. Rian walks along his foot, studying the beast with interest. Azi looks a little pale. Inside her collar, Flitt peers out at the dragon with wide-eyed interest.

Azi comes to stand so close to me that our shoulders touch. She offers me a reassuring smile that's very obviously forced. Together we take a few steps back and watch Mevyn, who flies up to hover by the slit of the sleeping dragon's eye. He looks over his shoulder at us and nods when he's certain we're ready.

"*Keep your knives sheathed,*" a voice echoes in my mind. Not his. Someone else's. A woman. Mindspinner, maybe.

"Old friend," Mevyn says quietly. The eye snaps open, fiery red and savage. It narrows and the dragon's snake-like neck shivers and shifts. The shadows hold him, though, and he can't do anything other than growl and sneer and glare at Mevyn. I watch in awe as the fairy, the size of a gnat to the beast, flies closer. Mevyn steels himself even as Valenor struggles and thrashes beneath his bonds.

"Valenor," he speaks the name with a commanding voice, and the dragon's black slit of an iris contracts and expands. "Valenor," Mevyn says again, this time soothingly. Affectionately.

Valenor's great nostrils flare and huff and smoke. Azi puts her arm out in front of me. Guides me back until we're pressed against the jagged rocks of the chasm wall. Rian doesn't seem to notice. He's crouched at the dragon's foot. His eyes trace every scale, every line. Azi stares at him and he snaps his attention to her and looks at the smoke and rushes to our side.

Up above in one of the openings, someone shifts. Sends a cascade of rocks tumbling down the wall. The rocks rain over the dragon, pelting his frostbitten wings. Valenor scrabbles and screeches and lets out a great, fiery breath. It blasts the wall in front of him and flames billow back toward us. Rian casts a shield just in time to block the blaze.

"Mevyn!" I cry as the flames clear.

"*Quiet,*" the woman says again. I search the air around the eye for him, but he's gone. Azi grips my shoulder. We watch together as the dragon settles again. Wait for Mevyn. He doesn't appear.

"Mevyn," I whisper.

"There," Rian points and I see it. A glint of gold peeking out from behind an ink-black horn. Mevyn flies up and back to the eye again. It blinks as the dragon huffs impatiently.

"Valenor," he says again. The name placates the dragon. There is a long silence as something about the creature shifts. He's thinking. Remembering. Finally, he lowers his head. Bobs it into what can only be a nod of consent. We watch the golden strings lick out. They stream into the fire red eye, filling it. Strengthening it. Warming it. The ice that crawls up the sides of the beast melts into knee-deep pools so that Azi and Rian and I have to climb onto a pile of rocks to keep from getting soaked. The shadows remain, though. Holding him. Binding him.

The stream of memories flows between the fairy and the dragon for what feels like an hour. With each one, Mevyn seems smaller. Paler. Less impressive. By the time he's through and they break from each other, he's reduced to little more than he was at the roots. Skeletal. Shrunken. White. Nearly naked.

Valenor, on the other hand, is no longer bony and cracked. His muscles ripple beneath black, glistening scales. His eyes flash with clarity. He opens his mouth and I brace myself for the flames, but none come. Instead, he speaks.

"Mevyn, my friend. My confidant. My guide. I have waited for you these long years. You are my savior. Lifebringer." He breathes a long sigh and closes his eyes. I feel his relief wash over all of us.

"Dreamstalker," the dragon calls to me. Azi's grip on my shoulder tightens, but Mevyn sinks down toward me and comes to rest on my forearm. He looks awful. Like he used to when we started out.

"What happened to you?" I ask him.

"What was meant to happen all along," Mevyn says. "Do not concern yourself with me, Tib. Speak to Valenor. He shall explain everything."

"Here, Mevyn," Flitt pops up from Azi's collar and darts to his side. She beams her light across him and he looks a little better, but he's still white and thin and without his armor. I raise my arm to look closer at him.

"Mevyn," I whisper. Sure, he's been irritating. He's been controlling. He's made me do things. But now, seeing him back this way again makes me sad. Angry, even. Why did he have to go and do this? Why did Valenor need to be so greedy?

"Dreamstalker," the dragon calls again.

"Go," Mevyn says to me. "He will explain."

I creep through the pool of melted ice along the dragon's massive foot to face him. His nostrils stream with smoke. He could breathe right now and burn me to a crisp. I could die. But something about him tells me that he won't. He isn't the desperate empty-headed creature we first saw anymore. With Mevyn's magic, he's changed now. He lowers his head to me, like he's bowing. I don't know why but I do the same. Mevyn still clings to my arm.

"I have seen your bravery," Valenor says to me. "Your courage has borne Mevyn to me. For that I am most grateful. I shall reward you, Dreamstalker, in due time." Each time he uses my title, I feel a tightening in my chest. A speeding of my heart. It makes me believe I'm more than just a boy with knives and vials. It makes me important. It changes me from the slave in the dye fields to a warrior. A hero. Each time he says it, the shadows that bind him shrink a little, like they're afraid of what it means.

"My fate is in your hands, Tibreseli Nullen, Dreamstalker, Bearer of the Guardian. Release me from these bonds, that I may fight beside you against the impostor who calls himself Dreamwalker in my stead. The thief, the wretch, the unworthy filth. Help me take up my mantle once more, and together we shall end him." He tips his head lower so I can see the desperation in his great red eye. "Please," he says, "release me."

I tear my gaze from him and look back to Azi and Rian. They glance at each other and then nod to me slowly. In the openings above, the rest of them nod, too. A dragon would be a good friend to make, I think. Still, I'm not sure he's telling the truth.

"How can I be sure you won't hurt any of us once you're free?" I ask him. "You could be lying, just to get yourself out of this."

"Wise child," his eye slowly closes and opens again. "Look, and I shall show you."

"No." I cross my arms. I know about looking. I've fallen for that before. The eye slides to Mevyn, who even as weak as he is, chuckles.

"Did I not show you? The boy has spirit," Mevyn says to Valenor.

"Indeed," Valenor looks at me. I wouldn't have believed that a dragon could smile, but the corner of his scaly mouth lifts slightly as he looks to me. "I give you my word, and something more. The gift of knowledge. Two gifts, in fact. The first is this: The Dreamwalker cannot be defeated from within his own realm. He must be drawn out completely, or as he sees it, released into this realm. The second…" he turns to look at the others. "Azaeli, come forward."

She sloshes through the frigid water to come to my side, where Valenor bows his head to her and she returns the gesture.

"Take your sword. Strike the bonds, Azaeli." Valenor says. Azaeli looks from me to Rian. Both of us nod. She raises her sword and slashes it through the shadow that binds the dragon's foot to the floor. It does nothing at all. The shadow isn't even aware of her. "Tibreseli, coat her blade with the liquid from your yellow vial."

Azi nods to me and offers her blade. I'm a little hesitant to do it. I don't have that much left and I'll need it later. I think of how the shadows screamed and fell when my yellow-coated dagger struck them. I don't want to give it up. Don't want to waste it.

"Trust him," Mevyn says weakly. Reluctantly, I pull out the stopper and streak a thin yellow line down the length of her blade.

"Again, Azaeli," Valenor says with a watchful eye. Azi swings her sword against the shadow and I wait for the shriek, but nothing happens.

"Now, Dreamstalker. Do not coat your blade. Strike the shadow." He tips his head toward me. I creep into the binding shadow and draw my dagger. I plunge the bare blade it into the darkness expecting nothing just like Azi, but the bindings writhe and twist and let out an earsplitting shriek that echoes through the chasm.

All around us, shadows seep from crevices and dive at me. They whip and lash from the dragon's back, legs, and tail. The bonds that held him drive toward me. They swirl around me, closing in. Lashing. Striking. I'm protected though. They can't touch me. I stab at them. One. Two. Three. Six. Nine. Twelve. Twenty. I jab and slice and growl and plunge and they keep coming, swarming me like a flock of birds, like crows at the dead.

I can see nothing but darkness. My ears ring with the shrieks of shadows as they die. I fall into a rhythm, turning and swinging and piercing. It's mindless work, almost like picking blossoms. They can't touch me, and all I do is swing. Swing and think.

Think of the knowledge Valenor has given me. The yellow vial held no power. The power was within me all along. I am the Dreamstalker. Slayer of Shadows. No longer the boy at the end of a whip. I'm so much more now. I was never meant to remain in Sunteri. I was meant to be here, in this chasm, fighting darkness. This is my fate. Tib. Dreamstalker. Bearer of the Guardian. Slayer of Shadows. Liberator of Valenor.

Chapter Thirty-Two:

INTO THE SKY

Tib

Blinded by darkness and deafened by screams, I fight. I lose count in the thirties somewhere. The shadow wraiths seem endless as they charge at me. They whisper things, wicked things that I know are lies. Everyone else is dead. Stop fighting, or Saesa will be next. I don't, though. They can't fool me. Outside of the shadows and below the screams I hear them encouraging me. Cheering. Applauding.

I'm getting tired. My arms and legs ache from fighting. Mevyn knows. He clings to my shoulder. He sends me the little strength he has left. I slash out again but meet nothing. I'm not blinded, my eyes are closed. I open them as Azi rushes me and claps me on the shoulder.

"You did it," she grins. "Look, Tib," she whispers, and turns me toward Valenor.

He raises his head, stretching past the openings where the others watch. His wings open slowly, up toward the small crack of white that slashes the black far above. Sky. He screeches and blows his fire. Terrible. Magnificent. Free.

A shift distracts me. A change in something within me. Something is fading. Leaving.

"Tib," Mevyn whispers in my ear. I tear my gaze from Valenor to him as he slips down my arm. I can barely see him. Barely feel him. "Look at me."

His eyes are dark and empty, like they were under the roots. Almost lost. Almost gone. Still they pull me in. Show me things. The Wellspring in Sunteri, filled with golden liquid to the brim. Fairies dance around the rim, laughing and singing like the ones in Kythshire. Blurs of color and sweet music. Sweeter than Mya's, even.

Another place. A circle of bright red mushrooms in a dense oasis. Fronds of rich green leaves that drip clean, clear beads of water.

More fairies perched on mushroom caps, like the ring in Kythshire but more vibrant. I recognize these fairies. One has a long fabric draped over his arm and a needle in one hand. The others are here, too.

At the center is a beautiful lady with enormous wings that sparkle with their own silver light. Mindspinner. She raises her arms and starts the dancing and they come. Dozens. Hundreds of fairies, in all shapes and sizes. A ball. A Celebration. Laughing. Their joy makes me grin. I want to join them. Be as happy as they are.

"This is what it once was," Mevyn says in a whisper, "and what it shall be, when restored. I shan't see the day, Tib. My time is nearly at an end."

I look away to break the connection and then look back. He's nearly gone. Flit comes to perch on my arm. She places a hand on him and closes her eyes. Her light flows to him, but doesn't do much. Makes him a little more solid, maybe. Azi and Rian come closer. Valenor dips his head to us.

"Fairies," Flitt says as she looks up at me sadly, "are like people. They only live so long. Some have easy lives and live for a very long time. Others work very hard, and their lives are much shorter. How old are you anyway, Mevyn?" she asks.

"One hundred seven full turns of the seasons," Mevyn takes her hand.

"So young," she whispers mournfully, shaking her head.

I can't wrap my head around what they're saying. Mevyn is bold and strong. He's a warrior. He knows things. He showed me so much. He brought me to this place with dragons and fairies and friends who protect me. Saesa, Azi, even Rian. People who value me. All that and still he carried the others with him, too. He's my friend. At the end of all of it, past the anger and frustration, he's my friend.

"I didn't understand," I say to him. "I was angry because I didn't know."

"I would have told you," he sighs, "but they had to remain safe." He leans his head into the crook of my arm. Closes his eyes. "Bring them home, Tib. For me. Restore it, and bring them home."

"I will," I say. "I swear."

"Thank you," Mevyn says. "My journey ends here." With the light given to him by Flitt, Mevyn is able to lift himself on his wings. "If you are ready," he says to Valenor, who gives a somber nod. The dragon tips his head down. His long black horns scrape the wall above us.

"Farewell, Tib," Mevyn says, resolved. He brushes my cheek with his hand. Looks into my eyes one last time. Shows me everything we've done and seen. Everything we've accomplished. New things, too. Secret things I must keep to myself. When he's through and without warning, he dashes up. Straight into Valenor's forehead. Disappears.

I feel it right away. An emptiness in my heart. A hole that gapes. He's gone. Truly gone. I stumble back against the wall. Sink to my knees. Before me, Valenor begins to transform.

The oily black scales at his forehead are the first to change to shining golden plates. The color spreads down the bridge of his snout, flashing brightly. The scales at his chin and throat flare to deep sapphire blue. Blue at his chest going to green along his shoulders. Green like the jungle. Like Saesa's eyes. Green to yellow along his sides, yellow to orange at the spines along his back. Sharp orange, tipped with red. Not like the blossoms. Like blood, rich and dark.

He turns a green face to me and tips back on purple hind feet. His wings open slowly over his head. They shimmer white at first and then burst into splashes of every color. The edge of every scale is trimmed with gold. Mevyn's gold.

"By all the stars," Rian whispers. Azi stands beside him, her mouth open in disbelief. Above us in the chasm, the others whoop and cheer.

"Did you see that?" someone cries out. I think it was Bryse. They don't know Mevyn is gone. I can't feel him anymore. Can't hear him in my head. He's part of Valenor now. He left me. Flitt drifts up to my face. Pats my hair comfortingly. Glows brighter. It makes me feel better. Not all the way, just a little.

"Come," Valenor says. "It won't be long before he discovers my escape, and there is much to do. We must go." He nudges me with his nose. Tells me to climb up.

I wipe my eyes on the edge of my vest. The vest Mevyn gave me. Step onto his enormous snout. Climb with my boots. The boots Mevyn gave me. Gifts. Not tricks. Things to help me. To help us. To help Sunteri. I'll have to go back there. Back home, where I never wanted to return. I made a vow, though. I'll do it for Mevyn. For his people.

Azi and Rian climb up behind me. We each cling to a spine on Valenor's back. He rears up on his hind legs. Drives his claws into the rock. Starts to climb. We pause to gather the others.

There's discussion about levitating us out, but it's short-lived.

They faced a fight in those openings. Gaethon and the clerics are drained. It would be too much for Rian alone. So we tighten our grip on Valenor as the others climb on. When they're all safely on board, he plunges his claws again and scales the icy rock all the way to the top of the chasm.

The wind billows and bites as Valenor spreads his shimmering wings at the crest of the mountain.

"Oh no," I hear Azi over the roar of it. "Flying. Why must it always be flying?"

We rise above the wind and clouds where the only sound is the rhythmic swish of the dragon's enormous wings as they push us forward. Everyone is quiet. Most duck their heads against the wind but I raise mine to it. Feel it cold against my cheeks. Let my eyes tear up and be blown dry. Think of Mevyn and the hole he left behind.

The air grows warmer and more pleasant. The craggy snow caps flatten out. Turn to green. Far below I see a castle. It sprawls low and sturdy along the shore of a great green lake. Lake Kordelya, I think. All around it are trees and long stretches of meadows dotted with colorful flowers.

We soar over it and lower and lower and finally land in a sun-splashed glen at the edge of the lake. I stretch my neck to see the castle but it's not close to here. This place is far away. Secluded. Valenor flattens himself to the ground to allow us to slide into the warm grass. The others seem shaky and grateful to be on solid ground again, but not me. I want to be back in the sky. Completely free.

Once everyone has climbed from his back, Valenor lumbers past us and plunges into the lake. He disappears beneath its surface and comes up again, splashing merrily. When he returns to the meadow, he rolls in the sunlight onto his back and twists and wriggles to dry off.

All the while, he groans with pleasure as his tail lashes dangerously and his wings splay out beneath him. Thoroughly clean and dry, he stays on his back and slides his head toward us so that he's regarding us upside down. His tongue lolls out of his mouth and he grins at us.

"I have dreamed of such a moment," he says mirthfully, "for seemingly endless days and nights." He sighs and wriggles again in the warm grass, closing his eyes. The others sit in the grass to rest while the clerics check each of them over.

"Now that it is done," he says after a while, "we must act quickly." He rolls to his stomach and turns to me and Azi, who is still looking a little green.

"The blood binding must be broken," he says. "Jacek will leave the dreaming then. He will consider himself freed, but he will be vulnerable here. The girl," he says. "The one that Mevyn showed me. Saesa. She must be brought into the dreaming. Only she can break his bonds."

"How?" I ask him. "Will it hurt her?"

"No," Valenor says. "It must be done willingly, and with cunning. He cannot know that I am waiting for him in this realm. He must think it is his own doing. You must let him take hold of her. Let him convince her. He cannot know the truth."

"It's too horrible," Azi says. "Letting him take hold of her. I've been in the Dreamwalker's grips. I know what that entails."

"You will bring me to her first," Valenor says to her. "I will give her protections."

"Wait a minute," Flitt pipes up, "you want to go to Kythshire?"

"That would be most prudent. Dreamwalker cannot seek us there. The borders between the dreaming and the land of the fae are too strong."

"But Jacek had his hold on me," Azi says quietly. "I was in Kythshire and he was still manipulating me."

"But he took hold of you in Sorlen River Crossing," Rian says. "You were already in his grips when I brought you to Kythshire."

"Indeed, that would make it easier for him."

"Nope, can't do it," Flitt says. "Sorry. No dragons allowed. I'm pretty sure I'd get in big trouble bringing you back with me. Even as nice as you are."

While they're talking, I reach absently into my vest pocket and run my fingers over the fringe of the scrap of fabric Shoel gave me what feels like so long ago. I pull it out and smooth it over my knee.

"What about Ceras'lain?" I ask. "We could bring her there. It's guarded from the Dreamwalker too, isn't it?"

"The elves?" Gaethon thoughtfully scratches his beard.

"I have friends there," I say. The others turn to me with looks of disbelief. I show Gaethon my scrap scrawled with elf writing and painted with the cygnet.

"The White Line, no less," he looks at Mya.

"Well, you are full of surprises aren't you, Tib?" she laughs and moves closer to see it. On my other side, Rian is already eyeing it in his Mage way. Reading the words I can't read.

"It's imbued," he glances at Gaethon. "What does it do, Tib?"

"Shoel said if I'm in trouble I should whisper into it," I explain, "and he'll hear."

"Shoel has become White Line?" Valenor rests his chin in the grass. His voice is a low purr. "Tremendous."

"You know him?" I move closer to Valenor. Lean against his foot. Trace the golden edge of his scale with my finger. I don't feel any closer to Mevyn, though. The hole still gapes.

"Many years ago," Valenor blinks his great red eye at me, "I traveled throughout the waking realm. I was curious, you see. Curious about the dreamers and the lives they lived when they left my realm in the day. I was welcomed by most. Dreamwalker, you see, did not have such dark connotations then. I traveled to Ceras'lain and Stepstone Isles and Elespen and First Sunteri. Even Cerion." His eye slides to rest on the others.

"How many years?" Benen asks. "I don't remember ever hearing of a dragon sighting in Cerion."

"Oh," smoke puffs from his nose as Valenor chuckles. "I did not appear this way at that time. With my mantle I can take any form. Dragon was my last before Jacek stole it from me. When I visited these places, when I traveled, I was a falcon, or a great cat, or a man just as you are."

"Why is it that you were able to walk in these lands?" Azi asks. "Jacek can only observe and make suggestions. He can't be fully here in this realm."

"Those are the bindings holding him," Valenor says, "set by his parents. When the girl releases his bonds, he will most certainly be able to walk freely among us." He looks at me, "I should like very much to see Shoel again, if the others have no disagreement with your calling him."

The only one who seems to have a problem with it is Bryse, who grumbles something that sounds like "elves again," but Cort whispers something and Bryse shrugs and nobody else argues.

"Okay," I turn the fabric over in my hand and raise it to my lips. "Should I do it now?" I look over at Rian.

"The writing says, 'Whisper my name, friend, though the distance between us might grow. We are never far apart, call upon me wherever you may go." Rian says. "It's actually more poetic in Elvish, but that's it essentially."

"Your translation could use a little work, Rian," Gaethon says with that haughty Mage's tone. "But essentially, yes. That is what it says."

"We shall fly closer, and then you may call him, Tib," Valenor says, "So that he won't have to travel far to us."

Azi glances at Rian. She doesn't seem to like the thought of another flight.

"Perhaps Rian and I should go to Saesa," she says. "We can discuss things at the Ring and bring her to you after.

"Very well," Valenor flattens himself into the grass and jerks his head to invite us to climb up again.

Azi and Rian say their farewells and walk off together toward the forest. From Azi's collar, Flitt waves merrily. Her light dances across the knight's face and sparkles against the blue flecks in her armor. I look away to the lake. She reminds me too much of Mevyn. Of the hole that seems to be opening instead of closing since he left me. I think about the fairies that are with me. They're silent. Not like him. They keep hidden. I wonder as my companions grip his horns and Valenor spreads his wings to lift us to the sky, how will I know what to do? Why did I promise him that?

The shoreline blurs beside us as we streak across the water southward. My thoughts turn to my sister as I follow it along. Her necklace is cool against my chest, tucked into my shirt. Iren's blue light glows softly as Valenor glides into the wind. Something in the lake calls to me. Pulls me. I slip to the side slightly and lean to peer into its silvery depths. Gaethon clamps a hand on my shoulder to keep me in place. As he does, the necklace slides toward the water's silvery surface. I catch it, but it feels wrong.

"*Drop me*," Iren's voice booms in my mind. I tighten my grip on it reluctantly as we speed along. Ki's necklace is all I have left of my sister. It's my only way of finding her. As we pass across the water's surface, I see things. Visions.

She's trapped. Buried. No, not buried. Drowned. No, not that, either. Captive. In a tower. But the tower is filling up with water. She's running out of time. She's scared. Screaming. Fighting. Others are there, watching. A prince. A shadow. Waiting for something from her. Something she refuses to give. I peer into the water. Try to see, but can't. There's nothing, only a dark form deep beneath the surface. What good would it do to drop it? It would only sink and be lost forever.

Then I see it in the distance. Fleeting. A flash of red bobbing in the water. Red-orange hair. Fox-colored, even as a man.

"Elliot!" I cry over the rushing wind. Mya scrambles across Valenor's back until she reaches my side. She squints into the water. Her eyes light up. She sees him too.

"Drop me," Iren's voice booms again. If I do it, if I let go, my link to her will be gone forever. If I drop it, I'm putting all of my faith in someone else. All of my trust in a stranger. Elliot waves his arms as Valenor dips lower.

"Drop it, Tib," Mya says in her soft, commanding way as she reaches for my hand. "Trust in them."

Behind him in the lake, dark forms drift in wait. They're man-like. Ominous. One of them lashes out at Elliot with a splash of silvery fins. A spiked weapon thrashes toward him. Valenor banks and circles. Mya and I slide to the other side.

"Elliot!" she shouts, and then begins to scream. Her scream is eerie. Not a sound of distress. More like a hunter's call for some strange bird. The dark forms pause.

Overhead, thunder crashes, sending streaks of lightning stabbing toward us. Valenor dodges it deftly and it strikes the surface of the water below with a loud sizzle.

"Give it to me!" Mya holds her hand out for the necklace.

"Mya you are not considering—" Gaethon starts, but a swerve from Valenor sends him off balance. He slips across the dragon's back and nearly falls into the water, but Bryse catches him with his giant fist and clutches him tightly as Valenor evens out.

"He needs me. We'll find you," she shouts to Gaethon. "Tib, the necklace!" She holds her blue-gloved hand out desperately, sparing a glance over her shoulder at the lake. Thunder and lightning crack over us again and Valenor swoops to dodge it.

"Jacek. We cannot remain here," the dragon rumbles as he circles. "Do what you must do, but quickly!"

"Tib!" Mya cries. Below, the forms are closing in on Elliot again. Above, the lightning crackles. I tug the necklace from my neck and just as I'm about to put it in her hand, Valenor banks. The trinket glows brightly all the way to the murky surface of the water before it disappears into the depths with a tiny splash. Mya's larger splash comes just after it.

"They'll need help," Gaethon looks over his shoulder. Donal nods and drops away. The others cling to Valenor as he moves to dodge another strike, but not quickly enough. His left wing is hit, pierced through with a searing bolt. He screeches and flaps and struggles, but eventually manages to right himself and push up.

We go higher and higher, leaving the lake and the castle and the mysterious dark forms far below. Soon we're soaring high above the clouds, where the blue sky stretches out above us and the world below is blanketed in downy white as far as we can see.

Chapter Thirty-Three:

LETTING GO

Tib

The others tuck into Valenor's spikes and settle themselves for the long journey, but I can't. I think of Ki. Just when I'm through convincing myself that I should have jumped in after Mya, I think of Saesa. She'll need me. I think of Mevyn. I promised him I'd see Sunteri restored. I hate myself for turning my back on my sister, though. I hate myself for letting go of that necklace. I want to be the one who sees her safe, not them. She saved my life. I should be there to save hers.

Gaethon keeps a hand on my shoulder even though the lake is far behind us now. I don't know what he expects me to do, jump off through the clouds? Still, it's obvious he's keeping an eye on me. Keeping me with the rest of them. I hate him for holding me here. For stopping me from helping Ki.

Mevyn showed him a lot of things. My thoughts wander to their meeting in the inn room. I wonder how much of it had to do with me. I hate him, but I understand. Aside from Valenor, he might be the only other one who knows what I'm supposed to do.

The clouds streak below us, endlessly white. The blue sky that stretches overhead slowly changes to red and purple and orange as the sun sinks low. The others have closed their eyes. They lean against the spines of Valenor's back and doze. Not me. I could never get tired of this view, this feeling.

I used to watch the birds, back in Sunteri. I used to envy their freedom. They could go anywhere, see anything, and do whatever they wanted. I dreamed that one day I could fly away, too. And now I'm here, soaring on the back of a dragon. Flying, just like them.

"We are nearing," Valenor says all too soon. "Tib, be ready to send word to Shoel."

He starts his descent, bringing us closer to the clouds. Droplets of mist collect on my arms and in my hair. I close my eyes and close my fingers around the sigil as we sink lower, waiting for Valenor's word. Waiting for the mist to clear. It only thickens, though. Drowns out all sound. Chokes me.

A blast that sounds like a canon rumbles nearby and a streak of red light shoots up through the clouds, striking Valenor from below. Gaethon's hand slips from my shoulder. Valenor screeches. We're falling. Plummeting. I cling to a spine but when he rolls, my grip slips. We're rushing toward the ground, fast. There is no movement from the dragon. No flap of a wing or effort to right himself. He's out cold. Around us, the clouds are strangely yellow and green.

I fight to keep hold of the slick spine, but Gaethon has more trouble than me. His robes flap chaotically around him, entangling his arms and face. He's the first to let go. The first to fall away, to disappear into the dark smudge of ground beneath us.

"No!" I shout.

"Benen!" Lisabella screams from somewhere across the dragon's vast back. I feel a charge of peace rush over me. "Valenor!" she shrieks, and his scales shimmer blue and gold. "No, Benen!" she cries again, and I cast a glance over my shoulder to see a streak of yellow plummet past me into darkness. She lets go not long after. The glow of her longsword is all I can see through the thick cloud mist.

With all of my strength, I wrap my arms and legs around the spike. It's red, deep red. Deeper than the blossoms. Almost black. I hold on and wait. For what, I don't know. Mevyn's voice, maybe. Telling me what to do. Telling me the right thing. Climb.

Yes, climb. I pull myself up. Across the dragon's back I can see Bryse doing the same. He's got a foothold on Valenor's scales. Cort and Dacva are slung across his back like merchant sacks. I do the same. Shimmy up the spike like the tall ship's mast. Grip a scale like the bricks of the tower. Hoist myself up. I'm a fair climber. I reach the dragon's belly before he does. The ground is getting closer, faster. At least now I won't be crushed beneath the dragon's weight. At least now I won't plunge to the ground like the others did. Bryse isn't far behind. He flattens himself against Valenor's stomach. The others slide from his back and do the same.

"Valenor!" I scream and pound at the dragon's thick chest scales with my fists. "Wake up!"

He does, and I realize my mistake all too soon. There's nothing here to hold onto. Nothing but smooth, stone-like scales. Valenor is oblivious. With a start and a scrambling, dangerous thrash of his wings he rights himself too quickly for me to find a grip. The four of us tumble off and plummet toward the ground.

As I flip and roll and fall, I'm vaguely aware of Valenor diving beside me. He swoops past and I reach out. His scales graze my fingertips, but he isn't close enough for me to grab hold.

"Here!" I shout, but my voice is drowned out by a strange, dark sound. Laughter, deep and cruel. It comes from everywhere. The clouds, the sky, the ground. It closes around us like the mist. I'm still falling. The ground is coming even faster.

Valenor circles away. I trust he'll come back. I trust he'll catch me. My cloak flaps violently around me. A scrap of white catches my eye as it flutters from my belt. The White Line's sigil. I reach out, but like Valenor's scales it's just out of my reach.

"Shoel!" I scream as my fingertips graze its frayed edge.

The ground is closer now. I'm just the distance from the top of Cerion's cliffs to the ocean. I see Valenor racing toward me. Far away, too far away. His strong, powerful wings push him fast, but not fast enough. He won't reach me before I hit the ground. I close my eyes. Curl myself into a ball. Wait for the impact.

It comes sooner than I think. Knocks the breath out of me. Stars burst across my vision. Someone grabs me around the middle. My direction shifts and my stomach drops as I feel the rush again. The rush of going up.

"I have you," Shoel says as he tightens his arm around me. "Catch your breath."

His cygnet's call drowns out the lingering doom in the clouds. I open my eyes to see the forest wall stretched out before us. Its great white tree trunks seem to spread their arms to welcome us. Something vast hovers over and I look up into Valenor's chest with relief. Bryse and the others peer down from his back. Following him are Julini and Zevlain on their cygnets, each bogged down with several more bodies. From this distance I can barely make out cloaks of blue and yellow. Flashes of chain mail. The blue glow of Lisabella's sword.

Shoel raises his free hand and gives a series of gestures. Below us on the wall, the White Line lower their bows and allow us to pass. At first I'm surprised when we don't stop at the wall, but as we glide along it I see a battle taking place on the ground. A small group is trying to fight past the border. Shocks of magic crash into the white trunks and travel up into the leaves, making them rustle and tremble.

Their attacks are answered by the elves' own Mages, who send bolts of purple and red to singe and stun the men below.

"Who are they?" I call up to him as we soar past, narrowly missing one of the bolts. "What's happening?"

"Cly Zhrel the Third," he answers. "Eighteenth Foray." I have no idea what it means, but there's no time to ask. He gives another signal and a quick wave and beneath me I see a series of colored flags raised by elves that line the top of the wall. The signal must mean something to him. He banks quickly and instead of landing on a perch like the last time we were brought here, he goes up over the wall and glides past it into the fields beyond.

Our cygnet is the first to land, then Julini and Zhevlain's follow. Valenor settles softly in the grass beside us, and right away he flattens himself to the ground. Before there's time to react, we're surrounded by at least twenty elves. They're tall and white and regal, just like Shoel and the others, but these are different. Haughty. Powerful. Mages, dressed in flowing robes of white that are open in the front all the way to their belts to show their bare chests. Even the women. They raise their hands all at once and beams of silver wind from their fingers and slide over Valenor, binding him to the ground. He doesn't fight or struggle. He just lies there and lets them do it.

"Stop it!" I shout. It reminds me too much of the roots. "Let him go!" I try to run to him, but Julini steps in front of me and crouches to my level.

"Tib," she gives an apologetic smile. Her voice reminds me of Mya's. It's kind and soothing. It makes me calm. She rests a hand on my shoulder and I feel my worry draining away. "They are not hurting him. They are merely ensuring the safety of our realm. He has consented to this."

"They're binding him! Why? For how long?"

"Until they can be assured of his good intentions and true identity. If he is who he claims to be, then there is no need for concern. Come. The others need healing." She tries to guide me away, but I don't let her.

"I'm not leaving him," I scowl. "I don't care if he agreed or not."

"Then we shall bring the others to heal, and you may remain." She pats my cheek and stands again. I can tell that she expects me to change my mind and go with the rest of them, but I don't. I creep closer to Valenor instead, into the silvery bonds that have no effect on me. Trace my finger along the scales' golden edges. Mevyn's gold.

They take the others away: Lisabella, Benen, Bryse, Cort, Dacva, and Gaethon. Take them to heal. Most of them can walk, but Gaethon and Benen have to be carried. Shoel stays with me while I wait for the spell to be done. I want to ask him about the battle and the cloud that knocked Valenor out, but he sits outside of the Mage circle and waits, and I feel like it would be wrong to shout across to him. Instead I follow the long line of Valenor's neck with my eyes. Gaze at his closed eye. It opens slowly, just enough for me to see a narrow slit of the red orb within.

I'm shown something new. Another battle. A different one, between a man and a boy. The man wears a cloak of stars that billows behind him like a torn piece of night sky. The boy is in tatters, skinny and dirty. His eyes are cruel and filled with hate. His fingers are twisted and claw-like as he thrusts them out to unleash his magic. He bares his teeth like a wild animal.

Behind the man, creatures emerge from the darkness. They scrabble over him and tear at his back and he screams in fury and pain as he tries to fight them off. There are too many, though, and it isn't long before he's overcome. The shadows chew and claw at his shoulders, pulling the cloak away. When he looks at the boy again, the betrayal he feels is plain and raw on his face. It quickly turns to rage as the cloak is ripped away, leaving just a thread behind.

The thread whips around the man and he thrashes and claws and roars as his body begins to change. His arms and legs stretch and twist and darken. His neck grows long. His back and head sprout horns and spines. He grows taller, broader. He roars into the boy's face.

"Return that which is mine, Jacek," he bellows. His words have little effect. Jacek holds his hands out to the shadows, who rush to deliver the cloak of stars to him. "I trusted you. You were to be my apprentice, my heir. How could you betray me?"

"Why should I be made to wait? You see?" he drapes it over his shoulders with a haughty sneer. "You've lost your hold, old man. They're loyal to me, now." The air around him shifts. The mantle changes, growing up over his shoulders, attaching itself to him. Flowing out like a stream of darkness behind him. Smoke and shadow. Ink and water. When it settles, he's taller somehow. His eyes are dark and grim. His body stronger. His stance bolder. The shadows collect around him, bolstering him. He raises his chin to the dragon, who blasts him with a breath of fire. When the smoke clears, Jacek is unmoved. His laughter is just like the laughter in the clouds.

"Your throne is crumbled. Your crown destroyed. You are nothing," the boy says. "You are no one." He strokes the cloak lovingly, taunting Valenor with it. The dragon backs away, shaking his head as if to clear the darkness. "I'm the Dreamwalker, and I banish you. Your kingdom is mine, now. *My* will is done."

His words strike me hard, like a punch to my throat. I feel myself falling again, this time together with Valenor through the sky, through a crevice in the mountains where he crashes hard and the shadows lash out around him and hold him. Fill him with despair and regret. Empty him of hope. Drain him of memory.

"*The mantle.*" The voice that echoes in my mind as I open my eyes is a blend of Valenor's and Mevyn's. I understand. The mantle is my quest. I'm the Dreamstalker. The only one who can recover it.

"I understand," I whisper as I walk along the length of him and stop when I reach his enormous head. His eye closes again and the silver streams start to rise and arc into the space above him.

From the ground at the elf Mages' feet, sprouts push up through the soil. They grow and thicken into beautiful white tree trunks exactly like those that make up the Forest Wall. For some reason, I'm not afraid of these as they grow and twine together to create a great circular room with a high domed ceiling. They are trees, yes, but their energy is different. Light and airy. Perfumed with flowers that droop from vines all around us, and lit by the glow of thousands of sparkling bulbs.

With a soft word from one of the Mages, the grass is covered over with a thick gray carpet. Another Mage creates ornately carved chairs with comfortable overstuffed cushions. Another commands a table. Food. Water. Fire for warmth. When the magic is done, they bow to the center. The silver beams fade away. Valenor slowly sits back on his haunches and twists his neck around to stretch.

There's plenty of room for him in here. There's even a door large enough for him to leave through if he wants to, draped with green vines that sway in the breeze. His scales glisten handsomely in the soft light. His tail flicks back and forth as he bows to each of the Mages in turn.

"Even in my darkest times, I never forgot the hospitality of Elves," he says. "Thank you, friends. Thank you."

"Would that we could do more," one of the Mages says. A woman.

“Yes, we would see you restored, friend. Your usurper vanquished,” says another.

“That is the goal, and your protection will be most helpful.” Valenor smiles.

“It is your protection,” a third elf says, “that has allowed us to thrive.”

Without another word, they all bow again and file out. Each one of them stops to look me over as they leave. Their silvery eyes bore into me. They nod. When they’re gone, I turn to Shoel.

“Are all elf Mages so scary?” I ask him.

He shakes his head and laughs, and the sound mixes with Valenor’s chuckle. The echo of the two together reminds me of the more sinister sounds coming from the yellow-green clouds.

“You have nothing to fear from our Mages,” Shoel says after a moment. “They are pure of heart, and filled with Light. They dedicate their lives to purity, kindness, knowledge, and the protection of Good. You saw it yourself. There is not a Mark upon them.”

I think of the Sorcerers of Zhaghen, with the blue-black curls that creep over their skin and slash across their faces. A sign of selfishness, of wicked overuse of magic. Those are the ones I hate. The ones who would waste their power without concern for anyone in their path. When she was younger, Viala told me that it starts at the heart.

“That’s why their robes were so low in the front,” I whisper thoughtfully, remembering the bare white skin of their chests. “I wondered.”

“Practice of the Arcane is a strict and hallowed art among our people. Any hint of the Mark is not tolerated here. A Mage will be stripped at the first sign of it,” Shoel says. He looks off into the distance and gives a half-hearted smile. Valenor looks away from him.

I can feel the tension between them enough to know that I shouldn’t ask what it’s about. There isn’t much to do now but wait for the others. I sink into a chair and look out the open door, toward the wall that blocks us from the battle raging on the other side. There’s no sign of it from here except for the rustle of leaves high above. Otherwise, it’s just as silent and peaceful as it was the first time I came with Raefe and Saesa.

“What did you say that’s about, the battle?” I ask Shoel.

“Cly Zhrel III,” his reply is word-for-word the same it was the first time. “Eighteenth Foray.”

“Who is Cly Zhrel?”

"A man who believes himself above the need for order and government. A man who sees boundaries as things to be broken and crushed. A Sorcerer and a Necromancer. A Warlock. A brigand."

"But how can he be all of those things?" I shrink away from the door, even though I'm well protected by the wall and those fighting there.

"He is what he calls himself, and what others call him. Titles. Names. They hold power, Tib, as you are well aware," Valenor says.

"But why?" I ask. "What does he want?"

"He seeks our source." Shoel says simply. Valenor looks at him. Looks at me. Looks away.

"Your source? What do you—" my question is interrupted by a slew of curses and a rustle of robes as the vines at the door are shoved aside.

"Azi?" Rian calls as he rushes inside, followed quickly by Lisabella. "Oh, Tib, excellent, you're here. Is Azi? Have you seen her?" he asks me, disappearing behind Valenor to search.

"No, I haven't…" I trail off and shake my head as he reappears on the other side of the dragon.

"Told you! She's not here!" Flitt squeaks as she darts around his head.

"Saesa?" he asks, his face going pale.

"No, she was supposed to be with you!" I jump to my feet, my heart racing. "What do you mean? What happened?"

"Calm down," Rian says, more to himself than to me. He paces across the floor, back and forth. "I'm sure this can be explained. We were preparing to leave the Ring. Saesa had her hand. I said 'Okay, to Mum, right?' and Azi said, 'Right!' So we stepped away into the Half-Realm and I…"

"Aha!" Rian claps his hands and grins. "I know what happened! She thought I meant my mum and I thought she meant her mum, so I ended up here, with you," he points to Lisabella, "which means Azi, of course, must have gone to my mum! That's a relief," he laughs. Nobody else does. Lisabella goes pale.

"So where is she, then?" Rian asks. "Healing up with the others? I heard about your flight on the way here. Good thing we weren't on it. Azi would have been…" he trails off as he looks from me to Valenor.

"She isn't here, is she?" he asks, turning around. "Where is she, Lisabella? Where's Mum?"

Chapter Thirty-Four:

LAKE KORDELYA

Azi

My first concern as we tumble through the Half-Realm is that Rian's hand has slipped from mine. My second is that we have arrived neck-deep in water, encased by some sort of stone. My armor seems to have magical qualities that keep me afloat, but Saesa isn't so lucky. Even though it's just studded leather, her armor is a heavy weight that threatens to pull her under.

I struggle to keep my hold on this girl who I swore to protect, who made her vow to serve me only moments ago among a ring full of fairies, her eyes brimming with tears. My squire.

Thankfully, my feet find a ledge. I guide her to it and we wait for the water to go still.

"Did you hear that?" she whispers as she clings to me. "Voices."

I nod. A tunnel is carved into the stone. It stretches ahead of us, though it's difficult to see how far. It's so deep that my helm scrapes the ceiling as the water reaches my chin, and there's little light here aside from a soft blue glow in the distance. Beyond that, everything is black. I keep my grip on Saesa and turn my head to listen to the voices in the distance.

"Bound by words, heart, deeds, and darkness. Never to be undone, except in death. We swore it together, Viala."

"Viala is dead," Ki's weak voice is extinguished by a splash and a struggle. The water's surface ripples along the tunnel toward us. Saesa's eyes go wide. She looks up at me and I shake my head slowly as I try to make sense of it. How did I end up with Ki and Eron if we were trying to reach Mya? Is she here, too? But why would she be? How could she be?

A palace guard crosses the mouth of the tunnel ahead and

shines a lamp to peer down at us. Saesa and I press ourselves against the wall, but he looks right at us. My heart leaps into my throat when the light shines over his face. Jac. He squints in our direction as the light passes over, looking hard. For a moment I think he sees me, but he keeps going. I slowly let out the breath that I didn't realize I'd been holding and look at Saesa.

"He didn't see us," she whispers. That's when it dawns on me.

"We're still in the Half-Realm," I reply under my breath.

"So we're invisible?" she holds her hand in front of her face and turns it this way and that.

"Not invisible, but they won't notice us unless we give them a reason to believe we're here. A noise, or a disturbance of something they can see." I pull my hand through the water and watch the ripples fan out behind it. "Like that."

"What about the Dreamwalker?" she whispers. "He can see us either way, right?" she shifts herself on the ledge and looks up along the ceiling at the shadows.

"I don't think so. Uncle gave me a talisman, and you're still under Mevyn's protections I hope." We both go quiet as Ki splashes and coughs beyond the tunnel.

"But you said Mevyn…" she lets her whispers trail off.

"I don't know. It was like he was absorbed into Valenor. Maybe a part of him is still alive, enough to keep his protections on you and your brother." I put a finger to my lips and nod toward the voices.

"Get her out of there. Put her with the others and leave us." Eron says.

We take advantage of the splashing that comes next to move further along the ledge, closer to them. It's slow going at first, but we reach the mouth undetected. What greets us at the end turns my stomach.

The tunnel opens up into a circular room with a low, dark ceiling full of hooks and chains. A stone walkway runs all the way around it, and in the center is the deep pool of water that connects to our tunnel. Just beneath the water's surface there is a fine grate with shackles attached to it. The room is bathed in blue light, and I follow it to the source: a heap of bodies across the way. Mya, Elliot, and Brother Donal lie bound and motionless, and the blue light glows from between Mya's fingers. Hers is the only face I can see from this angle. Her eyes are closed. Silently, I pray that they're all only knocked out.

Iren's light comforts me somehow. I wonder how she came by

it. The last I knew, Tib had it. I hope he's safe. I shudder to imagine how any of them came to be here. Even more curious is that neither Eron nor Jac have noticed the glowing trinket.

Jac drops Ki against the wall and binds her to it. With another glance in our direction, he gives Eron a respectful bow and lets himself out of a heavy door to the left of the bound Elite with a deafening clang. I keep an eye on the others. None of them react to the sound aside from Ki, who shudders and shivers as Eron stalks toward her. The look in his eyes is that of cruel desperation.

When he turns his back to us, Saesa and I shift slightly closer. When he reaches Ki I expect him to strike her or shake her, but instead he drops to his knees and takes her face gently in his trembling hands. Ki never takes her eyes off him. She squares her shoulders and sets her jaw, bracing herself as he lifts her chin. This time when he speaks, his voice is shaking. Even this close, it's difficult to hear him.

"I have searched for you. I've risked everything. My birthright, my marriage, everything. For you. For the plans we had. For the vows we made. Kythshire. The Wellspring. They'll be ours. We'll rule it, all of it. Cerion, Kythshire, Ceras'lain, Sunteri…everything. You gave me this hunger. If not for you…" He trails off as he leans closer to her, close enough to kiss her. Ki's expression is cautious, like a fawn caught in the wildcat's stalking gaze. "Look deep inside yourself. I know you can. Please, Viala. Please."

Ki raises her chin and locks her eyes with his defiantly. "My name is Ki. Viala is dead."

"Stop saying that!" Eron growls and slams his fist into the wall right beside her head. Ki flinches and he grasps her by the hair and forces a kiss on her. The blue light washing over the room seems to swirl together and concentrate on the two of them. Ki's eyes glow bright with it. They search back and forth and around as Eron continues to force himself on her. They see things unseen by any of the rest of us. I remember what Iren told me just before we left Kythshire. *When the time comes, if she is faced with it, she will remember. This is her final test.*

Saesa and I cling to each other, watching Ki's demeanor change from frightened and tortured to relieved and hungry. She's changed. I see Viala in her now. Her eyes close slowly. She presses herself into Eron, drinking in his kiss, trying to slide her shackled arms around him, surrendering to his touch. Aware of the change in her, he pulls away and scoops her hands into his, searching her eyes.

"Bound by words, heart, deeds, and darkness. Never to be undone, except in death," she whispers to him. "I remember."

"Yes, my love, my love," he buries his face in her hair and trails kisses along her neck.

"No." Ki says sternly, giving Eron pause. Her voice goes cold. "I was never your love."

"Truly you were, Viala. You are. You always will be." He draws her closer and tries to kiss her again, but she turns her face from him.

"Lies so deep, so dark that you believe them yourself." Ki says as Eron slumps back on his heels. "You aren't capable of love. Think hard, Prince. You have forsaken your own father, your king. You would have him killed so you could rise to his throne. You wanted me to do it, or have you forgotten? You begged me, but I made him fall ill instead.

"I hoped you would see reason, but you were already too far gone. You say it was Viala who led you astray, but did she lure you across forbidden borders? Did she convince you to betray the trust of the elves and the fae? No. That happened long before you met her. That was your own greed. Your lust for power. Your desire to control more than you were entitled to.

"The consequences that followed were your own to bear. The fairies' curse frightened you, but you were too proud to admit your cowardice, even to those who cared about you. Until she came along, and then it was your lust more than anything that made you drop your barriers.

"You kept secrets. Your heart grew dark and twisted. Wasted. You turned everywhere for comfort but never found it. Empty actions. Wicked pacts. You depended on her for power. You allowed her to control and manipulate you. You let her bewitch you and draw that hunger out of you.

"Little did you know that she was only a puppet. Her strings were plucked by another. Someone even more wicked than you. Someone dangerous and clever. Even after she was gone, he watched you, molded you. You were too proud to see it. Even now, you're too proud. You think every action, every brilliant idea is your own, but it isn't. Think carefully. It isn't." She shakes her head disdainfully and slides away from him. "My name is Ki. Viala is dead."

With every accusation, Eron's shoulder slump further. His head sinks into his hands and he rakes his fingers into his hair. Ki's chains jingle softly as she tucks her knees to her chest, watching. Waiting. I've never seen the prince this way. Curled into himself, he looks so small and vulnerable. Almost child-like. His shoulders shake with sobs as the depth of the truth sinks into him.

"It isn't too late," Ki whispers. "Your wife, your family, they still love you. Your father sent you here to clear your name. He still has hope for you. You can redeem yourself as prince. You could still rule Cerion in time. You'd be a fair king."

Eron shakes his head, not in denial of her words, but in what I can only describe as some sort of manic episode. He pushes himself to his feet and pulls at his hair and paces along the walkway, muttering to himself.

"It isn't too late," he says over and over, coming to stop at Ki again. "Bound by words, heart, deeds, and darkness. Never to be undone, except in death." He pulls her to her feet and draws his sword in one swift movement. "So I will do it alone."

His blade flashes in the blue light as he drives it through her stomach and holds her impaled by it. Saesa and I clap our hands over our mouths to keep from crying out.

"And now it is undone," he sneers into her shocked face, pushes her from the blade and watches her slump to the floor. For a moment he stands there watching, waiting for her sputtering breath to stop. As soon as it does, he shoves her with his foot into the water and stalks to the door, slamming it behind him.

"Ki!" I whisper and scramble to her side on the grate. Saesa struggles beside me. As I pull Ki's face out of the water her eyes stare vacantly into the ceiling. "No. Please, no." I whisper as I roll her onto her back to look at the wound.

It's all the way through from front to back, a quick killing blow. I could have stopped him. I should have, but it happened so fast. I can't accept it. I shake her, I call her name, but there's no waking her. She's gone. Saesa and I drag her out of the water and rest her on walkway. When I reach to close her eyes, they reflect the blue light so strongly that I have to look away. My gaze rests on Mya's wrist. "The stone," I say to Saesa, pointing in Mya's direction. "Iren."

She races to retrieve it for me and when she places it in my hand the light glows brighter. It seeps toward the wound as if reaching for it, so I place it there. The light brightens, stretching out over Ki, encasing her in soft blue ribbons. When she is completely covered in them they begin to fade away, and her with them. In a moment she's gone, leaving Saesa and I behind with our unconscious allies.

I fight the urge to sob for her loss, and instead I push myself on. Ki is in Iren's hands now. My guild needs me. I rush to them and I'm relieved to find them all alive. Alive, but sleeping so soundly that I'm not able to rouse them.

"Sleep spell?" Saesa whispers.

"Or—" my thought is interrupted by the eerie squeak of the door as it opens again. Jac enters alone and slams it heavily behind him. He stands with his hands on his hips, surveying first the water and then the pool of blood left behind by Ki.

"Didn't think he had it in him, did you, Lady Knight?" His eyes follow the line of the walkway to us and rest on me. He smiles. "But he's coming along well. Quickly, too. I see you've cleaned her up already. Good of you," he walks past me to the pool of blood and crouches. "Valuable thing, life's last blood," he takes off his glove and places his palm into it. "It holds memories, you know."

When Jac raises his other hand to gesture a spell, I catch within the shadows the echo of a figure, like a shroud around him. In that moment, Jac's features shift darker. I see him clearly now, his cloak of night billowing behind him, his eyes bright and curious. He whispers the spell and the pool goes sickly red and black. Smoky forms rise from it, showing things that I can't discern.

"Ah, you haven't kept your promise," Jac and Jacek's voices blend together. "You were to touch the Wellspring, or have you forgotten? And alas, Ki never had the chance, either." He watches the smoke intently, quietly. "Hm." He turns to peer at me. "You have someone else with you, too. It's her, isn't it?"

My heart starts to race. Somehow, despite Uncle's talisman, he can see me. Not only that, but he knows about Saesa. Or at least he thinks he does. Something in the smoke must have shown him.

"Come now, Lady Knight. Isn't it exhausting, always hiding away? Let us see each other plainly. Step into the waking. You were fond of Jac once, weren't you? Or are you more comfortable there, in the Half-Realm?"

As he steps away from Jac to move closer to me, the guard drops to his knees and collapses limply into the bloody puddle. Jacek is a ghost of himself here in the Half-Realm, but I don't underestimate his power as he approaches, searching the space around me for my squire. I don't know how it is that he can see me and not her, but whatever the reason, I'm grateful for it.

"Sister," he coos, still trying to see her, "so grown now. And a swords woman. You wish to be a knight some day like this one who fails to keep her promises? I can make you one now, if you'd like. Surely you know what I ask of you. Free me, Sister. Free me and you shall have all you desire when we walk this plane together."

I don't dare reach for her or even turn my head in her direction, but I feel Saesa shift closer to me. For a moment I consider grabbing her and taking her away to Kythshire or to Ceras'lain through the Half-Realm, but I don't know if that would reveal her to Jacek. That, and I can't bring myself to leave the others behind to be at the mercy of the prince and the Dreamwalker.

"Let them go," Saesa's voice makes me jump. Jacek's eyes widen with triumph. He moves closer. "I'll come with you if you release these three and allow them to leave with Sir Azaeli."

"Saesa, no," I whisper, gripping her arm behind me.

"We knew it might come to this," Saesa whispers to me. "You told me yourself."

I go over in my mind what we discussed in the Ring. She's right. She knows of Valenor's plan to allow her to be taken and to release Jacek willingly, but we aren't ready now. She was supposed to have protections placed on her. We were supposed to have a plan to thwart him once he was released into the waking plane. I never intended for her to go alone. We aren't ready for this.

"I agree to your bargain, Sister," Jacek grins. "I will wake them and allow them to go on their way, and you will come with me. On one condition. The Lady Knight must swear to keep her promise to me regarding the Wellspring."

"Hello!" Flitt pushes to me suddenly. I fight the instinct to whirl around and look for her. Instead I shift closer to Saesa, protecting her. Jacek hasn't noticed Flitt's arrival. I hope it stays that way. *"Glad I found you! Stay here. Stall him. I'll let them know."* I don't have to worry for long. She's already gone before I finish the thought.

"How did you see through the talisman?" I ask him. "You were inside Jac, weren't you? He saw me in the tunnel. How?"

"My dear Azaeli," Jacek grins within the shadows, "The Dreamwalker isn't governed by the same rules and laws of those on your plane. I see what I want, when I want to."

"That's not true," I argue. "You couldn't see Saesa. You still can't. You couldn't find me in Cerion when I was in the guild hall. You couldn't follow me to the palace."

"To be honest, I was expecting you here. Always the hero. It was only a matter of time before you came looking for Ki. For Mya and the others as well. Don't worry about them. They're having quite an adventure in the dreaming. Amusing, really. I do hope they stay for a while." His laugh sickens me. This is a game to him.

"You're trying to frighten me," I say. "To anger me. You're not as powerful as you'd like me to believe." I watch his eyes narrow, his anger build.

"I am more powerful than you can fathom, Azaeli. You should fall to your knees in awe of me. A whisper of a command, a step to the side, and I can travel anywhere in this world. I can suggest war. I can compel fire. I can rule princes and Sorcerers and rebels.

"I can move mountains and breach borders, and all of it done with such a perfect subtlety that the men who follow me believe it is their own doing. I step to the side and I am standing before Ceras'lain, compelling men to crush its great wall. I step to another and whisper, and a prince becomes a murderer."

"You're blinded by your pride," I shake my head. "I know the truth. All of us do. You're a prisoner, trapped in a realm that bores you. You yearn to be free. You want to be here where you belong, and that is something you can never do without Saesa."

Just past him behind his back, the air shifts subtly. Rian appears there, a finger pressed to his lips.

"You're a fool to underestimate me," Jacek laughs again and shakes his head, "and to think you could surprise me, Mage." He spins around and lashes out at Rian with a whip of a shadow that cracks through his wards and catches him around the neck.

Rian gives a half-grin and steps back.

"Your shadows aren't real," he smirks. "They're imagined. I figured it out. You feed on confusion, anger, loneliness, fear. If I come to expect it, you lose the mystery. Therefore, you lose the power." Rian shakes his head. "It becomes more difficult for you then, doesn't it?"

Jacek growls in anger and raises his shadowy hands up, plunging us into darkness. His cloak billows out behind him and as I cry out and charge at the shadows, I'm aware of something else. Another presence in the space between us, small and bold.

My attention is drawn away from it by the sound of a scuffle in the darkness ahead. There's a thud, and Rian grunts.

"No!" I shout. Rian casts a spell, and in the moments following the blinding flash I see that Jac is on his feet again, his sword drawn and raised to strike Rian. As it plunges downward, I push my mind into the guard's, trying desperately to stop his arms.

Rian looks into Jac's eyes, my eyes, but I'm too late. Jac's sword comes down, slashing, and the look in the eyes of my love shatters my heart. Pain, disbelief, emptiness. I can't bear it. I pull myself away from Jac and watch through my own eyes as Rian falls without a sound. I can't move. I'm frozen in terror as he crumples to the floor, his blood spilling into the singed puddle of Ki's.

Chapter Thirty-Five:

THE MANTLE

Tib

It's a good diversion. Rian is down. Azi is stunned. The Dreamwalker is watching gleefully. He doesn't notice me. Saesa charges the guard, the one who struck down Rian. Jacek turns his attention to her. Everything is dark again, but it doesn't matter. I don't need to see him. I can sense him. I just know. This is the best time. This is my chance.

I slip toward him, this man of nightmares and shadows. Formless but not. It isn't him I want, it's the cloak. The mantle. That's my goal. It's just within my reach, and still he doesn't know I'm here. He's too busy gloating over his kill. Rian was always good to me. He was a kind Mage. Azi drops to her knees beside him, weeping. Saying his name over and over. Shaking him. Sobbing. I brush past her, slip her a pink vial. Look away. I try not to think about it. I can't get distracted.

This was all part of the plan. I have to do it right, like Valenor told me. Thoroughly. There can't be a thread left behind, not a scrap. My title rings over and over in my mind. Dreamstalker. He can't see me. He can't sense me, thanks to Mevyn. The shadows and stars of his cloak swirl around me as I step into it.

Time seems to shift around me. Everything else slows. My heart races as I reach to his shoulders. I feel the rush of it: excitement, danger, control. He still doesn't see me. He's too swept up in Saesa's fight. He's too busy controlling Jac. My fingers rest on the mantle. It's complex, Valenor told me. Molded to the wearer. There are no clasps, no buckles. There is only will.

I know what I have to do. I start to close my eyes as my hands rest lightly upon it. The fight between Saesa and the guard grows more furious. I try to block it out, but Saesa is struck. She cries out and I have to look. She's been stabbed in her sword arm. Blood trickles down her bracer and along Feat's blade.

It doesn't stop her. In her rage, something shifts around her. She presses on, fighting bravely. Jacek sees her. Watches her. I can feel his hatred for her. He wants her dead, but he knows he needs her. Still, he forces Jac on her. The guard is nearly twice her size.

Don't be distracted. Your mind must be clear. Your intention must be set. The mantle is your right. You have been marked for it. You have been sealed. It is yours to take. It will be easy for you, if you will it. I've repeated Valenor's instructions over and over so many times since he gave them to me that I barely have to think about them now. I can't worry about Saesa. This is important. I'm the only one who can do it. For her. For Mevyn. For Valenor.

I push my hands up under the mantle. Raise my arms. Close my eyes. Tell it that it's mine, that it belongs to me. Believe it in my heart, like Valenor told me to. Jacek finally realizes the threat against him, but it's too late. The power that he stole is Valenor's by right. I'm only a steward, a messenger, but the mantle knows. It never belonged to Jacek. The mantle frees itself from the Dreamwalker and slips over me. Rests heavy on my shoulders. The cloak of stars billows around me and I feel a rush like I've never felt before.

I can do anything. No one can stop me. The darkness is my slave. The stars are mine to command. Every wicked thought, every hint of fear is something to collect and control. I turn to Jac first. I don't even have to say a word. I imagine him dropping his sword and he does it. I show him terror. I make him believe that Saesa is a monster who could crush him with her fingertips. He cowers from her.

There's no time to be amused, though. Jacek, stripped of his mantle, screams at me. He tries to rip and claw it away from me, but he has no claim. His power here is fading. He's slipping back into the Dreaming, just like Valenor said he would. Behind him, Saesa sees me for the first time. She dashes toward me, starts to throw her arms around me, but Jacek reaches for her as she passes by. With his last wisp of strength, he grabs her arm and pulls her with him. Together they disappear into the Dreaming.

"Saesa!" Azi and I scream together. She jumps to her feet and runs to the place where Saesa disappeared. Behind her, Rian pushes himself up weakly. She rushes back to him and helps him stand.

"A few holes in that plan," Rian mutters sheepishly. "Nothing major. Didn't have much time to iron it out. Sorry. You did it though,

Tib. Excellent."

"Nothing major?" Azi exclaims as she hugs him close. "You just nearly died!"

Both turn to watch as the cloak settles around me. Whispering Jacek's dealings. Stretching out from me like roots to all of those he's touched. Distracting me. Overwhelming me. Princes. Sorcerers. Necromancers. Maids. Thieves. Weeping. Pleading. Begging. Fearing. Something else. A determination. A push. A battle.

I close my eyes and focus on it and I'm there, floating above the Forest Wall. I am the storm, thundering and rumbling. Watching Cly Zhrel's army of Sorcerers battle the White Line. Watching them cast their magical attacks back and forth, back and forth.

"Stop," I say. "Enough." To my shock, they do. Cly lowers his hands. Shakes his head. Kneels in surrender to the elves.

"Tib." Rian says sternly, pulling me back to the circle room. Back to Azi and the sleeping Elite. I don't even feel the shift. It was like I was simply taking a step.

"You're not supposed to use it," Rian says. "Remember? Just bring it back to Valenor."

"But…" I stare from him to Azi. "I just stopped a war. Just like that."

"It's not yours," Rian says. "You have to be careful."

"What about Saesa?" I ask him. "She's stuck there with him. He'll do terrible things to her."

"We'll bring it back to Valenor and make a plan," he says and I can feel the anger in him. He looks over at the pile of his guild members, sleeping on the edge of the walkway. Crouches beside them. Gestures to me and Azi to join him.

"Ready?" he asks.

"What about him?" Azi points to Jac, who's still cowering against the wall.

"What about him?" Rian scowls.

"We can't just leave him. He didn't know what he was doing through all of this. Jacek was controlling him. If Eron comes back and finds everyone gone, he's sure to be blamed for it," she whispers.

"You…" Rian shakes his head and bends down and kisses her. "I love you, know that? Come on, then, Jac." He jerks his head toward the others. Against the wall, Jac blinks.

"Sir?" Jac says, a little vaguely. "Name's Patyr actually. Third rank. Royal Guard." He looks around a little warily. "Where'd that girl go?" He shivers. "The one with the claws and sharp teeth?"

Rian turns to me and raises a brow.

"I had to," I say, shrugging. "Saesa was losing."

"Don't do it again. You don't know what could happen. Come on," Rian turns to the guard. "We'll get you back to the palace." As Patyr comes to join us, Rian and Azi link arms with the others. I hold on to Azi's shoulder.

"Ready?" Rian asks. Azi's eyes meet mine as she nods. Sorrowful. Apologetic. I see Ki in them. Look down at the others. As Rian pulls us away into the Half-Realm back to Ceras'lain, I realize my sister isn't with us. The mantle flutters and drifts around us as we plunge toward the waking, and I know I'm not supposed to but I can't help it.

I look into it. I search along the vast fabric for my sister, for Ki. I see her in many places, but the last is through the eyes of a prince, at the end of his sword. Dropping away. Gasping. Dying. Pulled lifelessly out of the water by the knight and her squire.

We hit the ground hard and I tuck my knees and roll straight into Valenor's scaly leg. I push the mantle from my shoulders and shove it at him, desperate to clear my head of the image I just saw.

"Why didn't you tell me?" I scream and spin to face Azi. I throw myself at her, punching her stony chest plate until my knuckles bleed inside my gloves. She takes my wrists and sinks to her knees and holds me. Rocks me. Comforts me as she cries tears of her own.

"I'm sorry," she keeps saying again and again until I want to punch her stupid face and tell her to shut her mouth. I try to shove away from her but she won't let me. She just holds me tighter and rocks and rocks until I break down, too. Lisabella shows up at some point. She puts her arms around us both. Her peace washes over us. Allows me to let go. I cry hard. For Mevyn. For Ki. For Saesa. For Nan and Zhilee.

I'm only half aware of what's happening around us. Gaethon and Rian are working to wake the others. The elf Mages are here, too, trying to help. Nobody notices Valenor. Maybe it's my connection to the mantle that pulls my attention to him. I wipe my eyes on the shoulder of Azi's damp cloak and watch in disbelief as the mantle swirls and grows around him like a giant cocoon.

"Azi," Flitt pokes her cheek and points. The Mages look up from the others who are still caught in sleep. Together we watch in awe as Valenor starts to transform.

The mantle shifts from midnight blue to the colors of twilight and daybreak. It swirls and glitters and bursts with light that dances around the dragon's enormous form. He begins to shrink, wrapped in his cloak, to the size of a curled up man. The cloak pile lies motionless and lumpy for a long, breathless moment. Azi gets up slowly. Carefully. She pulls me up, too. We watch as the cloak shimmers to grass and flowers and silk and gold.

The center of it comes to a point. It changes to look like a man. A long braided beard spills down the front of his robes. He pushes his hood from his face and blinks at us. His eyes are white as snow. He's old. Really old. Not frail, though. Stern-looking, too, just like a Mage. But he smiles at me. Right at me.

"Valenor?" I whisper.

"Well," he says after a lot of throat-clearing. His voice is gravely. Unsure, like he's getting used to it. "I think I'll go fetch Saesa. Who's coming with?"

We all stand there staring at him. Even the Mages have stopped their efforts in order to gape. I'm the first one to move. I push away from Azi to move closer to the man. He's tall, like an elf, and slender. His cloak moves around him like something alive.

It isn't like it was before, though. It's brighter. Cheerful. Filled with promise. Possibilities. Hope. He reaches out to me as I approach. His eyes stare blankly ahead. That's when I realize he's blind. But I remember the cloak. He isn't, really. He can see everything. More than any of us can.

"They will not wake," he says quietly. Puts a hand on my shoulder. Guides me to the Mages who turn back to Mya, Elliot, and Donal.

This close to him, I can feel something else. Something familiar. A sense of guidance. An old friend. Mevyn. His presence is stronger, maybe because Valenor is so much smaller now. It reminds me of the fairies I'm carrying. They've been so quiet. I had almost forgotten about them.

"What do you mean?" Rian crouches beside his mother. Strokes her arm. I look at the rest of them. Donal and Elliot. The guard that stabbed Saesa.

"They are caught in the Dreaming. Much like you were, Azaeli. Not this one, though." He points to Jac.

"He is under my spell," Gaethon says. "For safekeeping. He will remain so until we can return him to Cerion."

"Very well," Valenor says. "As far as the other three, we must return to my realm and seek them out. We must recover Saesa. I fear what she might become in Jacek's grips. We must find him and put an end to him once and for all."

The elves vow to watch over those sleeping while we're gone. Gaethon and Lisabella will stay behind with them. This is where we'll send Jacek when Saesa releases him. The elves have magic that can bind him. They'll all be waiting. Azi and Flitt, Rian and I step into the folds of Valenor's cloak. He tells us to stay close.

It doesn't take much. Just a step to the side and we're off. Into the Dreaming. The last time I was here, it was dark. Shadows lurked around us. Rian went half-mad in our search for Azaeli. Everything was confused and strange. This time, it's different. Maybe it's because it's daytime. Maybe it's because Valenor is the Dreamwalker now. Everything is bright. Blinding, almost. The sun is warm overhead. It makes me want to throw off my cloak. The air is thick with the perfume of flowers. The sky is deep blue.

"It's so beautiful," Azi breathes as she holds tight to Rian's arm. Flitt darts among the flowers, laughing and shining her own light. Even Rian looks better. He was sunken and tired when we arrived in Ceras'lain. Here, he seems like he's gotten some strength back.

"It's completely different from the last time we were here," Rian says as he looks around in awe.

"The tyrant has been knocked from his throne," Valenor nods. "Still, we must proceed with caution. Do not be falsely comforted by the light and the warmth. This remains the Dreaming, and as with all the world, there is darkness to balance the light. Jacek has been stripped of his mantle, but he remains a Sorcerer, bent on freedom and vengeance. He is hungry for power. Our victory over him will not be an easy one."

"Speaks of it like it's a certainty, he does," a voice pipes up from the grasses. I remember this one. He showed us things the last time we were here. He helped us get to the castle. "An eventuality. He hasn't seen the new one. The warrior. He doesn't know."

"What's this, little one?" Valenor crouches in the grass. His cloak floats around him white and airy. Glittering, like a soft mist. Azi watches on. Clings to Rian. Looks wary or ashamed. Maybe both. Stubs pokes his head out of his shell. Peers at Valenor with wide, dark eyes.

"Red Glen," he whispers. "You'll see."

A sweep and a step, and we're there. Red Glen. Red trees. Red sky. Red, spindly vines with thorns that grab and pull at us. Red like the blossoms. Red like the blood that spilled from my sister. Red everywhere, mocking me. Taunting me. And at the center, a warrior just like Stubs said. Armor of black and red like a scab. Broad at the shoulders and intricately patterned. I lose myself in the metalwork. It entrances me. That and the red, which stirs so much anger, so much need for revenge, makes me unable to move, to think.

Not Azi, though. She's focused on something else. The two-handed sword slung across the warrior's back. It looks like Feat, but much larger. I remember what Saesa said all that time ago. How Feat was modeled after Azaeli's old sword. The one she lost.

"That's mine!" Azi screams and charges, drawing her own blade. The trees echo with Jacek's laughter as the two clash together. Their battle is short. The warrior bests Azi with barely an effort. Drives her to the ground. Pins her with a foot. Raises Azi's lost sword to strike the killing blow.

"Not anymore," the warrior's cold voice shocks me. Sets my blood running hot. I look closer, at the slits of her helm. At her eyes. Green. Jungle green.

"Saesa?" I croak. "No!" I cry, but she doesn't even turn. It's like she can't hear me. Like I'm not even here.

Something snaps in Rian, bringing him to his senses. He casts a spell, throwing Saesa back into the brambles. Together, he and I scramble through the red and pull Azi back. Valenor wraps his cloak around us all. Hides us. When he does, the red doesn't seem so bad anymore. Saesa turns, looking for us. Stalking through the thorns. I can hear her breath through the slits of her helm. Panting. Wild.

"Careful," he warns us with a whisper. "Steady your emotions. Azaeli, she is your squire. Remember your vow to her. She is not your enemy. Jacek is."

We see him then. Jacek. He looks different now that he isn't the Dreamwalker. I expected him to be less intimidating, less frightening, but he isn't. He's just as scary. More, even, because of how wasted he looks. Like a shell of his former self. Dark hair. Sunken eyes. Bones poking from his skin. Skin Marked with blue-black curls. He moves to the center of the glen where Saesa stands, her shoulders rising and falling like a hunting cat. Sword drawn. Feral. She glares at us as he whispers to her.

"You see? I told you they would turn on you." His voice is soft. Velvety. "You belong with me, Sister."

Saesa's eyes flash with betrayal and hate as she stands beside him, looking for us. She isn't the girl I met anymore. The kind one who draped a cloak over my shoulders in the freezing cold. That Saesa is gone. He changed her. He created something else out of her. Even if we can stop her, help her, I don't see how she can be that same girl again.

I try to heed Valenor's advice. I try hard, but it's too difficult. I want to be the one to end this. I want my dagger to be the last one he feels. I want my eyes to be the last he looks into as his life leaves him. I want him to feel all the pain he's caused others.

Beside me, I know Azaeli feels the same way. Rian's got a hand on her arm. He's holding her back. Jacek turns slowly. His eyes are narrowed. Black against black. I back into Valenor, sinking into his cloak as Jacek peers right at us and then keeps on looking.

"It is useless to search with your eyes. You know that, Jacek." Valenor says with a hint of amusement. "Or have you already forgotten the secrets you'd stolen?" Something shifts around us. The cloak, blue like the sky and green like the meadow licks out toward Jacek. Whispers things that are only meant for him.

Jacek tilts his head. Listens. Lets Valenor's words influence him. His face relaxes. He seems like he might smile. His eyes close slowly. Saesa lowers her sword. Looks away from Jacek. I see the girl in her again. Unsure. Afraid. Valenor is talking to her. His whispers echo in my thoughts. His voice blends with another, more familiar one. One that I've longed to hear. Mevyn. He's still with him. The two speak together.

"It is time, Saesa. Break the binding. Release him and end your nightmare. Think of Ceras'lain. Focus on the elves. They are prepared and waiting."

Saesa gasps. Looks at Jacek, whose eyes snap open again.

"Whatever he's told you is a lie," Jacek seethes. "He is a master of deception and false thoughts. Who do you think I learned it from? Who do you think I looked up to after my parents abandoned me in this place? And now he seeks to destroy me. For what, old man? To put me to sleep and forget about me? Lock me away? You see now, Sister, why it isn't safe to remain here. If we are to live, if we are to survive, it must be away from this realm."

Saesa steps closer to Jacek. Links an arm through his.

"You're right," she says. "You have shown me so many truths. I could never trust them again. Let's leave this place together. The blood binding is no more. I release you, Brother, into the Waking." The air around them starts to twist and shimmer and suck them in. They spin like they're caught in a dust storm. She clings to him. Just before she disappears, her eyes meet mine, jungle green. Pleading. Gone.

Chapter Thirty-Six:

MUNDANE SPELLS

Azi

Saesa and Jacek's departure is so fast I barely have time to figure out what happened before a blur of blue streaks past me and dives into Rian. I draw my sword in a flash and spin to swing so quickly that Flitt protests loudly in my ear as she nearly loses her grip on my pauldron.

"Will you calm down?" she shouts with annoyance and I stop myself short. "Look who it is before you hurt someone!"

When I do, I'm shocked to see Mya. She looks up into Rian's face and takes it in her graceful hands to turn it this way and that.

"Is it you? Is it really you? You're alive! Oh, Rian! Oh, I thought..." her voice is husky as she chokes back her tears and pulls him into a hug. From the far end of the glen, a fox comes bobbing over the grass. His red coloring fades into the scenery so that all I can make out are his white chin and the brown tips of his ears.

As he approaches, his form shifts. He walks upright on two legs and begins growing. Fur becomes soft leather clothing, a bow, a quiver. His snout and ears shrink into his head, and his hair grows to cover his eyes with Elliot's familiar fringe. He flashes me a quick grin that's a mirror of his son's before throwing his arms around his wife and Rian.

"Have faith, I said," Elliot whispers. "Didn't I? I told you I could smell him here. I told you he wasn't..." he shakes his head, unable to finish.

"This way, this way," Stubs says as he hobbles excitedly through the red grass. Behind him, Brother Donal fights through the brambles as they catch his robes. I rush to help carve a path for him and offer my arm to pull him through.

"Thank you, my child," says the healer, sounding shaken and

hoarse. "It is good to see you well. Very good. Bless you, bless you." He can't seem to meet my eyes, but he pats my arm through my armor and clings to me as if letting me go would lose me forever. "And thank you, kind one, for leading us to them."

Stubs nods quickly and rushes to Valenor, who crouches to stroke the creature's grassy back.

"Well done indeed, little one," Valenor smiled at Stubs, who gazes dreamily into his eyes for a long moment. "Thank you," the Dreamwalker says before sending Stubs away through the brambles once more. Valenor stands slowly and turns to the rest of us.

"While it warms me to see you all well, I'm afraid there is little time for happy reunions," he says apologetically. "We are here physically," he gestures to me, Rian, and Tib, "but the rest of you are here only in dreaming. When you wake, you shall be in Ceras'lain, where your comrades await. Where Jacek now walks free."

"Who are…?" Mya trails off, tearing her gaze from her son's face as she peers at Valenor. Elliot turns to him as well, his nose twitching.

"Valenor," he says. "It seems we've missed some of the adventure."

"Quite." Valenor smiles. "Wake now, and we shall meet you momentarily in Ceras'lain."

Under Valenor's instruction, Donal is the first to fade. He's followed by Mya, who leaves her son reluctantly. Elliot offers Valenor a bow and a knowing smile before he joins the other two. Before I can make sense of the gesture we, too, are spinning away. Valenor's way is different than ours when traveling from one realm to another. It's less chaotic. It feels more like we're soaring. I cling to Rian and bury my head into his chest as he folds me into his arms and bends to kiss my lips. It always amazes me how being so close to him makes every worry, every fear, every bit of anger fade away. For this short moment, it's just him and me. Us, together, is all that will ever matter.

We land with a soft flutter of Valenor's cloak on the grassy carpet of the dome where we left Mum and Uncle just moments ago.

"What happened?" Mum asks. She smoothes my hair back and looks me over, her eyes filled with concern. I take her hand and squeeze it reassuringly. Mya, Elliot, and Brother Donal are being tended to by the elves as they stir in their white chaises. One by one, they sit up.

"Saesa released him," Rian explains to the others gathered

around. Together we gaze about warily as if expecting Jacek to pop out of a shadow and lunge for the attack. The elves seem especially on edge.

"They are not here. She was to focus on Ceras'lain. I told her as much," Valenor says. He tilts his head, listening to the sky. I wonder, as the Dreamwalker with his mantle restored, how much he can actually hear.

"Ceras'lain is a rather large place," Uncle offers. "Perhaps her thoughts led her elsewhere within its borders."

"Brother," Tib murmurs. Everyone turns to him and he looks up from his thoughts. "It's obvious, isn't it? It was the last thing she said: Brother. She went to Raefe."

One of the elves gasps and looks to her comrades.

"She has taken him to Felescue," she says. At once, three of the guardians who have been standing vigil whistle. Outside, a rush of wings and the soft rustle of grass tell me that their cygnets have arrived. I glance at Rian. Flying again. He gives me an apologetic shrug and a grin that makes me feel a little better.

"We'll meet you there," Valenor says to my relief. "Bring as many as you can muster. The rest of you, with me."

"I'll get the others," Mum says. "Donal, come with me." She gives me a quick kiss and rushes off just as Valenor flares out his cloak.

"Quickly," he says, and as the elves rush out with Mya and Elliot to mount their cygnets, the cloak settles over us and we step away to Felescue.

We're greeted instantly by the sound of a sword fight, and I have barely enough time to take in our lush green surroundings and the perfect sparkling waters that trickle from white stone outcroppings all around a silver pool. A woman kneels close by, unmoving. Red-gold hair tumbles down her back in tight, shimmering curls. Her eyes are open and streaming with tears as she watches the battle taking place just steps away.

"Evelei?" Tib whispers. He reaches to nudge her shoulder but Valenor catches his hand and shakes his head. He rest his other hand on my shoulder to keep me with him as I follow the woman's gaze.

"You never believed in me," Saesa cries as she brings her sword down in a heavy arc. By his coloring alone, it's obvious the boy she's fighting is her brother. He parries her with the slender blade of his rapier and spins quickly. When he does I can see that his tunic has been slashed and stained with red.

"Raefe," Tib says under his breath. "Saesa, what are you doing?"

Valenor raises a finger to his lips as Saesa swings again. He's watching the woods beyond and I look and see him too. A shimmer of a shadow, hiding among the lush ferns, laughing.

"*This is what he does with his freedom*?" Rian pushes to me.

"Just when I think I'm starting to understand you people…" Flitt whispers.

"I admit," Raefe says breathlessly, "you've improved. How much of it is really you, though?"

Saesa lunges at him again, slashing at his knee with the blade. The attack slices through the strap of his leg armor, which flaps around as he stumbles toward the water.

"See?" he says as he steadies himself and she presses toward him again. "You let yourself move before you think. An inch higher could've taken off my leg." His teaching words don't do well to cover his true feelings. There's an underlying pain and fear in his voice as he speaks to her. Saesa doesn't reply. She swings again, this time cutting across his chest with a heavy slash that blooms quickly with blood. The blow knocks Raefe to his knees, but he scrambles quickly to stand again.

Beside us, Evelei chokes on her sobs. I glance back at Valenor and wonder why he's not doing anything to put a stop to this.

Raefe presses his free hand to his chest and throws up his rapier to block another swing from Saesa. When I look closely I realize that she's crying, too. Her face has changed. I've seen that look in her eyes before. It's the helpless look of someone whose body is being forced to do something they would never do.

"Valenor," I whisper.

"Yes I know," he bends to me. "Do you see them? The threads? Look closely, Azaeli. Break them."

I can feel Rian's eyes on me as I stare into the space between Jacek and Saesa. It's difficult to focus at first. I'm too distracted by the battle between my squire and her brother. I'm too afraid of the outcome. If Saesa comes out the victor, she'll never forgive herself. If Raefe wins, then I failed to protect her.

I close my eyes for a moment and try to focus on the first time I used this magic myself. I see Stubs running through the grass, his eyes filled with pleading, his little legs pumping. When I open my eyes again, the threads are there plain as day. The thrill of magic rushes through me, filling me with power.

I'm not sure what I'm supposed to do, so I do what makes sense to me. I imagine myself charging them, my own sword raised. To my shock, a golden figure rushes forth from me, a mirror of myself, her sword raised. She charges the threads, severing them. Saesa instantly throws her sword away and drops to her knees. Raefe does the same and holds his sister, rocking her and stroking her hair. Among the ferns, Jacek gives a frustrated growl.

My golden knight isn't finished. She whirls toward the woman beside us and swings her sword again. The magical bindings holding her break away, and the woman jumps up and rushes to the children as the knight fades away. The rush of energy drops, leaving me barely able to stand. Rian seems to anticipate it, and slides his arm around my waist to keep me upright.

"Whoa," Flitt whispers. "That's a neat trick, Azi." She shines a little light on me and it helps some. I can stand now at least, but I might be in trouble if I have to draw my sword and fight.

"Fool old man," Jacek's voice thunders through the trees, causing their leaves to shiver. "Do you think that a victory? I was merely playing. Waiting for you. You see, I know now. I know how weak you are in this realm and how strong I am. I know exactly what I can do and what you cannot do. What you won't do. Such a waste of power."

"Tib." Valenor whispers. He gives him a nod and Tib steps from view, his dagger out and ready to strike.

"Don't you wonder," Jacek addresses us, "why he hasn't attacked me yet? It's because he cannot. He can only work through others to achieve his victory, and he won't. His kindness is a weakness. That mantle is going to waste. Don't worry though. I don't want it anymore. I don't need it. I have followers who have been waiting for this day. Armies amassing to seek me. You've fought some of them before Azaeli, Rian."

Within the ferns he raises a hand to show a flash of red stone.

"Poised at Zhagen. Cresten. Belvitch. Yes, even Cerion. Our influence is everywhere. You heard your prince on the stone you discovered. Who do you think put the words in his mouth? Who was Ornis scribing to at the Keep in Kythshire all those months ago? Not just me, no. My mother's work. My father's. So many others. We have been lying in wait for our moment. Readying for the right time to strike. That time is now." He raises the stone to his lips and starts to whisper into it.

"Rian," Valenor whispers, and beside me Rian thrusts his hands forward. His fingertips crackle with purple energy that shoots across the pool at Jacek.

I'm disappointed for Rian at first. The spell does little damage to the Sorcerer. Then I realize that wasn't the intent. It didn't hurt Jacek, but it utterly destroyed his shield ward. As he raises his hands to cast the protective spell again, Tib emerges right in front of him and swiftly drives his dagger into Jacek's chest.

Jacek screams and thrusts his hands at the boy. Black tendrils shoot toward Tib but fizzle around him instead of taking their effect. Jacek is too shocked to react. Tib thrusts again, this time driving the dagger into his side.

"Julini. Shoel. Zevlain." Valenor says quietly, and the three elves drop from the sky and land lightly to surround Jacek. Tib looks tiny beside them, like the child he is. One of the elves whispers something fiercely as the three raise swords and spears to strike. Tib does the same with his dagger. Shoel moves to stand in front of Tib, to guard him. They block my view of Jacek, whose ragged breathing fills the otherwise silent area.

He whispers a spell and the group of attackers are thrust back. Two of them land in the pool. Shoel crashes against Tib and they fly into the ferns. They jump back to their feet. A short distance away, Saesa pushes herself to her feet. She lays my old sword down with reverence and draws her own from her hip to stalk toward Jacek.

Raefe tries to follow with his rapier, but Evelei holds him tightly and presses her hands to his bleeding wounds. Julini steps in front of Saesa to keep her from charging.

"You are utterly alone here," Valenor addresses the Sorcerer. "Surrender, and we shall spare your life."

"Why doesn't he just leave?" I whisper as Jacek stands with his hands out and ready to cast at the next person to approach him. The others circle around him warily, well aware that he could easily end them with a spell before they could close the distance to charge him. Tib is fuming to charge him again, but Shoel won't let him go alone. I try to unclasp my sword, but my use of magic has drained me too much. I can't lift it.

"He has no way to," Valenor replies. "He cannot travel as we can through the realms. He has only mundane methods of travel now. As well, the borders of Ceras'lain are too well-guarded to permit him to cross. He is biding his time here. Waiting for an opportunity to present itself. Essentially, this Sorcerer who considers himself all-powerful is trapped." Valenor explains loud enough for Jacek to hear. "Not an eventuality you considered, was it, boy?"

"It makes no difference," Jacek sneers. He seems undeterred by the blood from the two wounds Tib inflicted seeping through his black robes. His eyes are wild and determined as he raises his hands to cast again and the shield ward shimmers around him. Tib breaks Shoel's hold and charges, his dagger raised mid-strike as Jacek casts again. This time a globe of flames shoots from his hands and blasts Tib straight through the chest. Saesa and I scream but Tib only laughs.

"I thought Sorcerers were supposed to be smart," he says. "How many times are you going to try to blast me before you figure out it doesn't actually do anything?" He smoothes his vest where the flame ball struck. It isn't even singed.

"There are ways around that," Jacek whispers. "You have a thing against roots, don't you? A fear. I remember. It's such a simple spell. It's almost child's play."

Jacek swirls his fingers toward a nearby tree and a thunderous splintering and crackling fills the air as the roots break free of the earth and shoot toward Tib. He tries to run away but they catch him and bind him and squeeze him until he's gasping for breath. Saesa rushes to hack at the bindings but Jacek flicks a finger and the earth before her shakes and rumbles and forms itself into a man that drives a rocky fist at her.

"Thank you for the reminder," Jacek smirks. "I'd forgotten about these mundane spells. You are a master of them, aren't you, Rian? I've fought one of yours before. Glass. So fragile."

Jacek casts again and the trees crack from their foundations. Trunks split into legs and arms. Chunks of earth and stone form immense creatures with enormous fists. Water swirls from the pool and forms a dozen crystalline figures. Golems. They plunge toward Rian and me, splashing and gurgling. I draw my sword and ready myself as Rian's shields bolster us.

"Elementals," Valenor murmurs. "Think opposites."

All around us is chaos. Tib is turning blue as he's squeezed by the roots. Saesa and the elves hack at a dozen giant tree-men who lash and stab with their branches. One strike catches Shoel under the arm and flings him away. Another stabs a ragged splinter into Saesa's thigh. Above us, the cygnets circle and cry out eerily. The elves pause in their battle and look up.

"We're needed at the wall," Zevlain shouts.

"No, it's a trick," says Julini.

"Let's just kill one Sorcerer," Shoel grunts, eyeing Jacek, "then we'll go and check." They bolster themselves and try to force their way through the mass of moving trees to get to Jacek, but they're thrown back again. I hear a rustle in the woods and see Donal and Dacva push through the brush into the clearing.

Another sound emanates from the woods around us. Mya's song of Strength. It fills me up just in time to slash at the water creature that has finally driven itself through the shields with the force of a rogue wave.

"Air," whispers Rian beside me. He shouts a spell and a cyclone of wind bursts forth from him. It catches the water in its grips and sends it spraying in all directions. Elliot charges through the ferns and spins a kick at another of the water elementals, splashing it into raindrops.

Raefe and Evelei narrowly escape being crushed by a stalking birch. He deposits her into the safety of the ferns and creeps around toward Tib, who is still fighting for breath. Valenor leaves our side to hide her away, and I'm left feeling suddenly vulnerable.

I have no time to fret, though. Three more water elementals surge toward us. Rian calls another cyclone to spin at them but I can tell he's growing tired. A battle this heated is taxing for a Mage, and he was already exhausted when he arrived. I find myself wishing for Uncle and wondering why he hasn't arrived yet.

Valenor's mantle billows out over all of us and suddenly I feel refreshed and empowered, as though I've had the most perfect night's sleep and I can face anything. Finally, I find the strength to draw my sword. Beside me, Rian squares his shoulders and casts again. Across the way, the elves and the others fight harder. Even Tib gets a little color back. Still, the roots are relentless and I realize that he's too defeated even to panic at this point.

"Come on," I call to Rian, who stays close to me as I rush to Tib.

"Opposites. Fire." I say to Rian as I slam my blade into the thickest root.

"It'd burn him too," Rian spins and casts another wind gust at an approaching water elemental.

"He's immune," I say.

"To magical fire," Rian flings a spell mid-sentence as I hack again at Tib's captor. "Once it catches on the wood, it's not magic anymore."

"*I'll be right back*," Flitt pushes to me. I nod.

I swing again and take another chunk out of the root, but it's too slow. By the time I'm through even this one, Tib will have suffocated for sure. I glance up at him. He's turning blue again.

"How, then?" I growl as I hack in anger. All around us, the trees and the earth and the water pommel our allies. Saesa is sprawled on the ground nearby. Shoel and his companions are bloodied, but still determined to get through the line to Jacek.

"Kill the spell caster," Rian narrows his eyes. Beside us, Elliot takes out two waters and an earth, punching and kicking until he's soaked and muddy. He drives on toward the trees, but a false step and a lucky swing by a branch sends him soaring over us. He lands with a sickening thud in the ferns beside Valenor.

"Da!" Rian screams and stretches his hands out before him. Shards of glass spray from his palms, shooting toward Jacek in a blur. Two of the elves fall as we're swarmed by trees and stone and water. Beside us, Tib's breath goes ragged and frantic. The third elf falls. There's no one left but Rian and me. Even Mya's song has ended. Valenor's influence stretches over the area, doing all he can. Protecting. Bolstering. Convincing us that we still have a chance.

A rock being swings its fist at me and I duck, but Rian is right behind me and he takes the full blow. I scream as he crumples to the ground. When I swing my sword, the strike against the stone jars my arms. There's no time to check on my love. The attack is relentless. As I swing again and again, I peer through cracks toward the Sorcerer who stands undisturbed and grinning as he surveys his near-victory. His shields are down. If only I could reach him. One more blow would end his life.

Valenor's cloak flicks out to the fallen. He's trying to keep them alive, somehow. I know it. It's all he can do to help.

There is no way, though. I'm the only one still on my feet, and my opponents are too many. Beside me, the roots crack and move. I imagine them constricting, crushing poor Tib. He doesn't make a sound, though. He hasn't for a while. I want to look, to check on him, but I can't risk it. I force myself to keep fighting.

Trees and stone and water bear down on me, but suddenly I'm not alone anymore. A gust of wind as strong as a storm blows the water golems back, bursting them into droplets. At first I think it's Rian, but he's still lying behind me in the grass. Then I see a glint of iridescent green hovering beside me and feel the winds die down.

"Ha, no match for me, are they?" Shush whispers hurriedly. "Swing, Azi! I've got the water ones, no worries."

"And I've got these," Twig pops up on the other side of me. He shakes a scolding finger at the trees that crackle and bear down, and they settle where they are and stretch their branches up to the sky. "Good girls," he says with a quick nod. "And you, stay still," he says to the rock golems. Grass and roots spring up around them, covering them, holding them, breaking them down to earth again. Of course. Twig is an earth fairy.

"Get Tib," I call to him, "He's in the roots!" There's no time to hear his reply. More water golems come. Shush makes a cyclone to break them apart. The force of it crashes into the trees, shattering them.

"Told you I'd be right back!" Flitt says cheerfully while Shush sends yet another windstorm. "And I brought friends. Oh! Azi, look out!"

I don't see the shard of wood until it's too late. It splinters through my neck, sending pain searing up into my skull and down my spine. My knees buckle. My breath comes in short gurgles. My mouth fills with warm, thick blood. The tree comes to life again. It raises its foot, ready to stomp and smash and end me.

As my vision fades I'm aware of Twig beside me, taming the great creature again. I hear something else. Arrows. Several of them flying at once.

Through the dark blur that closes in, I focus hard on Jacek. His face is locked in a grimace. Five arrows neatly line his torso from his neck to his navel. Five more strike him at once as a blue light bathes the forest. Tib appears in front of him again, freed from the roots. He plunges his dagger into Jacek's robes. The black char of fairy fire spreads from the blade, crackling slowly, consuming him.

"You think this is over?" Jacek hisses through the blood on his lips as the charcoal creeps up his chest. "It has only begun. The wheels are in motion. The Order lurks, waiting to strike. You feared *me*," he laughs, gurgling blood. "You have no idea. Bask in your cursed victory." He reaches for Tib but his blackened arm crumbles. "May it forever blind you to the truth."

He falls backward into the ferns with a heavy thud and a puff of soot and smoke. The blue light nears as I struggle to keep myself awake. If I don't panic, if I breathe slowly, I can live.

"Azi," Shush whispers. My bangs rustle in the breeze as he hovers over me. "I'm sorry."

"Azi," Twig pulls the great splinter of wood from my neck. I feel the blood gush warm over my shoulder.

"She'll be all right," Flitt says, but she doesn't sound very convinced. "She's strong." Her light floods my vision, blocking out everything around me. I feel her land on my chest. The wound at my neck tingles. "Hang on, Azi. The healers are coming."

"Rian," I whisper. If it's going to end this way, I need him. Need to hold his hand and know he's safe. I try to look for him but I can't move much. Valenor's cloak flicks over me and I feel a hand squeeze mine. It's Rian's, I know it is.

The thought that he's okay gives me the strength I need to hold on. I blink through Flitt's bright light. I can't see Rian, but I do see Tib. He's standing over the spot where Jacek fell. He holds his arms out to someone. Her black hair shimmers in Flitt's light. The bow at her shoulder glows soft blue. The arrows make sense now. Ki. Flitt strokes my cheek. Someone approaches. Brother Donal. I sigh with relief. It's over. The healers are here. We're safe.

Chapter Thirty-Seven:

LIFEBRINGER

Tib

Alone on the widow's walk of the Ganvent manse, I sit and watch the ships come and go. I like it up here, where I can see for leagues and leagues. The cool breeze of Springsdawn rustles my hair. A group of ships catches my eye. Three of them coming in. I raise my new double spyglass. The one the Admiral brought me. I get a good look at them. Banners. Sunteri banners. Prince Vorance's ships. One is faster than the others. I focus on the crow's nest. The ratlines. The sails. I imagine Cap at the helm. Remember sitting up there, watching. Remember Mevyn.

Memories, Ki says, are precious. Hold on to them. Keep them safe. I think of the moment we became brother and sister again. Back in the battle at Felescue. Back when I thought all was lost until Twig spoke to the roots and set me free.

I couldn't believe my eyes when I saw her. At first I thought it was one of Jacek's tricks. It couldn't have been, though. He was dead now. Her arrows and my dagger made sure of it. I watched him turn to dust.

She smiled at me and ran to me, slinging her bow over her shoulder. Hugged me. Held me close. Not like before in the Ring. This time, she really knew me. This time she remembered. I wanted to keep hugging her and never let go. But Azi lay at our feet, cold and still. Rian, too. In fact, everything was silent. Even the elves were down.

Flitt was working healing over Azaeli. She was covered in blood but I couldn't see from what. I healed her with my vials. Healed Dacva, too, and Donal. Kept a tight hold on Ki's hand, though, just in case. She leaned toward me. Told me she was proud of me. Told me she was sorry for leaving me. Her eyes flashed blue.

The little door to the ladder creaks, and Saesa pops through it excitedly. She's still dressed for training. Her blue and gold squire sash flaps in the breeze.

"Tib, look what's come!" she says excitedly. She waves a couple of scrolls at me. One is tied with a purple ribbon. It has Princess Margary's seal: a tiny fairy perched over a flower.

"The royal wedding invitations," she says before I open mine. "One for you and one for me. We're to be Margary's special guests. Isn't it exciting?"

"That's great," I say. The fairy symbol reminds me of Mevyn. Of Flitt. I let my mind wander again, back to that same day.

Ki and I had gone to Valenor's side to settle in the ferns. After a while, Flitt tore herself from Azi's side to hover in front of me. She held out a stone.

"I'm supposed to give this to you," she said. "It was meant for Mevyn. Crocus said you earned it. She said it's up to you now. We'll help you if you need it."

She dropped the stone into my palm and right away I felt a stirring inside of me. Images of fairies flashed through my mind. Mindspinner. Weaver of Threads. Keeper of Songs. All of them sang to me. My heart began to race as I watched Flitt dart back to Azi and shine her light.

"As will I," Valenor said, patting my shoulder, "Lifebringer."

Saesa stands beside me on the widow's walk and we look off together toward the south. She doesn't say anything. Her shoulder presses against mine. She knows when I'm quiet, it's because I'm thinking back. She knows how important my memories are to me. I picture what's beyond the horizon. Elespen. Sunteri.

Heat. Sand. Wind. Stones. Sweat.

I never wanted to go back to that place. When I left, I swore I'd never return. It was different that last time, though. Not frightening or sad. Maybe because I knew it wasn't my home anymore. The distant fields of red were only memories. I have friends. People who care about me. Saesa. Ki. Azaeli. Rian. I chuckle at the last. Never thought I'd name a Mage my friend.

The rest of them were there, too. They earned a place. Mya and Elliot, who fought bravely against Jacek. Lisabella and the rest of the Elite who held back attackers at the Wall while the elves fought beside us. Everyone was there. All of my friends.

Valenor, too. His cloak billowed around us. Kept the dust and the heat away.

We stood together on the edge of the great empty bowl that once held all of Sunteri's magic. The drained, dead Wellspring. Ki rested a hand on my shoulder. I remember being so glad that Iren let her stay with me, just for that moment. After that, we'd say goodbye. They offered to let me stay with her in Kythshire. I thought about it a lot, but I didn't want to live among fairies every day.

Ki's eyes flashed blue and I knew the Spirit of the Shadow Crag was with us, too. There to witness what was about to happen. I reached into my pocket and looked at the others, who nodded to me.

I remember how the stone glimmered in my hand as I held it over the wasted spring. I closed my eyes and waited. I felt the stirring inside me, the fluttering of wings. It was the same as when Flitt first gave it to me.

One by one, they left me. Sage of the Known, with his scrolls and strange orbs. Keeper of Songs, who hummed softly as she parted. Warden of Sands, which swirled around him like a dust storm. One by one they placed a hand on the stone until all of them were reunited. The last to join them was Mindspinner, who turned and blew me a kiss before she rested her hand on the pebble. They weren't solid. More like ghosts or apparitions of who they once had been.

Together they drifted away from me until they were centered over the Wellspring. The rest of us waited and watched as the fairies poised themselves in place. Nothing happened. They bowed their heads and looked toward us.

"What's wrong?" Azi whispered.

"They are incomplete," Valenor said quietly by my shoulder. I felt a shift in him and watched in disbelief as another tiny apparition formed over his outstretched hand. "Old friend."

I let go of Ki's hand as a wisp of Mevyn turned to bow to me. He was barely visible, but it was absolutely him. When I reached out to him, he moved away from me and shook his head. I understood. A touch from me would have made him fade. He'd be no more. He drifted to join the others, but still nothing happened.

"They need a little boost." Flitt chirped from Azi's shoulder. She flew to hover in the center of the rest of them and as her colors touched each one of them, golden light shot over their heads in streams like a fountain. It flowed from the stone into each of the fairies and spilled over into the drained spring to fill it.

It filled to the brim quickly and flooded over. The banks of the pool turned green and burst with flowers of yellow and white and purple. Saplings sprouted from the sand and grew and stretched overhead. The restored magic crept onward as far as we could see. Dense palms and thick vines created a canopy of cool green shade. Water dripped from the leaves. Birds sang. I remember turning around and around to watch in awe as the oasis grew and flourished. Waterfalls trickled nearby. Frogs croaked.

"Come now," Valenor said fondly. "It is ready for you." He opened his arms beside me. Orbs of light no bigger than my fingertip emerged from his cloak. Dozens. Hundreds. A thousand, maybe. Pink, red, orange, blue, yellow, and green. They floated around us curiously. I could hear giggling and singing from them. Whispering. Chattering. Excitement. Relief.

At the center of the pool, the pebble was spent. Its magic was thick in the air around us now, just like in Kythshire. The fairies holding it sunk lower and lower until they disappeared into the Wellspring. I turned to look around, hoping to see Mevyn. No one else was looking. Their attention was on the Lady Knight and her Mage.

At the Wellspring's edge, framed by glittering gold, Rian knelt before Azaeli. He had her hand in his, and he was gazing up at her, smiling. Flitt's light danced over them brightly as she hovered between them, grinning. I remember how it made Azaeli's eyes sparkle.

Rian pulled something from his vest that glinted in the light. A ring. The others gathered around them and I edged closer to watch.

"Azaeli Hammerfel," Rian said, clearing his throat. He was nervous, anyone could see that. "Here in this place, surrounded by magic, all I see is you. All I ever see is you. You have stood beside me through doubt, through adversity. In battle and in happiness. I can't imagine my life without you. I can't imagine a day without you. Azi, with your parents' blessing and with all the love in my heart, I ask you. Will you be my bride?"

Saesa clung to my arm, her eyes wide. Everyone around us seemed to be holding their breath. Even the fairy orbs were silent as they drifted and bobbed nearby. Azi grinned down at Rian. She nodded, but didn't say anything as tears streamed down her face. Then he took her in his arms and when they kissed, everyone erupted into cheers and whoops. Even the fairies.

In the midst of the celebration, the quiet pool of the Wellspring rippled. No one else noticed but me as tips of golden wings appeared in the center of it. A spear tip followed. I nudged Saesa and pointed as the familiar head of golden, waving hair emerged, followed by shoulders of leaf-like golden armor, a broad chest, and stout legs. I watched in disbelief as Mevyn floated over the surface of the Wellspring toward us.

He stopped before Azaeli and Rian, who were still being hugged and congratulated by the others. They slowly fell into a hush as one by one they noticed him.

"You have done us a great service," Mevyn said gravely. "We are grateful to you, one and all." He opened his arms to them. Behind him, the others of his kind hovered in a group to watch and listen. Mindspinner glanced at me and smiled. Weaver of Threads gave me a nod.

"Our gratitude is such that we gladly name you as allies, as long as you act in the interest of the Wellsprings. If you should need us, then you will come to remember us, and we shall allow you passage. We hope that you understand the measures that must be taken at this time."

Valenor nodded beside me. His cloak caressed all of us. Made us move closer together in a bunch so that Mevyn could see us all properly.

"It is essential," said Mevyn, "for us to protect our restored Wellspring." He looked from one of them to the next, his golden light glinting in their eyes. He didn't look at me, though. He kept his promise. Never again would he meddle with my mind.

The rest gazed into his eyes. Even Saesa. Even Ki. He never made such a promise to them. The blue stone of her engagement ring glinted and sparkled in the golden light as Azi stood hand in hand with Rian, agreeing to the spell that would make them forget.

"And now," Mevyn began, "for the preservation of my people and for your own protection…"

"What are you thinking about?" Saesa asks, jarring me back to the present. I look at her. Meet her bright green eyes.

"Old friends," I say quietly. I'm not sure exactly what she remembers and what she doesn't, so don't go into details.

"Well," she says, "let's go in." She picks up my spyglass and tucks the invitations away. "We don't want to be late for supper. Nessa's invited My Lady Knight. I think she's going to try and get her to talk about the accusations against Prince Eron. Oh, and my mum made a cake."

I let her take me by the hand and pull me through to the ladder. The roots, the trees, they're only memories. The closed space doesn't frighten me anymore. After everything I've been through, not much does.

The End

CHARACTER GLOSSARY

Amei (Ay-mee) Princess Amei Plethore: Prince Eron's wife.
Asio *(Ah-zee-oh)* King Asio Plethore: The first king in the Plethore Dynasty.
Azi *(A-zee, A-zay-lee (Not OZZY)* Sir Azaeli Hammerfel: A Knight of His Majesty's Elite, and Ambassador to Kythshire. Daughter of Lisabella and Benen.
Stenneler *(STEN-nel-urh)* Baron Marcel Stenneler: Custodian of Kordelya Keep.
Benen *(Ben-in)* Sir Benen Hammerfel: Knight of His Majesty's Elite, Azi's father, and Lisabella's husband.
Bette *(Bet)* Bette Hansley: A cook at the Ganvent Manse.
Brother Donal *(DON-ol)* Brother Donal Vincend: Healer of His Majesty's Elite.
Bryse *(Brice)* Bryse Daborr: Shieldmaster of His Majesty's Elite, partner to Cort.
Cap *(Cap)*Captain Odell Ali: Captain of the Royal Sunteri Navy Scout Ship who hired Tib on.
Celorin *(Sell-OR-in)* Celorin Treftora: Elf healer on the White Wall.
Cly Zhrel *(KLY zrell)* Cly Zhrel III: Warlord leading the attacks against the White Wall.
Corbin *(Core-bin)* Master Corbin Mordale: Sorcerer who fought at Kythshire, married to Dinaea.
Cort *(Court)* Cort Finzael: Member of His Majesty's Elite. Swashbuckler and partner to Bryse.
Crocus *(Crow-cus)* Chantelle Rejune Cordelia Unphasei Seren: A plant fairy. Leader of the Ring at Kythshire, partner to Scree.
Dabble *(DAH-bull)* Dabble: A fairy. Overseer at the Maker's Tree, creator of Flitt's Diamond.
Dacva *(Dock-Vuh)* Dacva Archomyn: Apprentice healer to Donal, Azi's former rival in training.
Dinaea *(Dine-AY)* Mistress Dinaea Mordale: Sorceress who fought at Kythshire, married to Corbin.
Diovicus *(Dye-ah-vik-us)* King Diovicus Srisvin: The Sorcerer King of legend, who nearly overtook Kythshire.
Dorian *(DOR-ee-un)* Captain Dorian Evret: Captain of Cerion's Navy scout ship, messenger for Admiral Ganvent
Dub *(Dub)* Wade Cordoven: A thug for hire.
Dumfrey *(DUM-free)* Dumfrey Pilsen: A bumbling Mage in the employ of the Royal Family of Cerion.
Edsin *(ED-son)* Edsin Merribane: The driver of Tib's carriage on his journey to Ceras'lain
Elliot *(El-ee-oht)* Elliot Eldinae: Member of His Majesty's Elite. Husband to Mya, and Rian's Father.
Elmsworth *(ELMS-worth)* Davin Elmsworth: Captain of Arms, in charge of the royal armory and arsenal.
Ember *(Ember)* Ember: A Fire fairy, and high-ranking member of the Ring in Kythshire.
Emmie *(EM-mee)* Emeliana: The only officially adopted child in the Ganvent house.
Emris *(EM-riss)* Master Emris Boled: Sorcerer who fought at Kythshire and was destroyed by Iren.

Eron *(Err-ohn)* Prince Eron Plethore: Son of Tirnon and Naelle. Prince and Heir of Cerion.
Errie *(AIR-ee)* Eron Kreston: Child of Maisie, a resident at the Ganvent Manse.
Fenston *(FEN-stin)* Captain Gabriel Fenston: Captain riding with the Elite to Kordelya
Finn *(Fin)* Isaac Finnvale: A member of the Royal Guard, and Princess Margy's favorite.
Flitt *(Flit)* Felicity Lumine Instacia Tenacity Teeming: A Light fairy who has befriended Azi and bonded to her.
Freland *(FREE-lund)* Justin Freland: A member of the City Guard.
Fresi *(FREZ-ee)* Fresintal Plethore: A cousin of Prince Eron.
Gaethon *(GAY-thon)* Gaethon Ethari: Headmaster of the Academy, Member of HME, Azi's uncle, Rian's mentor.
Ganvent (GAN-vent) Admiral Tristan Ganvent: Nessa Ganvent's husband, and Admiral of Cerion's Royal Navy.
Garsi *(Gar-SEE)* Garsi: A toddler, the youngest girl at the Ganvent Manse.
Gorgen *(Gore-Genn)* Master Kivin Gorgen: A Sorcerer who fought at the keep at Kythshire.
Grenis *(Gren-NISS)* Grenis: King Tirnon's servant in the treaty room.
Gruss *(Gruss)* Edwin Grusteven: Carriage guard for Tib, Saesa, and Raefe.
Hub *(Hub)* Filip Hubvenchlis: A swordsman. Saesa's Trainer.
Iren *(EYE-ren)* Iren: Guardian of the northern border of Kythshire, Spirit of the Shadow Crag.
Jac *(Jack)* Jac: A member of the Royal Guard who befriends Azi.
Jacek *(JAY-sek)* Jacek Mordale: A Dreamwalker.
Julini *(Joo-LEE-nee)* Julini Aluvren: An elf archer, and member of the White Line.
Ki *(Ki like eye)* Ki: Formerly Viala, an archer in the service of Iren, and Tib's sister.
Kris *(Kris)* Kristoff Plethore: A cousin of Prince Eron.
Lilen *(LILL-in)* Lilen: A Mage Apprentice, the eldest girl at the Ganvent Manse.
Lisabella *(Liz-uh-BELL-uh)* Lisabella Hammerfel: Knight of His Majesty's Elite, a Paladin, Azi's mother, married to Benen.
Luca *(LOO-kah)* Luca Savaneli: Groundskeeper for His Majesty's Elite.
Maisie *(MAY-zee)* Maiseline Kreston: A former palace maid, mother to Errie. Lives in the Ganvent Manse.
Margy *(MAR-jee)* Princess Margary Plethore: The youngest member of Cerion's Royal Family.
Master Bental *(Ah-NOD BEN-tul)* Anod Bental: High Master of the Academy, Mage-Advisor to the King of Cerion.
Master Rendin *(AY-brim REN-din)* Master Abrim Rendin: A high-ranking Mage at the Academy.
Mevyn *(MEV-in)* Mason Evret Valor Yester Numinous: The last of the Sunteri fae.
Mouli *(MOO-lee)* Mouli Savaneli: Housekeeper and cook for His Majesty's Elite. Married to Luca.
Muster *(MUSS-ter)* Muster: A half-giant thug for hire.
Mya *(MY-uh (not MEE-uh)* Mya Eldinae: A bard. Leader of His Majesty's Elite. Rian's mother, and Elliot's wife.
Myer *(MY-er)* Lars Myer: Captain of the King's Guard of Cerion.
Naelle *(Ny-ELLE)* Queen Naelle Plethore: Queen of Cerion.

Nan *(Nan (like Ann)* Ivenia Nullen: Tib's grandmother. A slave of the dye fields.
Nate *(Nate)* Nathen Kreston: A royal page.
Nessa *(NESS-uh)* Vanessa Ganvent: Wife of Admiral Ganvent. Foster mother to Saesa, Raefe, and many others.
Oren *(OI I-rehn)* Oren: Plant fairies. The Guardians of the Eastern border of Kythshire.
Ornis *(Or-niss)* Master Ornis Vanet: A Sorcerer who fought at the keep at Kythshire.
Patyr *(PAY-ter)* Patyr Ellings: A Royal Guard.
Pearl *(Pearl)* Pearl: Azi's Horse.
Prince Vorance (*Vore-ANS*) Prince Vorance Evresel: Prince of Sunteri, and Sarabel's suitor.
Raefe *(RAFE)* Raefe Coltori: A swashbuckling apprentice, Saesa's brother, lives in the Ganvent Manse.
Ragnor (RAG-nore) Master Halasan Ragnor: Azi's swordsmanship trainer.
Resh Alanso *(Rehsh Uh-LON-zo)* Resh Drish Alanso: A Sunteri Knight, and Prince Vorance's personal detail.
Resh Kanalal *(Rehsh KON-o-lol)* Resh Olian Kanalal: A Sunteri Knight, and Prince Vorance's personal detail.
Rian *(RI-an)* Rian Eldinae: Mage of His Majesty's Elite, Azi's childhood friend and love. Son of Mya and Elliot.
Ruben *(ROO-bin*)Ruben: An orphan living at the Ganvent Manse.
Saesa *(SAY-suh)* Saesa Coltori: An aspiring swordswoman, a friend of Tib, lives in the Ganvent Manse.
Sara *(SAY-ra-belle)* Princess Sarabel Plethore: Princess of Cerion. Middle child, betrothed to Prince Vorance.
Scree *(SCREE)* Subter Crag Rever Enstil Evrest: Earth fairy. A rock, son of Iren, leader of the Ring.
Shoel (*SHOHL*) Shoel Aluvren: White Line, section leader
Shush *(SHUSH like rush)* Soren Hasten Udi Swiftish Haven: A Wind fairy, and high-ranking member of the Ring in Kythshire.
Stone (*Stone* Cornesta) Stone: Leader of a band of thugs for hire.
Stubs *(Stubs)* Just Stubs: An earth and plant elemental who lives in the Dreaming.
Thurle *(THURL)* Garison Thurleft: Guard put in charge of Margy after Finn.
Tib *(TIB (like bib)* Tibreseli Nullen: A slave to the dye fields who escaped to Cerion.
Tirie *(Tee-ree)* Tirianne Costi: Margy's Nursemaid
Tirnon *(TEER-non)* King Tirnon Plethore: His Majesty, King of Cerion.
Twig (*Twig***)** Tufar Woodlish Icsanthius Gent: A plant fairy who has a special bond with Princess Margary.
Valenor *(VAL-en-or)* Valenor: A Dreamwalker.
Viala *(Vee-AH-lah)* Viala Nullen: A Sorceress who conspired with Prince Eron. Sister of Tib.
Zevlain *(Zev-LANE)* Zevlain Ivlindren: A Knight and Cygnet Rider of the White Line.
Zhilee *(ZI-lee)* Zhilee Nullen: Tib's younger sister.

ACKNOWLEDGMENTS

When I began writing this series, I wanted to create a story that could be enjoyed by both the young and the young at heart. I'm so grateful to God for the inspiration that came to me while I was writing. I'm thankful to my friends and family, who are always so supportive of me.

Call of Sunteri is dedicated to my mom, Bonnie Hatch, who is a constant source of support, inspiration, and encouragement for me. Thanks, Mom, for being my biggest fan and for keeping me writing by asking for more story every day.

To my husband, James, thank you for letting me escape into Azi's world as often as I want to, and for always being understanding and supportive when I get lost there.

To my son Wesley, you are an inspiration to me, and I love you so much!

To my bestie Emily, thank you for your general awesomeness and moral support.

I'm also very grateful to the following readers who were kind enough to take the time to read Call of Sunteri before it was published, especially Debra White, Jennifer Hicks, and Stacy Marans. Also J.A., J.M., and M.F., your enthusiasm to read more is a real inspiration, thank you!

Finally, thanks to everyone who has taken the time to read this book and the rest in the Keepers of the Wellsprings series. I hope you have enjoyed reading it as much as I loved writing it!